one

THE HEART REMEMBERS

It began like the soft haze of a dream that slowly washes over the senses, teasing, promising with half-formed images. The cool shadows of Ombre Rose surrounded her and she felt herself drifting. All about her she heard the murmur of the leaves, the sigh of the breeze through the overgrown shrubs and vines . . .

Promise me . . .

The words came from somewhere . . . she couldn't seem to remember . . .

It was then she felt it, or perhaps only imagined it; the lightest touch against her cheek, like the breath of the wind . . .

Forever. Promise me.

An incredible warmth wrapped around her, almost as if someone's arms had embraced her.

She might have struggled, except for the arms that held her. She might have cried out, except for the mouth that caressed her lips, her cheek, her closed eyes, then retraced each touch, each caress with a fiery heat so intense it left her breathless.

Was it a moment, an hour, a day? Was it even real?

LET PINNACLE BOOKS
LEAD YOU TO THE
SUMMIT OF ROMANCE

LOVE'S AVENGING HEART ($3.95, 17-302)
By Patricia Matthews
Beautiful Hanah thought only of escaping from her brutal stepfather, Silas Quint. When he sells her into servitude as an innkeeper's barmaid, Hanah faces the toughest battle of her young life. The fiery redhead faces cruelty and humiliation as she struggles for her freedom and searches for a man to fulfill her dreams.

LOVE, FOREVER MORE ($3.95, 17-244)
By Patricia Matthews
When young Serena Foster's parents were suddenly killed, she found one night's comfort in arms of young Rory Clendenning. But one night of passion cannot last forever, and when rugged Darrel Quick came into her life, Serena discovered a new and very different type of love. Serena finds a new vision of her destiny as a woman as she searches for *LOVE, FOREVER MORE*.

SWITCHBACK ($3.95, 17-136)
By Robin Stevenson and Tom Blade
When Elizabeth took her grandmother to a silent film retrospective, she never could have imagined the events to come. Dorothea saw herself in a movie starring the love of her life, Vernon Dunbar, yet she could not remember it all. If only Elizabeth could travel back in time and sort out her grandmother's secretive past . . .

Available wherever paperbacks are sold, or order direct from the Publisher. Send cover price plus 50¢ per copy for mailing and handling to Pinnacle Books, Dept. 17-433, 475 Park Avenue South, New York, N.Y. 10016. Residents of New York, New Jersey and Pennsylvania must include sales tax. DO NOT SEND CASH.

ALWAYS, MY LOVE

CARLA SIMPSON

PINNACLE BOOKS
WINDSOR PUBLISHING CORP.

PINNACLE BOOKS

are published by

Windsor Publishing Corp.
475 Park Avenue South
New York, NY 10016

First printing: October, 1990

Printed in the United States of America

Chapter One

St. Louis, Missouri
June 25, 1865

"Be sensible Amanda, the war has only just ended. Conditions in the South are absolutely appalling. Your brother, Stephen, would never allow it. What can you possibly be thinking?"

All her aunt Lenore's dire warnings engulfed her as Amanda Spenser slowly stepped down from the carriage into the chaos of the St. Louis waterfront.

"Good Lord! What have we come to?"

Her aunt's trusted maid, Mary Wilson, stepped down beside her. Wide-eyed, she clutched the crucifix about her neck as she had the last five days since they'd left New York.

The docks along the St. Louis riverfront were a tangled mass of cargo, wagons, and sweating dock workers. Sleek packets from the West Indies rode the water at deep anchor, like large, graceful birds at rest. Shallow draft sternwheelers were moored beside steam-powered ferries and tugs. Flatboats bobbed like fat, squat women. Roustabouts cut intimidating paths through arguing crewmen, hawkers, and passengers.

The late-morning air was ripe with a mixture of scents and odors. It was unbearably warm, a different heat that

5

was like a live thing blanketing everything with smothering humidity. Amanda had already arrived at the conclusion that her heavy silk gowns and traveling clothes were ill-suited to the hot, damp climate.

The jacket to her gray silk traveling suit was badly wrinkled, the shirtwaist underneath clinging to her skin as perspiration slipped down between her breasts to pool at her waist.

She blew back stray wisps of pale gold hair that dampened across her forehead and waved into soft disarray. Her cheeks were flushed and her brilliant aquamarine eyes stared in disbelief at the confusion of screeching, colorful parrots and equally loud, screeching vendors.

They sold everything from boiled crayfish, fresh fruit and aromatic coffee to spices and bundles of flowers. It all congealed with the steam from boiler-driven engines and the heat to thicken in the throat and sting the eyes. A woman's cackling laughter followed a stream of explosive curses.

It was worse than their journey south by train, when for days they were jostled aboard one train after another after leaving Grand Central Depot. They quickly learned the trains ran sporadically at best and were overcrowded in the least.

Amanda had heard rumors of the conditions in the South, but nothing prepared her for the battle-scarred landscape, cannons left where they mired down in muddied river bottoms, burned-out supply wagons, and still—two months after it was all over—there was an occasional carcass of a dead horse or mule. And always, at every station, each water stop, there were the soldiers.

There were masses of them in blue uniforms being sent north to their homes and families. Occasionally there were those in the tattered Confederate gray, but they were few, for they couldn't afford the fare. Instead, they crowded the towns and roads, hobbling alone, riding in wagons and carts, or astride a horse. Unarmed, defeated, they were simply trying to survive on the road home. And always there was the resentment and bitterness in their eyes.

Aunt Lenore was right. The conditions were appalling. Everywhere she looked there were homeless refugees on the move, leaving burned-out homes in hopes of finding someplace else. Only there was no other place. The entire South was in ruins.

Coming here so soon after the war wasn't sensible, or wise, and undoubtedly not safe. Amanda knew that, just as she knew her brother wouldn't have approved of her coming here. But like so many others in this senseless war, Stephen Spenser—first in his class at West Point, captain in the Union Army—had not returned. He was buried in a nameless grave beside some remote battlefield in Virginia.

The pain of grief was sharp as she thought of Stephen. He had been both mother and father to her after their parents died. He'd soothed her fears over countless scraped knees and childhood injustices. And he promised he'd never leave her. But as she knew so well from the loss of their parents, life was fragile and uncertain. Now, Stephen was gone, too, and no amount of tears or anger could bring him back.

Perhaps it was because of Stephen that she had made her decision to accept Lacey's offer. Dear Lacey, southern through and through, from her sultry accent to her magnolia-pale complexion that she guarded from the sun with a vengeance.

They had been as close as sisters for six years, through the trying years at Van der Poole's school, through all the schemes they could get themselves into, and all the trouble they could possibly escape. They were fifteen when the war started and Lacey's father insisted she return immediately to Baton Rouge.

Amanda remained at Van der Poole's while Lacey finished her education in England. But through all the years in between, in spite of a war, blockades, and all the righteous political passions, they somehow had remained friends. Then their letters to each other became infrequent. At one point she didn't hear from Lacey for almost an entire year only to learn she had already returned from England.

Lacey's last letter arrived three weeks after the surrender

7

was signed and read simply:

"I wish you were here. I need you so. Lacey."

Amanda made her decision first and thought of the consequences later. There were still restrictions on travel. It was impossible for Lacey to visit her in the North. Therefore there was only one logical conclusion. She would go to Baton Rouge. It took quite a bit of finagling to make the arrangements. She had to ask a special favor of a classmate of Stephen's from the Point. Strings were pulled, special permission obtained, and she was on her way.

Lacey was to accompany her father upriver as far as Louisville. He had business there and they would be stopping briefly in St. Louis before returning to Baton Rouge. Amanda was to join them in St. Louis for the remainder of the trip downriver to Baton Rouge.

A telegram was waiting for Andy at her hotel when she arrived in St. Louis. Lacey and August Kittridge would meet her this morning at pier eleven. But at the moment that seemed impossible as she and Mary pushed their way through the mass of pressing, jostling bodies.

Transportation in the South had practically come to a standstill during the war. Now that travel had resumed on the river, every port, each dock was filled with anxious travelers desperate to reach another destination. It was worse than anything she could have imagined.

Andy gasped as a hand slipped intimately down her backside and gave her a light pat. She whirled around, several well-chosen words on the tip of her tongue, but the culprit had already disappeared into the crowd.

"I saw the fella, Miss Andy. And don't you worry none." Mary nodded sharply as she wedged through to her. "I gave 'im a good poke with me umbrella in a right critical spot. He won't soon be takin' liberties with another lady real soon."

Amanda's cheeks flamed at Mary's obvious meaning, but it was apparent that with the woman along, she had little to fear. She grabbed Mary's wrist and pulled her from harm's way as a roustabout pushed past them, precariously jug-

8

gling a large crate on his broad shoulders.

They squeezed past barrels, hogsheads, and countless cartons. Clumps of bananas from the West Indies vied for space with kegs of Irish whiskey. Good Lord, Andy thought, as she struggled to hold on to both Mary and her own valise, how on earth would she ever find Lacey in all this confusion?

She stretched onto her toes trying to see the names of the ships moored at the dock. Lacey had mentioned they would be traveling on the *Iron Queen,* but there must have been at least a dozen sternwheelers in various stages of loading or unloading tied up at the docks.

The names painted in bold block letters read like the class roll at Miss Van der Poole's school; the *Francis K.,* the *Lettie Jeanne,* the *Lady M.* Andy's gaze fastened on one nearby — the *Delta Queen.* And beside it, the *River Queen.*

A feeling of utter helplessness washed over her. How was she ever going to find the *Iron Queen* in all this confusion.

"Well, I declare! If it isn't just the most ravaging, beautiful creature I ever saw!"

The words stopped Andy in her tracks. It couldn't be! She smothered a giggle. There was only one person in all the world who could absolutely murder the English language to such perfection.

"*Ravaging* creature?" Andy choked with merriment as she spun around to find Lacey Kittridge contemplating her with something that could only be described as smugness. "Don't you mean *ravishing?*"

"Well of course. That's exactly what I said." Lacey waved an impatient hand through the air. Then she stood back, hands folded demurely in front of her and gave Andy thorough inspection.

"Just look at you. Daddy always did say you would be a late bloomer. I should be pea-green with envy." Her mouth was turned into a pretty pout.

Andy bit back laughter, as she vividly recalled how Lacey was always so poised, so graceful, while she was gawky at best, "with oodles of promise," as Lacey would always console her.

"Good! It's about time, don't you think?"

Lacey gave her a look of cool appraisal. "I absolutely refuse to be envious," she declared flatly. "People might think I was jealous."

"And of course you've never been jealous a day in your life." Andy tried to keep a straight face.

"Of course not. That is a weakness of character, and we both know I have absolutely none," Lacey concluded with a satisfied smile.

"And of course, you're very humble, too."

Lacey smoothed her bright-red hair with a properly gloved hand. "Well, I do have my rare moments," she replied matter-of-factly.

"Rare indeed!" Andy pulled her bottom lip between her teeth and bit back more laughter. Her eyes filled with tears of merriment.

Lacey gave her one of those fey, southern belle simple looks. "How can you say such a thing, when we haven't seen each other in ever so long? You should be absolutely dripping with kind words." She pouted playfully, then with a mischievous glint in her amber eyes, she leaned forward to whisper. "You have made some improvements. I see you took my advice." She gestured discreetly to the bodice of Andy's gown.

"Handkerchiefs work all right in the bodice, but they're a little flimsy, and if you ever have the need of one, then you have to go digging for it. A nice, round ball of cotton works best for stuffin'." She stood back with that same sweet, innocent expression plastered on her face. "But of course, you have to make certain they're the same size or else you'll be uneven."

Andy almost choked at the direction of their conversation. They hadn't seen each other in over four years, and how did Lacey greet her?

Not *hello, I've missed you dreadfully* or *Andy dear, I am so very glad to see you all this time.* Not that she really expected that sort of greeting. Lacey was . . . well, she was Lacey—spon-

10

taneous, flirtatious, sometimes outrageous. Her father always insisted it was because she'd lost her mother at such a young age and hadn't the advantage of a firm hand.

The truth was, Andy was a little apprehensive about seeing Lacey again after all this time. Four years was a long time. They had both been through a great many changes, including being on opposing sides of a conflict that had literally torn the country apart.

The thought had nagged at her the entire trip from New York that Lacey might have changed. Her attitudes and feelings toward Andy might be different.

When they parted, they'd sworn to be friends forever, but recalling the promise her brother once made and couldn't keep, Andy realized that time had a way of altering childhood vows.

But in these few minutes, she knew this was one promise that had been kept. Lacey hadn't changed. She was still just as unpretentious and outrageous as always. She had certainly managed to shock Mary Wilson.

"Lacey Kittridge! You're absolutely indecent," the maid scolded. "Here the two of you haven't seen each other for four years and the only thing you can talk about is things no decent young lady would talk about in public!" Pure indignation narrowed the woman's eyes.

Lacey looked at Andy with mock pity. "And you traveled all the way from New York with her? You do have my heartfelt sympathy."

"Mercy sakes alive!" The horrified maid rolled her eyes. "You haven't changed a whit."

"No, she hasn't!" Andy giggled with pure enjoyment. "Thank heavens!" And with that they collapsed into each other's arms.

They laughed, they cried, they both tried to talk at once. Every time they drew a deep breath and tried to compose themselves it began again, until tears streaked their aching cheeks. Their noses were red, their eyes were red, and neither could find a handkerchief. They leaned on each other for support, completely oblivious of the attention they were drawing.

Lacey sniffled indelicately as she drew back to take a look at her friend. "If I'd known you were going to turn into such a pretty thing, I'd have thought twice about invitin' you down here. It's difficult enough to find an able-bodied man without invitin' more competition." Then she turned to Mary. "I shouldn't tell you that I've missed you. It will only give you a swelled head." But she did anyway, giving her a long, hard squeeze.

Mary drew back and sniffed her disapproval. "Both of you are behavin' like hooligans!"

Andy bit back another wave of laughter. Just like the summer out at her aunt's summer house on Long Island. They were fourteen and Mary caught them putting sand crabs in the water pitcher. Then there was the frog they put in the bread basket set out for one of her aunt Lenore's dull afternoon tea parties.

"Well, naturally." Lacey looked at her as if it were the most natural thing in the world. "Andy taught me everything I know." Which was a lie, of course, and they all knew it. Then Lacey took Andy's hands in hers and became quite serious. "I was afraid you might change your mind."

Andy shook her head. "I thought I'd die if stayed in New York just a week longer."

Lacey giggled with delicious excitement. "Well, imagine my surprise when I got your letter."

She looped their arms together, chatting excitedly as they walked to the end of the dock, where the *Iron Queen* rolled gently at her moorings.

"All the arrangements have been made," Lacey explained. "Daddy will be along shortly. He had to talk to someone by the name of Peabody or Peterson, or somethin' like that. Good heavens! Do you believe all this confusion?" Then she went on, hardly pausing to catch her breath.

"I was afraid you might have trouble gettin' to St. Louis. Let me tell you, no, I mean absolutely no one in their right mind, is goin' south. Everybody I know is tryin' to leave. Except for thievin' Yankee carpetbaggers and politicians."

Talking to Lacey was like trying to keep up with a locomotive at full speed. A frown shaded Andy's soft eyes. "Is it really that bad?"

Lacey tilted her lovely head. "Things are almost worse now that the war is over. There are shortages of everythin', boats are delayed. They have only just begun repairs on the railroad. A lot of the river ports were either burned or shelled when the Yanks rode south. And travelin' alone? Daddy won't even let me go into downtown Baton Rouge without one of the servants along for protection. The town is filled with riffraff. Mercy sakes, I just can't believe Stephen let the two of you come all this way by yourselves." Then her smile brightened as she cast a searching glance around both Andy and Mary. "That is, of course, unless Stephen came with you and he's tryin' to play some sort of trick on me. That would be just like him, hidin' and savin' the surprise to the last moment."

Lacey turned to Mary. "Is he still as handsome as ever?" Her dark eyes twinkled merrily. "I am a loyal southerner, of course, but I could forgive Stephen almost anything, even bein' a blue-belly Yank."

She looked at Andy expectantly. "Well? Did he come with you? Tell me! Oh, that would make everythin' just perfect! I mean, after all, if we have to have Yankees in Baton Rouge it might as well be Stephen." She glanced from one to the other expectantly.

Andy bit at her lower lip as tears threatened. She struggled to find the right words, but they all seemed to catch in her throat.

Lacey seemed to sense what it was that was so difficult. Her hand flew to her lips as all color drained from her face. "Dear Lord!" she breathed, her voice trembling with dread. "Please say it isn't so! Not Stephen!" Her eyes flooded with tears.

"It happened at a place called Morgan's Landing in Virginia, two days after the war ended," Andy whispered.

Lacey seemed to visibly crumble before her. Andy's arm

13

went around her trembling shoulders just as her legs seemed to go out from under her. "We've got to get her aboard the *Iron Queen*," she said.

Mary nodded. "If only Mr. Kittridge were here."

Andy looked up at Mary as she shifted Lacey's head to her shoulder. "We can't wait. We'll go aboard now."

With one of them on either side of Lacey, they crossed the last few paces to the lowered gangway connecting the sternwheeler to the docks.

"Hold it right there!"

Andy looked up in surprise at the soldier in the imposing blue uniform who blocked the gangway.

"We need to get Miss Kittridge aboard," she explained, then turned to assist Lacey.

"I'm afraid that's not possible, miss."

Andy looked up in surprise. The man obviously didn't understand. She smiled as she began to explain.

"Miss Kittridge is not feeling well. She's had a very bad shock. We're simply taking her to her cabin. Now if you'll please stand aside."

He thrust out a stocky arm to prevent them from boarding.

"I'll need to see papers, miss." The words snapped out from thick lips pinched into a bulldog expression beneath the dark-blue billed cap.

"Papers? What are you talking about? We're passengers aboard this ship." Patience was fast giving way as Lacey moaned softly against Andy's shoulder.

"That may be, miss, but I still have to see passage documents." His mouth snapped shut.

She tried once more as politely as possible under the circumstances. "Sergeant, I don't know anything about official documents. We are passengers on this ship and we are going aboard."

"Andy, please . . ." Lacey implored softly. "All passengers have official boarding passes. The military requires them for travel."

"What seems to be the problem, Sergeant?"

14

Andy looked up as the cool, officious voice cut through the stifling waterfront heat. The officer in the brilliant blue uniform slowly strode toward them, the gold braid epaulettes of the Union uniform winking in the midday sun.

Her eyes fastened on the twin rows of embossed buttons, then came up slowly to the blunt clean-shaven chin, high-planed cheeks, and hooded, cool eyes. Beneath the sweep of the brimmed hat with the gold braid tassel, his hair was almost jet black. The mouth was expressionless, with precise military emotion. In other words, none at all.

"I explained it was necessary to see their boarding passes." The sergeant's straightforward stare never wavered as he repeated his instructions.

Andy felt the captain's icy appraisal. "I'm Captain Durant. The sergeant is acting on my orders. Official papers are required by all passengers."

She wanted to scream. Most of all, she wanted to strike that smug, official expression right off both their faces.

By-the-book soldiers, her brother called them. Long on orders, short on judgment. They were so full of themselves and their sense of duty, nothing else mattered. And they always did everything by the book. The book, of course, being the military handbook of rules and regulations.

It was obvious to everyone that Lacey was not well, yet the captain seemed to take some sort of detached pleasure in carrying out his orders. It was there in the efficient energy of his movements, the flawless line of the crisp uniform. She'd seen countless men like him at Stephen's graduation from West Point. Everything about Captain Durant bespoke New England, university education, and an impeccable family background that practically guaranteed an officer his commission.

The blue of his uniform set him dramatically apart from everyone else on the docks in this southern city, and he used it to full advantage. It was a sense of power. Some men respected it and used it judiciously. The contemptuous way he looked at them suggested he knew or cared little about either.

15

"Andy please, don't make trouble. I have the papers in my reticule." Lacey weakly handed the drawstring bag to her friend.

Andy quickly found the papers and handed them to Captain Durant. He slowly read through them. Then that hooded gaze came up, regarding her from beneath the brimmed military hat with an expression that was subtly changed.

"You're from the North." There was surprise in his voice.

Andy frowned slightly. "Yes, New York."

The captain touched his gloved hand up to the brim of his immaculate hat. "My sincerest apologies, Miss Spenser. I assumed . . ."

So that was it! He had assumed she was a southerner. That explained the barely concealed hostility. But now that he knew she was from the North, everything was changed.

She started to say exactly what she thought of his conduct and his attitude but Lacey gave her a warning look.

Captain Durant handed the papers back to her. "You should keep these with you at all times," he suggested in a remarkably congenial tone. "Unfortunately, things are very difficult in the South right now. I'm sure you understand."

"I'll try to remember, Captain," Andy answered coolly. "Now, if you don't mind, I would like to take Miss Kittridge to her cabin."

"Of course. I'll escort you aboard."

Andy stiffened. "That won't be necessary. Miss Wilson and I can manage very well."

"Nevertheless, I will accompany you." The authority was unmistakable. "I wouldn't want it to be said an officer refused to help a lady."

A scathing reply was on the tip of her tongue, but she felt the faint warning pressure of Lacey's weak fingers.

"Allow me," the captain insisted.

Before Andy could object, he stepped in front of her, carefully lifting Lacey into his arms.

"It will be a much safer journey this way," he explained, carrying Lacey across the length of the gangway.

When Lacey was carefully deposited in her cabin, Andy turned to bid the captain good-bye.

"Thank you for your assistance." With cool dismissal she refused to meet his gaze. What she really wanted was to slap that expression of cool superiority right off the captain's handsome face. But he wasn't about to be so easily put off.

"I knew a fellow officer named Spenser from New York. We were cadets together at West Point," he suggested.

Andy replied stiffly. "My brother Stephen was at the Point."

"And he's not with you?"

He might have been a handsome man if not for the coldness behind his eyes, a coldness that seemed to reach his very soul. Now it was carefully hidden away behind that perfect facade.

"No," she answered simply. "Now, if you don't mind . . ."

He smiled as he tipped his hat. "We will be seeing more of each other, Miss Spenser. I'm making the return trip with you as far as Baton Rouge. If there is anything you should need . . ." He seized her hand where she gripped the latch to the door.

"I would feel honored if you would call me Chandler. After all, I've been acquainted with your brother."

Andy pulled her fingers from his as she practically choked on her words. "You've been more than kind." And then refusing the invitation of familiarity, she added with obvious meaning, *"Captain* Durant."

Andy stood on the upper deck of the *Iron Queen*. It was late morning and Lacey still hadn't come up on deck yet. She smiled to herself. Some things never changed.

Something else that hadn't changed was Lacey's father. August Kittridge was the same. He was a tall, robust man with a florid face and a boisterous enthusiasm for everything. His coppery hair and mutton-chop whiskers had once rivaled Lacey's hair for brilliance but had lightened with faint streaks of gray. He never sat still very long, constantly

17

leaping up and running off to greet some long-lost friend—he seemed to know everyone aboard the *Iron Queen*. He had a keen sense of humor, making jokes about Yankees and Confederates alike. But behind the boisterous humor was a keen sense of judgment and a sharp business sense. He was a successful businessman before the war and his business had survived. He would be successful again, for he was a good judge of character—even when it came to his daughter, whom he adored. He indulged her, spoiled her, and knew her as well as he knew himself, for they were like two peas in a pod.

Years before, he had considered Andy his "other daughter." That hadn't changed. Within minutes of being reunited he made her feel as if she had somehow come home and Andy knew she had made the right decision to come south.

They had left St. Louis four days ago, arriving in Natchez just after dawn this morning. She had seen Captain Durant often, more often than seemed necessary, but she was polite for Lacey's sake. Andy still didn't understand her fear of him. Lacey never had a cowardly bone in her body. She was always the bold one, willing to take a risk, or flaunt convention. But Lacey had changed. She had become cautious.

Andy was grateful Captain Durant was needed ashore this morning. After the first two days, she'd run out of polite pleasantries to exchange, and she hated playing the part of the hypocrite. Now she enjoyed her solitude and the balmy, late-morning breeze that came in off the river. She watched as disembarking passengers went ashore and roustabouts stripped bare to their waists in the pressing heat loaded and unloaded cargo.

The last crates were carried aboard and the final call went out for passengers to board. The riverboat's bell sounded a series of double rings and a whistle blew overhead. When they docked earlier, the twin smokestacks trailed lazy streamers of dying smoke. The huge steam-driven paddle wheel slowed, reversed, then stopped altogether as mooring lines were thrown ashore. Now those stacks were like sleeping twin dragons that had awakened.

Clouds of billowing black smoke churned from each stack as furnaces were fed in the engine rooms and steam built up. They would soon be under way. The following morning they would arrive in Baton Rouge.

Andy turned toward Lacey's cabin, determined she had slept long enough. But voices from the dock below caught her attention. The sergeant stood at his post at the end of the gangway. One by one, he checked remaining passengers aboard and asked for their boarding passes.

An older couple was passed through with only a brief nod from the sergeant. He didn't even bother to inspect their papers. The last passengers were two men. Andy watched as the sergeant barred their entry.

"Let me see your papers," he ordered gruffly.

The words drifted up to her on the warm, humid air, and Andy felt her own irritation rise. She watched the exchange intently.

The first man, taller by several inches, handed him the papers. There was something defiant in the gesture—a moment's hesitation as he extended the papers yet refused to release them immediately when the sergeant reached for them.

Andy held her breath. It was almost imperceptible, but she sensed it—like a silent challenge, or threat.

Dangerous. That described the man, and a frisson of fear mixed with excitement tingled across her skin.

She couldn't see him clearly, only the lower part of his face beneath the wide brim of his hat. But there was a stubborn angle to his chin, obscured by the closely cropped, rich brown beard. Andy was certain if she could see his eyes, she would see the defiance reflected there as well.

His stance suggested an almost animal wariness, as if he could either lean back and engage in casual conversation or spring forward with powerful energy. She saw it in the deceptively relaxed set of his shoulders beneath the dusty, worn black frock coat. The faded gray pants were snugged over lean, muscular thighs and tapered down just over his knees to disappear into the tops of scuffed black boots.

Was it possible he was a Confederate soldier? She'd seen a great deal of tattered gray uniforms since arriving in the South—the torn and faded remnants of a defeated army. Nothing about this man so much as hinted at defeat. Quite the opposite, Andy concluded. This was a man who wouldn't know the meaning of the word—and wouldn't accept it under any terms. And that made everything else about him all the more fascinating.

Andy leaned over the railing, almost hoping he would look up so that she could see his face clearly—and more importantly, his eyes. They would be cool, she decided. Possibly blue, or gray, but capable in a single glance of chilling straight through a person . . .

Again that tingling sensation ran through her, and Andy's hands tightened on the railing until her knuckles turned white.

Chapter Two

"Captain Durant?" The sergeant called for his superior officer.

Every muscle in Coleton James's body tensed at the sound of that name, the name of a man he knew but had never met . . . until today.

The sergeant turned to the captain. Coleton's hand eased down toward the service revolver hidden under his coat. From behind, he felt Rafael Kelly's restraining hand.

"Easy, my friend." Rafe warned, the words faintly accented with Spanish. "We knew the Union Army would take these precautions. Do not be foolish and give yourself away."

"Of all the people it had to be Durant," Coleton muttered under his breath as the man turned to his commanding officer.

"Ah, but you have the advantage, amigo," Rafe whispered discreetly, "for in all the time he chased the infamous Gray Fox, never once did he come face-to-face with his quarry. And now, thanks to this bumbling, worthless excuse for a sergeant, you have the advantage. Of course, that furry face of yours helps as well." He chuckled softly as he lightly ran his fingers over his smooth-shaven chin.

He went on, enjoying himself at his friend's expense. "It is my good fortune Captain Durant did not swear a blood oath to see *me* hang. I don't much care for the heavy beard you must wear as a disguise. It is too hot in my native Mexico. I pitied you on our visit there."

"Your sister didn't seem to object to my appearance," Coleton shot back at him, knowing the remark would hit home. Rafael Kelly was passionate about few things in life, but the virtue of his beautiful sixteen-year-old sister was one of them.

"Ah, my friend, I will not let you make me angry. If I didn't trust you, I would not have fought by your side for General Lee these past four years."

"You fought because you were paid to fight, and paid very well."

"That was true enough for the first two years. The Confederate gold was plentiful then. But in the end, we both know it was my abiding love for you—a man I consider as my brother—that kept me at your side when General Lee had only the worthless Confederate bonds and empty promises of French gold. I liked your General Lee very much, but I have never cared much for the French. They have a habit of breaking their promises."

Rafe's dark eyes danced at his enjoyment of their current predicament. "Even now, if this does not go well, I will be more than happy to kill both Durant and his fat, stupid sergeant for you."

"You would do that?" Coleton rocked back on his bootheels, easing the tension of the wait while the soldier showed their papers to Durant—papers that were forged and dearly paid for.

Rafe shrugged good-naturedly as he took a long, thin cigar from his inside coat pocket and lit it. "Of course. It is the least I can do for a man who has intervened with fate and saved my life on at least two occasions."

"Three," Coleton corrected, his eyes never leaving Durant.

"The last time does not count, because you were the cause of the trouble with that cowboy down in Texas." He made a clucking sound with his teeth.

"That was because I stopped him from shooting you in the back as you headed upstairs with his woman."

Rafe shrugged. "Two times, three. What does it matter?

22

The point is I am willing to overlook certain things, as long as you stay away from Victoria. For that I would kill you." He grinned wide at the last statement.

Coleton stared up the gangway at the man who had pursued him for four long years and had, until now, failed in his attempt. "How many men do you suppose Durant has aboard that riverboat?"

Rafe shrugged. "I've spotted at least a dozen. There are undoubtedly many more ashore, as we've seen these past few weeks since leaving Mexico."

"This is just like that night we stole the battle plans for the Wilderness campaign—right under Durant's nose. There were a lot of soldiers that night."

"The odds were a thousand to one," Coleton reminded him. "And we were almost caught." He still carried the scars from a bullet he hadn't dodged quickly enough.

Coleton weighed the alternatives. They could simply leave, even though he knew there was little possibility Durant would suspect who they were.

Amnesty was granted to all officers who'd served the Confederacy when the surrender was signed at Appomattox Courthouse—that is, to everyone except the Gray Fox and his men who had escaped to Mexico along with hundreds of other southerners who refused to accept the surrender. They'd lived with Rafe's family, at their rancho just across the border from Texas. But now he had to come back, no matter how great the risk, for he was about to lose the one thing in this world that still meant something to him.

Durant checked and rechecked the papers. Coleton thought of the gold they'd paid for those papers and vowed to cut a certain man's throat if this didn't work. Then Durant looked up and slowly walked toward them. He nodded, his gaze hooded and his expression completely unreadable. He might have been about to ask for a cigarette or order them hanged.

"You're from California."

Coleton nodded once, his gaze boring right through Durant. Before he could answer or so much as acknowledge

Durant's statement, Rafe pushed past him, placing himself between them.

"My family has a rancho in Los Angeles. We are cattle-men."

"This says your name is Kelly." Durant looked skeptically at the papers.

Rafe grinned wide. "*Sí, señor.* My father is Irish."

"And you, sir?" Durant directed his question at Coleton.

"Kelly," he said simply, while every muscle in his body tensed. "James Kelly."

"We are cousins. Our fathers were brothers," Rafe offered by way of explanation. Only Coleton saw through his easy manner to the dark intensity that glowed in his black eyes.

"You are a long way from California," Durant observed as he continued scanning the official papers.

"The war is over, señor." Rafe went on to explain. "Now is the time for rebuilding. There will be a need of cattle in the South."

"Yes," Durant answered thoughtfully, "we could've used more of your cattle in the last months of the war. I don't care if I never eat another chicken."

Coleton's fingers constricted. He remembered the faces of the haggard Confederate troops those last weeks before Appomattox. Beaten, without horses, most without weapons, half starved because there was no food after the Union Army swept through and confiscated everything in sight, more dead than alive, they'd rallied behind General Lee, and to a man they were willing to go right on fighting. He ached when he thought what a few chickens would have meant to those men. And he wanted to kill Durant for it.

Rafe saw the cold fury that glittered in Coleton's eyes, and knew what he was thinking. But his smile for Durant only deepened.

"So perhaps we may be able to do business with the Union Army as well. Perhaps directly with you, capitán." His voice was smooth as silk with all it implied. "That is, of course, if everything is in order."

Durant's head came up and he looked at both men intently, as if weighing some inner thought. For several long moments Coleton waited, almost hoping Durant did suspect they were lying. It would give him a great deal of satisfaction to kill the man who'd dogged him for the better part of two years.

From the top deck of the *Iron Queen*, Andy watched the exchange. Fascinated, she saw what Durant couldn't see—the subtle interplay between the two men trying to board the riverboat, the careful maneuver as the shorter man interceded to speak with Durant, the clenching and unclenching of the taller man's fists as if he struggled with some great emotion that could only be anger.

For just a moment the breeze seemed to die in the morning heat, there was a lull in the noise from the docks, and she found herself holding her breath.

"Very well, Sergeant. You may let these passengers board." With that same military efficiency, Durant handed the papers back to Rafe and nodded curtly.

"Good day, gentlemen. I hope you have a profitable stay in the South."

With that he slipped his military gloves on and stepped down onto the dock to speak with one of the men loading cargo.

Without understanding the reason for it, Andy was relieved as she watched the two men board the *Iron Queen*. She slowly released the breath she'd been holding.

They were directly below now, just stepping up onto the lower deck when the taller man stopped and looked up. For the first time she saw him full in the face.

Without knowing how, Andy had been certain his eyes would be light . . . blue, maybe gray, and piercingly cold, like the man himself, hinting at danger.

She'd expected it, even anticipated it. She had studied art in school and knew how to watch people. By watching him, she understood in those brief moments that here was a man who had his secrets, who walked and carried himself as if he expected danger, might even welcome it. The eyes of a man like that would be cold, unreadable, and as impenetrable as stone.

She sensed all of that even though he was too far away for her to be certain, and she was convinced his eyes would be gray—intense, cold, ruthless. But she saw something else as well, something unexpected and almost frightening. For in that brief moment as he stood looking up at her, Andy was certain she had looked into the past.

Coleton saw her leaning against the rail of the upper deck. She was silhouetted against the brilliant white heat of a midday sky. The wind caught at her bound hair, freeing pale tendrils to dance on the air like spun gold, and for just a moment Coleton remembered another afternoon so many years ago, when a beautiful young woman had stood waiting for him.

Durant was forgotten. The war was forgotten. There was just this moment, caught in time—part of the past, yet so real.

The memory was so strong, the resemblance so profound that for a moment he almost believed it was *her.*

"Sunny?"

She couldn't have heard anything. It was only the whisper of the wind. Yet Andy was certain she had heard something or perhaps sensed it—a name.

It was so brief, it might never have happened, yet so intense, Andy was certain it had. Instinctively, she jerked back from the railing, and in spite of the summer heat she was cold, unbearably cold, as if something . . . or someone . . . had touched her soul.

Andy had all but forgotten the incident in the days that followed their trip downriver. She saw nothing more of the gray-eyed man, and almost believed she *had* imagined that brief encounter.

Now it was early morning and cool. Streamers of night mist lingered on the water. They moved like silent spirits toward the distant shore and wrapped around water oaks and bald cypress trees that lined the water's edge. Shrouds

26

of Spanish moss dripped from outflung branches and made them look like so many old women who clutched their shawls about sagging shoulders as they gathered along the banks of the river.

It was an odd illusion that sprung from her artist's mind as Andy watched from the deck of the *Iron Queen*. Her fingers itched to take up paper and charcoal pencil and sketch her impressions so that she would have them to put on canvas later. Then it occurred to her she truly wanted to paint for the first time in months.

Her art was always the one thing that gave her solace, like a healing balm as she expressed emotions, thoughts, impressions on canvas. Monsieur Perrot, the instructor at Van der Poole's school, encouraged her talent. But recently she had little desire to paint, especially after Stephen died.

Now she found herself wishing she had thought to keep the small case packed with paints, pencils, paper, and canvas with her. It would take too much time to retrieve it from the bottom of her trunk. They would be past this point in the river before she could return, and the light would be changed. Instead, she committed the images to memory while she waited for Lacey.

She'd slipped a message under Lacey's cabin door earlier. From experience she knew there was absolutely no point trying to wake Lacey before she was ready. As Andy knew all too well, she had a nasty disposition if she didn't get enough sleep and would make everyone suffer dreadfully for it.

Andy looked up. Would wonders never cease? Lacey Kittridge was up and about and it was only a little after nine o'clock in the morning. This certainly had to be a momentous occasion.

"Don't say it." Lacey held up a delicate gloved hand as she approached. "Daddy already lectured me about bein' so late. I swear, Andy, no one in their right mind gets up as early as you do. It's absolutely disgustin'. But that's not the reason I'm so late. I ran into *that* man." Her eyes widened meaningfully.

27

Andy was again reminded of a train at full throttle. "What man?"

"What man, indeed!" Lacey gave her a narrow look. "Why, just about the most excitin' thing on two legs, and with the most unsettling dark eyes I ever saw. And the way he looks at a woman . . . Lord, I swear I come undone every time I see him!"

For emphasis, Lacey flipped open her fan and proceeded to cool herself in spite of the chill that still clung to the morning air.

"Who are you talking about?"

"Who?! Why, that dark, handsome man who came aboard in Natchez." Lacey snapped her fan shut and thrust the tip at Andy for emphasis. "Which I might add, you couldn't be bothered to tell me about at the time."

Andy knew exactly who she meant — the man who had come aboard with that tall stranger.

"I simply forgot," she murmured softly. "I didn't think it was important."

"Not important!" Lacey was aghast. "Good heavens Andy, you simply must reexamine your thinkin'."

"Such as?" Andy quipped with a faint quirk of smile.

Lacey pretended to glare at her. "You simply have no appreciation of the situation. I turned down an English viscount because he was too old. Then when I got home, I found every available man was either my daddy's age or still in short pants. Let me tell you, the pickin's are mighty slim."

Andy could only shake her head. She remembered how coy and flirtatious Lacey was when they were younger. "It's not like you to make a fool of yourself over a man. You usually have them falling at *your* feet."

"Yes," Lacey agreed, "but times bein' what they are, a young lady has to realign her thinkin'. What difference does it make so long as the results are the same?"

Andy pretended to be shocked, although nothing Lacey did had ever shocked her. "Why, Lacey Kittridge, whatever happened to all that refined southern breeding and good manners?"

Lacey gave her a smug, elegant smile. "They're still there. I've simply changed my way of goin' about gettin' what I want. The trick is to take the initiative but make the man think he's the one in control."

Andy leaned against the rail and smiled as she turned her face toward the sun's warming rays. "And I suppose you've already made the first move."

All Lacey's aloofness and composure evaporated in an instant, and she became the giggling girl Andy remembered so well. "Well, of course." She grabbed Andy's arm with a sense of conspiracy.

"I overheard him talkin' with that friend of his . . . the tall one?" Lacey babbled on beside her.

"His name is Kelly. Although for the life of me, I can't imagine where he got a name like that with those dark eyes and black hair. It must be Irish, but I swear he looks like he could be Spanish. And he's devilish handsome, and when he smiles . . . Oh, Andy! He looked right at me. And well, he has just the most scandalous smile, like he knows just what a person is thinkin'."

"He probably knew *exactly* what you were thinking," Andy pointed out, fighting back a smile. "And you should be ashamed for eavesdropping."

"He did not know!" Lacey replied, immediately indignant. "And I was not eavesdropping. I just happened to turn around and there he was. Besides . . ." She looked off across the water with an air of detachment, "I was enjoyin' the scenery and the early-mornin' air."

Andy practically choked at that one. Lacey hated mornings, she made no pretense about it, and avoided them at all costs . . . until now.

"You've never been up this early since we attended school together. And then you were positively horrid," Andy reminded her.

Lacey sniffed indignantly. "Well, as I said, times bein' what they are, a girl has to rearrange her thinkin'."

Andy shook her head. She only half listened to Lacey

chatter on about Mr. Kelly as she watched the distant shore-line pass by. She already knew exactly how she would paint it if she had her paints and a canvas. Then Lacey caught her attention once more.

"I went to your cabin first. You have a note from Captain Durant," Lacey said, giving Andy a meaningful look. "Andy, you mustn't antagonize him. He's left you countless messages and you haven't answered one of them."

"I'm not trying to antazonize him." Andy threw bits of bread crust she'd saved from breakfast to the water birds that dipped and careened above the boat. "What he did at the docks in St. Louis was unforgivable." She cast another crust into the gentle breeze and watched two birds dive for it.

"I'm ignoring him," she announced simply.

Lacey leaned on the railing beside her. "Perhaps in your eyes it was unforgivable, but you had better get used to it, Andy. I tried to explain things are bad down here. Feelin's run deep since the war. Southerners hate the Yanks and the Yanks hate southerners. But we have to get along, even if we don't like it. Either that or go right on fightin' the war."

"Peaceful coexistence?" Andy suggested.

"Most of the time." Lacey went on to explain. "After all, Louisiana has been under Yankee control since the second year of the war. But every once in a while, the Yanks seem to enjoy stirrin' things up. They're in control of the government and they take advantage of that."

"Thievin' Yankee carpetbaggers and politicians?" Amusement tipped Andy's lips as she recalled Lacey's exact description.

Her friend looked a little chagrined. "I know everyone isn't that way. Daddy always says you can't judge a book by its cover. Maybe he's right, but I swear sometimes it feels like we're all sittin' right on top of a powder keg, just waitin' for someone to light the fuse. And there are some people you just can't afford to offend."

"People like Captain Durant," Andy concluded thoughtfully.

"He's powerful, Andy. General Sheridan is in charge of the military occupation for all of Louisiana. Chandler Durant is his right-hand man. They *are* the law right now in Louisiana, and for God knows how long. They have the power to do just about anything."

"And you're frightened of him."

"Yes, I am. Oh, Andy, so many innocent people have been made to suffer. Every politician, judge, anyone in any official capacity before the war, has been treated like a criminal. Sometimes the military comes in the middle of the night and takes people away, sayin' they're part of spy activities. Homes are confiscated, people lose everythin', their belongin's thrown out in the street. Some go to jail," her voice dropped, "or get hanged. Lord, Andy! People are just tryin' to survive! All I'm sayin' is be careful."

"And you're afraid Captain Durant might be offended and take it out on you."

"It's not me I'm worried about. It's Daddy. All his warehouses and boats operate under special license from the new provisional government. The war all but ruined him. Now he's put everything he has into building the company back up again. But that doesn't matter one whit to men like Chandler Durant. They don't need a reason to close down somebody's business. It was hard on him during the war. It would just about kill him if he lost everything now."

"I see," Andy murmured softly. "Of course my being in Baton Rouge might work to your advantage, too. After all, Captain Durant wouldn't dare insult the hosts of a northern lady."

"Oh Andy, don't be so flippant. He can be dangerous."

"By the book," Andy murmured thoughtfully, then smiled as she covered Lacey's hand with her own.

"I'll be careful," she promised.

They stood, each lost in their own thoughts as the river slipped by. A persistent sun tried to penetrate the veil of mist on the water. The huge paddle wheels churned rhythmically, the water sighing before it was cast back to the river.

31

Further downriver charred pilings protruded from the water. Blackened timbers were all that remained of a boat landing that had been burned to the water line. Water oaks and cypress cluttered the water's edge. They thinned, then broke in uneven clusters, clinging to the shore. The mist broke, rolled away, and Andy caught sight of the winding strip of road running parallel to the river. Beyond, unkempt grass swayed in the morning breeze like a green satin banner, then converged on a wide lawn that spread up the gently sloping hill.

One stately column appeared briefly through the mist. Then there were six, ten, twelve columns before they were once more blocked from view by the lane of trees that lined the road.

Andy leaned far over the deck railing and strained for a better view. Neatly lined groves and a long row of buildings spread along the base of the hill to the south, then open fields beyond as far as the eye could see. To the north and east, heavily wooded forest were belted in dark green.

The trees ended as the road turned off into a wide avenue that swept up the hill, and the house she'd only barely glimpsed before now came into full view.

Andy gasped. She had never seen anything like it. Those dozen columns supported the facade of the house and sweeping second-story balconies. Double porticoes spread to either side, then broke and extended back into huge wings. There wasn't one main entrance but two, she saw, as the driveway completed a wide circle before the house. Two sets of steps were positioned one at each end of the wide front veranda.

"It's beautiful," she breathed, completely awed by the very size of the house. "It must have at least fifty rooms!"

"Sixty-two, not counting the main ballroom," Lacey provided with a mixed sense of pride. "It's called Ombre Rose."

"Ombre Rose," Andy whispered, enthralled by the beauty of the name as well as the house. "It's magnificent."

"That it is," Lacey agreed. "But then, that's what Patrick James intended."

Andy was enchanted. She'd seen countless elegant homes and fine mansions in New York. Some of her friends lived in them. But none could compare with Ombre Rose. It had a sprawling, peaceful serenity that hinted at wealth, pride, and enduring strength.

"There is no other like it. The architect came all the way from France to design it. Then he burned the plans so no one could copy it. It used to be the finest plantation in this part of the state."

Andy was staring intently at the house in the distance. "Used to be? What do you mean?"

Lacey nodded sadly. "Before the war. The family's gone now. No one lives there anymore."

As the grand house slowly disappeared behind the thick cover of trees at the water's edge, she went on to explain, "Patrick James tried to hold everything together. It was once one of the largest sugarcane plantations in Louisiana, but most of the workers took off during the war, and it just got to be too much. Mr. James had a bad heart and just wore himself out tryin' to work the fields with the handful of people who stayed on. His widow, Marilee, lives in Baton Rouge. She only went back once after he died." There was coolness of disapproval in Lacey's voice. "That was when she took it upon herself to open Ombre Rose to the Yanks. The Union Army had their headquarters there for a long time. They burned every other large plantation straight to the ground, if you get my meanin'. But Marilee lived right up there in that house with all those Yankee officers. I'm certain she was the *perfect* hostess." Her words were bitter.

Lacey's meaning was all too clear. She obviously believed Marilee James had struck some sort of bargain to save her home.

"But why doesn't she live there?" *I would*, Andy thought.

"She always hated the place." Lacey spat out disgustedly. "Everyone always said it was because Patrick James had it built for his first wife. He never really got over her death."

It was all so sad. "Weren't there any children?"

"There was a son from the first marriage. He was almost

33

as old as Marilee. They didn't get along very well," Lacey explained.

"Later on, he went off to school in England. He came back just after the war started and joined up with the Confederacy. He never came back. Now Marilee can finally be rid of the place." Lacey's voice was filled with disgust as she looked out across the water at Ombre Rose. "It's to be auctioned off. Marilee claims she can't afford the taxes. Between you and me, I think she has plenty of money. The Yanks were very generous with her for lettin' them use Ombre Rose."

"Even with the war on and everybody starvin' to death, Marilee wore gowns from Paris and entertained her guests with the finest wine. She was always drivin' about in a fine, shiny carriage with a matched team of horses, when everything else on four legs was confiscated by the Yanks. Now it looks like she'll make a pretty penny off Ombre Rose. Patrick James would never sell it. It's just too bad his son didn't come back from the war. He'd never let her sell the place. Now some filthy carpetbagger will probably buy it." She looked at Andy. "I'm sorry, it's just hard sometimes. But I just can't bear the thought of people like that at Ombre Rose."

"I think I understand," Andy whispered as she stared out over the water. The *Iron Queen* completed a slow, wide arc around the bend in the river, and she caught one last glimpse of that distant hillside through the crowning treetops at the riverbank. Her hands grasped the wooden railing until the skin stretched white across taut knuckles.

It was like a perfect white pearl set in the green velvet of the distant hillside — remote, abandoned, and breathtakingly beautiful. Some emotion equally remote and abandoned pulled at her.

Ombre Rose. The name whispered back to her on the breath of the wind and she knew she had to see it again.

Coleton James and Rafe Kelly stood at the railing at the

stern of the *Iron Queen* as the riverboat slowly rounded the bend in the river. The shoreline was only a hundred yards away. With Durant and his men aboard, they agreed it would be wiser to go ashore now rather than to continue on to Baton Rouge. They spent the night avoiding another confrontation with Durant. Now the riverboat approached the eastern shore of the Mississippi River.

He knew the river; the swim would be easy enough with the current slowed by shallow sandbars. The rolling mist on the water would shield them. But more important, he wanted to see Ombre Rose.

There were so many memories, but the strongest was of a morning just like this. Images drifted back to him—fragments, like bits and pieces of a torn picture scattered on the wind. He remembered the mist that shrouded the land and wrapped about the trees.

The cold gray dawn spilled into the glade. Shadows lengthened and separated as they stood shoulder to shoulder. The mist swirled around their legs like a live thing. The silver light gleamed dully off equally silver barrels of identical pistols.

Slowly the paces were counted off. One, two, three . . . eight, nine, ten. At the count of twenty they slowly turned to face one another. For a brief moment he stared into the face of the man whose pistol was aimed at his heart.

He saw the beads of fear that glistened across the man's forehead, sensed the sickening copper taste of fear in him, and saw the end of barrel of the pistol waver unsteadily.

"No, please! Coleton!"

Sunny.

She broke free and ran across the open glade as it erupted with the roar of gunfire . . . ran into his arms. He caught her as she fell. She clung to him as he slowly lowered her to the damp ground.

"Coleton? You're safe?" she whispered softly as her fingers twisted in the front of his shirt.

Gently he cradled her. "I'm safe."

She smiled faintly. "I was so afraid. I couldn't let him hurt you." Then her breath caught in her throat and her blue-green eyes widened. "Coleton?"

"Yes." His hand at her back filled with blood.

"Tell me again. Please say it."

She was cold now, so very cold. He held her against him to make her warm again.

"I love you." His voice ached in his throat and he cradled her in his arms. "I'll always love you. I promise."

"Forever?"

"Yes, Sunny. Forever. I swear it."

Forever.

Coleton's hands trembled against the railing. The memory was so real he could almost feel her skin beneath his fingers. Then he pushed the memory back even farther and reached inside his coat for a cheroot. The flame was unsteady. Finally the tip glowed and the smoke curled back to sting at his eyes.

The morning breeze whispered over gently swirling eddies, churning lazy whitecaps in the water, sighing like whispered promises.

He'd promised her forever—a promise he couldn't keep, a promise stolen from them in one blinding moment at dawn.

He'd believed in forever once. He didn't believe any longer. Forever was a lie.

Coleton flicked the cigarette into the water. When he turned to Rafe, his voice was hard, his face expressionless.

"Let's go."

They both climbed over the side, slipped silently into the water, and kicked away from the stern of the riverboat. With determined strokes, Coleton swam for shore.

Chapter Three

Andy's first week in Baton Rouge was hectic. Twice she tried to persuade Lacey to take her out to Ombre Rose, but something always seemed to interfere. Lacey had arranged an endless round of teas and social gatherings to introduce her to family friends in Baton Rouge.

She was amazed that even in the aftermath of war, with everything in such short supply, the polite functions of society went on as before. The simplest ritual seemed to give the ladies of Baton Rouge something to look forward to — a bright moment in an otherwise bleak existence. Of course, their reception of a Yankee in their midst was met with cool disdain. Lacey ignored them and plowed straight ahead. Andy couldn't decide whether the dour matrons failed to intimidate her or whether Lacey was determined to intimidate them by openly flaunting a Yankee guest.

Andy had become the center of controversy, embarassingly so, but she could hardly refuse to attend a barbeque or a small soiree. Lacey would have been devastated, and it would only have fueled the contempt that everyone seemed to feel toward the "snooty, thievin' Yankees," as everyone north of the Mason-Dixon line was referred to. So she deferred out of consideration to her friendship with Lacey.

And then there was Captain Chandler Durant. He had called on her twice since he arrived back in Baton Rouge four days ago, and was most persistent in a way that made

Andy feel uneasy. He seemed to assume that she should fall willingly at his feet merely because they were both from the North and he had attended West Point with her brother. His supercilious air of superiority made her uneasy, and she had coerced Lacey into making an excuse for her on both occasions. She had no doubts he would call again.

But she wasn't concerned with Captain Durant or Lacey's exhausting social schedule this morning. She was determined to go to Ombre Rose if she had to sneak out to do it—which at the moment was precisely what she was doing.

The first shafts of gray light fell weakly to the floor as Andy slipped from the bed. It was deliciously cool this time of morning. Even the humidity didn't seem so oppressive, and a faint breeze gently lifted the faded damask curtains at her window.

She caught her breath as a floorboard creaked underfoot. She stopped and listened for any indication that someone might have heard her, but there were just the normal sounds of the house this early in the morning.

Down the hallway, beyond her closed door, she could hear August Kittridge humming to himself. She knew it would be at least a half hour before he walked past her door on his way to breakfast.

The room next to hers was silent, of course. There was no amount of bribery or threat that could have driven Lacey Kittridge from her bed at this hour. It suited Andy's plan perfectly, for if Lacey was awake and knew what she was up to there would be no end to her objections.

She had learned which of the other floorboards creaked and carefully tiptoed around them, stepping across an especially disagreeable one to the wardrobe.

The shadows were heavy in the room, but she decided against turning up the bedside lantern. She didn't want Mary or Cassie to know she was up.

Andy shivered as she pushed her nightgown down over her hips and stepped out of the pool of delicate lace.

Opening the bottom drawer of the wardrobe she pulled out silk underdrawers and a lace-trimmed camisole. She slipped into the undergarments, tying the satin ribbon closure over her breasts.

Searching all the way to the back of the wardrobe she found the package she'd hastily hidden. She winced as the stiff paper wrapper crinkled loudly in the stillness of the room.

"A lady must never go out unescorted," she whispered aloud, and a slow smile tipped the corners of her mouth as she held the contents of the package aloft for inspection: blue cambric shirt, sturdy denim pants, and a black felt hat.

She had convinced Cassie to purchase the small-sized, man's clothes for her on a trip to market a few days earlier. The garments were a necessary disguise.

Andy giggled as excitement swept through her. "And a *lady* is not about to go out," she announced to her reflection in the full-length cheval mirror beside the wardrobe.

The shirt fell to her knees, the sleeves dangling at least eight inches below her fingertips, but that was of little concern. She would simply roll up the sleeves and tuck the tails into the pants. But they presented an entirely different problem. They were more than big, they were huge!

Buttoning the shirt, Andy pushed up the sleeves and stepped into the pants. Good Lord, she could almost fit into one leg! And even with the thickness of the shirt tucked in, they still fell to the floor at her feet. Andy hitched them up and looked around for something to use as a belt.

She groaned. All her belts were either attached to dresses or wouldn't fit around the extra fullness of the denim gathered in at the waist. Her gaze fastened resourcefully on the braided satin tie that bound the curtains back from the window.

When she was dressed, Andy studied her reflection once more. All signs of her feminine figure were hidden beneath the padded excess of shirt and pants. In fact, she resembled a lumpy, overweight boy. Shirtsleeves were rolled back to her wrists, the collar was discreetly buttoned. The one real incongruity was the green satin tie at her waist, but there was nothing to be done for that. Then her gaze fell to her feet.

For the time being, she would simply wear her own high-topped riding boots. They were the most practical thing she owned.

Andy gathered her long hair at the nape of her neck and twisted it into a thick coil, tucking it under the black hat. It dipped down low across her eyes, making it impossible to see anything unless she tipped her head back and looked down her nose, where the hat came to rest. She shoved it back on her forehead. After all, she had to see where she was going.

She checked the clock that sat atop the rosewood chest of drawers. There were still ten minutes before August Kittridge went downstairs. She seized the canvas and paints, wrapped in a neat bundle, took a deep breath, and opened the door. All clear. She stepped out into the hallway.

Actually, getting downstairs was easier than she expected. She heard the distinctive clinking of silverware in the dining room as the maid, Cassie, set the table. Mamalu, the large black woman who ruled the kitchen, was busy cooking breakfast. She couldn't understand what she was saying, but by the rise and fall of her voice Andy suspected she was lecturing Tallman. He was the Kittridge's driver, butler, and all-around handyman. He always ate early, then went out to harness the mare to the carriage while August Kittridge ate his breakfast.

Her hand was on the parlor door when Cassie's voice stopped her. "What you doin' in here, boy?"

Andy swallowed convulsively, keeping her head low, the brim of the hat almost at her chin. What should she do now?

"I told you to take dem things on 'round to the kitchen." She clucked her tongue. "You know you ain't supposed to come in through the front door. Now get!"

Andy smothered a giggle. Her costume had worked. Cassie thought she was the delivery boy bringing fresh foods from the marketplace.

She ducked her head as she ran for the kitchen. "Yes, ma'am," she said, lowering her voice as she altered her course and shot past Mamalu and Tallman in the kitchen.

Mamalu was standing beside the small breakfast table, hard in the middle of a lecture directed at Tallman. She paused once, midsentence, finger waving in the air to give Andy a strange look, only to launch back into her tirade. Andy didn't worry about Tallman; he couldn't have escaped the kitchen if his life depended on it.

It was only when she reached the yard that separated the house from the carriage shed that Andy saw the boy disappearing around the corner of the house toward the street. He was dressed in a blue cambric work shirt and dusty denim pants. His feet were bare. The only thing missing was the black felt hat as he clamored aboard the wagon making early morning deliveries.

Andy didn't question divine providence, she simply kept on going until she reached the shed. The carriage stood outside, the mare already harnessed waiting to take August Kittridge to his office down at the waterfront. The ancient gelding was in the stall farthest to the back.

It was obvious he hadn't been ridden in some time. He shied at her first attempts to saddle him, then merely blew out disgustedly when she persisted. Lacey had mentioned how difficult it had been to keep horses during the last two years of the war.

A quick thought flashed as she wondered how the gelding and mare had avoided confiscation by the Confederate Army.

Out in the pale light of the yard after she saddled the gelding, she understood. The Confederacy had probably come to the same conclusion as she had. Poor Lucky didn't look as if he'd go more than a hundred paces without dropping. He must be as old as the hills, his back swayed dangerously, and bones stuck out in every direction.

41

Andy wondered if the animal's name had some significance for the horse itself or the person trying to ride him. Still, Tallman said he was reliable and surefooted.

"I wonder how long ago that was." Andy sighed. She would have to take Tallman's word for it.

There were two entrances to the yard, one off the front drive that cut in from the main street and another smaller one at the back of the property, turning into an alley that lined the houses along this block. Andy chose the back gate and sent Lucky along at a pace she fervently prayed wouldn't strain the poor animal. Riding to the end of the alley, she cut across the adjacent street, keeping her hat low to conceal her face as she passed a carriage.

She'd casually asked Tallman the day before which was the river road. Cutting down one tree-lined street, then turning onto another, she easily found the river road at the edge of town. The sun was a golden ball in the pale sky as she sent the gelding drumming down the road to Ombre Rose.

The plantation was about three miles past the edge of town. She considered cutting off the road where she would be less likely to draw attention. The trees were thick past the edge of town and would provide cover, but she decided against it. Lacey had mentioned the interconnecting bayous that wound in and around Baton Rouge, places where a person could wander for days and never come out.

"Come on, Lucky old boy. We'll just stick to the main road."

She urged the gelding on at a faster pace, excitement surging through her. At last she was going to see Ombre Rose. With any luck she might even be able to get in a couple hours of painting and still be back before Lacey made her first appearance in time for lunch.

There was hardly anyone on the road this early in the morning. She passed a farmer and his family on their way into town. Bundles of golden sugarcane stalks were stacked high in the back of the open wagon. She ducked her head, shielding her face beneath the brim of the hat in what must have seemed a casual nod.

The farmer nodded back, but kept his gaze trained on the road ahead, obviously uninterested in what he assumed to be a slender boy on horseback.

Several hundred yards off her left through the trees at the water's edge, she could see the morning sun shimmering on the brown water of the Mississippi. To her right the forest had thinned, giving way to clumps of oak and spreading cypress. She'd been riding almost an hour when she noticed a long break in the trees up ahead. She rounded a bend in the road and drew the gelding to a bone-jarring, stiff-legged stop. He snorted his displeasure, but Andy never heard it as she stared at the wide field of overgrown grass that swayed gently in the morning breeze, fanning back from the road and sweeping lazily up the gentle incline of the hill to Ombre Rose.

A wide road paved in brick cut through the overgrown grass. The sun was warm, wrapping the magnificent house in a soft morning haze. Her breath caught in her throat. It was even more beautiful than she first thought. Slowly, Andy guided the gelding up the road, his hooves making clopping sounds on the red paving stones.

As the road climbed that slight incline Andy could see the roofline of stables in the distance behind the house. They stood empty, individual stalls gaping open as if they only waited for their Thoroughbred occupants to return from an early-morning ride.

Lacey had mentioned some of the finest race horses were once bred here at Ombre Rose. But that was before the war. Now they were all gone.

Beyond the stables and exercise paddock were other low buildings and an enclosed yard.

"The kennels," she whispered, almost before she thought of it. And beyond were orchards.

Peach and pecan trees . . . She remembered running barefoot through the groves, the moist, rich earth pushing up through her toes . . .

"Of course they would have had dogs," she assured herself, but why was she so certain about the orchards? How could she possibly remember running barefoot?

Andy ignored her wandering imagination as she let the gelding set a slower pace. It took almost ten minutes to travel the road to the main house, and in that time, Andy realized there was far more to Ombre Rose than she'd seen from the river.

Unkempt fields spread to the north like a rusty brown carpet. A dark belt of green forest bordered to the east. What she originally thought was one continuous long building parallel to the fields was actually a row of small cottages. There was a small yard in front of each, the grass overgrown there as well.

One yard was fenced, the gate hanging at a crooked angle. A dried and broken skeleton was all that remained of a tree in another. The cottages stood empty and silent.

The workers and their families lived there. The thought seemed to leap from nowhere.

And they were paid for their labor, not slaves.

"Mr. James didn't hold with a person ownin' another," Andy whispered out loud. The unusual cadence in her voice startled her.

"Good heavens," she laughed, a little uneasily, "this place certainly works on the imagination, doesn't it, Lucky." She patted the gelding's neck reassuringly, laughing at her mood as much as the soft drawl that had seeped into her voice.

It did set her imagination whirling. With her artist's eye, she could imagine what life might have been like once at Ombre Rose.

She could almost hear the nickering of Thoroughbred race horses from the pasture that bordered the carriage road; voices calling out across the wide lawns; the wild barking of dogs as visitors arrived.

It required little effort to see ladies in their elegant hooped skirts strolling along the wide verandas and smell the dusky hickory smoke from the stone barbeque that mingled with the intoxicating sweetness of star jasmine

44

from the gardens.

It was like the games she'd played as a child, where she had imagined herself stepping into another place and time she'd read or heard about. Make-believe it was called, long before the war when Ombre Rose was alive with people and laughter.

The laughter echoed back and it was her own. Stunned, Andy blinked back the vivid scene. How could she possibly know what it had been like? And what the devil was a barbeque anyway?

Slowly the images receded, leaving only the grand, breathtaking house before her. And it was truly magnificent.

Lucky blew out wearily as she dismounted. If it was possible, Ombre Rose was even more beautiful than when she first saw it from the deck of the *Iron Queen*.

"Greek and Italian architecture," she murmured to herself, easily recognizing the brilliant blend of the two architectural styles she'd seen in countless gallery paintings.

"Well at least old Perrot the Parrot managed to teach me something," she mused thoughtfully as she looped the reins through the huge ring at the ornate iron hitching post.

She rubbed her hand slowly over the rusted, snarling lion's head. Something about a wish flashed through her thoughts and was then gone.

Her gaze fastened on the house. That day aboard the *Iron Queen*, Andy had counted twelve columns supporting the front facade. Now she realized additional columns spread around the side of the house to a semicircular wing. There were actually twenty-two Corinthian columns!

A veranda ran the full width of the house on the first floor with two sets of wide steps at either end made of polished granite. The upstairs gallery, enclosed by an intricate wrought-iron railing, looked out on the vast lawn toward the river and provided shade below. Andy slowly walked the length of the veranda.

The exterior of the house had been white originally, but it was in bad need of fresh paint. The overcoat was cracked in many places, flaking away to reveal a gray undercoat.

"A gleaming pearl," Andy mused, remembering how she'd thought of it when she first saw it from the *Iron Queen*. The soft blending of the white, peeling away to the gray had created the illusion from a distance.

Still, she thought to herself as she slowly climbed those granite steps, it was a grand house. She'd seen many opulent homes in New York, the austere and extravagant mansions that lined Eighth Avenue, the palatial estates out on Long Island, but none could compare with the breathtaking serenity and splendor of Ombre Rose.

There was a peacefulness here, an air of quiet expectancy, that seemed to spill over into the empty cottages, the deserted stables, and the soft sigh of the wind in the overgrown grass.

Her aunt Lenore used to say houses were like the people who owned them. Andy tried to imagine the people who had once lived at Ombre Rose. Surely they must have been as rich and fine and beautiful.

She continued her exploration. The veranda spread around each side of the house, broken only by those Corinthian columns. She followed it around the south portico, walking along the circular veranda under the magnificent wing of the house. From there the expanse of lawn rolled down the hill to the woods beyond. It was like an enormous park with tall pines, spreading oak, and flowering magnolia trees.

Row upon row of unkempt rosebushes were overgrown along this side of the house. Many had not survived and lay withered to thorny stalks. Of course, she thought with sudden realization, the plantation had been named for the roses!

At the far end of the park, an arbor broke the line of overgrown shrubs that formed the southern perimeter. Andy stepped down off the veranda and immediately found the footpath set in bricks. It curved back around to the front of the house, the direction from where she'd just come.

She frowned. There was another path here somewhere that led into the park.

Andy stood abruptly, a little frightened by the intensity of that thought. How on earth would she know whether there was a second path or not?

She almost turned around to follow the one path back to the front of the house but something stopped her. As the nagging persisted, Andy gave in to it. She pushed through the knee-high grass, pulling brush and weeds and scattered limbs aside. If there had once been a path here . . . Then she stopped as the toe of her boot scratched against a hard, solid surface.

Excitement poured through her as Andy tore aside brush and shrub, laughing excitedly as her fingers finally brushed against the coarse, hard surface of the interlocking bricks that formed the lost walkway. She couldn't imagine why the one path was clear and this one left to the weeds and brush. A better question was, who had cleared the first one? Supposedly Ombre Rose was deserted. The entire place should have been overgrown, but it wasn't.

The answer didn't matter to Andy. She'd found her secret path and intended to follow it wherever it led her.

Here and there it emerged through the overgrown weeds. Andy followed it into the park behind the main house. Several times she lost it and had to go back and begin again in a new direction.

Even though the park was overgrown to weeds and brush, it was still beautiful. In spite of the lack of care, the trees still flourished, spreading a cool green canopy across the gently sloping hillside. Occasionally the trees broke apart and sunlight filtered through. It was like walking through a private forest.

The path ended abruptly at a wall of shrub and trailing vines stretching overhead. She would have simply turned back if it hadn't been for the sun's reflection; something was concealed in the arbor that momentarily caught the bright light and glared into her eyes.

Andy pushed her way through the shrubs, low-hanging tree branches, and heavy underbrush. She pulled away the tangled vines that draped like a shroud.

Then her fingers brushed against smooth, cool stone. She traced the pillar up, until she was stretching on her toes. Andy tore away more vine, exposing the tall white column that was at least eight feet high and made of the most beautiful marble she'd ever seen.

With agonizing slowness, she worked her way around in a circular direction, pulling away clumps of brush and small limbs until her hands were raw.

Three then four columns were partially exposed, with delicate scrolled ironwork joining them together. At the fifth column she found the gate.

It must have been years since anyone had trimmed the wall of shrubs and vines. Andy jerked away the twining growth with mounting excitement. When the gate was fully exposed, she stood back wiping her sleeve across her forehead. Leaves and twigs were tangled in her hair. She must look a sight, but couldn't have cared less.

She wondered what this place was as she stopped to catch her breath. Only now could she make out the unusual design intricately worked into the ornate wrought-iron panel. It was made up of patterns of intertwined leaves and flowers—that were all roses, trailing end to end, woven into the design around the entire structure.

The latch at the gate was rusted but looked as if it might be persuaded. There was no lock. The moment her fingers touched it, Andy jerked her hand back.

A warm, tingling sensation spread from her fingertips to the palm of her right hand, like a wild, warm energy surging through her. It wasn't painful, simply unexpected, and Andy instinctively rubbed her thumb across the sensitized fingertips. Almost as quickly as she noticed it, it was gone.

She laughed at herself, remembering that as a child, when she knocked her elbow playing, a sudden numbness would shoot through her hand. She must have bumped her arm clearing away some of the shrubs and branches.

Dismissing it, Andy reached out to the latch. Once again, the tingling returned, with far more intensity this time. It was as if she'd somehow touched something pleasantly warm. Almost like touching someone's hand.

Staring at the wrought-iron latch, Andy decided it must have been warmed by the sun. Yes, of course, that was it. But looking up, she could see only the solid canopy of trees overhead.

This was ridiculous! Whatever the reason for the unusual sensation, it certainly wasn't anything to be frightened of. With that bit of mental taking-herself-by-the-shoulders, Andy seized the latch and jerked with all her strength. Several vines wove through the wrought-iron frame like tiny ropes. After much effort, the gate lurched open, the rusty hinges creaking reluctantly. Andy ducked beneath a tangle of vines as she stepped inside.

The structure was octagonal in shape, perhaps twelve or fifteen feet across, and each side was formed by the pillars that supported the roof overhead.

How extraordinary! Andy could see individual panes of glass through the vines that grew everywhere in wild profusion. The roof was made of glass! The individual panes were smeared with a dirty haze, making it almost impossible to see out. The sun shone feebly through, falling to nothing more than weak streamers of light on the marble floor. It must have been the reflection off the glass that caught her attention.

Andy was captivated as she slowly brought her breathing back under control. Now that she was inside, she realized it was some sort of outdoor terrace—a gazebo. She'd seen structures like it out on Long Island, only they were usually made of wood.

Andy slowly walked about the inside of the gazebo, stepping over trailing vines and broken twigs. The pillars were smooth white marble, the same as the floor. The intricate ironwork that formed each of the wall panels had once been painted white although there was little trace of it now. Several of the overhead panes had shattered as branches from the trees outside grew and crowded for room. The glass crunched underfoot.

Even in such a sad state, Andy could imagine it as it had once been—a beautiful place, private and cool, to escape the heat. The breeze would come up off the river. The surrounding trees would provide shade in the summer. And the glass roof overhead would provide shelter from the unexpected afternoon showers that seemed to come so often.

She wondered if this gazebo might once have been used to play hide-and-seek. It was a private place, where a person could slip away from the main house, just to be alone . . . *or to be with someone.*

The thought came unbidden, as if some faraway inner voice might have whispered it to her.

Andy clasped her hands over her arms and rubbed them, the coarse cambric shirt roughening her skin. She felt a momentary shiver, almost as if she were chilled. Except that it wasn't cold.

Still, she felt a strange inner trembling, almost anticipation. It was like special occasions when she was a child—like her birthday when she would wait all day for Stephen to return home with her present. He would pretend he had forgotten and act terribly surprised when she rushed to meet him at the door in anticipation. Then, when she almost thought he might truly have forgotten, he would reach inside his coat pocket, or retrieve her present from some hidden place. Even now she could remember that thrill of excitement, hardly knowing what to expect, certain only that it would be wonderful.

That was exactly how she felt now. As if she were waiting for something very special, in this extraordinary hidden place.

A half-formed thought crowded at the edge of her imagination: *as if she were waiting for someone.*

The strangest sense of something familiar and yet elusive at the same time swept through Andy. It was almost as if she were to close her eyes and try very hard, she might be able to see that person's face.

Andy laughed softly. It was complete foolishness, she chided herself, her gaze slowly following one draping vine as it lazily curled its way to the floor.

It was then she saw something she hadn't noticed before: a flower had grown through the wrought-iron railing, a small white rose. There was only that single bloom on the trailing branch as if it had poked tentatively through and now struggled in the dim light.

One rose, somehow surviving when no others grew nearby. How sad and alone it seemed. Had it grown here always, planted by the mistress of Ombre Rose? Or had it grown wild, defying the vines, lack of water, and sun to struggle out some meager existence where it should never have grown at all?

Promise me. The words seemed to rustle through the dried leaves as Andy bent to pick the rose.

"Who's there?" Andy whirled around, but there was no one there, only the breeze lifting the branches of the trees. She was alone.

It came to her again; that strange, inexplicable feeling that she could imagine what it was like before the war, when there was life and laughter at Ombre Rose. As if . . . she might have been here before. But that was impossible.

With a faint frown, she inhaled the fragrance of the rose. If she wanted to get any painting done this morning, she should get started. After all, that was the reason she'd come here today. But she wasn't ready to leave this place yet. She leaned back against a marble column. It was so peaceful and quiet.

The coolness of the stone penetrated her back through the shirt as she tilted her head and looked up at the soft glow of sunlight overhead. She closed her eyes, the quiet and the heavy fragrance seeping into her as images played behind her closed lids: horses in the pasture, their coats gleaming like burnished velvet; ladies in softly hued gowns, their voices tinkling on a warm afternoon breeze; a handsome young man, the sun in his soft brown hair, running through the park . . . running to the gazebo.

It began like the soft haze of a dream that slowly washes over the senses, teasing, promising with half-formed images. Cool shadows surrounded her, and she felt herself drifting. All about her she heard the murmur of the leaves, the sigh of the breeze through the overgrown shrubs and vines . . .

Promise me . . .

The words came again from somewhere . . . She couldn't seem to remember . . .

It was then she felt it, or perhaps only imagined it; the lightest touch against her cheek, like the breath of the wind, or a soft whisper.

Forever. Promise me.

An incredible warmth wrapped around her, almost as if someone's arms had embraced her.

She tried to open her eyes, but they were heavy as if she were tired, so very tired.

Forever.

The word echoed from very far away.

Promise me.

She might have struggled, except for the arms that held her. She might have cried out, except for the mouth that caressed her lips, her cheek, her closed eyes, then retraced each touch, each caress with a fiery heat so intense it left her breathless.

Was is it a moment, an hour, a day? Was it even real?

It didn't matter as she was drawn into some dark place of memory, void of sight or sound. There was only feeling, incredible feeling as heat swept through her, taking her where neither mattered.

His arms molded her to him. His kiss was stirring, possessive as his mouth shaped hers.

Her mind cried to deny what was happening. This wasn't real. There was no one here. She struggled to free herself.

Yet even as Andy felt the coarse chafing of the denim

52

against her skin, she gasped at the exquisite pleasure of those heated fingers stroking away the soft satin bodice of her gown.

Thought collided with sensation. Reality slipped into some far place beyond memory. It was as if she were two people: Amanda Spenser, who had come to Ombre Rose, hoping to capture it on canvas, and someone else, dressed in that satin gown whose flesh ached under those fevered hands. Someone who stepped from the shadows and became her.

"Love me." The words tumbled from her swollen lips as his hands stroked upward from her waist and those lean fingers brushed across her breasts, teasing her to aching need.

"I will always love you." His lips burned the promise against her skin as he slowly lowered her to the floor of the gazebo.

"You're mine. You will always be mine." The words were a fiery heat that seemed to sear her soul.

The marble was cool against her bare shoulder blades, the heat of his body pressing into her, his hands moving with deliberate slowness as they stroked her.

"Make me yours," she whispered into the heat of his kiss, abandoning herself to the need, the desire, this recaptured moment.

Tears slipped from beneath her lashes and they were kissed away. Words caught in her throat, so many words she'd longed an eternity to say. They were trapped by the lips that moved over hers. His hand came up, caressing her cheek with such tenderness.

Slowly she opened her eyes, staring up through the cool green shadows. Streamers of sunlight bathed their naked bodies in a pale golden glow. His eyes were the softest gray and dearly familiar. She reached up, tracing the curve of his mouth as the words seemed to shimmer through the sunlight and leaves.

"Promise me," she whispered.

His eyes were like quicksilver, shot through with fire and

light one moment, cool and restful the next. His fingers laced with hers, pressing their palms together, sealing the promise.

"I will always love you. Forever." Those simple words seemed to come from his soul, and she gave herself to the need that swept their young bodies. Then there was no need of words as those lips moved down her throat, lingering over the hollow at her neck. There was only the need as those hands moved over her with familiar longing.

"Yes." She didn't know whether she whispered it or wished it.

"Yes." She answered those questing hands as they ignited her body to flame.

It poured through her, consumed her until there was nothing but the intense pleasure of that lean, hard body pressing against hers, naked with need, hard muscles glistening as they came together, his hands enfolding hers, the whisper of passionate promise as those lips closed over the aching tip of her breast, filling her with a hunger as their bodies joined. And in that stolen time, she believed in forever.

Was it only moments or hours? Slowly, she felt the warmth steal from about her body. The glow of sunlight that had caressed their bodies slipped into the shadows. The gazebo was gone. A cool mist surrounded her.

She looked up, searching for those soft gray eyes and found only shadows. He was bending over her; she could feel his arms about her, hear the frantic pounding of his heart beneath her cheek. But in place of the desire and passion of moments before, there was an expression of such unbearable anguish on his young face. Something was wrong, terribly wrong.

"I love you," he whispered brokenly. *"I love you. I love you."* Over and over again, each time more desperately as if he must make her believe it.

She reached up, as panic and fear, achingly familiar swept through her. She couldn't breathe, there was such incredible pain. And she couldn't see him.

Her fingers grazed his face and he clasped her hand, pressing it against his cheek.

"I do love you." His voice was filled with such torment and pain. *"I will always love you, forever."*

"Promise we will always be together!" she cried out softly as the shadows slipped between them and his hand was torn from hers.

At first there was only darkness. Then a faint glow of light, and she was drifting toward it. It became stronger, pulling at her, bringing her back . . .

"Promise me," Andy whispered over and over.

She opened her eyes reluctantly. They slowly focused. The shadows seemed to fall away as she stared up through lazily curling vines that grew unhindered to dirt-smudged panes of glass in the skylight overhead. Patterns of dappled sunlight spilled across the marble columns. The single white rose was clutched in her hand. Everything was exactly the way she remembered it.

"Oh, God, what's happened?" she sobbed brokenly, struggling to breathe past the deep ache inside. She was laying on her side, knees drawn to her chest. The coolness of the marble penetrated the coarse denim pants and cambric shirt.

Tears pooled in her eyes and spilled softly down her cheeks. She felt such incredible loss and wept for it. She cried until she couldn't cry anymore.

A very long time later, she pushed to her feet, weakness pouring through her. It was several minutes more before she trusted her legs. Her fingers trembled as she brushed leaves from her hair. She hesitated, her hand above the latch at the gate.

Andy breathed deeply and slowed the frantic pounding of her heart. Almost daring herself, she seized the latch. When there was no recurrence of the tingling she had experienced before, she quickly ran down the two steps and retraced the path to the house.

She wanted to run, as far and as fast as she possibly could. *Just leave*, she told herself, knowing she shouldn't have come.

Forget the painting. It was a ridiculous idea anyway, she rationalized, slipping her foot into the stirrup and whirling Lucky about. She wouldn't come back.

Even as she told herself, another voice whispered from deep inside her:

I'll come back. I have to.

Chapter Four

Andy remembered little of the ride back to town. The first thing she was truly aware of was the change of Lucky's pace. It was hot, and the air was heavy with unspent moisture. The gelding had set a reluctant pace back to town. Now his ears pricked forward in what could only be an indication they were almost home.

. She dismounted inside the shed, going through the motions of stripping away the saddle and pad, forgetting that sort of thing was usually left for Tallman. Her thoughts were splintered, disjointed. The more she tried not to think about what had happened at Ombre Rose, the more it persisted.

Dear God. What had happened? Dream, fantasy, imagination? No dream had ever been so real, she thought as she twisted a thick handful of straw and wiped down the gelding. She'd never experienced anything that left her so emotionally drained—she was aching for something she couldn't explain.

Even now the memory of the experience left her weak and trembling, leaning against the gelding's warm neck as she tried to breathe strength back into her arms and legs.

The yard was empty, the sky overhead threatening as Andy made her way carefully to the house, the bundle of her canvas and paints carried under one arm. She must look a sight, she thought as she stepped up onto the service porch at the back of the house. She'd lost the black felt hat somewhere, her hair hung loose to her waist, and there was a tear in the shirt and smudges on the pants. She slipped upstairs unseen, and once safely back in her room, collapsed against her closed door.

An hour later, when Lacey finally rose at her customary time of almost noon, Andy had bathed and changed her clothes. Only the faint smudges of fatigue under her eyes betrayed she hadn't slept the morning through.

"You look a bit peaked, darlin'," Lacey remarked as they walked arm in arm down the staircase to eat a late breakfast.

"We can always postpone our shoppin' trip in town today to another time."

It was a generous offer and Andy would have loved to take Lacey up on it, but the disappointment was obvious in her friend's voice. And she did need more turpentine and pigments. She had begun a painting of Ombre Rose as she saw it that day from the riverboat. Now that she had been out to the plantation, she wanted to make several changes. She gave Lacey a bright smile. "I wouldn't hear of it. It will be good to get out of the house. You've been promising to take me shopping for days, and I do need some paint supplies. We can leave right after we eat, just as we planned."

Tallman had dropped them off over two hours ago, continuing on to the waterfront to meet August Kittridge. Lacey had made several purchases, and Andy had her neatly wrapped paint supplies tucked under her arm.

They stepped out onto the sun-bleached boardwalk in front of the mercantile store.

"You are behavin' absolutely scandalously," Lacey declared flatly, and with more than a little scandalized outrage. "Buyin' that piece of sugarcane from that boy and eatin' it like, like—"

"Like a piece of sugarcane?" Andy suggested, laughter dancing in her brilliant eyes. She knew exactly what Lacey was thinking. There was a definite code of conduct in the South between the gentry and the slave class. But she wasn't about to acknowledge it. Besides, she was curious about sugarcane. Like most people, she had never really stopped long enough to consider where sugar came from. She was fascinated by the fibrous stalk. It was sweet, juicy, and the watery syrup was running down her chin.

"You know what I mean! Honestly!" Lacey fumed as she pulled her own handkerchief from her sleeve and wiped Andy's chin. "I can't take you anywhere. I just don't know what you'll do next."

"It will probably be all over town that you were sittin' on the sidewalk eatin' cane with that boy like a common fieldhand," she proclaimed indignantly.

"He was all of seven years old. And I'm not sitting on the sidewalk," Andy informed her with a look of pure innocence. Lacey was right, of course. She'd discovered that since she arrived in Baton Rouge. It was bigotry pure and simple — something she never had any patience for, and it was a side of Lacey she'd never seen — as if she were afraid of what people might think. It almost seemed they'd changed places in their attitudes from the years they were in school together. Then, Lacey always had more daring than was healthy for anyone with a careless disregard for consequences. Now it was Andy's turn to be just a little outrageous, and she enjoyed seeing Lacey unnerved by it all.

But it was more than the girlish pranks they enjoyed as young girls. Andy reminded herself that things were different in the South. A war had been fought over those differences. She simply had to make allowances for them, but without compromising what she believed in. She felt confident it could be done. She and Lacey had always been able to bridge the gap with friendship. She was determined that wouldn't change now.

Lacey gasped as a man pushed past them without so much as a tip of his hat. She glared at his retreating back.

"Damn Yankees! They are insufferably rude and ill-mannered!" she fumed, waving the tip of her parasol in a threatening gesture.

Andy stared after the man. "Wasn't that the clerk at the bank you introduced me to the other day?" She was certain she recognized him.

"He was movin' too fast for me to recognize him." Lacey smoothed her gown with the proper amount of indignation.

"No southern gentleman would behave in such a manner."

Andy struggled not to laugh. "Of course it was he. You know the one—Mrs. Whitherspoon's nephew." She had met Mrs. Whitherspoon and doubted she would ever quite be the same after the encounter. The woman actually had the poor manners to ask her if she was taking delight in seeing the South in ruins. That got the afternoon tea off to a brilliant start. From that moment on it was as if war had been declared in the front parlor. She and Lacey left early.

"I know what you are tryin' to imply, Amanda Spenser—that he obviously lacks manners. Therefore, you may wipe that smug expression off your face. It is possible I was mistaken and that it was George Whitherspoon. If so, considerin' the direction he was goin' in, I would say he's probably goin' to the auctions?"

"What auctions." This was the first Andy heard about any auction. She thought all trade went on down at the waterfront as cargoes were shipped or brought in. August Kittridge had spoken of it often. Certain things were still so hard to come by people often began bidding for them right there on the docks before cargoes were even unloaded.

Lacey frowned. "Land auctions; properties seized by the new government."

"Why? What about the people who own them?"

"It's part of what's goin' on with the Yankees down here, Andy. Most people are dirt poor, without a cent to their names. Prices are sky-high. You know the outrageous price you paid for that turpentine. The merchants were forced to take out loans on their businesses. If prices are high and they can't sell their merchandise," she went on to explain, concisely, "then they can't meet the loan payments. The banks end up takin' the businesses back and some Yankee comes along and picks it up for a song, 'cause they're the only ones who have any money. But that's not the worst of it." Lacey's expression was grim. "Most of the men have been away for four years, fightin' the war. The farms and plantations are in ruins, there's hardly any crops comin' to market. Now the new government has stepped in and levied taxes on everythin'. Without crops there is no money."

"And the farmers can't pay their taxes," Andy concluded, grasping another startling reality of the economic ruin in the South.

Lacey nodded. "They lose their land and their homes. Many of them don't know anythin' else but farmin'." There was a soft catch in Lacey's voice. "So many of our friends have lost just about everythin'. That's why everyone is so resentful. It wasn't enough we lost the war, and so many of our boys died. Now the Yankees come down here and buy up all the land for practically nothin', throwin' people out of homes they've lived in for generations. Like a swarm of vultures."

"Surely it's not that way for everyone." They walked slowly as they talked, coming upon a group of men who crowded in the doorway of the building at the end of the street. Andy recognized several she'd met over the last two weeks, and many more that she hadn't. Some were nodding their heads sadly and moving on, their heads bent in whispers. Others remained, straining to see over the shoulders of those in front of them. Obviously there was a great deal of interest in the auction.

"Some manage to get by," Lacey admitted. "But the only reason Daddy is still in business is because of foreign investments he made before the war."

They stopped outside the City Hall Building. Notices were posted in the windows facing out onto the street giving descriptions of properties being offered in that day's auction.

"How often does this happen?" Andy read some of the brief descriptions; twenty- and thirty-acre farms, several businesses, all being offered at ridiculously low opening bids.

"Once a month. I try not to come into town on those days. It's just so awful." Lacey started to turn away. "All those good people losin' their homes. I know most of them. Ombre Rose is to be sold today."

Andy looked at Lacey in stunned surprise. Of course, Lacey had mentioned that the plantation would be auctioned off, but she hadn't thought it might be this soon. A week ago, it might not have bothered her. Now, something inside her died at the thought it would be sold.

"Andy! What are you doin'?" Too late, Lacey made a grab for her arm, trying to stop her.

"You can't go in there."

Andy slipped into the Town Hall meeting room, ignoring the few bemused glances that fell her way. She smiled faintly, catching a flash of pale blue as Lacey wedged through the crowd behind her. There was a look of exasperation mixed with horrified disapproval wrinkling her lovely brow.

"Andy!" Lacey whispered furiously, trying to get her attention and draw her away.

"We shouldn't be here." They stood together as an officious-looking gentleman with steely mutton-chop whiskers read from the podium the details of the next property being offered at auction. It was a tailor's shop. Behind the auctioneer another gentleman sat at a desk, making notations on various papers and documents. The bidding was opened at three hundred dollars which was to cover existing inventory, a five-year lease on the land, and mortgage payments on the building. Andy couldn't believe it.

The pace of the bidding was furious as it bounced back and forth between three men. She'd never seen any of them before. That could only mean one thing—they weren't from Baton Rouge. Andy had the feeling she was getting her first real look at Yankee carpetbaggers.

She jumped as the auctioneer's gavel slammed down on a final sales price of six hundred seventy-five dollars. Her gaze immediately fastened on a small, older man who seemed to shrink into his chair. The tailor? He looked absolutely stricken, and Andy felt a knot growing inside her at the lives that were passing before her eyes. The knot tightened with every crash of the gavel—farms, warehouses, an area of privately owned dock space down at the waterfront, one of the hotels, three restaurants, nothing was spared.

If money was owed, property went on the auction block. And with each sale, she could feel the resentment that crept into the room like a flowing current, constantly eroding.

"Good morning, Amanda."

Andy turned at the silky greeting. "Good morning, Captain." She smiled briefly up at Chandler Durant. She had seen him as she came in and hoped to avoid him.

"I must say I'm a little surprised to see you two ladies here." It was the first time he chose to acknowledge Lacey's presence, his lack of common courtesy grating on Andy's nerves.

"Is Mr. Kittridge here as well?"

Again there was that faint underlying tone of disapproval.

"Oh, no." Lacey carefully explained. "He's busy down at the warehouse. Several boats came in last night. Andy was the one who insisted on comin' on in."

"Is that so?" There was a faintly bemused expression on Chandler Durant's coolly handsome face as if he found Lacey's comment amusing. "I wasn't aware of your interest in auctions."

Andy gave him a quick smile in response. "Simple curiosity, that's all." *And none of your damn business,* Andy thought with a flash of annoyance. For Lacey's sake, she said nothing but continued to concentrate on the bidding.

"It should prove to be a very interesting morning," the captain remarked casually, glancing about the assembled crowd with those cool, appraising eyes.

"There seems to be more than the usual interest in this auction. Perhaps it's due to the properties we've confiscated."

Andy had been trying to ignore most of what he was saying. She found Chandler Durant overbearing and supercilious, but his comment brought her gaze back to his.

"I wasn't aware that was your responsibility."

"Merely one of many, Amanda." He took her hand, very much the gentleman. "I would like time to tell you about my responsibilities. My assignment here in Louisiana will be of great advantage to my military career."

Andy withdrew her fingers from his.

"The spoils of war for the victors, Captain?" she implied archly, remembering her first assumptions about men like Chandler Durant.

The response was guarded speculation behind that artificial smile. "In every conflict there are the victors and . . ." he looked briefly to Lacey, who chose to look away, as if she were concentrating on the auction, "the vanquished."

"It is a fact of war. Your brother was an officer. I'm certain he understood that. But it is easy to see how your impressions might be far more emotional."

More emotional because of her friendship with Lacey was undoubtedly what he meant to say.

"I shall try to keep my emotions under control, Captain," she assured him, wishing he would go away.

"Perhaps only where politics are concerned, Amanda." The warning was subtle but all too clear. Then his voice lowered to that first silkiness. "However, I should like to explore other emotions with you."

Andy pretended she didn't hear him as the auctioneer's voice rose above the noise of the crowd to announce the next property available for bidding.

"Gentlemen!" He roared over the conversation, demanding their attention.

"We have one last property offered today," he announced in a booming voice.

"Let's get out of here." Lacey pleaded. "I hate this." She turned and started toward the door as others parted to let them pass.

A tremor of excitement seemed to pass through the crowd, making Andy hesitate as the auctioneer's voice began the usual list of details.

"This is a particularly impressive property," he began. "We're not talking about some few acres of swamp land. We're talking about one of the most extraordinary properties in all of Louisiana." He went on listing the merits of the property, trying to excite the potential bidders and raise the opening price.

"Fifteen hundred acres; six hundred in valuable high land, five hundred in rich forest, four hundred in bayou and rich in game. We're talking about a piece of property that before the war was the single largest producer of sugarcane in these parts. The opening price includes a mill, sugar house, stables, workers' cottages, two streams, three ponds, two and one half miles of riverfront."

His words sent an inexplicable shiver down Andy's spine. Cottages, stables, and on the riverfront? The auctioneer had her full attention.

"And I haven't even spoken of the house," he continued. "This is not a house, gentlemen, but a castle built for a king; fifty-three thousand square feet under one roof, sixty-four rooms, a ballroom, gentleman's study, two kitchens, music room, sitting room, family reception room, two bedroom wings, and for recreation . . . a bowling alley. All surrounded by lovely grounds and orchards, befitting the life of a prosperous country gentlemen or a wealthy businessman. It was once one of the finest Thoroughbred farms in the South. It can be again."

Something inside Andy froze her beyond movement.

"Gentlemen, this grand estate was valued at over sixty thousand dollars before the war. But times bein' what they are . . ." He shook his head sadly and spoke with great difficulty.

"I am instructed by the current owner to begin the bidding at five thousand dollars." He held up a hand for silence as appalled whispers ran through the crowd. "That is an opening price of three dollars per acre on the high land, fifty cents per acre on forest and bayou property. The balance is for the buildings and the house. And gentlemen, I ask you to remember this magnificent house was built at a cost of thirty thousand dollars."

Silence fell across the stunned room.

"Gentlemen, please. The owner is faced with a very difficult situation. Is there anyone who will open the bidding for Ombre Rose plantation?"

"What the hell do you mean, it's being put up at auction!?" Coleton James's hand slammed down on the hard wood surface as he leaned over the desk toward Judge Tyler B. Ormsby.

The judge looked briefly to Coleton's companion and received only a cool, appraising stare. Both men had that lean, animal intensity he'd seen too many times since the war; a slow-burning inner fire of lingering hatreds and resentments.

"I sent you a telegram when I learned Marilee intended to put it up at auction." He went on to explain. "I tried to persuade her to hold onto the place, but there was no changin' her mind." The judge rose from behind the desk watching the man before him, trying to gauge how much of Coleton James's reputation was truth and how much was rumor.

"You know how she always hated the place. When I didn't hear from you . . ."

"I've been on the trail most of the last three weeks," Coleton admitted with tight-lipped fury, knowing there was no point in blaming the judge.

The judge flinched at the razor edge of bitterness and shifted his weight pondering the rest of what he felt Coleton should know.

"She retained Parker Rawlins to handle the sale,"

Ormsby added carefully.

Coleton's head snapped up. "Rawlins!?" His voice had lowered to chilling calm. "I thought he must be dead by now."

Or wished it? The judge chose not to speculate further on that little matter.

"When is this auction supposed to take place?"

The judge hadn't thought he feared any man considering some of the criminals he'd sentenced in his court. But he feared this man. He grabbed his high-crowned hat and nodded grimly.

"Right about now. They'll save it and the old Home Farm property for last. I asked around . . . There are a couple of fellas intendin' to bid on Ombre Rose. The idea is to split it up into smaller plots and sell 'em off for a profit. I hear tell one fella fancies the house for his octaroon mistress."

Coleton's hand slashed across the desk, upsetting the inkwell, spreading its ominous blackness across papers and wood.

"Damn 'em to hell! Damn Marilee and all of them! They won't have Ombre Rose!" In a fit of cold, blind fury, he swept his hand across the desk, sending stained papers flying. The judge never made a move to rescue any of it and simply shook his head as he watched Coleton stalk out of his office. Coleton James's temper was more than just rumor. Still, he'd been friends with the boy's father for nearly forty years.

Wheezing and wiping his beaded brow, the judge finally caught up with Coleton at the entrance to Town Hall. He seized him by the elbow. "What you goin' to do, son?"

"I'm going to put a stop to this auction." Coleton jerked his arm free and pushed into the crowd.

"And just how do you expect to do that?" the judge whispered pointedly, trying desperately to keep them from drawing any more attention than they already had.

"According to my father's will, Ombre Rose is rightfully mine. Marilee has no right putting it up for auction."

"She has the right if you're dead," the judge snapped, pushing Coleton and Rafe into a far corner.

"What the devil do you mean by that!?" Coleton spat back, his already-worn patience made more precarious still by the round of bidding that had already begun.

"Listen to me!" the judge insisted vehemently. "There was a price on your head. After the war, word came back you were dead, lost in some battle in North Carolina. I was the only person who knew any different and I just let it be. It seemed better that way." Judge Ormsby's face was flushed.

"I figured you could straighten everythin' out later on. I never thought Marilee would put the place up for sale. But the truth is, if you step in now and try to stop this auction, claimin' to be the rightful owner, federal authorities will have you arrested on the spot and hauled off to jail on some sort of trumped-up spy charges." He jerked his head meaningfully, indicating the soldiers in dark-blue uniforms interspersed among the bidders.

"They're just itchin' to get their hands on men like you. And you'll lose Ombre Rose anyway. Be smart about it!"

Rafael laid a restraining hand on Coleton's shoulder. "He is right, my friend. It would be foolish to lose everything by acting unwisely."

Fury burned through Coleton, but he knew they were both right. The minute he tried to stop the auction, he'd be tightening the noose around his own neck.

"All right . . ." The fury ebbed to a slow burning anger. "But there has to be another way. I won't let some damn Yankee take Ombre Rose!" As another round of bids was launched across the speculative noise in the Town Hall, a dangerous light filled his eyes.

"I think I just found it." He slowly made his way through the crowd.

Lacey gasped at the opening bid. "My God, I can't believe it! Ombre Rose is worth ten times that. But who could possibly come up with even five thousand dollars?"

"Five thousand!" came the shouted response.

The opening bid was shouted very near her, jolting Andy into another form of shock. Someone was actually going to bid on it! She leaned forward, straining to see who had bid through the crowd.

Conversation buzzed all around her, then one man whispered behind his hand to another and inclined his head toward a portly man in a gray suit with a garish, lavender brocade satin vest. His thumbs were hooked into his vest pockets with an air of self-importance. He wore more jewelry than was reasonably fashionable even for a woman and a self-indulged smile that rolled in a sea of flesh at his round face.

He looked exactly like the caricatures that appeared in the articles in Baton Rouge newspapers that vilified the Yankee invaders. It was clear he was the man who'd made the first bid.

Andy recoiled in horror at the idea of this man possibly being the new owner of Ombre Rose. Dear God! What would happen to that lovely house in the hands of a man who looked and smelled as if he'd just stepped from a pleasure house.

Her thoughts flashed to the gazebo, protected and hidden with its secrets in the overgrown park. Even now she couldn't begin to understand what she had experienced there. The thought of that man finding it, going inside as she had, made her cringe with revulsion.

"I hear tell he plans on splittin' up the good farm land into smaller plots and sellin' it off," one man in front of her mused to another.

The other man shook his head tragically. "Can't see him plantin' it to cane. Damn Yankees don't know the first thing about sugarcane. I heard he's got himself an octaroon mistress and plans to move her on out to the house."

"Absolutely appallin'!" came the drawled response. "Patrick James would burn it to the ground before he'd let someone like that even set foot on Ombre Rose. Now there was a man with a love of the land."

"I'm glad he didn't live to see this. Too bad his son didn't make it back from the war. This would never have happened," the second man added. "The widow always was too greedy, lookin' out for herself, not carin' two cents worth about anybody else."

The first man obviously agreed, leaning closer to his companion. "My wife heard Marilee James is still sleepin' with that Yankee officer she entertained at Ombre Rose."

Andy didn't care to hear the rest. She was too devastated. Tears flooded her eyes at the memory of the magnificent house, the surrounding park, the rich fields and pastures. It would all be gone, destroyed forever. And what would happen to the gazebo? Most likely it would be sold off, too, or torn down. After all, what practical use was there for marble? And the gazebo stood in the middle of the park. Yes, of course, she thought bitterly, the gazebo would be torn down, too.

"Fifty-three hundred dollars."

Andy was snapped from her thoughts at the sound of the challenging bid. Chandler Durant seemed interested as well.

"It seems there's quite a lot of excitement over this property."

"Fifty-four hundred," the garishly dressed Yankee countered. The auctioneer repeated the last bid.

"Do I have fifty-five hundred?" His gaze searched the room as he tried to drive the price up. "Fifty-five?"

Lacey tugged insistently at her elbow. Andy ignored her as she strained to get a look at this newest challenger who'd called out his bid.

"I'm not leaving," she whispered vehemently over her shoulder as she finally spotted the man.

He was of medium height with straight, dark hair in bad need of a cut that gave the appearance of having been carelessly slicked back. He wore the pants, shirt, and waistcoat common among the better dressed gentlemen, but he seemed uncomfortable, as if he weren't used to such finery. He kept glancing at a piece of paper in his hand. On the next round of bids that took the price of Ombre Rose to fifty-seven hundred dollars, he looked across the room in the general direction where Andy stood. Then his gaze fastened back on the auctioneer. Countless properties had been offered for sale that afternoon but he'd bid on none of them that she was aware of. It was obvious Ombre Rose was the only property he was interested in, and he meant to have it.

Who was he? and why did he so desperately want Ombre Rose?

Andy couldn't remember seeing him in Baton Rouge before today. If she had, they would have been introduced, because Lacey seemed to know everyone. That could only mean one thing—he wasn't from Baton Rouge.

Was he a northerner, possibly another carpetbagger like the first bidder, simply intent on picking up a piece of prime property to be split off and sold for a profit?

"Six thousand dollars."

Andy whirled around as yet another voice rang out in the hot, musty room. A man threaded his way through the crowd of people in careful, measured strides.

He was lean and tall with a tense wariness in his movements. The black, double-breasted shirt was open at the throat, exposing a muscular neck as darkly tanned as his face. Faded gray pants were tucked into worn knee boots. They were black, along with the belt that molded his hips.

A woolen poncho was slung casually over one shoulder and hung low to his knees, making it impossible to see whether or not he wore a gun. Instinctively, Andy sensed it was there even with the military's restriction against firearms.

But more than the animal intensity about him, the too-long, light-brown hair that was like a mane about his head and only heightened that impression, or the fact that he undoubtedly wore a gun into a room full of Union soldiers, it was the man's face with that rich brown beard that drew her attention back. She knew him! He was the man she'd seen aboard the *Iron Queen!*

She recognized the determined angle of firm chin. His mouth was almost obscured except for the slight curve of lower lip. His nose was straight between the thrust of equally dark brows. She stared at the pale scar that slashed his cheek, disappearing into his beard. As it had been that day, her impression of him now was that of hard, straight, unyielding lines reflected in his stance and his features. Except for his eyes . . .

Watchful, intense, guarded. She saw all those things in his gaze as he quickly scanned the room and something more as those disconcerting gray eyes came briefly back to her—the brief, unguarded flash of recognition.

It was more than that brief encounter aboard the riverboat. It was something she felt deep within that stirred ellusive memories of another time and place. And with it came an unreasoning fear, and some another emotion from earlier that morning in the gazebo—desire.

"Be careful, my friend," Rafe cautioned Coleton, following his gaze and glancing meaningfully at the uniformed officer who stood several feet away.

"Our friend Durant is here."

Coleton nodded. "I saw him."

The moment he made his bid, several people turned his way. It was her gaze that lingered and flashed with memory—twin blue pools of liquid heat above the angle of faintly flushed cheeks. Then, as she openly studied him, he could see her eyes weren't really blue, but a shade closer to green, fringed with long dark lashes, several shades deeper than the pale-gold hair that framed her face.

His own memory stirred as he recalled a slender young woman staring down at him from the upper deck of the riverboat. His first impression struck him, as it had that day, that she reminded him of Sunny, painfully so.

She was small and slender, dressed simply in a pale-blue gown that spoke of understated elegance—a lady with pale gold hair that escaped the tight coil atop her head to curl softly about her face in the damp heat. A beautiful lady with faintly flushed cheeks who returned his gaze without the coy affectations of the women he was used too. Almost as if . . .

"I applaud your taste in women, my friend," Rafe commented as he saw the direction of Coleton's gaze. "But I think you would be wiser to keep an eye on Durant and make certain he does not recognize you."

Coleton's attention snapped back to the stunned silence in the Town Hall as the auctioneer repeated his bid.

"Is that correct, sir?"

He nodded with a determined frown. "The bid stands at six thousand dollars."

The bidding soared. Six thousand three hundred, six thousand seven hundred. It topped seven thousand dollars as it volleyed back and forth between the three men. The auction had now taken on the atmosphere of a marketplace.

Andy wanted to scream at them to stop. What did any of them know or care about Ombre Rose? Except for the man with those penetrating gray eyes that seemed to see everyone and everything. His bidding was quietly spoken or given with a curt nod to the auctioneer.

"Nine thousand dollars." One of the men yelled his bid.

Coleton considered his last opponent. He'd already eliminated one bidder. This other man was different. He had the air of someone who knew the value of what was at stake and intended to have it. But he would never let anyone else have Ombre Rose. He called out his answering bid in a firm voice.

"Ten thousand dollars."

A low speculative murmur swept through the crowded hall as the auctioneer repeated the bid to make certain it was correct.

Andy bit at her lower lip. An intense feeling of panic she couldn't begin to understand slipped through her as the auctioneer's gavel hovered over the podium. Images of Ombre Rose flashed through her thoughts—the gently waving grass, the untilled fields, the abandoned cottages, and the cool, beckoning quiet of the park. Then the house itself, like a magnificent luminous pearl, to be treasured and loved. Tears pooled in her eyes and she bit down so hard on her bottom lip that she tasted blood.

She realized what she had to do. There had never really been any choice at all, not since she'd first seen Ombre Rose from the decks of the *Iron Queen*. Andy's voice rang out clearly across the buzz of conversations that filled the Town Hall.

"I bid eleven thousand dollars for the Ombre Rose plantation."

Chapter Five

The auctioneer blinked uncertainly. "I beg your pardon?"

Beside her, Lacey gasped. Andy felt the collective weight of everyone's attention as one by one all the men in the room turned to stare at her. She cleared her throat, her voice strong and certain as she squared her shoulders.

"Amanda, surely you aren't serious." Chandler Durant added his surprise. He started to make a gesture to the auctioneer that it was all a mistake.

"Please don't." Andy stopped him with cool determination. "I'm completely serious." And then she repeated her bid for the auctioneer's benefit.

"I bid eleven thousand dollars for Ombre Rose."

"Oh, my God!" Lacey cried out, reaching out to Andy in what could only be a gesture to steady herself against fainting. The room burst into immediate uproar.

"I never heard of such behavior," was one outraged response.

"Who the devil is that young lady?"

"Undoubtedly no lady at all. I can't imagine how she got in here."

"Amanda, this is complete foolishness," Durant warned her icily.

"Perhaps, but then that would make me a fool," Andy bit off, no longer trying to be polite. "And I'm certain you wouldn't want to be seen with a fool." She saw the struggle for control behind those guarded eyes.

75

"You haven't had time to think this through clearly. You were simply caught up in the excitement of the moment. I'll explain it to the auctioneer."

"I don't want you to explain anything at all," Andy insisted. When he finally seemed to accept that she wouldn't change her mind, he nodded stiffly but refused to leave.

"Gentlemen! Gentlemen!" The auctioneer pounded his fist on the podium as he shouted to bring the room back under control.

"Gentlemen! Please! I must have silence! Silence!"

At last the uproar began to subside. Yet Andy could still feel the weight of every gaze in the room. The auctioneer thrust his gavel in her direction.

"This is serious business. Do I have your meanin' clear, young woman? Is it your intention to submit such a bid?" He looked at her as if he was certain she must have experienced a moment of light-headedness and by now would have gotten hold of herself.

"Oh, Andy, what are you doin'?" Lacey clung to her arm with trembling hands. "I think I'm goin' to faint."

Andy whirled on her. "Don't you dare faint on me, Lacey Kittridge," she warned in a voice Lacey had never heard before. "If you do, I swear I'll leave you right where you fall." The solemn promise in her friend's threat snapped Lacey out of her swoon, afraid she might do exactly that. And a little embarrassment was nothing compared to looking like a complete fool on the floor of the Town Hall meeting room.

"You wouldn't!" But the stunned surprise in her voice indicated she believed there was just the smallest chance Andy might do just that. She swallowed hard, her eyes as wide as saucers.

"I do believe I am feelin' better now," Lacey whispered, still holding on to Andy's arm with a death grip.

Andy turned back to the auctioneer. "Sir, I bid eleven thousand dollars for the Ombre Rose plantation." It was madness and she knew it, yet even as she dared a look at the man she'd bid against, Andy felt an overwhelming sense of calm. The only question now was, how high was he willing to bid for Ombre Rose?

"Gentlemen, please!" The auctioneer begged once more for silence.

"Are you aware of the law, miss?"

Law? Good heavens, what was he talking about? Andy thought. Was there some restriction that forbade her bidding.

"If you are successful in this bid, your husband or guardian must take title himself to the property," the auctioneer provided.

Andy slowly released the breath she'd been holding as Lacey began to protest.

"Amanda, this is crazy. What on earth can you be thinking?"

"I fully agree." Chandler Durant added his support. It was obvious he hadn't considered her serious when she made her first bid.

Andy slowly untwined Lacey's bruising fingers. "I mean to have Ombre Rose."

"You don't have to do this, just to see the place," Lacey bemoaned. "I'll ask Daddy to make arrangements for us to go out there and you can paint it all you like. You don't have to do this!"

"Yes, I do."

Andy turned to the auctioneer. "I handle my own affairs, sir. My bid stands."

Tight-lipped fury pushed Coleton to the edge. The exact sum of money he and Rafe brought out of Mexico was eleven thousand three hundred and eighty-seven dollars.

"I am with you all the way, my friend." Knowing what it meant, Rafael gave his assent for Coleton to bid every last cent.

"After all," he shrugged, "it is only money. We can live off the land for a while until we can bring the rest of it out of Mexico."

Coleton nodded his gratitude as the auctioneer repeated the bid.

"Eleven thousand three hundred dollars."

Andy could feel his eyes on her, that penetrating speculation, the icy contemplation. It was that lean intensity that was almost animallike, wary and vaguely threatening.

The warning was there, felt rather than seen, subtle and dangerous. Fear might have served her better, but she wasn't afraid. She was recklessly fascinated, and equally dangerous. She was determined.

"Eleven thousand five hundred dollars." Andy spoke crisply so there could be no misunderstanding.

Rafe quickly stepped in front of Coleton. It was a casual gesture, but it didn't go unnoticed around the room. "Easy, my friend. This is far too dangerous. There is too much to be lost here," he quietly warned with a restraining hand.

White-hot fury uncoiled deep inside Coleton. He'd bid every last cent he could lay his hands on, and she'd immediately outbid him. One moment he could almost feel the warm, moist earth of Ombre Rose within his grasp; now it was literally slipping through his fingers.

He took a step toward her and immediately felt the restraint of Rafael's hands, his shoulder blocking him further. "Don't be a fool!" his friend hissed at him. "Would you hand yourself over to the blue-bellies after everything we have been through? It isn't meant to end here, my friend. There will be another day. I promise you!"

"Don't do it!" Judge Orsmby added his argument. "This isn't what your father would want!"

Coleton's eyes blazed with impotent fury as he listened to the auctioneer. There was nothing he could do. When the man looked to him again, Coleton simply shook his head.

"Eleven thousand five hundred dollars," the auctioneer repeated when there was no challenge. "Once, twice." He slammed the gavel down onto the podium.

"Sold. For the sum of eleven thousand five hundred dollars to the young woman."

"You are to see Mr. Rawlins about payment and the necessary documents," the auctioneer instructed Andy as he indicated a distinguished gentleman sitting slightly in back and to his right.

"And . . ." he paused meaningfully, "I hope this is no trick."

Andy merely nodded that it was not, and the auctioneer immediately announced the final property offered for bidding.

There were several murmured comments about outlandish behavior and a "woman's proper place." Andy chose to ignore them all. She turned to Lacey only to find her friend had slumped into a vacated chair.

"I can't believe you did that," Lacey whispered, stunned. She was pale, absolutely every freckle in existence popping out on her translucent skin.

"Have you lost your mind?"

"I don't think so. Now, if you'll just sit right here. I have to see the gentlemen about some property. I think they'll be wanting their money."

"Amanda!" Lacey grabbed at her arm. "They'll throw you in jail when you can't pay."

Clearly her friend didn't yet understand. Andy patted her hand gently. "They won't throw me in jail. I have enough money, Lacey. I inherited half my father's estate when I turned eighteen. The other half went to Stephen. Then when he . . ." She caught herself.

"Anyway . . ." she reassured, "I have more than enough money."

"But why?" Lacey persisted, and then her voice lowered so that no one else would hear. "Your home is in New York! Why did you do it?"

How could she explain? "That is my aunt's home, not mine. It was never really my home. It was simply where I went to live after Stephen and I lost our parents. And now that he's gone . . ."

She couldn't tell her about the experience at Ombre Rose. Not yet.

"Lacey, I can't explain it. Now please, just wait here while I take care of everything."

"Allow me, Amanda." In spite of all his objections, Chandler Durant escorted her to the gentleman she was to see about the papers.

It was more simply done than she expected. Because she had no husband or living male relative, Andy was allowed to take title in her own name. She was to deliver a draft for full payment before three o'clock that afternoon. Payment for Ombre Rose could be easily taken care of with a visit to the bank president. Before arriving in Baton Rouge, she had considered the possibility of traveling abroad afterward, perhaps even persuading Lacey to accompany her. With that in mind, she'd had a substantial amount of money transferred from New York. Now her plans had changed.

Andy smiled down into Mr. Rawlins's somber blue eyes, thinking he was certainly a very distinguished-looking gentlemen. His sandy hair was only faintly gray at the temples. He looked to be approximately her aunt's age, yet his eyes were deeply lined and there was an unhealthy pallor about his skin, as if he were not entirely well. Still, he was an attractive man.

She grew uncomfortable as he stared at her for the longest time, a stunned expression on his face. He seemed not to have heard her reply.

"Is there something wrong?" Beside her, Chandler Durant was growing impatient.

"No. It's . . . nothing." Mr. Rawlins smiled quickly, too quickly, looking back at her with a puzzled expression before returning his attention to the papers before him. "It's just that for a moment I thought perhaps we might have met." He was looking thoughtfully at Andy. "You remind me of . . . someone." He drew trembling fingers across his forehead, making her certain he was not well.

Andy felt uneasy. Whoever that person was must have meant a great deal to him. She smiled softly and impulsively laid her hand on his. She knew what it meant to lose someone very dear.

"I hope the memory is a pleasant one, Mr. Rawlins."

His gaze came back to hers with such anguish, it took her breath away.

"I wish to God that were true, Miss Spenser."

In the next moment that flash of vulnerability was gone as Mr. Rawlins once more retreated behind the careful barrier of his profession. The smile did not return.

"Everything should be in order, Miss Spenser."

"Thank you." She was about to leave when she turned back abruptly.

"Do you know anything about Ombre Rose?" she ventured on a sudden impulse.

Mr. Rawlins immediately stiffened, his mouth thinning to a hard line. "Everyone in these parts knows of Ombre Rose."

"I thought perhaps you could tell me a little about it," Andy suggested, at a loss to understand why a simple question should affect him so deeply.

"Yes, of course," came the stiff reply. "It was once the largest sugarcane plantation in Louisiana. But then . . ." He hesitated, and the hands that shuffled the papers before him into a neat pile shook visibly. He flattened them on the desktop to still the trembling. "That was before the war," he concluded, choosing to say no more.

"I see," Andy replied quietly. He'd said nothing she didn't already know from the auctioneer.

"Perhaps you could introduce me to Mrs. James. I have a great many questions about Ombre Rose."

"Yes, I'm certain you do, Miss Spenser. But Mrs. James was rarely there. She didn't care for life in the country and chose to live in town."

"Thank you, Mr. Rawlins," she replied softly. "I'll see that you have the proper payment on time."

The dismissal in his tone was only too obvious. Then, as if he seemed to reconsider, he added, "If there is anything else I can help you with, please feel free to call on me."

Andy smiled, light filling her eyes. "Thank you, I will."

She gathered her papers and put them in her reticule and Chandler Durant escorted her back to Lacey. "I'm certain that in a few days, Amanda, when you've had a chance to think all of this over . . ." he began.

Andy cut him off. "Captain, please."

"I only wished to say that in the event you should change your mind, I'm certain I can arrange to take care of the details for you and see that your money is returned to you."

It was then she saw him across the room. His eyes followed her with a look of such intensity it took her breath away.

The room seemed to whirl away from her into a black void of time and space. The voices and faces around her disappeared until there were only those eyes. A memory flickered through her thoughts . . .

eyes like quicksilver, shot through with fire one moment, cool and resting the next, filled with secrets, memories, and longing

In the breath of an instant, the memory came back to her from the gazebo and another time she couldn't quite remember, making her fingers ache with sudden longing . . . to touch. And the words ached through her from some hidden place

promise me

"Amanda? Amanda, are you all right?"

"What?" Andy jerked back to reality. When she looked up, he was gone as well as whatever she had experienced. She felt so empty and alone.

Chandler Durant's voice grated irritably. "I was simply trying to explain that I can take care of this for you, in the event you should change your mind. Which I would strongly urge you to do."

By the book, Andy thought as she turned on him. "I have no intention of changing my mind, Captain. And I don't wish to discuss it further." She took hold of Lacey's arm and propelled her out into the glare of midday.

"You will change your mind, dear Amanda. I will see to it," Captain Chandler Durant softly vowed before signaling one of his men. He pulled him discreetly aside.

"Find out about that man who bid against Meachum and Miss Spenser. I want to know everything."

* * *

Coleton's chestnut stallion was shiny with perspiration. There was a feeling of heaviness due to more than just the moistureladen air as he cut through the trees.

The bank was high and grassy, spreading to huge oaks hung with long gray beards of Spanish moss to his left. On the right the bayou itself lay black and sluggish, broken occasionally by the rippling from water bugs or an alligator's bony snout.

He turned down a half-forgotten path, the ground spongy beneath muted hooves, returning to swamp with no one to tend the intricate pattern of levees and drainage ditches that wove across this dearly familiar land like a spider's web.

It was years since he'd been here, but Coleton didn't misjudge the trails as he sent the chestnut across a shallow feeder creek and followed its meandering trail. A snowwhite ibis broke the smothering solitude, thrusting into the air, slowly gaining altitude over the treetops, then disappeared in a low, swooping glide.

He listened for the sounds of the bayou: the water thrust of an alligator, the sharp cries of other water birds, the almost rhythmic chorus of bullfrogs. This time of day, early in the morning, the bayou was alive. As heat set in, it would slip to lazy slumber with only the incessant buzzing of insects.

Slowly, the bayou worked its sultry magic, soothing, uncurling the knot of tight fury deep inside him. Now the cypress bay thinned and the stream opened into a wider lake. He followed the eastern rim, knowing deep swamp lay in the other direction.

The tree cover broke to open field, unplowed, the last stalks of some forgotten crop now withered to dry death. But beyond the fields and the double row of empty white cottages lay the main house of Ombre Rose. The symbol of so many lost dreams sat in silent splendor, and the ache deepened.

Coleton simply sat there, filling his senses with Ombre Rose. Home. His home. He didn't care what the documents said. No one would ever take it away from him.

"I promise," he vowed, his voice breaking with sudden emotion. Then he turned his horse back along the lake edge and continued into the forest of bald cypress and aging oak.

At least Home Farm was his, signed, sealed, and delivered. The official documents might carry Rafe Kelly's name for the purpose of keeping his own identity secret for now, but the other deed Rafe had signed back to him was in the safety-deposit box at the bank. It would remain there for the time being.

He almost laughed at the bittersweet irony of being forced to buy back land that was his in the first place. If nothing else, his stepmother was certainly thorough. In one morning she had managed to rid herself of all that had belonged to Patrick James and the life he once hoped for with Coleton's mother. First Ombre Rose and then Home Farm, the original land where his father started out when he came over from Ireland with nothing but the clothes on his back, two strong hands, and iron-willed determination.

Home Farm started out as nothing more than a fifty-acre plot of almost-impossible bayou land that was mostly water. Serving a five-year indentured bond to a country gentleman, Patrick James learned a great deal about the land. He learned to cut in drainage ditches and build levees so that he could control the flow of water that dominated his property.

Within three years those fifty acres had grown to three hundred, and his father planted the first cane crops. At the end of five years, he tore down the crude shack he'd lived in with a young colored man who worked for him. Together they built the solid bayou house that became Home Farm. It was there Patrick James took his bride, Angeline Forestierre, and all his dreams.

Coleton had been born at Home Farm along with a brother who hadn't survived infancy. But still the dream persisted; another fifty acres here, two hundred there, until Home Farm spread to that gentleman planter's borders.

Eventually Patrick James bought that as well. It was, Coleton surmised, the ultimate symbol of what his father had achieved. The old, rambling planter's house, half fallen down with rot, was leveled. On a distant hillside, high and safe from seasonal floodwaters, his father and mother planted row upon row of her precious rose cuttings. The dream of Ombre Rose was born.

His mother lived long enough to see the first roses bloom, but not to live in the house his father lovingly built for her. And then there had been Marilee; cold, calculating, offering his father just enough affection to make a solitary man aware of his loneliness. But Ombre Rose was never her home.

The cypress bay thickened and clogged the almost invisible trail. Coleton urged the chestnut through the creeping veil of vegetation. Then the bay opened into a sunlit clearing.

Solid, built on thick upright timbers, cypress wood gleaming in the early-morning sun, Home Farm lay sprawled like a welcoming haven. Coleton was so intent on the flood of childhood memories washing back over him that he didn't hear the faintly whispered change in the sounds of the bayou. He heard nothing until the sharp rasp of metal cocking back to meet metal.

"Hold there, mister," came the warning words, as dangerous as the cold steel of the gun Coleton sensed at his back.

"Move slow. I got a real unsteady finger."

Coleton let out a long, low breath, slowly raising his hands, reins dangling from his fingers. How could he have been so stupid as to ride in here blind?

"Now, just cross one leg over and slide off that horse." The order echoed across the clearing. "And make it real slow and easy. Don't let me see those hands drop an inch or I'll blow 'em clean off."

Coleton hesitated, sensing the very real danger if he stayed where he was, or worse, if he moved too quickly. Slowly, he brought his breathing back under control.

"You still totin' around that damn 'coon gun? Or did you shoot off your own foot yet and trade it in on a reliable gun?"

The tip of the long single shot rifle wavered. The head

moved, the dark eye sighting down the barrel squinted in the morning sun.

"I got the gun and both feet," came the hesitant reply. "And I got two hands, and right now they got this gun pointed right at your back!"

Coleton almost laughed. To think he'd been this careless after four years of learning to listen for every sound.

"Well then, use it on me, or to find some dinner. Preferably muskrat stew," he shouted back, his shoulders beginning to rock with laughter.

"Muskrat stew? Muskrat stew!" The eyes concentrating down that long barrel lifted in astonishment.

"Mr. Coleton?" Stunned surprise mixed with disbelief.

"I am if you don't decide to shoot my head off first." With an easy grace, Coleton swung his right leg over the pommel of his saddle and slipped to the ground. Hands still held at shoulder height, he turned, a wide grin lifting the tips of his mustache.

"As I live and breathe! It is you, Mr. Coleton! It is you!"

Coleton leaned back in the chair on the front porch and kicked his heels up on the cypress log railing. Eyes closed with the first truly peaceful feeling in years, he drew deeply off the freshly rolled cigarette, letting the soothing curl of heat penetrate deep inside. Muskrat stew was better than he remembered; better than the first time when Cairo took him deep into the swamps to learn the ways of the bayou, living off the land and the water.

His eyes slowly opened and he contemplated the older man across from him. Cairo; black as night, tall with almost regal bearing. His name had come from the land of his origin, Egypt. Somewhere in his distant past, he had been well educated. An unfortunate twist of fate had cast him aboard a slaver at the age of fourteen. Supposedly he was descended from some nubian nobleman. That was the story that went back to when Cairo and his father first knew each other.

The black, frizzed hair was steeled to gray now, but those eyes that seemed to see through the swamp mists with unerring accuracy were still the same. With some sixth sense he always knew where lay dangerous water or solid ground. Cairo had been his father's friend, and because of something in their shared past, Patrick James had given Cairo his papers of freedom years ago.

They'd worked the land at Ombre Rose together, reclaiming it from swampland, and when his father built the big house, he gave Cairo his own plot of land and a home of his own, sharing the wealth with his friend. They sank their roots down deep on this land, raised their families and lived well in an odd friendship few people understood and even fewer tolerated.

Coleton squinted up into the morning sun that shafted across the porch. "I wasn't certain I'd find anybody still around," he remarked thoughtfully.

Cairo sat in a chair beside him, contemplating the smoldering tobacco in the bowl of his pipe. "This is where I belong. When the soldiers came and told us we were all free to leave, we simply laughed at them and told them Patrick James made us free a long time ago. We chose to be at Ombre Rose."

"But it was hard after he died. We tried to keep the crops going, knowing you would come back. First the Yankees burned the mill, then they burned the fields. Without crops, there was no way to pay the people. Some of the men joined up with the Confederate Army in the last months of the war. The families stayed until the last time the Union Army came. There was trouble and most simply left."

"Where did they all go?"

Cairo's eyes gleamed. "The Yankees tried to drive them off. Some families were scared and decided to go North. But the others . . ." Cairo's smile deepened, "they hide out in the bayous and they wait. I stayed here at Home Farm, like it was in the beginning. I knew you would come back." Cairo tapped his head with his forefinger. "I know it here, and feel it here." He laid his flattened hand over his heart. "I know

Patrick James's son come back to Home Farm."

"It is good you are back." Cairo puffed from his pipe, the smoky fragrance wrapping a lazy curl around his gray head. "The war was a bad thing. Look at the land." He gestured wide with large, eloquent hands.

"It lies fallow. Too long there have been no crops. But now . . ." The older man nodded his approval. "Now we will turn the fields and plant the cane. The way it was in the beginning with your father. I have continued his work. Even now there are new experimental cane shoots to be planted."

Coleton rolled his head back along aching neck muscles. He sighed wearily, the truth bitter in his mouth. "It's been sold, Cairo."

It was the first time he'd actually said it, and somehow those words made it seem so final. At the same time they brought back all the frustration and impotent rage that had eaten at him for days. It brought back other thoughts.

Amanda Spenser was her name, and she was from New York. A damn Yankee! What the devil did she want of Ombre Rose?

For a long time there was only the echo of sounds off the bayou, the startled cry of a bird, the distant thrashing of water that could only be the successful hunt of an alligator.

"I got back too late." His voice wasn't all that calm. "Marilee had already put it up for auction. Most of my money is still in Mexico. I thought it was just the taxes . . ." His eyes closed wearily, retreating behind closed lids, but the truth followed him there as well.

Cairo had risen from his chair and walked to the edge of the porch. He stood there for a long time, saying nothing, his own weariness carried in the sudden droop of his shoulders.

"It is good your father did not live to see this day." He shook his great regal head, holding in the emotion Coleton knew he must feel.

"His wife always hated Ombre Rose." Cairo frowned, with only a faint deepening in his voice to betray any emotion. "I suppose this is her revenge."

Just as Coleton knew he wouldn't, Cairo didn't ask who the new owner was. If Ombre Rose was gone, then he chose not to know. But Coleton wanted and needed to talk about it.

Coleton came slowly to his feet, gazing out across the clearing toward Ombre Rose.

"Ombre Rose is mine. No one will take it away from me," he solemnly vowed. "I have to find a way to get it back."

"Yes." There wasn't a trace of surprise or doubt in Cairo's reply.

For the longest time, they simply stood together at the railed porch, letting the rhythmic water sounds of the bayou soothe and ease the anger.

"What about Home Farm?" Cairo asked at last.

Coleton's laugh was hard and cynical. "For twelve hundred dollars it's mine. But the way things are, for the time being, no one is to know I'm back. It has to do with a little matter of my wartime activities." He'd become somber, but now the laughter was there and it turned razor-sharp.

He pounded a fist against a thick timber, shaking his head at the cruel irony. "I had to buy back my own home."

"How much land did you get?"

Some of the bitterness eased behind a faint smile. He knew Cairo was already calculating when they could plant the first cane crop at Home Farm.

"The house, the lake, and the original three-hundred-acre tract."

Cairo beamed. "The land your father and I started with, forty years ago. It's good land, Coleton."

"It's all good land. And I mean to have it all back. What can I do to help?"

He felt Cairo's steady gaze and knew the man would do whatever he asked.

"For now, I want you to go to the big house . . ." Coleton stared out across the lake that shimmered peacefully at the edge of Home Farm. Beyond lay Ombre Rose and all his dreams. "To welcome the new owner and keep an eye on things. And remember, if you should see me . . . we've never met before."

Cairo's knowing eyes met his.

Lacey tried to talk Andy out of it. August Kittridge gave every logical argument against it. Captain Chandler Durant called on her twice and left each time in tight-lipped fury. Quite simply, Andy refused to sell the Ombre Rose plantation.

Now, this morning, Lacey had given every possible excuse to delay their departure. Mary and Cassie sat opposite Andy in the carriage, waiting patiently. Tallman checked the mare for the third time. When she absolutely refused to wait any longer, Andy nodded to him that they were ready to leave.

It was then Lacey finally decided to make her grand appearance. Andy suspected she'd been watching from the windows all along; a silent battle of wills.

"All right." Lacey agreed disagreeably as she fussed with the strings of her wide-brimmed hat. "If you're so damned set on goin' through with this, I suppose I better go along with you." And with that she flounced into the open carriage and refused to speak to Andy the entire ride out to Ombre Rose.

The moment it came into view from the river road, Andy knew she'd made the right decision. The granite steps, the wide, sweeping veranda under the gallery, each gleaming pillar that curved around to the wings of the house—all seemed to reach out, welcoming her. It was almost as if she weren't a stranger, but someone who'd only been away for a very long time and now had returned to this magnificent house. Like an unfolding memory, she felt as if she'd driven up that long, climbing drive a thousand times.

Tallman swung the carriage around in front of the main steps. Before he could step down to assist her, Andy anxiously climbed down. The keys Parker Rawlins had given her the previous afternoon were clutched tightly in her

90

hand. Like an excited child she scampered up onto the wide porch, her anxious steps tapping back echoes along the portico.

The large door was made of gleaming mahogany and shone lustrous in the afternoon sunlight that spilled across the veranda. A glare caught her eyes, much as it had on her previous visit, reminding her of another door she'd opened. The sun reflected off leaded glass that formed the arched sunburst over the entry.

The ornate key fit easily into the lock. But before Andy could turn it, the door opened, spilling afternoon light onto lustrous wood floors in the entryway and the most imposing man she had ever seen.

For the longest moment they simply stood there staring at each other, both equally stunned.

He was of an equal height with Tallman, only not as heavy. His head was finely sculpted, his bearing regal and aloof. The impression was completed by the long flowing white robe he wore that fell to his ankles. His feet were wrapped in leather-thonged shoes that left most of the foot bare.

His eyes were warm liquid brown behind wide hooded lids, yet she sensed he saw everything and knew even more. His first surprise was quickly masked behind a closed expression that gave nothing of his thoughts away, yet she sensed he was studying her.

"I . . . beg your pardon." Andy drew back uncertainly. "I wasn't aware there was anyone here." She felt as if she was babbling nonsense under the scrutiny of the keen-eyed gaze that seemed to take in everything about her without ever leaving her face.

"I am about to perish out here in this heat!" Lacey came up behind her abruptly. She stopped, stared at the dark-skinned man, and gasped.

"Good heavens! Cairo!"

Andy looked at her sideways. "Do you know each other?"

Lacey's eyes were wide as saucers. "Well, of course, it's just that you gave me such a start." She smiled at the tall man. "I didn't expect to find you here, Cairo. It's good to see you again."

The man called Cairo simply bowed his head slightly and without a word turned and preceded them into the house. They followed with Andy whispering furiously over her shoulder. "Who is he? What is he doing here?"

Lacey made a warning gesture with her hand as Cairo stopped and waited for them. "He used to be with the James family. I thought he left with the others. I'll explain later."

Cairo promptly led them on an inspection of the main rooms on both the first and second floors of the house. The immensity of Ombre Rose defied imagination.

There were indeed fifty-four rooms, although Andy didn't see them all. She peeked briefly into the formal sitting room, library, one of two kitchens, the main dining hall, music room, and gentleman's study.

Most of the rooms were closed off, cloths draped over sparse furnishings. She expected dust, spiderwebs and mustiness. But the rooms were cool, orderly, and immaculate.

It reminded her of her first impression days earlier, when she found the path in the gardens cleared of weeds and underbrush. Someone had been caring for the house as well. Was it Cairo?

Two hours later the mysterious, robed man led them out onto the cool shaded gallery that opened off the upstairs sitting room, Lacey collapsed into one of the white wicker chairs ringing the small round table.

Andy stood at the wrought-iron railing, fanning herself lightly against the afternoon heat as she gazed out over the park that bordered this side of the house.

"Who is he?"

"His name is Cairo," Lacey informed her. "He's a free man of color. He owned property and used to live near here. Supposedly he and Patrick James knew each other from way back. I was just as surprised to see him as you were. After the Yankees confiscated all the property, I figured he took off like the others. I haven't seen him in ever so long."

"What others?"

Lacey shrugged. "Ombre Rose was a workin' farm before the war. Patrick James used to employ a lot of field hands. Many had been with him for years and raised families here."

Andy remembered the double row of white cottages.

"He didn't own slaves?"

Lacey shook her head. "He didn't believe in slavery. Probably had somethin' to do with his own beginnin'. Daddy said he was dirt-poor when he first started. His people were loyal to him. Even after he died, they stayed on, tryin' to keep the place goin'. That is, until the Yankees came through and took the property."

"Where did they all go?"

Lacey shrugged. "Maybe up north. Most folks seem to think they took off into the bayous."

"But why would they go there?"

Lacey sat up. "Because at least they can survive there. I tried to explain all of this to you." The anger was back.

"Times are hard, Andy. The farms are in ruins. Look at this place. There simply aren't any jobs for the Negroes or any way to pay 'em if there were. And most people down here don't want to give 'em the chance for anythin' else."

Andy frowned. She'd heard some of the dreadful stories of slavery. She'd witnessed some of that cruelty on the streets of Baton Rouge. But good or bad, everything these people had known of their previous way of life had been taken from them.

Now they were expected to make their own way in an economy completely unsuited to support them. And that sad reality was made all the worse by the bitter resentment of just about every southerner she'd encountered.

Change hadn't come with the end of the war. It had only just begun. It was as if an entire civilization had been torn apart.

She stood at the railing and was about to turn around when she saw him—a lone rider sitting atop a chestnut horse at the edge of the park where it was bordered by a thick wall of bald cypress and water oaks. For the longest time he simply sat there, looking toward the house.

Andy couldn't see his face from this distance, but there was something familiar in the tall, lean angle of his body as he sat astride.

"Andy? Have you decided to be angry with me after all?"

She glanced back, unaware Lacey had been talking to her. "I'm sorry." She accepted the lemonade Cairo placed before her, but when she looked again the lone horseman was gone.

Lacey chose to stay with her at Ombre Rose over the days that followed. They explored the house by day, and fell into exhausted slumber at night.

Andy discovered her first day at Ombre Rose that the plantation had indoor plumbing. It was something she expected of New York City, but not of a Louisiana plantation. Obviously Patrick James had been intent on having the latest and most innovative conveniences for his grand home.

Cairo showed her the huge boiler located behind the kitchen that was fueled by coal. When needed, hot water was forced through copper pipes into a ground-floor bathing chamber and four additional bathing chambers on the second floor. One adjoined her suite of rooms. Another surprising feature were the indoor water closets instead of the usual country outhouses.

Fresh water was supplied by two rainwater cisterns located at the rear of the house. Each was capable of holding ten thousand gallons of fresh water, and with the frequent rains, the supply was constantly replenished.

Andy was delighted to find the chandeliers and light fixtures were all lit by piped in gas. Now she discovered the source—a fifteen-hundred-cubic-foot gas holder. It was located in a small brick building also at the back of the house. Cairo explained this small plant produced acetylene gas from calcium carbide. Andy was fascinated.

She saw the brick sugar house where the cane had once been processed into raw sugar. Rats scurried over the debris. It was obvious others had been here as well. The four huge boiling vats had been hacked apart. The mechanism of the mammoth grinding stone, brought all the way from the West Indies, had been dismantled and carried off by the Yankees.

They wanted to make certain the plantation couldn't produce any income to support the flagging Confederacy. Destruction was the most certain remedy.

There was further destruction. She walked all the way around what was left of the sugar warehouse where cane was once stored. All that remained were blackened timbers that gaped out of the foundation like scorched skeletons. It reminded her of the boat landing she'd seen from the river.

And then there were hundreds of acres of open fields lying fallow in the burning July sun, miles of levees for watering, the banks collapsed, wooden gates for releasing the water either badly damaged or missing. It was clear Ombre Rose plantation had once been a huge agricultural enterprise, undoubtedly requiring hundreds of workers to plant, maintain, and harvest the sugarcane. She had only a glimpse of it all, and it was completely overwhelming.

Lacey's father had warned her, and now it was becoming abundantly clear that even if she knew what she was doing, which she didn't, making Ombre Rose plantation operational again was a monumental task. She couldn't do it alone.

Andy suspected that was why he'd promised to try and get someone who knew something about farming out there to help her. But knowing how people in Baton Rouge felt about northerners in general, and herself specifically, Andy didn't hold out much hope.

If she was the sort of person who indulged in self-pity, now would have been the time. But whenever she looked about her at this magnificent house, felt the welcoming warmth of its walls, it all faded.

She would simply have to find a way to make it work. That's all there was to it.

It was almost noon when she returned to the main house and Cairo disappeared. She slipped into the gentleman's study.

She'd spent a great deal of time there the last few days trying to find the plantation records Parker Rawlins had mentioned when she picked up the keys to the house.

From everything she had been able to find out, the former owner of Ombre Rose was a meticulous businessman. She needed those records to understand fully what she was up against.

Andy's gaze came up as Lacey whirled through the double doors. Her face was smudged with dirt and soot, as was the large apron that covered her gingham gown—and most of her gown, for that matter.

"What are you doin'?"

"Trying to find journals, records, anything that tells about running a sugarcane plantation." Andy was standing on a small stool in front of a massive bookcase and reached for another unmarked leather book.

"There has to be something here about the crops."

"Oh, for heaven's sakes." Lacey rolled her eyes. "You simply plant the stuff in the ground and wait till it comes up. Then you cut it and send it off to market. Simple."

"Lacey, what am I going to do? There isn't anything here about sugarcane."

A large smile dimpled Lacey's cheeks and made every freckle dance. "I was hoping you'd ask that. I have the perfect solution." With that she reached up, seized Andy by the hand, and pulled her down off the stepstool.

"You have to see this. You're just never goin' to believe it! It's so excitin'! Absolutely the most beautiful room in the entire house!" She took a deep breath and rushed on. "You'll have to plan a party. A big one. Oh, I just couldn't believe it when I went in there. I can't imagine you hadn't seen it yet!"

"Lacey, please!" Andy held up both hands in surrender.

"Will you stop long enough to tell me what you're talking about?"

Lacey drew a deep breath. "The grand ballroom, of course. Come on!" And with that she seized Andy by the hand and pulled her down the hallway, past the study and formal dining room into the circular east wing, then dragged her past the music room to a set of closed double doors.

"Close your eyes, and don't open them until I say you can," Lacey instructed excitedly.

"Can't this wait? It's almost lunchtime and I'm starving."

"Oh, pooh, you can eat later. I want you to see it now."

Making certain her eyes were closed, Lacey stepped around her.

Andy could hear the doors being opened. Then Lacey turned to guide her through the doorway. The grand ballroom, she thought with a faint smile. It sounded elegant and romantic.

"All right, open your eyes." Lacey sounded like an excited child on her birthday.

Elegant? Yes. Romantic? Yes, and more. Andy could only stare at the enormous circular room.

Floor-to-ceiling windows along the curved wall were hung with diaphanous curtains, giving it an almost ethereal quality. Sunlight filtered through to the hardwood maple flooring, catching spinners of dust, and creating golden sparkling pools that whirled away from the opened doorway.

The room was painted white, with elaborate, handcast ceiling medallions and breathtakingly beautiful frieze plaster. Even the windows were slightly bowed with the curve of the walls flanking them. A triple archway with plaster friezework and Corinthian columns graced the middle of the room. Lighting was provided by two enormous crystal-and-brass chandeliers and a multitude of smaller light fixtures. When they were all lit, it would be dazzling.

"Isn't it absolutely breathtaking?" Lacey breathed excitedly. "I can just imagine what it must have been like havin' a grand party here."

"It's beautiful," Andy whispered, and it truly was.

But now there was only the late-afternoon sun casting the entire ballroom into a softly muted half light, like the mist that often accompanies dreams. She could almost imagine what it must have been like at a fancy dress ball.

She slowly walked about the edge of the ballroom, her footsteps curling the dust into soft clouds.

Yes, Andy thought with a faint stirring inside. She could imagine what it might have been like. Listening to Lacey, if she simply closed her eyes . . .

It began slowly, images slipping in and out of focus in the muted half light just as Lacey had described;

brilliant lights from the lanterns flickered faintly then brightened, creating golden pools of light off gleaming white walls and reflecting in wall mirrors;

at the far end of the ballroom she could see the velvet draped dais and the musicians dressed in matching, elegant black formal coats and pants;

then she felt the sultry evening breeze that whispered through curved windows that had been thrown open wide;

she saw the vivid colors; blues, greens, lavenders, and pale pink, all in shining satins, elegant brocades, and clouds of the finest silk;

around and around they whirled and spun, these magnificent ladies and their handsome escorts; laughing, talking, flirting, risking a glance, a flirtatious smile, a secretive whisper;

and she was part of it. The music seemed to drift among the dust and shadows and then it became louder, the musicians taking form, the soft strains of a waltz whirling the dancers until they were a magical blur of light, color and movement;

and she was whirling and dancing with them, laughing with breathless abandon, smiling and flirting as those faces spun past her in wild phantasm;

she felt the throbbing pulse in her veins, the breathless excitement, the heat that coursed through her, the almost chaotic movements of her feet, stepping faster and faster until it seemed she would be swept into oblivion;

she heard the gaiety of her own laughter;

felt, touched, saw everything until it was a wild, maddening kaleidoscope that spun past her, and she was spinning with it;

It was then his arm closed around her waist and his hand folded over hers, and slowly, the spinning, the colors, the laughter all whirled back to the present.

There was only his face, the dearly familiar, careless fall of his light-brown hair across his forehead, the taut strength of his body guiding her through the floating waltz, teasing as he brushed against her, then moving away to tease even more.

Heat flowed into her fingertips where their hands joined, the beating of her heart keeping wild accompaniment to the music. His soft gray eyes were filled with light and love and laughter and cool shadows of promised passion.

It swept through her, surrounded her, until there was only his face, lean and tanned, and so very young, and the fire in those haunting gray eyes, stealing through her with promises and words and memories.

"Tonight," he vowed, pulling her close until their bodies touched and disapproval was mirrored in the matronly faces that whirled at the edge of the dancefloor.

"Tonight," he whispered against her cheek, luring her with his boldness, until she turned and felt that aching sweetness against her own lips, mindless of those who watched.

And then they were whirling past the light, and sound and color out into the cool air on the gallery. They slipped into the night shadows and his arms drew her full against him as his mouth came down to hers with such reckless energy and deep longing.

"I will tell them tonight and then we can be together forever . . . forever . . ."

His hands slipped into her hair. She could feel the lean intensity of his young body pouring through her. Dear God, she loved him, wanted to be loved by him, this way, forever.

"Yes!" Her soft-sweet cries whispered from her swollen lips.

"We will be together, forever." And the shadows closed around them, making the passion sweeter, the need more intense for these few stolen minutes.

A voice was calling her, distant at first, then insistently.

"No," she whispered wanting to make this moment last. But the voice came more insistently, pulling them apart.

"Sunny?"

"Sunny!"

"Andy?"

"Andy!"

Someone was bending down beside her. An arm was across her shoulders and she was being shaken.

"Andy? Please!"

The frantic words sliced through the dark shadows around her. Someone was calling her. No, they weren't calling her. They were calling someone else. . .

"Are you all right?" The voice was urgent.

She shook her head, trying to push those insistent arms away. She had to go back wanted to go back. He was going to tell them all tonight . . .

"Andy!"

Slowly the room came back into focus. She was kneeling on the hard maple flooring. Soft pools of dust scattered as she gasped for air, deep, cleansing breaths of it, as if she'd been submerged for a very long time.

"Lacey?"

"Yes, darlin'! My heavens, you scared the life right outta me."

Andy slowly raised her head. What was she doing on the floor? Had she fallen?

She remembered coming into the ballroom. Lacey was so excited about showing it to her. And then . . . Dear God, she felt so weak.

Lacey's arm went around her waist as she slowly helped her stand.

"I'm the one who's supposed to faint all the time, not you." She laughed but her voice was shaky.

Andy brushed her fingers across her forehead. Lacey's chattering was bringing her back. The room had changed.

100

It was silent, dusty and darkening with late-afternoon shadows. Empty.

Andy stared at the cavernous ballroom. Gone were all the finely dressed ladies and their escorts. Gone was the music and the brilliant glow of lights. And gone was the handsome young man with those compelling gray eyes.

She breathed out a long sigh, and it caught, painful in her throat. For a moment, just a moment . . .

"I don't know what came over me."

Strength slowly flowed back into her numb arms and legs. "For a moment it seemed . . . It was all so real."

Lacey laughed, a nervous little sound. "It must have been somethin'. You were sure talkin' about it."

Andy rubbed her hands over her arms. Her fingers felt warm, and tingled. She looked up in confusion.

"What did I say?"

Lacey giggled uneasily. "You were sayin' all sorts of strange things, laughin' a little, like you were real happy about somethin'. And then you looked up, as if you were lookin' right at someone, and you said, "We will be together forever." And then you just slumped to the floor. It scared the peewaddin' right outta me."

Andy let out a shaky breath. It had happened again, just like that morning in the gazebo, when she thought she had experienced . . . something.

No, she was certain she'd experienced something. But what?

Lacey wrapped an arm around her shoulders. "Come on, we'll find Cassie and get you somethin' to eat. You've been workin' too hard." They started toward the large double doors to the ballroom.

They both stopped.

The tall, imposing man stood framed in the large gaping doorway of the ballroom.

"The man outside said I would find you here."

Perhaps it was the way he said it. Or perhaps it was the words themselves. Maybe it was neither of those, but the way he simply stood there, bathed in the half light that filtered through the ballroom and spilled out into the hall, his face obscured.

He seemed to come from the shadows as if he were part of them—his height, the width of his shoulders filling the doorway, making the cavernous room seem no longer empty or so sadly abandoned.

His voice seemed to linger in the large circular ballroom, echoing across the white walls, reaching up to the frieze ceiling medallions until it slipped to the curved windows.

The words brushed across Andy's skin, bringing back the dreamlike scene she was certain she had imagined earlier. Now her breath caught in her throat. The sound of his voice was achingly familiar and real. The notion flashed through her startled thoughts . . . She knew him.

Chapter Six

"Well, as I live and breathe. You scared the livin' day-lights right outta me," Lacey bubbled excitedly, jarring Andy back to the here and now.

"Forgive me. It wasn't my intention to frighten you." Again those deeply silken words played along the walls, slipping back to play havoc with Andy's already shaken composure.

"I came to speak to someone about a position."

"Position?" Lacey turned to Andy uncertainly. They both recognized him as the man who'd bid against Andy at the auction.

"I was told you needed someone familiar with managing a plantation," he explained briefly.

Andy recovered slowly as she tried to compose herself.

"Yes . . ." She hesitated. "Mr. Rawlins did say he would try to send someone out. But I don't really think . . ."

"A place this big requires someone with experience," he stated. "I've got a lot of experience with sugarcane."

Andy thought she caught the faintest change in the man's expression when she mentioned Rawlins's name, but then it was gone.

"Perhaps we should discuss this in the study," Andy suggested.

Lacey frowned. "You certain you feel up to it?"

Andy took a deep breath. "I'm fine," she assured Lacey, then turned to the man, daring a quick look, thinking again that he looked like the man she thought she'd seen. *That was just it,* she told herself, *you "thought" you saw someone.*

"Well, if you're certain, then I'll go on ahead and have Cassie bring in tea," Lacey suggested.

"That will be fine." Andy turned to the stranger.

"The study is this way, Mr. . . . ?"

He pointedly ignored her question. "After you, Miss Spenser."

She hesitated, a little irritated at his advantage in obviously knowing her name—but then, he would have gotten it from Mr. Rawlins. Andy preceded him, hesitating as she remembered the doors to the ballroom. When she turned back, he'd already reached to close them. His hand seemed to linger on the gleaming brass latch, and then he turned to her with that quiet, penetrating gaze and followed her down the hallway.

The doors to the study were left open. As soon as she entered the room, Andy turned to face him.

"I don't know what you're doing here, but I really don't think this will work . . ."

He walked slowly about the masculine room, pausing before the large desk to run his fingers across the dark, rich wood before turning to her. It wasn't the gesture of appreciation for something obviously valuable, but rather a disconcertingly tender gesture, as if he were truly feeling the rich texture of the wood.

"As I said, I came about the manager's position." He fastened those hooded gray eyes on her, forcing Andy to look away unexpectedly.

"I know who you are," Andy announced as she rounded the desk, feeling the need to put some sort of solid, safe barrier between them. She thought she detected something in his eyes, perhaps a momentary uncertainty. Then it was gone.

"You bid against me for Ombre Rose."

The uncertainty was gone, replaced by a brief smile, only faintly more open than those watchful eyes.

"An error in judgment," Coleton admitted with ironic humor. What he should have done was step in and stop the auction like he'd wanted to do originally. Then none of this would be necessary. No, and he would undoubtedly have spent the last days in a military stockade facing trial. Much as Coleton really didn't care to admit it, this was the only way.

"An error in judgment? I don't understand. You did bid on it."

The smile deepened, but only slightly, never fully reaching his eyes. She found herself wondering what might happen if it did. Then she thrust the thought from her mind.

Coleton retreated to the safety of lies.

"I was bidding for my friend. Occasionally his judgment doesn't measure up to his . . . financial resources."

Andy vaguely remembered the handsome, dark-eyed young man with him that day. Oh, yes, the one who'd made Lacey's knees turn to jelly. She considered his answer and seemed satisfied with it.

"Just what are your qualifications, Mr. . . ."

"Kelly. Miss Spenser." Coleton provided. He might as well use the name a little while longer.

"Yes, Mr. Kelly. Are you from Baton Rouge?" She thought she detected a faint softness to his words, but it wasn't the thick drawl of Lacey's southern accent. It was something else she couldn't quite place. He could be from anywhere.

"I've been traveling a great deal the last few years." Coleton smiled. The lies were so easy, and not really lies, just slight variations on the truth. Whatever it took to get what he wanted!

Traveled. That could mean anything, Andy thought. "Are you familiar with this area?"

In spite of the fact he was fully prepared to resent Miss High and Mighty Damn Yankee, Coleton found himself almost amused by the way she questioned him. She was trying to ask all the right questions without really knowing what they were. All right, little miss, let's see what you've got. Would it take weeks or only a matter of days to drive her off Ombre Rose?

"I lived near here several years ago."

That was about as clear as mud. Andy decided to try again. "Have you ever worked on a plantation?"

"Most of my life, before I started traveling." Coleton enjoyed seeing the faint spark of exasperation in those unusual blue-green eyes.

"Perhaps it would be easier if I told you what I'm looking for," Andy suggested, feeling as if they were getting nowhere with this line of questioning.

He leaned back, resting one hip on the corner of the desk with such casual familiarity that it unnerved her. She got up, no longer feeling safe behind the desk. He'd very handily managed to remove that barrier of security. She moved away from him and went to stand before the expanse of windows that lined the adjacent wall.

"I don't know what you've heard in town, Mr. Kelly, but it's probably everything but the truth."

She stood with her back to him, arms crossed over the bodice of her simple gown, hands clasped over her upper arms, as if she were faintly chilled, or uneasy.

"I was born and raised in New York." He could see her take a deep breath before continuing. No airs, no high handedness that he expected of a Yankee. In spite of himself, he was a little surprised at her openness with someone who was no more than a stranger to her. Resentment shifted just a little. He was curious.

"The North," she clarified. "A Yankee."

She turned, pinning him with those magnificent eyes that had now shimmered to a shade that was more green than blue. "At least as far as some people are concerned. They can't seem to get past the fact that I'm from New York. But that is precisely the point, Mr. Kelly."

"I'm *from* New York. I no longer consider it my home. Ombre Rose is now my home. I don't expect you to understand any of the reasons." She found herself thinking of her earlier experience in the gazebo, and again just a short

106

while ago in the ballroom.

"The reasons aren't important to anyone but myself. The point is . . ." She found herself watching him, no longer unsettled by those contemplative eyes. "I must find a way to make Ombre Rose self-supporting. I will be perfectly honest with you, Mr. Kelly. I don't know the first thing about farming, or this land. But I am willing to invest everything I have to make it work. I want to raise cane."

For the first time since he'd followed her into the study, Andy saw that impenetrable barrier slip just a little. His mouth curved faintly beneath the soft sable of his mustache, giving a hint of just how devastating his smile might be. For a minute, the thought occurred he was going to laugh at her. Then the thought occurred that she would love to hear him laugh.

Andy looked away, certain one moment she was completely in control of this conversation, and then equally as certain she wasn't.

How had she done it? Coleton wondered. In the space of twenty minutes, a half hour at the most, Miss Amanda Spenser, Damn Yankee, had managed to give him pause to think. She was open, unguarded, completely without pretension. She was vulnerable and knew it. What's more, she knew exactly what everybody, including himself, thought of her and didn't give a damn. She so much as said it.

She was articulate, if a little nervous, determined with an almost endearing shyness, and Rafael was right; she was one of the most beautiful women he'd ever seen, hauntingly so, almost more than he wanted to admit. And he was struck again, as he had been that day at the auction—in little ways, gestures, the unguarded way she smiled and then tried to hold it back. Dear God! She reminded him so of Sunny.

And she wanted to raise cane? By the gossip running rampant in Baton Rouge, she'd already raised a little Cain.

Laughter warmed deep inside him, forcing him to put tight control over it. He hadn't felt like laughing in a long time. It was another of those emotions so carefully hidden away for so long. Oh, he could laugh with Rafe, enjoy an off-color joke or crude humor. But this was something else.

It was a simple, purely enjoyable feeling for what she'd said . . . and for the pleasure in finding her to be so very unpretentious and breathtakingly beautiful.

These were new and disconcerting feelings. He wondered about them, then pushed them aside. It was his turn for questions.

"What do you know about sugarcane, Miss Spenser?"

It caught her so off guard that he would suddenly ask something of her that it took a full, long moment before Andy recovered enough to answer.

"Very little, I'm afraid. I haven't been able to find any of the plantation records or journals."

"How little?"

Suddenly she felt completely chagrined. "It grows in the ground." She winced at how inane that sounded even to herself. She rushed to add, "But I'm willing to learn. And I can work hard—"

"And you think you're going to plant it, care for it, and cut it all by yourself." Coleton cut her off.

"Well, no. Not exactly."

He liked the way she straightened her back with a faintly defiant gesture, as if she were mentally taking herself by the shoulders.

He remembered the first time Sunny tried to ride that damn stallion her father brought down from Louisville.

The thought came unbidden. It was just that same little kind of gesture, as if to say the whole, entire rest of the world could go to hell in a basket.

"I am perfectly aware that I will need workers. I am prepared to pay them a fair wage. But if you were to be my manager it would naturally be your responsibility to hire the people you need—"

Again he cut her off, more than a little irritated at the

way she'd so innocently slipped under his skin.

"What are you prepared to pay me?"

"I beg your pardon." He'd done it again, turning the entire conversation around on her so that she didn't know who was asking and who was answering. He certainly had the most aggravating way of . . .

"One hundred dollars a month and a percentage of the first cash crop when it comes in." He announced his demands. He'd meant to disarm her; instead, he was the one disarmed as color flooded into her cheeks and those magnificent eyes flashed to brilliant aquamarine.

"Fifty dollars a month, and we will negotiate the percentage on evaluation of the first crop," Andy blurted out, fighting back anger and a whole multitude of wildly churning emotions. Of all the . . .

"Agreed," he called over his shoulder as he turned and walked out of the room.

"I don't know if you're qualified," she shouted after him. "I didn't agree to anything yet." Her fists clenched into tight balls. Good riddance, she thought, not even attempting to show him out.

"How many others have you seen?" echoed back to her from the hallway. He didn't even have the decency to come back to speak with her.

Andy started to the door. She absolutely refused to carry on a shouting conversation.

"None!"

"I'll see you in the morning."

That was it. It was so quickly done, Andy hardly had time to recover before she heard his bootsteps echo down the wood hallway, hesitate, then disappear in the shudder of the front door slamming behind him.

"What was that?" Lacey only just now returned, Cassie in tow with the silver tea service.

"I think I just hired a manager."

"You think?"

"It's hard to tell. I didn't say yes, and he didn't say no."

"Wasn't he the man at the auction?"

Andy knew what was coming; another of Lacey's warnings.

"Yes."

"I don't suppose he just happened to mention that man who was with him." Lacey motioned Cassie to set the silver service on the desk.

Andy's gaze came up in surprise. "There really wasn't time."

"Honestly, Amanda. Sometimes I wonder about your behavior."

She wasn't at all certain she was hearing correctly. "I thought you were scandalized about the way that man looked at you."

"Well, yes. At first. But it's just that it caught me unawares. Normally that sort of thing wouldn't have bothered me at all."

"I see. And because it did bother you, you're upset that I didn't find out his name," Andy shot back at her.

"I didn't say that. And why are you bitin' my head off? I should think you'd be absolutely thrilled to have someone now who can help you with this place."

Andy was thrilled. Add to that, baffled and worried, not to mention increasingly more frustrated and absolutely livid in the week that followed.

She'd hired Kelly, or Mr. Kelly, she wasn't certain which, on Wednesday. That wasn't exactly right, either. He'd more or less insinuated himself into the position of plantation manager. When she thought back on it afterward, she wasn't really certain how it happened.

The following morning, unable to sleep, and certain she'd made a very grave mistake, she went in search of Mr. Kelly to tell him just that. She found him in the study, poring over the plantation journals, all thirty of them, give or take a couple, one for each year since the plantation was built in 1831 until the last year of operation, 1863.

He mumbled some vague excuse that Cairo had found them, informed her they would need capital available at the bank for equipment and supplies, gave her a long speculative look, and then simply left.

When she went after him to find out just how much capital he was talking about, he was nowhere to be found. Not in the stables, the sugar house, or the fields. And there was no answer on the door of the long, low bungalow where the former manager lived. He reappeared briefly around noon, remaining long enough to eat in the kitchen.

"I need to discuss finances with you," she insisted.

Again that long, speculative look from penetrating gray eyes, as if he were seeing something more, or trying to see something more.

"We can go over it later. Start with ten thousand dollars. I'll need a line of credit at the hardware and lumber stores. And we need mules."

With that, he got up, replaced his hat, thanked Cassie for the lunch, ignored her, and strode out the kitchen door.

By the end of the first day after hiring him, Andy was baffled.

She didn't see him again until Saturday when she was awakened by a loud crash that splintered through the early-morning quiet, quickly followed by a round of articulate cursing and other voices.

Oblivious to her state of dress, or lack of it, Andy threw on her dressing gown and ran downstairs.

Mr. Kelly was in the middle of the yard at the bottom of the hill. Six wagons stood in a long line arching all the way down the lane to the river road. They were loaded with barrels, crates, and stacked lumber. He was shouting orders, waving each driver to a specific location.

Cairo stood nearby dressed in his flowing robes, tablet in hand before a crowd of men and women. Workers? As each stepped forward, he made an entry. She'd been desperate to hire workers, with no success. Where had these people all come from? "What is going on here?" Andy demanded as she reached Kelly, choosing to ignore what she

111

thought was a faint flickering of appreciation in those cool eyes as he glanced her way. In the next moment it was gone, shifted behind that impenetrable mask he wore over his emotions, and Andy fought back a sliver of regret.

"Materials for construction of two caning sheds and levee gates, four plows, eight mules, fencing materials to repair the pastures so we don't lose the mules." His tone was condescending, as if he considered that she would even ask, an intrusion. "Various small hand tools, hoes, shovels, spades, harness, and two flatbed wagons. Here's the bill." He reached for her hand and slapped the paper into her palm.

Andy only stared at him. She'd arranged the line of credit as he asked. And now this extensive bill. Did this mean he'd already used the credit?

"Mr. Kelly, we must go over these expenses. If you'll come up to the house when you're finished here—" She tried to pin him down to a specific time but in the next moment was cut off as he turned to her, seized her by the shoulders, and virtually lifted her up and set her down out of harm's way as a wagon loaded with lumber rumbled through the yard.

He hesitated, hands on her arms. Surprise at that contact shifted in those mercurial gray eyes, surprise almost as great as her own.

"Later," was all he said before whirling back around and disappearing across the yard, shouting orders to six people at once.

Later! Right! Andy thought, wadding the bill into a tight ball. That was when she began to worry, really worry, and about a great many things; such as money, money, and money. And all three came back to Mr. Kelly. She worried about that decision the most.

It was the question of money that really started her thinking. One thing was abundantly clear. She knew enough about sugarcane to know that any new crops planted now wouldn't be ready for harvest until the following year.

112

There was a two-hundred-acre section of cane that would be ready in the next few months, but the fields had been left virtually unattended. All manner of pests had ravaged the fields, the crop yield would be limited. Still, there would be some cane to harvest for processing yet not enough to warrant building two caning sheds. They had one argument over that obvious fact.

Another argument came from another suggestion she made the day she went for a long ride along the perimeter of the forest at the east rim. She was so excited as she returned to the main house, more excited still to find Kelly just turning his own horse into the pasture to graze at the end of the day.

"I think I've solved one of our problems," she joyfully announced, sliding out of the saddle and ignoring his frowned greeting. He was always frowning at her.

"Which problem would that happen to be?"

She ignored the trace of sarcasm in his voice. Kelly was always sarcastic.

"Capital."

"I didn't realize there was a problem with capital."

"Obviously!" She couldn't resist the opportunity for a little sarcasm of her own. "Especially since you don't mind spending all of mine." It was obvious he wasn't really interested, but she was determined that he hear her out. Besides, she'd already spoken to Cairo about it.

As he turned, saddle in his arms and headed for the tackroom, there was that faint shift to his shoulders that she'd become very familiar with over the past weeks; dismissal.

"Lumber," she announced to his arrogant back.

"We had a shipment delivered yesterday."

"I'm not talking about buying it. I'm talking about selling it to the lumberyard in Baton Rouge, or any other customer who wants it." She heard the distinct sounds of the saddle being placed in the tackroom.

"Kelly!"

"I heard you."

113

"Well? What do you think?"

"Where are you going to get lumber?"

Andy inhaled, warming to her idea. It would work, she just knew it would.

"The forest at the east rim of the property. It's good pine, and so thick some of it can't even grow. We could send some of the men over with equipment and the mules. There's a tributary of the river that runs right through there. They could take down the lumber along the river and just float it downstream. Cairo says it joins up with the bayou. And I talked to the men. They know that whole area in there, and several of them know how to take down trees. It would work. I know it would. And we could get a good price for it. We could float it right out to the levee and from there into the Mississippi. If I spoke to Lacey's father, I'm certain we could get flatboats from him to take the logs to the mill in Baton Rouge."

"Wait a minute. Hold on!" He came at her, holding up a hand. "Just how much do you think you could get for the lumber after you pay your own men and Mr. Kittridge?"

"A lot. I've worked it all out on a piece of paper." She started to pull it out of her pocket. "I checked all the figures, plus the prices being paid for lumber in Baton Rouge. All that lumber is just sitting there rotting on top of itself because there's too much of it."

"It might be a possibility," he admitted grudgingly. Andy was more than certain.

"I know it would work."

"But not now."

"Now is perfect. We could have the men working starting tomorrow."

"I'll think about it."

Andy was stunned. "What is there to think about?"

"A great deal, Miss Spenser." He turned on her. "In the first place, those cane fields have to be planted and there's a great deal of work to be done in the existing fields so that we don't lose the cane we have."

"But I thought we could spare some of the men—"

"The problem is you didn't think." He cut her off. "If you had, you would realize we are already short-handed." Then his tone inexplicably softened, as if he realized he might have been too harsh. "We'll talk again about it later." And with that he stalked off, leaving her to mentally throw darts at the back of his arrogant head.

There was that word again. Later. Anger burned slowly as she returned to the house, mentally trying to decide just how much she needed Mr. Kelly. In the end, she realized she needed him a great deal.

Lacey talked her into going into Baton Rouge on Monday. She agreed with great misgivings. That didn't begin to describe what she felt as they were leaving and Kelly appeared on that chestnut stallion of his and thrust a piece of paper into her hands.

"A list of supplies we need." Without another word, he whirled the stallion around and was about to ride off.

She stopped him. "Mr. Kelly. We need to have that talk. I want to—"

"Rebuild Ombre Rose into a self-sufficient plantation." He did it again, taking the conversation in an entirely different direction, and, as usual, to suit himself.

"Well, yes, of course . . ."

"And all you have to do is see to it I have those supplies." He was looking at her in that strange contemplative way of his as she met his gaze directly. Then his eyes shifted to her mouth.

"Will that be all?" Coleton asked, abruptly cutting his gaze away. He was aware—vividly aware—that Miss Amanda Spenser was a maddeningly desirable woman. As it was that time aboard the *Iron Queen*, his natural response to her as a woman was all tangled up with memories of the past. She bore an uncanny resemblance to Sunny. Because of it, or in spite of it, he focused on the anger.

"Yes, until this evening," Andy informed him curtly. "I shall expect you up at the house for supper. Afterward, we will discuss the operation of the plantation."

He pulled his hat lower over his eyes, turned his horse

115

about, and rode off, leaving her with the same feeling she'd had that first afternoon—not yes and not no, just that cool contemplation of his which made her wonder who was really making the decisions. Frustration was beginning to set in.

Later, when she and Lacey were in town, they learned that Kelly, or Mr. Kelly, whichever he chose, had persuaded the bank president to increase the original line of credit to the amount he initially wanted—ten thousand dollars. Most of that was now gone, and then there were the other bills that were steadily mounting.

Then they had the pleasure of formally meeting the other Mr. Kelly, Rafael Kelly with those scandalous dark eyes. Supposedly they were cousins. *Cousins, my foot!* Andy thought all the while Lacey was literally falling over herself under his charming smile. He was only too happy to accept Lacey's invitation for supper at Ombre Rose that evening. Andy could have joyfully strangled her.

And that is exactly who was present for dinner that evening—Lacey, the "devastatingly handsome" Rafe Kelly, and herself. Her Mr. Kelly was glaringly absent. Not that either Lacey or her guest seemed to mind. Andy's frustration rose a notch to quiet fury.

She managed to suppress it for two hours while Lacey alternately babbled and swooned over their guest after he left. When she could stand no more, she went up to bed.

Unable to sleep, Andy paced her room, wandering out onto the moonlit gallery. Still restless, she went downstairs and closed herself into the study, intent on going through the plantation records. Unable to concentrate, she opened the wide glass doors to the rose gardens beyond, questions and doubts turning over and over in her mind.

It was then she decided to visit the gazebo. Everything was so frantic she hadn't had a chance until now, or wanted one. She slipped silently down the cleared path, her gown whispering softly about her bare ankles, her feet silent on the paver stones.

The gazebo was there, just as she remembered it, pale

116

and softly illuminated where the columns were bared to the moonlight. A sweet, heady fragrance drifted through the heavy foliage as tiny blossoms of star jasmine wound their way like weaving fingers through the wrought iron. This time the gate opened easily. She stepped inside.

Andy took tentative steps, lightly stretching her bare toes to feel for pieces of broken glass. She should have remembered to wear shoes.

It was a haven, safe, secret, private, taking her into its shadows. She remembered that first day weeks ago and looked for another rose blossom. There was only the sweet scent of jasmine, slowly smoothing out the anger, the evening breeze, rustling the leaves and wiping away the tight knot of doubt.

She had no idea what time it was when she finally turned to leave. She gasped as a long, dark shadow stepped through the filtered moonlight. Then she saw those pale, contemplative eyes, felt the anger that immediately replaced his first surprise.

"What are you doing here?" The words came low, almost painful.

Andy cringed. "I was just out walking." Good heavens! She sounded foolish even to herself. "I couldn't sleep." Then her gaze shifted nervously to the thin gown she was wearing. Wrapping her arms about herself, she stepped carefully but quickly toward the gate. His hand caught her.

"Aren't you going to ask why I wasn't at supper tonight?" His mood was now dangerous. It hissed through the air.

"I don't think so. Not now." Andy tried to move past him.

"Aren't you going to ask me about the expenses? You wanted a full accounting." His fingers tightened.

Andy's alarmed gaze came up to his. Why was he angry with her? He was the one who'd chosen not to show up. Was he questioning her right to go over the costs? And what was he doing here?

117

A subtle warning went off in her head. "Not tonight. The morning will be sufficient."

"Sufficient!?"

The word came out faintly slurred. My God! He'd been drinking!

"There won't be time in the morning, Miss Spenser!" He spat out her name as if it offended him. "We're planting the first cane starting tomorrow. The cane you ordered me to plant."

Alarm replaced the anger. She tried to pry his fingers from her arm.

"The morning will be more than sufficient to discuss the financial situation, and a few other things," she repeated, trying to sound calm and collected and not the least frightened, which she was rapidly becoming.

"Good night, Mr. Kelly. If that really is your name." Thrusting his hand from around her arm, Andy started through the gate. His other arm prevented escape.

"Not quite yet, Miss Spenser."

Chapter Seven

Coleton used the anger as a defense against her, but now she'd turned it against him, and he could feel that safe wall of resistance crumbling. He wanted to hurt her for it. More than that, he wanted to touch her.

His warm fingers grazed her skin, then became bruising as they slipped beneath her jaw, jerking her around to face him.

"There's something I need to know."

Before she could think, before she could breathe, his mouth crushed down over hers.

His kiss was intense, anguished, searing, as if he were trying to hurt her. This was ravagement pure and simple, and it left her choking, gasping for air, her bottom lip faintly salty with blood at being crushed against her teeth.

As violently as it began, it ended. He jerked her away, the expression in his eyes stunned and disbelieving.

"Get out of here," he whispered harshly, shoving her through the gate so that she stumbled.

Andy fled for the house. She didn't look back until she'd thrust the doors to the study tightly shut and bolted them. Then, fearing he might come after her, fearing even more the flickering of hope that he might, she stumbled up the stairs in the darkened house. She flung her door shut and bolted it as well, collapsing across her bed in a sea of anger, pain, and humiliation—and something else less easily understood.

Regret? She thrust it away, refusing to even think about it, much less acknowledge it.

"Damn him!" she cried, pounding her fist into the coverlet and feeling as if she'd made a bargain with the devil. This had been coming for days.

Tomorrow. Her shattered thoughts came briefly together; tomorrow she would fire Mr. Kelly.

As far as all her well-laid plans, tomorrow didn't come. For the entire next week, the first acres were systematically plowed and planted. The people she'd hired, or rather Kelly had hired, labored in the fields from sunup to sundown, their bronze bodies glistening in the sweltering heat.

For the first time, Andy stayed away. She didn't want to see Kelly, and she knew he was always in the fields. Better to wait until the cane was planted. She needed him for that much. She would handle the rest after he was gone. At least that was what she told herself.

She became irritable, preoccupied, and, as Lacey informed her one morning as she prepared to visit her father in town, downright disagreeable.

All afternoon, as clouds rolled in from the gulf, frustration simmered to anger and then boiled over into livid rage.

Who the hell was this Mr. Kelly anyway to take over as if he owned Ombre Rose? Forget the fact that he had workers in the fields and small, tender cane shoots in the ground. What made him qualified?

Disregard his plans for repairing the levee system to control watering and drainage. Anyone could have thought of that.

And the more she thought of it, all of it, Andy seethed. By early evening, as distant thunder began to rumble through the darkening evening haze, she was as unsettled as the coming storm.

Andy knew rain was frequent, even through the hot summer months. It was what made the bayou country so tropical the year round. It would rain for a couple of hours, clear up, and the sun would come out steaming everything lush and green. But this storm didn't stop after a few hours. It went on through the day, keeping the planters from the fields. It ran off the sloping overhangs of the house, into downspouts and gutters, pooling into small rivers that flowed to the bottom of the hill.

It splattered incessantly on the exposed granite steps while she stood watching the workers race about like ants.

Uneasiness settled over the house. Cassie retreated to the kitchen to bake yet more bread. Mary decided to clean rooms that were already spotless. Lacey was still visiting her father and undoubtedly wouldn't attempt to return until the storm was over.

Late afternoon, as the storm continued without any sign of letting up, Cairo appeared at the back door off the kitchen. Andy had come in for yet another cup of tea. It was the first time she'd seen him in days.

It was the first time she dared voice her own fears. "How bad is it?"

"This is one of the worst storms I've seen this time of year. It's hard on the new cane we just planted. It floods the fields then washes it away."

"Can't it be drained away?"

"Not fast enough. Mr. Cole . . ." He caught himself as she looked up.

"Mr. Kelly has the field hands laying canvas. I just came up to get food for the workers."

"Canvas?" Andy frowned. What was he talking about?

"They spread it over the fields, to keep the rain off."

Andy shook her head. It seemed an impossible task. "How can they hope to cover it all?"

"Not all, just the newest fields. The cane hasn't set down yet. The other will probably be all right."

"What about the men?"

"They're just about wore out, but they'll keep workin', as long as Mr. Kelly says. Problem is, there aren't enough men."

Andy swung around and headed for the door to the hallway. "I'm coming with you."

It was worse than she thought. Everyone was soaked to the skin. Workers scrambled with rolls of canvas tarpaulin. A vague thought flashed through her mind about the cost, and was then quickly dismissed. She thought she saw Kelly, but he was quickly gone, shouting orders through the pouring rain. Everyone was wet, like gray shadows moving across the muddied landscape.

Dressed in her denim pants, cambric shirt, and boots, Andy stumbled into the nearest field. It was one that had been planted only yesterday. She could vaguely make out the beaten young stalks thrusting out of the ground. She seized the rolled end of a piece of canvas as two men darted past. In the gray, soaked gloom she became one of them, struggling, fighting, trying desperately to save the tender cane shoots.

More than once the mud sucked at her boots, pulling her down with amazing tenacity. Each time, she jerked them free. She lost count of the pieces of rolled canvas she carried. There was only the aching fatigue in her arms and shoulders, and then she didn't remember that, either. Every part of her was wet, soaked to the skin, her unbound hair plastered in thick streamers to her head and shoulders.

She recognized some of the workers; others were strangers. It didn't matter. She worked until the fading gray of afternoon deepened to evening and she couldn't even see their faces.

Lightning cracked overhead and it seemed the sky opened even further. A hand pulled her around.

"What the hell are you doing here!?"

Kelly's face was momentarily illuminated, the anger unmistakable.

"Trying to save my sugarcane."

"*Your* sugarcane?"

"Yes, mine!" Andy spat back at him, then reached for another length of canvas.

"Go back to the house!"

"I will not. If everyone else can work, so can I."

"You don't belong here."

She was certain he meant the fields, equally certain there was hidden meaning as well.

"Ombre Rose is mine. I'll stay," she shouted as thunder rolled over them.

"Not today!" he shouted above the roar of wind and rain and thunder. "Get back to the house."

"No!" All the anger and frustration of the past days coiled inside her. She wouldn't quit, she wouldn't let the rain destroy her cane.

"Damn you!" he cursed, grabbing her by the arm and jerking her roughly around. He pointed as another flash of lightning lit up the eery landscape. Steady streams of water poured through the furrows of the field. She saw Cairo outlined against the night sky as he waved the workers from the fields. They scattered into the night darkness.

"You can't stop it! We've done all we can!" He jerked the canvas out of her hands, threw it to the ground, and pulled her along behind him at a full run. Andy was helpless to do anything but follow him.

He stopped for a moment, hesitated as if uncertain, then cut across the end of the field in a different direction.

Andy stumbled, then fell and was immediately hauled to her feet. Mud filled her boots, oozed out the tops and filled them again. Where was he taking her? She'd ridden down in the wagon with Cairo from the main house. She couldn't see where they were going but instinctively knew they were heading away from the house.

She gasped as rain came down in pelting, driving sheets, forced to hold on to his hand as they ran.

The rain broke, hit them again, then broke. They were running under the cover of trees. Thunder rolled a crashing symphony, then burst into another chorus of light and exploding sound. For the flash of an instant the gazebo was outlined in the stark white light. Kelly thrust the gate open, pulling her inside. And then he turned on her.

"Damn you! I told you to go back to the house."

Her lungs aching, Andy gasped out at him, "And I told

123

you . . . I wasn't going . . ."

"There was nothing more to be done."

"I had to try to help."

"Why?" The one word stung viciously.

Why was he so angry with her? For trying to save her sugarcane? For trying to save Ombre Rose?

"Ombre Rose is mine. I've got to make this work. I can't fail. And if I have to plant, cut, and crush the damn cane myself, I'll do it! And without your help, Mr. Kelly!" She dashed rivulets of water away from her eyes.

"Meaning?"

"Meaning, I want you off my property in the morning. I will pay you one hundred dollars for your time, and then it's finished!"

"Finished? Finished!" The words whipped at her. His arm snaked out closing around her waist as he pulled her full against him. "Not just yet, Miss High and Mighty Yankee!"

Andy gasped at that remembered contact. But it wasn't the danger in his words that frightened her. It was the compelling danger in the touch of his body. The strength of his arm about her was faintly bruising, warning what might come if he simply chose it.

"Let me go!" Andy hissed at him. Her other hand snapped back to strike at him, only to have her wrist seized painfully in those strong fingers.

"Do you really want that?" he whispered as his fingers tightened and he pulled her intimately against him. Those gray eyes were filled with such secret shadows and something else that echoed out of memory.

"I . . ." Andy's breath caught in her throat. "Oh, God," she whispered from fear, anger, and all the other inexplicable emotions that had driven them at each other for days, ever since that moment in the grand ballroom when she had looked up to find him simply watching her.

"No!" It poured out of her in a wild tempest that matched the storm. Her trapped hand twisted the soaked fabric of his shirt as her other hand stole behind his neck, bringing his mouth urgently down to hers.

"No!" she cried out in aching need she hardly understood. She didn't want to understand.

The storm outside became the storm within.

To Andy it seemed as if all the violent forces of nature followed them into the gazebo and now surrounded them.

All the doubt and anger of the last days were concentrated in the fiery heat of that one burning kiss.

And then he jerked her away from him, his fingers bruising her upper arms, his eyes wild with something she hardly recognized let alone understood.

"Damn you!" he cursed, his lips thinned beneath that sable mustache, his eyes cold and dangerous.

"You couldn't leave well enough alone."

She stared at him wild-eyed, seeing all the frustration and anger mirrored in his gray eyes. But there was something else behind the anger, something dangerous, barely controlled. Was that a reflection also? Was she seeing her own emotions once more? Dear God, it was frightening.

But there was no time for fear or regret as he came at her this time, pinning her against the cool marble pillar with his body.

Andy gasped. "You're hurting me."

"I want to hurt you," he said, voice low. "Damn you. It wasn't supposed to be this way."

No, it wasn't. She knew that and even as she knew it, was powerless to stop it.

But this time it wasn't a curse but a caress, and Andy shuddered as his mouth plunged down over hers.

Unlike the first time he kissed her, there was no pulling away, no chance for escape, no hope for it. His fingers imprisoned her face between his hands with almost desperate strength. His mouth moved over hers with equal strength, smothering back any protest, his lips almost cruel, the thrust of his tongue as he probed between hers, perilously violent.

Retribution or need? Andy sensed both, refused the one and felt the other shudder through her. Dear God, what

125

was happening to her?

His lips burned across her eyes, her cheek, the curve of her neck, the indentation where her pulse felt as if it would burst from her skin.

With a groan of anguish and despair, Coleton's hands plunged into the wet gold of her hair. As if he could take her inside him, he molded her slender body with his. For one agonized moment his eyes searched hers, knowing yet refusing to accept, glimpsing something from his past in those shimmering aquamarine depths. And then his mouth bruised down over hers once more. He wanted to hurt her, crush her arrogance, foolish pride, and unbending determination with fear and pain.

The fear and pain were his. He'd never wanted anyone the way he wanted her, the way he'd wanted her from the first moment he laid eyes on her. The last weeks it ate at him like a disease tearing at his insides. He hadn't even wanted Victoria Kelly with all her innocence and smoldering, youthful passions the way he wanted this woman. He hadn't wanted anyone since Sunny.

Sunny.

Somewhere in the shattered recesses of his mind, Coleton knew it wasn't possible. But the longing within his body, the memories that had alternately starved and fed him for all the long years, refused what he knew. It was the same; the feel of her, the taste, the sweet fit of her body against his.

Lightning burst bright as day through the panes of glass overhead and across his stark features. Andy gasped, but it became a whispered sigh as his mouth reclaimed hers with fierce urgency.

Shuddering with a need that had lain too long in his soul, Coleton's hand spread down her back, feeling the slender indentation at her waist, the enticing roundness of her bottom beneath the sodden pants. And from memory, his hand moved farther still, cupping her to him as the need came alive. A sound that was part groan, part sigh escaped as his other hand imprisoned her chin, his fingers turning her face so that there was no escape.

His lips pinned hers, the warm velvet of his tongue alternately stroking and plunging in such wild assault there was no other awareness until she felt the rush of cold air against her bare skin as those fevered hands separated the front of her shirt. Her cry of panic was swallowed by the heat of his kiss.

With a silent moan of despair, Andy's hands plunged across his hard-muscled shoulders and down his back, answering the need with her own.

When did her lips part willingly, welcoming the searing heat of his tongue dueling with hers?

When had shock, disbelief, even outrage subtly changed to other less easily defined emotions?

And when had resistance become the compelling hunger to be closer, to touch, to feel even as his hands bruised her?

Now the sounds that whispered from her throat were sweet endearments of love as her hands moved over his face, her fingertips grazing the sable softness of his mustache, then tangling into the long hair at his temples, bringing his mouth back to hers with a soft cry.

His lips parted hers, then teasingly withdrew, then plunged deep inside, again and again until the violation was complete, fueling a deeper, more primal hunger. His fingers burned across her skin where the shirt parted to reveal the lacy camisole. His lips followed, caressing her sensitized skin as it was slowly exposed.

Andy cried out softly. Somewhere in some dark place within her, memory and desire unfurled. Her body came alive as the delicate fabric of the camisole was stripped away. She shivered in the warm, damp air as first his hands, then his mouth replaced the fabric at her breasts. She closed her eyes, reveling in the assault, shivering with anticipation, her skin fevered beneath his hands and mouth.

When did it begin, that first faint essence of time whirling and expanding about them, and then ceasing to exist at all.

She seemed to turn into the soft, cool shadows behind her eyes, as if she were looking in on herself all the while feeling his hands on her body.

A single image, then another and another moved slowly before her, as if she were watching them all joined together in one, long, drawn-out sequence that became movement, color, and light.

Feelings, sight, sound awakened under his stroking, taking her back through the shadows and then joining her there as if they'd both moved through some invisible barrier into another time and place. Only the *place* was here, in the softly muted shadows of the gazebo; this dear, treasured secret place, where . . . *they'd first met, first loved* . . .

She heard the voices; faint whispers at first, then louder, joined by breathless laughter. And then she saw them, as if she were inside the gazebo looking out.

He was young, his wide shoulders contrasting with his narrow waist and hips. He wore riding pants, and gleaming brown boots to the knees. The snowy white shirt was carelessly open at the neck, revealing bronzed skin. His hair was long, windblown, falling lazily over his forehead and the same color as those light-brown brows. But it was his face that took her breath away, lean, handsome, the jaw wide and sharply angled, his mouth curved in a dangerous, compelling smile.

He turned as he ran, holding his hand out to the girl, and for that moment his gaze was shielded from her. Then, as he caught at the girl's hand and brought her to him, she saw his eyes, and it seemed her heart stilled beneath her breast.

They were wide-set, fringed in thick, dark lashes, and the most unusual color she'd ever seen; a mixture of shadows and light all blended together in a soft shade of gray, flecked through with gold when he laughed.

Dear God . . . she knew him . . . Coleton. Recognition was sharp, painful, mirrored out of the past.

Andy tried to turn away, but she couldn't, as if some invisible hand prevented it. It was as if she had stepped through some invisible door to another world and couldn't find her way back. The images played through her thoughts like looking through a window.

He whirled her around and around, her feet barely touching the ground, their laughter weaving in the warm, sultry air.

The girl was slender and small, her honey-blond hair tumbling free at her shoulders as she was lifted high, her hands braced at his shoulders.

The young man gently released her, letting the girl's slender body slide down his with aching slowness, his arms encircling her possessively. Color spread across her cheeks, but the girl didn't pull away. Instead, she tilted her face up for his kiss.

Andy watched as they ran toward the gazebo, laughing as they raced up the steps toward her. She shrank back but there was no escape. Fear was replaced by a new awareness. Time slipped into the shadows, and she became that girl. And the boy she saw through the haze of some long-forgotten memory became the man who was with her now.

Laughter slipped to soft whispers as they embraced. Whispers became soft sighs beneath fevered kisses as they caressed and then kissed again.

Her cheeks were flushed as she whispered to him. His hands trembled as he slowly lowered the capped sleeves of her gown, exposing first one young breast and then another.

Her hands fumbled at his shirt buttons. He bent her over his arm, his mouth closing with such exquisite tenderness over the bud of first one nipple and then going to the other, taking it into his mouth with such worshipful need.

"You're so beautiful. I love you."

"And I love you," Andy cried out as her head twisted back and forth, her body set afire by the assault of his lips. And then her hands slipped into that mane of light-brown hair, bringing his mouth back to hers.

"Please, love me. Make me yours, forever."

His hands trapped her face. "I love you. I would never ask you to do anything . . ."

"I need you," she breathed into his kiss. "I want you, for always."

He looked at her with such anguished need.

129

"If I make love to you, it's forever," he solemnly vowed.

"Yes, forever." Andy whispered with closed eyes as the words came from some deep, inner place. She could feel the heat of his mouth against hers—real, demanding, giving.

Reality and dream blended, the present slipped into the past. She saw it all happening at the same moment as she felt it. They slowly undressed each other, and when they were both free of their clothes they came together. And there was no more dream, only reality and this man.

He slowly lowered her to the floor of the gazebo, the smooth marble cooling their fiery bodies.

Her sighs slipped through the soft leaves of the gazebo, building with each stroke of his hands, until she lay wide-eyed and flushed beneath him.

"Please," she begged softly as desire warmed through her body.

The skin at his shoulders gleamed bronze across hardened muscles, a faint wedge of dark-brown hair spreading across his chest, then narrowing to his belt. She watched the path her fingers took through the downy softness, marveling at the clearly defined muscles that worked beneath her touch.

Their bodies were light and dark; hers pale, small, the fragility accentuated against his tanned, heavily muscled limbs. She wanted to stroke every muscle, touch every part of him.

And then he was touching her, as only he had ever touched her, with that faintly tender urgency that seemed to leap between them.

His hands caressed through her hair as he bent over her and it seemed they were moving together through those dark shadows of time and place.

"I love you."

He was so close; the heated gray of his eyes was nothing but a soft blur, like the rising mist off the bayou.

"Promise me." The words were so achingly tender, echoing from the dark corners of memory.

"I promise," Andy whispered, her mouth hungry under his as he moved over her, his body stroking hers with fiery heat. She felt that hard thrust at her hip and turned questioning eyes to him.

His leg moved between hers. And then it was as if they were the storm as she opened to him, sliding her legs along his, heat melting into heat.

She moved with him, the muscles of her young body enfolding him as he pushed full inside her. Andy turned her cheek against his shoulder, tasting the heady sweetness of him as they slowly began to move as one.

There was no gentleness in him. There was only the driving need that had lain buried too long within him. Instinctively, she understood it, for it mirrored her own need.

Somewhere in the vague recesses of his mind, Coleton knew this was all wrong, but he was powerless to stop it.

Everything seemed to whirl away from him. He felt her hands moving over him, heard her soft cries beneath his kisses, knew regret for the pain that shuddered through her and then winged away as he drove deep inside her. And he saw those brilliant eyes smolder to green, saw the wild torrent of honey-colored hair shimmer to pale gold as it tangled about them. And he knew. In his soul, he knew.

"Sunny." His throat ached with tears.

Slowly, they moved together, driving the pain away as their bodies felt the need and raced to quench it.

Again and again, he thrust deep inside her, almost as if he could lose himself in her, and find the past.

Memories, dreams or reality. Beyond reason, all logic, beyond everything he believed in, hatred splintered away. There was only this moment and this woman, arching to take him more fully, her head thrown back, her hair fanned like molten gold across the white marble.

And those compelling eyes watching him. They seemed to see right through him, drawing him in even as her sleek body drew him and sheathed him.

She gasped, feeling as if her soul would shatter at the

131

sensations that swept through her.

"Coleton!"

Dream or reality? He heard her softly whispered cry and didn't try to understand. He couldn't wait . . . he'd already waited too long—weeks, years, a lifetime. Her nails raked the bunched muscles at his shoulders, her eyes shimmered to deepest blue, and everything spun beyond his ability or desire to comprehend. There was only this moment, and this woman, so much like Sunny that he could believe she was Sunny.

His mouth bruised hers to a soft cry as his fingers dug into her slender hips lifting her to him.

The need in him was violent, hungering, demanding to be fed. His climax was equally violent, like fire searing through him and into her. He could feel it in her skin, in the fevered caress of her body as she turned those magnificent eyes to him in wonder and pulled him closer still, heat burning to heat, threatening to consume everything in its path.

Coleton stared up through the broken panes of the skylight. The rain had stopped. Heavy clouds tumbled over each other in the midnight sky, rolling, chasing, breaking around a crescent moon. It cast silver light into the gazebo, shining off white marble, illuminating the pale strands of her hair wrapped about them.

He eased from her side. Without waking, she curled into a small silken ball of pale skin and soft curves. He dressed in the shadows, willing himself not to look at her. The cold clamminess of the pants against his skin helped jar him back to reality.

Fool! he berated himself.

He left the shirt. Then, glancing back briefly to the quietly sleeping form on the marble floor, he went to her.

Fool—This time it came with less conviction. He reached for her shirt. It was still damp as he drew it over her shoulders. His fingers ached against the heat of her skin. God, she was so soft, so beautiful.

Gently he lifted her and she curved into his bare chest,

132

instinctively seeking warmth as her head tucked beneath his chin. She weighed no more than a child.

Coleton made his way through the gardens to the stairs at the end of the gallery. The doors to her room were unlocked. He carefully slipped inside, crossing the room from memory. She'd chosen his rooms. Coleton gently laid her on the large four-poster bed. Its voluminous softness seemed to swallow her. He pulled the coverlet up over her.

His fingers brushed a bare shoulder and his breath caught as she turned over on her back, the dark crescents of her lashes fluttering sleepily.

Perhaps it was the color of her hair, spread in wanton disarray across his bed. Perhaps it was the way her lips parted slightly as she breathed, or the way her small hand lay across the pillow, fingers slightly curled.

Shadows of feelings washed back over him; all those feelings and images as they'd made love in the gazebo.

He reached out, tentatively touching her fingers, something unfolding deep inside as they instinctively wrapped around his. It seemed so natural.

He could almost believe . . .

Then his fingers curled into a tight-fisted knot of denial. Without looking back, he slipped quietly through the door and made his way along the gallery, fighting the betrayal of images, memories, and the desire that coursed through him.

Coleton stole through the early-morning shadows to the stable and saddled his horse. He had to get away, to think, sort things out after what had happened.

He wanted to go into town, but it was late. And then there was Durant. There were Federal patrols everywhere. He couldn't risk another encounter with the man; there was too much danger he might be recognized. For that reason he'd buried himself at Ombre Rose the last weeks.

Ironically, he realized if he hadn't, last night would never have happened. But it had. And suddenly everything was very complicated.

From the very beginning she turned it all against him.

It began the first time he saw her at Ombre Rose, standing in the grand ballroom. She was so pale and beautiful, her hair like spun gold, her eyes wide and dark. He'd surprised her, and in that one moment before she recovered, he'd seen something he hadn't wanted to confront.

It came to him over and over in the weeks that followed after; that faint, elusive quality. It came unexpectedly; in the turn of her head, a look, a glance, the soft laughter in her voice, or a spark of anger in those eyes. Shadows, of another time, another place, someone else.

Christ! He shoved his hands back through his shaggy hair. What came over him last night during the storm? He should never have taken her to the gazebo. But she had made him so angry, standing there in the middle of the damn cane field in the pouring rain, arguing with him.

He'd simply grabbed her and looked for someplace to get out of the rain. Then the anger exploded, shattering what little control he had left, and there was no holding any of it back. He wanted to lash out at her, shake her until her teeth rattled. He wanted to shout at her that she had no business being there in the first place. He wanted . . . her.

So he'd given in to it. After all these years, after countless whores and a number of mistresses whose faces he didn't even try to remember.

But it hadn't been enough. There was something in her eyes, something about the way she responded to him.

Desire and innocence. A deadly combination. He was totally unprepared to find out just how innocent she was.

In spite of it, or maybe *because* of it, he'd stayed there in the gazebo with her when it would have been far wiser to leave. But he couldn't. And he couldn't stop touching her, stroking her, fascinated with the way she came alive underneath him. He wanted to make love to her over and over, closing out the world outside the gazebo, wanted to forget all the memories. And for a time he had.

Even now he could remember everything about her—her slender body entwined with his, the stark contrast of her flawless pale skin against his scarred body, the rapid rise and fall of her taut breasts beneath his hand, the bruised fullness of her lips that became hungry under his even in sleep.

She'd turned it all against him, and that started a slow-burning fury deep within him. Anger and betrayal collided, feeding off one another.

Ombre Rose was his home. He'd sworn to have it back and would do whatever it took to get it. No damn Yankee, not even a beautiful one, was going to stand in his way. That was the anger, and he understood it. The betrayal was less easily understood.

Nineteen years ago, in that cold, misty dawn, he was certain he'd lost everything he knew of love when he lost Sunny. He'd lived with it and learned to accept it, building a careful wall around his emotions, holding on to the memories of everything they'd shared in their brief time together, living off it. He believed it was enough . . .

That is, until last night. There had been that recognition, a momentary flash deep inside that it was more than just a passing resemblance to Sunny. For just those few moments frozen in time, he knew he was touching her, making love to her. Those few hours, he was able to block out the pain of the past.

He swung out of the saddle as the first gray streamers of light filtered through the trees. The chestnut stallion blew out nervously, but he ignored it. Turning the knob, he slipped into the house. Crossing the large main room, he reached for the lantern at the table. A long form separated from the shadows in the darkened room.

"Cairo?"

Living constantly on the edge of danger during the war had taught him to be careful. All it took was one time; relaxing his guard, doing something foolish or stupid, like now.

Metal clicked against metal. Coleton felt the unmistakable hard thrust at the middle of his back.

"Slow and easy, friend. Don't make this any harder than

135

it has to be."

He breathed in slowly, willing his nerves back under control. Then he moved; quickly, to his left, out of the line of firing and away from that first figure in the shadows. His plan was to hit the floor, roll into the darkness at the edge of the room at the same time he drew his own gun.

It was only when he felt the sharp blow and stars burst in his head, Coleton realized how badly he'd miscalculated.

Several things registered briefly; there were more than two men—Durant—and something one man growled just before everything went black.

"Christ! I hope you haven't killed him!"

Chapter Eight

At first Coleton thought he was dead. Everything was dark. There seemed to be no feeling in his arms or legs. Sight, taste, smell all blended into a sensory void of nothing.

It began slowly, that distant drumming in his ears, coming on in wave after wave of pain so intense that it shot jagged flashes of light across the back of his eyes, making him wish he was dead. Still it continued, wildly, rhythmically, pounding. Blood-red color pulsed images through his head. It was then he recognized the pounding, the chaotic beating of his own heart. He wasn't dead! But felt damn close to it.

He heard a low sound, someone groaning, then realized it was himself. It was then the world burst into a chaotic flash of brilliant, piercing light as the darkness, a coarse blindfold, was torn away.

White, gold, a burst of blue, faces. All swam before him in painful disarray refusing to come together in any recognizable form.

"What's the meaning of this? I was told he wouldn't be harmed!"

The voice was indignant, filled with quiet authority and vaguely familiar. *Give 'em hell!* Coleton cursed through his dazed thoughts as his head rolled uncontrollably forward, his eyes closing momentarily against the painful slash of light.

"It was unintentional. We weren't expecting that much resistance."

"God Almighty! What did you expect? That he would come with you willingly? I protest this kind of treatment. If you want my cooperation, sir, I suggest you do everything in your power to make him more comfortable."

There was a faint drawl and a lazy cadence to that almost-familiar voice. Definitely not Durant, as he first thought. But if not Durant, then who? And why?

There was a moment of silence. *That's right,* Coleton thought. *If you're not going to kill me, then make me more comfortable.* He would have said it, except for the little fact that his tongue refused to obey the feeble commands his brain was sending out. That and the fact that it felt swollen to three times its normal size, and dry as cotton.

"Loosen the bonds and get him some water," came the curt orders.

Whoever belonged to the first voice, Coleton reminded himself to thank the man when he was feeling a little more like himself. His arms fell forward, numb to the fingers, his shoulders aching with strain from being jerked back, his wrists bound behind his back. That accounted for the numbness.

A cup was thrust into his face. He felt, rather than saw it, the metal cool against his parched lips. But when he tried to lift his hands to accept it, they simply hung limp at his sides, refusing to obey. He forced a wry grin.

"You'll have to excuse my lack of manners, gentlemen," he croaked around his thickened tongue.

"For Christ's sake!" That first indignant voice again, Coleton thought, with that same nagging of familiarity. He squinted as a shadow fell across him, turning his head as much as his cramped neck muscles and the pounding in his temples would allow. The cup was held to his lips and he drank long, quenching gulps.

"Easy goin', son." One hand rested gently on his shoulder.

Easy goin'? It lodged somewhere in his battered

138

thoughts and held. Someone had once said just those same words to him. The man's shadow eased the pain behind his eyes as he looked up, the face cast in that same shadow. But the lionine head, the white hair, and neatly manicured beard were unmistakable. As were the somber blue eyes that regarded him evenly as his own vision cleared.

"General?" Coleton rasped from between parched lips, the water momentarily forgotten.

"Private citizen, Robert E. Lee nowadays," came the familiar voice. "You feelin' better?"

"Yes, sir." Out of habit and respect for his former commanding officer, Coleton struggled to sit up straighter, wincing through the pain in his strained shoulders.

"What the hell is going on!?" Coleton growled. "Are you all right?"

"You're goin' to have a lot of questions. But just take it easy for now." Lee's hand still rested on Coleton's shoulder as he turned to the shadows at the back of the small room.

"You'll not have my cooperation unless you release him and see that that head wound is properly taken care of." There was a moment of hesitation.

"I'll walk out of this car and there's absolutely nothing you can do to stop me, sir." The threat was unmistakable, with that same air of quiet dignity and authority with which General Robert E. Lee had commanded the army of the Confederacy.

"Sergeant! Do as he says," came the orders from the shadows. "See that our guest is well taken care of, fed and rested. Then we'll talk."

Coleton discovered the medical care was adequate, the food better, but the badly needed rest consisted of the single hour he dozed while someone, who he wasn't certain, sewed up the gash in his scalp. He was given laudanum for the pain, a stiff whiskey, and was rejoined by General Lee and the "voice" from the shadows.

"Major Coleton James of the Army of Virginia," the

voice recited from the spread of papers that fanned across the desk before him.

"Entered service the tenth of June, 1861, 3rd battalion of the North Carolina regulars. Transferred to a special detachment under General Robert E. Lee, October 17, 1861, and promoted to the rank of captain, duties 'unspecified.' "

Coleton shot a glance from Lee to the man in the shadows and waited. The numbness was gone; he flexed his fingers. The food had done wonders for his strength. His vision had cleared, and he slowly scanned the small room.

A railroad car? Lee had mentioned something about that earlier. What was this place and where were they? He remembered returning to Home Farm. That's when someone turned out all the lights.

He did a quick mental inventory—four men besides the general and the voice from the shadows. And all armed. Military training had taught him to evaluate every situation, then take appropriate action. The problem was, he didn't yet know what he was dealing with. One thing was clear, if they intended to kill him, they would have already done it. The pain throbbing through the back of his skull was a nagging reminder they hadn't wanted that. At least not yet. And what the hell was Lee doing here?

More surprise as he saw the hands that went with the voice. They were strong, with long, tapered fingers, blunt-tipped, moving through the papers with quiet efficiency. The next question that registered was immediately answered by the thrust of brilliant blue coat sleeves cut to perfect precision over strong wrists with gold braid trim winking in the light from the lanterns. Christ! A Union officer! But not Durant.

The information was read from the reports in that cool voice. "Apprehended and escaped, always one step ahead of the Union Army. Rumors of securing vital information prior to the battle of Shiloh, the Wilderness campaign, and with all due respect, General . . ." The man nodded

140

to his now civilian guest. "Rumors of providing information vital to General Lee's invasion of Maryland. Promoted to the rank of major."

"Rumors, sightings, secret documents, crucial information leaked." The silhouette of that head came up and Coleton could feel the man's eyes boring into him. "An illustrious military career. If the Confederacy had a half dozen more like you, the war might well have gone the other way, Gray Fox."

"I was merely obeying orders."

"And after the war you continued to elude the Union forces, by fleeing south to Mexico."

Coleton pushed back in his chair with a deceptive ease of calmness. "I was merely taking a friend up on his invitation to visit his home."

"Ah, yes, Lieutenant Rafael Kelly, citizen of Mexico, mercenary to the Confederate Army," came the curt reply.

"He likes adventure," Coleton replied just as coolly, wondering if his friend had also been picked up. He thought it unlikely. Only he knew that Rafe had left several days earlier to return to Velez as part of a business transaction they were arranging with Rafe's father. He was to send word when all arrangements had been made and then return to coordinate everything after that. He didn't expect to hear from him for a few more days. It would be at least two to three weeks before he would return.

"Colonel, I think we are all well acquainted with Major James's military record. He was a good soldier who followed orders. Just like the rest of us," Lee interjected politely but not without definite meaning.

Coleton's thoughts churned back through all the Union military officers he'd encountered or heard of the last four years, trying to scrape together something that would give him the identity of the man who now leaned across the desk, arranging newspaper articles, recent military reports, all in chronological order.

"You can read these if you like. General Lee is aware

141

of their contents. I'll go over them briefly."

"A military supply depot broken into, May 17, of this year. Six crates of rifles taken from a railroad siding outside St. Louis the night of June 3, more rifles, mortar, and countless rounds of ammunition stolen June 10, Alexandria, Louisiana. The frigate, *Gallant,* with a manifest of cannon, gunpowder, and explosives lost off the Gulf coast June 14, U.S. Army supply wagons attacked outside the military battery at New Orleans and cargo confiscated June 23. The latest was a midnight raid, eight days ago at Morgan City. Several crates of rifles and ammunition seized." The colonel's voice fell silent.

"And in every instance, except for the disappearance of the *Gallant,* this insignia was found." He turned a piece of badly wrinkled and soiled paper toward Coleton.

Coleton glanced at it briefly, masking any reaction to the familiar fox-head emblem. He waited. Just what the hell was he expected to say? *Yes, I confess, I did it?* He looked to Lee. His former commander and one of the few men he trusted completely merely nodded. The colonel's next statement was even more confusing.

"We're fully aware, Gray Fox, that except for the last incident, you were in Mexico and are not responsible for any of these crimes."

Coleton shot a glance to Lee. Except for Rafe Kelly, Lee was the only other man alive who knew where they were headed after the surrender. That meant Lee had provided them with that information. As if reading his thoughts, Lee came to his feet and approached, taking the chair opposite Coleton.

"The situation is very grave, Coleton. The surrender, peace for this nation, the lives of countless soldiers and innocent people may be in very grave jeopardy. Because of that, and because I believe that true peace is the only way this nation can now survive, I've agreed of my own free will to lend my support to Phoenix and his superiors."

Phoenix? So the colonel had a code name as well. Coleton's gaze shot back to Lee. "Go on." He was willing to listen.

Phoenix came around from behind the desk. He was taller than Coleton had originally thought. He immediately took in the gaunt look on the even features, faint streaks of gray in the light-brown hair, light-blue eyes that seemed to pierce a man through, the angled frown as if Phoenix cared for this no more than he did. He moved stiffly around the desk. It was then Coleton saw the cane and noticed the hard expression that masked the obvious pain. A war wound?

He made several quick assessments. Phoenix was thorough, intelligent, and careful. And he was trusted, implicitly. If this was as critical and vital as Lee said, it meant Phoenix's orders probably came straight from the top in Washington, or damn close to it.

Phoenix relaxed back against the front of his desk, only inches from Coleton. A definite ploy to gain his trust, or a show of superiority. In spite of the fact that the man was obviously military all the way, Coleton was inclined to believe it was the first.

"It seems someone wants us to believe the Gray Fox is responsible for these stolen weapons—"

"It's a perfect cover, Coleton," Lee interjected. "You're a known Confederate spy, who became somewhat of a legend. Unfortunately there are still many in the South who hope the Confederacy will rise again." He spoke bluntly.

"There are many, like yourself, who chose not to surrender." The man called Phoenix held up a hand. "I'm not going to argue the choice of words. The facts are, there were many who fled into Mexico. We know about them. Our sources also tell us there is every reason to believe these stolen weapons could be part of some kind of conspiracy to raise a new Confederate Army."

Robert E. Lee stood, hands folded at his back. He slowly walked around the small room. "If four years of war taught us one thing, Major James, it was that we couldn't continue to fight. Our men were beaten, be-

143

leaguered, and weary. We had no armaments or supplies. The South was and is in virtual ruins. It will be years, perhaps decades, before we can ever recover fully. But idealism has no room for the harsh facts of reality.

"An army is not made of a few stolen rifles. I know that. It is for that reason I signed that surrender at Appomattox. It is for that reason that I now offer my unconditional support. The South will not survive another war, not one more battle, not one more skirmish. If there is such a conspiracy, it must be ended at all costs before it's begun, in order that the South can survive!" He slumped wearily into his chair and Coleton saw again the ravages of the illness that had plagued Lee the last months of the war. He was tired, his eyes sunken, his cheeks above the flowing white beard hollow beneath prominent bones. Yet he was still the most dignified and powerful man Coleton had ever met.

Lee leaned forward in his chair. He rested one hand on Coleton's shoulder much the same way a father might when he was about to ask something of his son. His eyes were crystal-clear, somber, filled with complete conviction.

"I'm no longer your commanding officer, Major James. I'm an old general with no army to command. Therefore I can only ask that you please don't turn this man down without considering very carefully what he's asking and exactly what is at stake."

Coleton nodded gruffly. "All right, sir." He didn't like it, but he agreed.

"Good." Phoenix stood and walked slowly across the room to ease the pain from his stiff leg.

"This is our proposal: We have a list of all Confederate officers who refused to accept the surrender. We're convinced the man behind the conspiracy is on that list. He's posing as the Gray Fox because it will stir sympathy for his cause and it provides a perfect disguise for his true identity. We want you to find the man impersonating the Gray Fox."

Maybe he was thinking a little slowly, because of the

pounding in his head, but Coleton was at a loss to understand just why he should do it. He wanted to stretch his legs and find out if he could still walk on his own. He thought better on his feet, felt less vulnerable. As he stood, four armed guards came out of separate corners.

"At ease." Phoenix immediately ordered them back.

Coleton relaxed and slowly loosened his aching muscles. He gave Phoenix a long, steady look.

"When the general signed that surrender at Appomattox the war was over as far as I was concerned. I went to Mexico simply because I needed money. My home has been taken, my father is dead. All I wanted then and still want is to go home and try to put those four years behind me. I don't give a damn about your little conspiracy or your stolen rifles, and I sure as hell don't see any reason to risk my neck for the very same people I fought against and who, by the way, are responsible for my home being put up for auction."

Phoenix and General Lee exchanged looks. "I was afraid that might be your initial response," the Yankee officer responded grimly. "I think you'd better look at this." He pulled yet another paper from the leather portfolio on the desk and handed it to Coleton.

Spread across the top in bold letters were the words "Warrant for War Crimes" followed by several paragraphs and Coleton's name, rank, place of birth, and residence in the lines provided.

"If you accept this assignment as a joint effort by both our representatives, the United States government will dismiss all charges for war crimes and issue you a full pardon with complete restoration of rights as a citizen of the United States of America."

A full pardon. So that was the bait being dangled. And as far as Phoenix was concerned, it was just payment for the right to walk around and breathe the same air as everyone else without the fear of arrest, imprisonment, or hanging. Coleton gave Phoenix a long, cold look. He seemed to hold all the cards. He had him under guard, he had the list of charges, and he had the offer of the pardon. The choice was Coleton's. But there was really no choice at all. And then of course, there was the fact that the general believed in it all.

Obviously there was no coercion involved. He knew his former commanding officer well enough to know if there had been, he would have made it public. Lee was an honorable man whose word meant everything. Damn! Coleton silently cursed. Why did they have to bring the general in on this? Quite simply, because they knew he was the one man who could convince Coleton he should do it.

"I'd like a cigarette." Coleton sat back in his chair. He needed to think, and neither time nor his head were cooperating. One of the guards stepped forward, offered the cigarette, and lit it.

The searing smoke helped steady Coleton's nerves. He squinted up at the man called Phoenix through the blue-gray haze. They knew he'd do it and he knew he'd do it. It was merely a matter of establishing the price.

"I want more," Coleton stated flatly. He was immediately aware of the look that passed between the general and Phoenix.

The Union major stiffened. "You're not in a bargaining position."

"Oh, but I am. You want this Gray Fox, whoever he is. You want the conspiracy stopped. You're offering a full pardon if I survive. If I don't, you're not out anything. But you and I both know you came to me because I'm probably the one man who can find Gray Fox. If you could find him, you would have already done so. Am I making myself clear so far?"

"Go on."

"These are my terms. I'll find this Gray Fox, because no one has more reason to see him stopped than I do. When I deliver him to you, I want a full, unconditional pardon of all crimes and full restoration of rights."

"I already offered you that."

"In addition . . ." Coleton's voice lowered with deadly meaning, "I want my home returned to me."

Phoenix's eyes narrowed. "It's my understanding you were living at your home."

"Only as an employee. My family home was sold at auction in Baton Rouge over a month ago. The federal government drove the taxes up so high on it that it was put up for sale. I bid on it, but most of my funds are still in Mexico. I was outbid by a Yank—" He caught himself, a slow smile spreading in spite of the driving pain in his skull at the stony expression on the major's face. "A northerner."

"That's my price—my freedom and my home, the Ombre Rose plantation . . . completely restored as it was before the Yankee Army came through Baton Rouge."

Phoenix drew a long breath as he met Coleton's cool stare evenly. Then he looked to General Lee. "The choice must ultimately be yours, Colonel, but I would give him what he wants. It seems a small price to pay to ensure peace."

Phoenix nodded. "All right. You'll have everything you asked for, provided you deliver this Gray Fox impersonator to me."

"I want that in writing and signed by your commanding officer and your secretary of war."

"I don't suppose you'd like the President's signature as well?" Phoenix bit off sarcastically.

"President Johnson? No. After all, he's a southerner, a gentleman, a man of honor. I'll just take his word for it."

General Lee choked back a fit of coughing that sounded very much like laughter.

"Very well, James. I'll make all the arrangements. You'll have your signed agreement."

"Just give it to General Lee. I'll trust him to hold on to it for me. Now, if you don't mind, I'd like to get some sleep. Am I free to go?"

Phoenix rounded his desk, placing it once more between them. "You are free to remain here." The meaning was implicit. "I will personally brief you on all the information we have Gray Fox. We'll make everything available to you, but once you leave this train, there can be no further contact. I trust you understand."

"I understand."

"And I trust that as soon as you've had a couple of hours' sleep you'll be ready to leave."

"There are some things I have to take care of first."

"I'm afraid that won't be possible. We don't want anyone to know what you're up to."

"I'm sorry, Major. But that just won't work. I have to let least one person know I'll be gone for a while. His name is Cairo. He can be trusted."

Phoenix hesitated. "You may tell this Cairo you will be gone, but you must not reveal anything of what you've seen or what's discussed. Is that clear?"

"Perfectly clear."

"Good. And just to make certain it remains perfectly clear, I'll send the sergeant along. Sergeant!"

"Yessir!" One of the four guards, dressed in civilian clothes, stepped forward.

"You are to accompany Major James to the Ombre Rose plantation. He may inform this man, Cairo, he will be gone for an unspecified amount of time and then you are to immediately return here. Is that understood?"

"Yessir!"

"If he gives you any trouble, if he attempts to speak to anyone else but this person, you are to immediately shoot him. Is that understand?"

"Yessir!"

"Now, Major." A long, hard look of complete understanding passed between them. "You will need a way to contact me. There are only a handful of people who even know of this. You will not know their names. Like it or not, Major, you will have to trust me."

"And *you* will have to trust me." Coleton underscored the obvious.

"General Lee has assured me that I can." He sat down

148

at the desk. Unbuttoning the top closure of his uniform he pulled out a small gold medallion that dangled from a chain. He took it off and handed it to Coleton.

"When you find Gray Fox, or if you get into trouble, this will be your only way of contacting me. Take it to the Hotel Carillon on Canal Street in New Orleans. Ask for Deauville and show this medallion. And please . . ." For the first time the major's face softened. "Don't lose it. It means a great deal to me."

Coleton looked at the small medallion, no bigger than a nickel. As thin as it was, it was heavy, solid gold, with a small figure etched on one side—the picture of a bird, soaring into flight.

"It is a phoenix, the mythical bird that dies when it plunges into the inferno and is then reborn from the ashes. It was a gift from my sister. She would be very angry if she discovered I lost it."

Coleton smiled. "I'll see that you get it back, along with the Gray Fox."

Four hours later, Coleton rode away from the train on that deserted stretch of track outside Baton Rouge. He'd been given money, an identity, and the name of a man in New Orleans connected to one of those lost arms shipments. He allowed himself only one thought: Ombre Rose.

Andy turned over slowly. She felt the soft brush of fabric beneath her cheek and frowned sleepily. Her eyes adjusted slowly in the pale, muted light. Her hand spread across the cotton sheets and she jerked upright.

It was cool in the room, gray light cutting through the louvers at the large windows. Beyond the gallery she could hear the faint, slow drip, drip of water in the downspouts. It was a lazy, peaceful sound. The storm was over.

It was then she remembered; the rain pounding the freshly planted cane shoots, washing it away, the workers hurrying like frenzied ants to save as much of it as they could, the mud running small rivers of destruction through the fields, and Kelly.

She closed her eyes trying to block out the images that played back through her disbelieving thoughts. It was a dream. It must be. It had to be! None of it happened!

Andy threw back the sheet, frowning at the cambric shirt she wore instead of her nightgown. She must have been so exhausted when she came in that she simply fell asleep in it. Yes, of course. That was it.

She crossed the room. It was early, but she wanted to find out just how much damage the storm had caused. Then she stopped as if she were rooted to that spot on the floor.

Her soaked pants lay over a chair, depositing small droplets of water into a tiny pool on the floor. Her boots stood nearby. But what drew her attention were the louvered doors at the gallery. One was latched, but the other stood ajar, the cool, early-morning breeze slipping into the room. Her eyes fastened on the trail of wet bootprints left on the cypress wood floor. They were much larger than her own and marked the floor from the bed to the door.

Dear God! It wasn't a dream, or some fantasy like that time in the gazebo. It was real! She had gone to the gazebo last night with Kelly. It seemed there was something else she should remember, but it was elusive and slipped away.

She fought back the wave of liquid heat that seemed to seep into every part of her just at the memory of what they had done together. Her legs trembled violently as she went to the bathing chamber. Turning a faucet, she splashed cool water over her heated skin.

Andy struggled to compose herself. She had to think. Dear God, she had to think!

"It never happened." She rehearsed to the mirror as she smoothed her hair back into a tight, efficient knot at the back of her head.

"Of course. And just what will you say to him when you see him?" she flung back at her reflection.

"I'll simply explain that it was a mistake. It should never have happened."

"Of course, and knowing how agreeable, charming, and considerate the man is, he's certain to simply accept it as that and forget all about it."

Andy bit at her lower lip as she stared at her pale reflection. Two bright, fevered patches stood out on her cheeks. That was the problem carrying on an argument with yourself. Sometimes you came up with equally valid points. She knew damn good and well exactly what Kelly wouldn't do and that was forget about the matter, treat it as if it never happened.

Dear God! How could she face the man!? Just thinking about Kelly turned her knees to absolute quivering jelly. She could almost see that self-satisfied smirk of his, feel the slow inspection of those eyes. What would he say?

"How are you feeling, Miss Spenser? I hope you didn't suffer any ill effects from the storm." She was certain he would reserve that sort of remark for when the servants were present.

But what about when they were alone together, as they inevitably would be? What if he expected that anytime he wanted . . . ?

The color in her cheeks deepened. No, she simply wouldn't think about that. Surely the man wasn't that big a cad that he would assume simply because it happened once . . .

Oh, God! She couldn't go through with this. Andy's knees felt as if they would buckle.

And what was the alternative? The little argument began again. *Staying locked in your room for the rest of your life with food handed to you through a crack in the door? And what about what he might say to other people?*

The hairbrush clattered noisily to the top of the dresser at the knocking that came at the door.

Andy glanced down at the cambric shirt that was all

151

she was wearing and forced herself to her feet. A second, more urgent knocking drove her across the room and to her wardrobe. She stripped off the shirt and plunged her arms into the sleeves of the satin dressing gown, coming around just as the door was thrown open.

"Amanda?" Lacey poked her head tentatively into the room. "Are you all right?"

"Lacey!" she breathed with a combination of relief and genuine welcome. "What are you doing here?"

"I just had to come out this mornin' to check on you after that dreadful storm." She swished across the room in a wave of sea-blue silk. "Mary was absolutely beside herself when I got here, babbling something about you bein' ill. She said there was no answer from your room last night, and when she knocked on your door earlier this mornin', there was still no answer. I can't believe you went out in that dreadful storm. And here you are bright-eyed and bushy-tailed to greet the mornin'." She gave Andy an affectionate hug. "Although I will say you do look a bit flushed." She laid a hand against Andy's cheek. "Are you feelin' all right? You aren't comin' down with a fever, are you? The climate in Louisiana can be deceivin'. People are always comin' down with swamp fever."

Andy shook her head. There was hardly a chance to get a word in. "That's encouraging." She laughed, releasing some of her pent-up nervousness. "But I'm fine. It's just a bit warm in here already."

"Well that's true enough. The heat after a storm like that can be absolutely obsessive."

"Oppressive," Andy corrected her.

"That, too." Lacey waved a hand through the air as if to say it really wasn't important. And of course to Lacey, it wasn't.

"You go ahead and get dressed, I'll just go on downstairs and tell Mary you'll be right along. I swear that woman is gonna bust a gusset. She is simply too excitable." She gave Andy another quick squeeze and then

152

whirled back across the room, pausing briefly to flash her a devilish smile. "And then I'm goin' to steal you off into town for some shoppin'. If I don't get you outta here once in a while you're goin' to grow hayseeds in your hair, become all wrinkled and prune-faced from workin' out in the fields, and people will start spreadin' the most dreadful rumors."

"Rumors?" Dear God, did Mary suspect something about last night? Had she said something to Lacey?

Lacey laughed. "Maybe the rumor that you're really having a mad, passionate love affair with that handsome devil of a manager you hired," she suggested turning to leave.

"Whatever would make you think of that?" Andy gasped, color flooding once more into her pale cheeks.

"Darlin', relax. I didn't mean anythin' by it. Only that I might consider it myself if I were stuck out here all the time. You have to admit, he is one handsome devil. Although I must admit there is very little family resemblance."

"What? I'm sorry, Lacey. What were you saying?"

"That there is very little family resemblance between your Mr. Kelly and mine. They must favor their mothers. Well, I'll see you downstairs. And hurry! I came all the way out here without breakfast at this dreadful time of the mornin' just to see you. The least you can do is have breakfast with me."

"I'll hurry," Andy promised weakly as the door closed, her thoughts fastening on what Lacey had said: "your Mr. Kelly."

"Well, he's not 'my' Mr. Kelly!" she fumed as she whirled around in a sudden fit of temper. She was angry; at herself for being so foolish as to let something like that happen last night, and at Kelly for taking advantage of her. Damn him, anyway! But she wasn't so angry as not to realize that it would do no good trying to discuss such a matter with Kelly. His reply would undoubtedly be that they would discuss it later.

Plain and simple, the best course was not to discuss it at all; just pretend it never happened. In the meantime, Lacey mentioned going into town. She would pay a visit to Mr. Rawlins and speak to him about Kelly. Clearly, the man had to go.

Parker Rawlins's law office was on Chartres Street. It was small and poorly lit, with a small front area separated from Mr. Rawlins's desk by a wood railing. It wasn't quite what Andy expected.

"Ladies! What a pleasant surprise. I hope you haven't been waiting long. I just stepped out for a . . . breath of fresh air." He crossed the room in composed strides.

"Please, please come in and make yourselves comfortable. May I offer you some refreshment? I don't have much, just water, I'm afraid." He motioned to a water pitcher at the same time reaching to close a drawer at his desk. "It's a pleasure to see you again, Miss Spenser." He finally responded with genuine warmth. "You're doing well with your new home, I hope."

"It's about Ombre Rose that I came to see you . . ." Andy began, aware of the subtle change in Parker Rawlins at the mention of the plantation, almost as if he'd made his cursory inquiry without any genuine interest as to how she was faring at Ombre Rose.

"I see. Well, of course. If I may be of help. But there is really very little I can tell you about the place."

"It's not about Ombre Rose. It's about Mr. Kelly." She'd said nothing of her reasons for seeing Parker Rawlins to Lacey, and received two surprised glances.

"Mr. Kelly?"

"Yes, the man you sent out to take the position as manager." She took a deep breath, plunging on ahead. "The man obviously has some knowledge of a working plantation, but I'm afraid the situation simply will not work out. We are in . . . disagreement over several things, and I simply cannot keep him on. I was hoping

154

you might be able to help me find someone else to fill the position."

She was aware of Lacey's perplexed expression but chose to ignore it. There would be time enough for explanations later, although at the moment she had no idea just what she would tell Lacey. Certainly not the truth. Parker Rawlins's expression was one of complete confusion.

"Miss Spenser, I'm afraid I don't know what you're talking about."

"Mr. Kelly, the man you sent out for the position," she explained once more.

"My dear, I'm afraid I sent no one out. In times like these, a position like that would be very difficult to fill. I made several inquiries on your behalf but without success."

"I don't understand. He said . . ." Thinking back over her initial meeting with Kelly, Andy caught herself. He hadn't actually said Mr. Rawlins sent him out. His exact words were that he "came about the manager's position."

"Are you certain you don't know him? He's the same man who bid against me at the auction," she suggested. "He seems to know a great deal about sugarcane and Ombre Rose in particular. I got the distinct impression he was from around here. And Cairo seems to know him."

"Cairo?" Parker Rawlins looked genuinely surprised. "Good heavens, I had no idea he was still at Ombre Rose. You say he knew this Mr. Kelly?"

"Well, yes. It seemed they knew each other. They got along very well . . ."

He shook his head rather quickly, rubbing his hand across his chin. "I do seem to remember him from the auction," he remarked thoughtfully. "But I assure you I don't know the man and I certainly didn't send him out to Ombre Rose."

"I see." Andy was completely bewildered. If Mr. Rawlins hadn't sent him out, then who had?

155

"I would caution you to be very careful, Miss Spenser. A young woman in your position, alone, that is . . ." he began, then looked up, his gaze going beyond them to the door.

"Good mornin', Parker." A softly feminine voice brought both Andy and Lacey around. "Oh, I'm sorry. I didn't realize you had someone with you."

Parker Rawlins cleared his throat. "That's quite all right, Marilee. I'll only be a few more minutes."

Andy turned fully around, openly curious about the former mistress of Ombre Rose.

Rawlins coughed again, and Andy wondered if the man was not entirely well. "Miss Spenser, may I present Marilee James. Marilee, this is Miss Amanda Spenser."

A look of keen interest flashed in the woman's jade-green eyes. She had to be one of the most strikingly beautiful women Andy had ever seen. Her hair was jet-black, coiled high on top of her head in an intricate array of curls. The style emphasized her large, faintly slanted eyes that were almost catlike above high cheekbones, brilliant as emeralds one moment, glinting almost yellow the next. She was tall, with a well-curved figure beneath the cut of a very expensive gown of the latest fashion when most of the ladies of Baton Rouge were wearing gowns from the year before or older.

"So you're the one who outbid everyone else for Ombre Rose."

Andy felt the overlong appraisal, the cool assessment, and something else that was more vague. It was almost as if Marilee James were staring at her, as if in that first moment appraisal, she might have recognized her.

"Yes, I was just speaking to Mr. Rawlins about hiring a manager for Ombre Rose."

Now there was faint surprise mingled with the curiosity. "I see. Then you plan to stay. I simply can't understand why you would want the place. It's so remote and isolated. And there's absolutely nothing to do there. Just sugarcane and swamp." There was obvious disdain, al-

156

most bitterness, in her voice.

It was now Andy's turn for surprise. "Of course I plan to stay. It's my home now." She smiled. "I was hoping you could tell me about Ombre Rose. Perhaps you know Mr. Kelly."

"Kelly?"

Rawlins coughed again. "Yes, Miss Spenser was just telling me about a fellow who hired on out at Ombre Rose. It seems he's the one who bid against her for the place."

"I had asked Mr. Rawlins to help me find someone and I just naturally assumed . . ."

"Well, if Parker didn't send him out, then who is he?" There was just the faintest trace of something more than mere curiosity behind Marilee James's simple question.

"I . . . don't know very much about him. But he seems to know a great deal about sugarcane. However, I don't think it will work out." Why the devil was she stumbling over her own words? Why did she suddenly feel so uncomfortable under that vivid appraisal? Andy stood, driven by a sudden desire to leave.

"Thank you for your help, Mr. Rawlins. If you should hear of anyone wishing employment, please send them on out to Ombre Rose. I'm prepared to pay a fair wage." She turned. "Good day, Mrs. James."

There was now something else hidden behind the obvious appraisal. "Good day, Miss Spenser."

Lacey turned on her the minute they were out the door. "You never mentioned anything to me about letting Mr. Kelly go."

Andy glanced back over her shoulder. Marilee James and Parker Rawlins were deep in conversation.

"I didn't mention it, because it didn't seem important at the time."

"But he seemed so perfect. You said yourself, he knew more about sugarcane than even Cairo. He got equipment for you, hired workers, got those fields planted, even managed to save most of the new cane from that

157

storm."

"Lacey, I don't want to discuss it. It simply is not going to work out. I'll have to find someone else to manage the plantation."

"Who?"

"I don't know."

"The truth is, you won't be able to find anyone."

"Lacey, please! I don't want to discuss this."

"What is wrong with Kelly?"

Andy stopped at the corner. "We just don't agree on things."

"What's to agree about? He knows everything about sugarcane and you don't know anythin'. That seems pretty simple to me."

"You don't understand."

"No, I don't. Would you like to explain?"

"There's nothing to explain." They crossed the street, Andy determined not to speak of it further, Lacey equally determined that they would.

"Give me just one good reason why you're letting him go."

Reaching the other side of the street, Andy turned to her in exasperation, "He's arrogant. He doesn't bother to consult me about decisions," she was gaining momentum, "and he spends my money without telling me first."

"I think that comes under the heading of manager," Lacey hinted broadly. "You know, you hire someone who knows far more than you do about something and give him the responsibility of taking care of it. Manager."

Andy glared at her. "I know what a manager is supposed to do."

"Well, since he's been doin' all those things, I can't see that you have a good reason for firin' him."

"I will fire whoever I choose for whatever reason I choose. Besides, I don't trust the man."

"Why? Has he taken something?"

Andy whirled away from Lacey. God! If her friend only know how close she came to the truth. Taken something?

Yes, he'd taken a great deal in the gazebo last night. But she couldn't say that.

"Andy!"

"I thought you wanted to go shopping."

"I thought you were going to fire Kelly."

"I'll do that when I get back to Ombre Rose."

"All right then, let's go shopping. It'll give me time to change your mind."

"What do you think?" Lacey turned around from the mirror where she sat trying on hats.

"It makes you look like Eunalee Whitherspoon," Andy remarked dryly.

"You're just tryin' to be mean and spiteful because you didn't want to come shopping. Why don't you look around? You could use a few new things. After all, you can't go around in men's pants and shirts all the time." She gave Andy a pointed look.

Rather than argue with her, Andy decided she was safer looking about the small shop. The door sat between two display windows. The shop was long and narrow, cutting straight back from the door with long glass cases on either side of the single aisle. In the cabinet to the right were lace, ribbon, woven cording, eyelet, beads, and all manner of trims for fine dresses.

A pale-blue gown displayed in the one window drew her attention. It was a simple but elegant creation with the finest of hand stitching, small, looped satin braid trim decorating the heart-shaped neckline and delicately puffed sleeves that gathered at the elbows. It was a rather old-fashioned design, but of exquisite craftsmanship.

"My grandmother made that gown." The young proprietress beamed as she came from the back room and noticed Andy's attention. Lacey had explained the shop was owned by a young free woman of color who was amazingly talented with needle and fabric. By the few garments she'd seen displayed, Andy readily agreed.

"You must have inherited her talent," Andy replied warmly.

"Oh, I'll never be able to sew like Grandma. She learned a long time ago from a Frenchwoman in New Orleans. I've tried to learn everything she knows, but my work isn't as fine as hers. Just look at that gown. If I could only make tiny stitches like those."

"You must forgive my granddaughter," came the low, softly melodious voice behind Andy. "Her enthusiasm sometimes runs away with her. That is a very old-fashioned gown, not the style the ladies care for nowadays. Of course, with the war, most ladies haven't the means to buy new gowns."

Andy turned, drawn by that voice.

"Andy, this is Miss Angeline. Miss Angeline, this is my very dear friend from New York, Miss Amanda Spenser." Lacey made the introductions while she excitedly pointed out another hat she wished to try on.

"I'm very pleased to meet you, Angeline," Andy said haltingly, struggling with a memory that wouldn't come.

Then she smiled as she turned back to admire the gown. "Your work is exquisite. I've never seen anything so lovely or finely made." She touched the hem of the beautiful gown, caressing the fine woven satin trim. For several long moments there was only silence, broken by Lacey's excited chatter with Angeline's granddaughter from the back of the store.

"It was a very special gown," came the words so low as to almost be a whisper. "I made it a very long time ago, for a very special occasion."

Andy looked up at the sudden sadness in the woman's voice. "The young lady must have been very special as well for you to give such care to the detail." She smiled.

"She meant a great deal to me."

There was such an odd light in Angeline's large, dark eyes as she seemed to be staring at her.

"Are you all right?" She reached out, gently taking the woman's hand.

Angeline nodded. "I'm fine. It's just that for a moment . . ." She shook her graying head. "You have very beautiful hair. You reminded me of someone." She smiled past the moment. "You must forgive an old woman. It's not often I have someone admire my work."

"Are you sure you're all right?"

"Yes, child. Perfectly all right. Is there something I can help you with? A particular gown you would like to see?"

"Yes." Andy turned back to the pale-blue silk gown. "May I try it on?" She saw the immediate hesitation. "I'll be very careful," she added. "Please. It's so lovely."

Angeline's expression softened. "Well, all right, I suppose. It does look as if it would fit."

There was a small dressing room at the back of the shop. Andy's pale-yellow muslin gown buttoned down the front. She quickly unfastened the closure and stepped out of the voluminous skirt. Angeline's granddaughter brought the blue silk gown back from the display window. She helped Andy slip it over her head and shoulders. They were standing in front of a full-length mirror adjusting the sleeves as Angeline came back to see if they needed any help.

"Could you button it, Grandma?" the girl asked as she knelt on the floor to spread the layers of the wide skirt.

Angeline beamed as she came to help Andy. "It's such a lovely pale color, almost white. I remember when Miss Sunny . . ." She caught herself. "I remember when the young lady picked out that fabric. Sent all the way to New Orleans for it; she wouldn't have any other." There was a distinct emotional catch in Angeline's voice.

"She must have meant a great deal to you." Andy said softly.

"Yes, she did." She said no more as she began below the waist at Andy's back, using a button hook to lace the small, covered buttons through the tiny satin loops. She adjusted the back of the bodice, hesitating as her fingers brushed Andy's right shoulder blade.

"That is a most unusual mark," Angeline whispered,

her voice suddenly dry.

Andy glanced back over her shoulder, noticing the woman's deep frown at the small, almost perfectly round birthmark. It was about the size of a small coin, and a darker shade of her own skin.

"I was born with it. I always try to make certain my gowns cover it."

Angeline was very quiet, her fingers trembling as she smoothed the neckline at the back of the bodice and closed the last buttons. "It almost looks like a scar . . ." she began, then caught herself. "I'm sorry. You must forgive an old woman her curiosity. But you must not worry. You are so lovely, no one would ever notice it." She finished by gently turning Andy around and smoothing a stray strand of her hair back from her face, an especially tender and loving gesture.

"Ah, yes, you are so very lovely in the gown." Her voice was thick with emotion. "As lovely as the young lady I made it for."

Andy bit at her lower lip, certain she knew the answer before she asked. "Would you sell it to me?"

She could see that Angeline was stunned. "I never thought to sell the gown. I put it in the display window only to show my work."

"Yes, of course," Andy agreed with disappointment. "I shouldn't have asked. But perhaps you would consent to make me one like it."

"But it is so old-fashioned," Angeline protested with faint amusement. It was obvious she was very flattered.

"It's not old-fashioned. It's perfect — a grand, elegant gown." Andy complimented her with genuine feeling as she whirled around and around, letting the elegant silk swirl around her feet. She smiled up at Angeline.

The woman's expression was startled. "I will make one for you," she said. "In whatever color you like."

"Pale blue," Andy announced, admiring the gown. "Exactly like this one. If you can find the fabric."

Lacey simply shook her head in amazement as they left

the store a short while later.

"There are times, Amanda Spenser, I just don't understand you. First you didn't want to go shopping. I practically had to drag you into that shop. Then you end up buying several dresses. Just like Ombre Rose. I take you in to watch the auction and you end up buying the largest plantation in these parts. You are definitely becoming impractical."

"You mean impulsive."

"That, too. I am very serious about this Amanda. You've changed."

"What's wrong with that."

"What's wrong with it? I'll tell you what's wrong. I just never know what you're going to do anymore. It frightens me. It's as if there were two of you inside there, and I just never know which one is goin' to pop out. It's just a little misconcertin' that's all."

"Disconcerting," Andy corrected, amusement dancing in her eyes.

"That's what I said! And please don't go around correcting me all the time. You're always doin' that!"

"Someone has to. You'll get yourself into trouble one of these days saying things you don't mean."

"I always say exactly what I mean. It's you who's so confusin'. Now tell me, what are you goin' to do about Mr. Kelly?"

"He what?" Andy stared incredulously at Cairo. She and Lacey had arrived back at Ombre Rose and she'd immediately asked to see Mr. Kelly. The sooner this was all taken care of, the better. "But he can't be gone!"

"I am afraid so, Miss Spenser." Cairo regarded her with a closed, contemplative expression.

"When?" One word was all she could manage, Andy was so incredulous.

"He spoke to me shortly before you left this morning."

"Before I left? And you said nothing about this?"

"He explicitly asked that I say nothing. He thought it would be better."

"He said? He thought?" Andy was almost beside herself, she was so angry.

"And I suppose he left instructions as to the running of Ombre Rose in his absence?" Sarcasm dripped from her words.

"As a matter of fact . . ." Cairo began.

Her mouth fell open. Then she quickly closed it and began pacing back and forth across the study. "I can't believe this! He just leaves, without so much as a word—!"

"Andy . . ." Lacey interrupted hesitantly, "I hate to point out this little fact, but you were goin' to ask him to leave."

She was vaguely aware one of Cairo's dark brows arching in faint surprise.

"That is beside the point! He had no right to quit! Dammit!" Andy stomped her foot on the thick carpet. "I wanted to fire him!"

Chapter Nine

Andy applied a thick paste of the oil paint. With a palette knife she spread it for texture, filling in the line and form she'd begun weeks ago. She worked with a vengeance, telling herself she had to make good use of the early-morning light. She ignored the more obvious reason—frustration.

Damn Kelly! she fumed as she slapped another daub of paint on the canvas. Just who the hell did he think he was! Leaving instructions! As if she would give his instructions even the least consideration after he lied, spent her money as if there were no tomorrow, and then simply disappeared.

She picked up the coarse hog's-hair brush, stroking in the heavy bark of the oak tree she was painting. The problem was, of course, that was exactly what she'd done. She knew enough from the plantation records to see that the instructions he'd left with Cairo were exactly what any efficient manager would recommend. Perhaps that more than anything fueled her temper and goaded her until she snapped at everyone, finally driving Lacey back to Baton Rouge. Her only release was her painting.

When she wasn't painting she was everywhere about the plantation. The cane field lost the night of the storm was replanted. Another fifty-acre section to the east was cleared and prepared for planting. The repairs to the sugar house were progressing, but the mechanical drive that was stream-operated had to come from the West Indies. Andy tried not to worry. After all, harvest wouldn't start for another two to three months. Supposedly Kelly had ordered the necessary parts and they would arrive on time. She'd seen a receipt for the exorbitant cost and nearly fainted. No wonder her money was disappearing so quickly.

The caning shed was completed, fences mended. It seemed there was constant repair to be done on the house. Many of the rooms were still bare and closed off. Cairo mentioned there were furnishings in the huge attic, and Andy promised herself she would visit it as soon as possible.

She kept a close eye on her finances. With just a little luck and a decent harvest from the existing cane fields, she might be able to get through without touching the money Stephen had left her.

Andy wiped her brush with a cloth soaked in turpentine and stood back to inspect her painting. Only the trees and the outline of the gazebo had been present when she put it away weeks ago. Now the gazebo was almost complete, as were the trees. Yesterday she'd begun on the young man.

She went with her instinct, one line following another. He was young, wide-shouldered, with a restless energy that matched her own, except that it was caught momentarily on canvas.

Feeling. It came from that. It had seemed natural to paint the gazebo and the park, dense with moss-draped live oaks. They were a part of Ombre Rose and it was becoming a part of her. For Andy, painting was like creating something alive, capturing some moment frozen in time, a feeling, an essence of emotion. Even when she simply painted pastoral scenes or pieces of fruit, it was there. She could feel the breeze that lifted the draped moss or smell the lush ripeness of the peaches. In this painting, she had begun to feel the raw energy of this young man the minute she applied that first bold stroke.

It was there in the deceptive resting line of his body she managed to capture, leaning against the live oak. It was in the taut muscles that stretched beneath skintight breeches, in the careless way his shirt was open at the neck and the wildness of his hair caught by the breeze that lifted her imagination.

Without any conscious thought she began filling in the details of his features: sable brows, the wayward fall of lighter brown hair faintly streaked with gold that waved across his forehead, straight, strong features broken by the reckless curve of a devilish smile, the wild passionate light of youth in his gray eyes.

It spilled out of her, pure emotion coming to life on canvas. The early-morning light that she favored changed and lengthened across the room. Still she worked, with almost feverish movements, a slash of color, a soft blending of hues, the accent of dark against light. Her fingers cramped around the fine sable brush she used. The muscles between her shoulder blades spasmed and still she worked, defining, shaping with her brush and her imagination.

It was only as exhaustion seeped into her hands and fingers that she finally relaxed and noticed the light was gone. She stood back to inspect her work and frowned slightly.

"Ah good, you've finished." Mary whirled in through the door, a breakfast tray clutched in her hands. "I won't take any excuses. You're to eat!" she announced firmly, and turned around to place the tray on the small table nearby.

"Good heavens!" she exclaimed as she stared at the painting Andy had been working on. "It's him!"

"Him?" Andy looked up from cleaning her brushes. "What are you talking about?"

"It's him!" Mary pointed insistently at the painting. "It's Mr. Kelly."

Andy's head jerked around, her gaze flashing to the painting.

Mary went on. "Oh, it's a bit different. He has a mustache now and he's a bit older. But it's him, all right. I'd know those eyes and that smile anywhere." The woman beamed with satisfaction.

Andy stared at the painting of a much younger man, and started to deny it. But as she looked at the painting, she realized it was true. It was Kelly. Granted, he looked several years younger in the painting, more slight of build, but it was unmistakably Kelly, especially after he had shaved the rest of his beard.

"It's his smile," Mary confirmed confidently. "It hasn't changed a bit."

"His smile?" Andy gaped at her with disbelief. "I don't know how you can make a comparison." She bit off. "Mr. Kelly never smiled. All he ever did was shout, and give orders . . . and ask for money!"

Mary looked up in stunned suprise. "He most certainly did smile, and quite a lot. You've caught it just the same." She motioned to the painting. "A handsome smile, with sort of a rakish twist at the corner as if he were thinking wicked thoughts." She went about removing a teapot and a covered plate from the tray.

"You were always so busy arguing with the man you never stopped to notice." She crossed to Andy, tucking a heavy linen napkin in at the neck of her blouse as if she were a child. "Or perhaps you did notice," she suggested archly with a wise, knowing smile.

"I noticed no such thing." Andy snatched the napkin from her blouse and then jerked the cotton dust cover down over the painting. "It's all wrong. I shall change it tomorrow."

Mary gave her a long, straight look. "You've caught him just right. But if it's in your head to change it, I'll not be the one tryin' to stop you. But I will tell you this; you have to eat. You'll make yourself sick if you don't."

Andy threw down the napkin. Removing the silver cover from the plate, she selected a piece of buttered toast, then slammed the cover back into place and turned to the door.

"That's not enough to keep a bird alive." Mary started out after her, but she was already through the door and down the hall.

"Amanda! Amanda Spenser!" Mary fumed after her, then drew herself up indignantly when it did absolutely no good at all. "And you did capture him just perfect!"

Andy slammed the front door and went in search of Cairo, Mary's words ringing in her ears. He'd promised to ride with her into the bayou today. She wanted to explore her ideas about the lumber now that she didn't have to argue with Kelly about it.

Tired, hot, and weak with hunger, they returned from the east rim of the property well after midday. She took a long refreshing shower in that marvelous invention. And an hour later, dressed in a white muslin dress with her wet hair coiled on top of her head, Andy was just coming downstairs. Mary met her halfway.

"There's a woman here, says she brought some things you purchased in town."

Andy frowned slightly. She couldn't remember making any arrangements for anything to be delivered. And she was trying to watch her expenses. She followed Mary through the wide hall to the entrance at the back of the house off the service porch. She smiled radiantly.

"Angeline! How good to see you again."

"I brought those things you bought the other day," Angeline explained simply, indicating several boxes stacked just outside the door.

"When I'm workin' on somethin' I like, I jes can't seem to put it down till it's finished. And my granddaughter helped me, too. Fact is, Miss Amanda, business has been pretty slow for her. Besides . . ." she explained with an offhand gesture. "I had to deliver some other things nearby and I thought I would bring these."

"It's just that it's so hot today. Worse than yesterday, I think. I can't imagine anyone driving all the way out here."

"Oh, I don't mind. I have to get out of that shop. I don't like bein' closed in. So every once in a while I jes take off. I only help out when things get real busy. My eyes aren't what they used to be."

Andy smiled. "Please come in and get out of the heat. Would you like some lemonade or perhaps some fresh brewed iced tea with mint. We keep the ice in a storage chamber beneath the pump house."

"Yes, I know." Miss Angeline smiled. "The tea would be fine and then I'll jes be on my way."

Andy turned to her in surprise. "You've only just arrived. I won't hear of it."

An odd mixture of surprise and quiet contemplation crossed Angeline's face. "That is very kind of you Miss Amanda, but it just wouldn't be proper."

Andy knew exactly what she was talking about — that it wouldn't be proper in the eyes of southerners for her to entertain a black woman in her home. She straightened her shoulders.

"Ombre Rose is my home, Angeline. For as long as I can keep it," she added a bit wistfully. "I will have whomever I wish as my guest, black, purple, or with polka dots." The last was spoken with that unmistakable straightforward, no-nonsense determination.

Angeline's dark gaze was somber. She'd seen something in that flash of stubbornness and grim determination that she'd recognized briefly in her granddaughter's shop. She hadn't wanted to acknowledge it, the physical resemblance had been disturbing enough. And then there was the blue gown.

Miss Angeline pushed back the memory. Remembering was too hard and too sad. But in spite of the old grief that never truly went away, she felt a bond with this girl. It was undeniable, and it was the reason she'd come out here today.

"Please say you'll stay," Andy coaxed, smiling with genuine warmth.

"All right. I'll stay to help you try on those dresses.

Just to make sure of the fit," Angeline agreed. "But my grandson should go back to town this evenin'. I don't like Eliza bein' alone."

One day stretched into three, and then four. And somewhere along the way a silent agreement passed between them that Angeline would stay. Andy sensed that it had something to do with the blue gown. Perhaps it had begun with that, but Angeline's decision seemed to have been made when she saw the portrait.

When the next rains came, Andy again felt that panic she'd known during the last storm. But Cairo assured her the new plantings were well rooted in the fields. Their main concern was keeping the fields well drained with the series of newly repaired levees and gate systems that interwove Ombre Rose. He assured her all the gates were opened and the fields all draining as they should be. There was absolutely nothing for her to do. And that made her worry.

Of course there were other reasons her nerves were on edge with this storm. It brought too many other reminders she tried to convince herself she would much rather forget. As the rain continued, her restlessness grew.

Cassie had gone into town to visit her family, staying at the Kittridge house for a few days. The woman Maya now had full charge of the kitchen. Angeline was busy in the second-floor sewing room, mending the countless linens that had begun to show wear after many years of use. Mary was downstairs, closing some of the ground-floor windows as the wind shifted and blew rain inside to dampen the freshly waxed floors.

Andy came out of the study where she'd been going over the monthly costs for the plantation. She clutched the receipt for the new pieces of equipment purchased for the sugar house. They'd been ordered from a firm by the name of Bright and Son in the West Indies. The receipt was dated almost two months earlier with a promised delivery date in Baton Rouge that was already over two weeks old. She was beginning to worry.

She'd found the receipt after Kelly left. Against her wishes he'd gone ahead and ordered the equipment. A hastily sent telegram to the firm's New Orleans shipping office was answered by the information that the firm couldn't possibly cancel the order. The equipment was special ordered and had already been shipped. In addition, it appeared it was already paid for, the sum over three thousand dollars.

Andy had a choice. She could pay the additional expense to have the equipment installed and made operational when it arrived, or she could pay another mill downriver at New Orleans to process her cane. Either way she'd already paid for the equipment.

But as time ran out, it appeared her choice was fast disappearing. Not only had she paid an exorbitant amount of money for something that hadn't arrived yet, but it looked as if she would have to pay the high cost of taking her cane to another mill. Damn Kelly anyway!

She thrust the receipt into the pocket of the white batiste dress with black trim. She was tired of sitting and going over figures that constantly seemed to exceed her readily available cash. She was tired of the rain. Mary gave her a long look as she lowered one last window.

"It's too bad Miss Lacey couldn't come out from town to be with you. You need the company. You're just like a restless cat."

"I think Lacey's still angry with me," Andy remarked with only a trace of chagrin.

"She'll come around." Mary nodded her assurance. "The shoe just fits a little tight on her foot, that's all."

"I did invite her to come back with Cassie. But they won't try to come out in this weather."

Mary dried her hands on the apron that hung across her skirt. "You've been wantin' a chance to go through the attic upstairs. Today seems like the perfect day for it," she suggested.

"Cairo says there's all sorts of things stored away up there that belonged to the James family. Seems the soldiers didn't bother goin' up there when they stayed here. And Mrs. James didn't bother takin' much with her."

"Maybe I will go on up." Andy contemplated it. For weeks she had been curious to see what was up there.

"Take this lantern up with you. And see if you can find some vases. Cairo mentioned there used to be several very nice ones. Some of those roses need to be cut."

The stairway to the attic was behind a door at the far end of the gallery on the second floor. It was cool, faintly musty, and dark. She found one wall lantern just inside the door. She turned the knob, then lit the mantel. The flame sputtered then caught, glowing against the bright brass back plate.

The stairs were steep and narrow. At the top she found another lantern and quickly lit it as well. Light pooled a half-mooned arc across the attic floor, giving just enough meager light to outline various shapes and another lantern on the far wall.

Andy crossed and lit it, tripping in the process and bruising her knee. As the lantern glowed, sending light into this section of the attic, she realized she'd tripped over a child's rocking horse. It plunged back and forth, slowly coming to a stop. She smiled as she bent and ran a hand over the painted wood, the yarn mane, and the leather reins, remembering Lacey said there had once been a child here at Ombre Rose. Although it had been many years ago, and, as Lacey also told her, the child, now a man, hadn't come back from the war.

The attic was filled with the past. An old picnic basket, trunks stacked three high to the sloped ceiling, assorted boxes, crates and cartons, a covered loveseat against one wall, a child's furniture and toys. She found a complete set of cast-iron miniature soldiers all in field dress uniforms she didn't recognize.

There was a sailing vessel, also in miniature and to precise detail right down to canvas sails. She found boxes of books, too numerous to place in the crowded shelves in the downstairs study. In one crate she found a full set of exquisite gold-bordered china. In another she found silver goblets. The pattern on both were the intricately woven stems of roses.

The loveseat and two matching chairs were covered, as were the dining-room chairs. A delicate French writing desk was neatly tucked away and Andy made a mental note to have it taken down to her room. She found several porcelain vases. Most were in perfect condition. Only one was chipped. Their designs were in a variety of floral patterns set against the white bisque porcelain. She set two of the larger ones near the stairwell.

The attic was large. It covered the entire upper story of the house, extending back from the stairs in two directions. She'd only just begun to explore it. Lighting another gas lantern at the wall, she found what appeared to be a large mirror, also draped. She pulled aside the cloth, delighted to find the glass was still intact. It would be perfect in her sitting room.

Poking behind a small mahogany game table she found what appeared to be second draped mirror. She untied the cording that bound the cloth and carefully lifted one end. It wasn't a mirror at all but an exquisite cherrywood easel. Excitement poured through her as Andy tugged the remainder of the cording loose and pulled away the cotton cloth.

She stood back, eyes wide as her breath caught in her throat. She shook her head slowly, transfixed and at the same time disbelieving. It was an oil painting.

But it wasn't the fact that it was an oil painting that caused fascination and a tremor of fear to slip ice-cold across her skin. It was the subject of the painting: a gazebo, the canopy of spreading oak trees across the park at Ombre Rose, and, dear God, a young man, so handsome, so young, and filled with fiery passion as he stared back at her.

It was identical to her painting!

Andy clasped her arms tight about her waist, afraid to move, to even breathe.

"Dear God! What is happening?" her voice whispered through the soft pools of light from the lanterns.

She tried to turn away, yet it was impossible to break that contact. Her eyes refused to obey, and yet she felt that overwhelming fear that if she didn't look away, she would suffocate, unable to draw another breath of air. And yet the painting held her mesmerized. Those passionate gray eyes drew her in, refusing to let her go. That devilish smile seemed to deepen, so perfect were the proportions and the light that the young man seemed about to speak to her, looked as if he would extend his hand and reach out to her if she stayed.

It was then it began. That faint fading of everything else about her, as if the light had somehow become very dim, slipping to a soft glow that remained only on the painting and that handsome face, those haunting eyes, holding her, drawing her.

Andy tried to cry out. She couldn't breathe, and it seemed to have grown suddenly cold, so very cold. She gasped against the painful pressure on her lungs, the dry heat that clogged her throat. She tried to pull away, but couldn't. It was as if she were looking at everything through a long, dark tunnel and the only light at the end was the light on his face.

Unable to breathe, even to speak, much less move, Andy felt all strength seep out of her arms and legs. Like a lifeless doll she collapsed to her knees. She thought it must be a little like dying, slipping off into some dark void where there was no sound, no sense of feeling. And the pain was intense.

She was dying. She was certain of it. It was happening again, just as it happened that day in the gazebo and then again in the ballroom.

Sight, sound, touch; all ceased to exist except for the painting and the young man who stared down at her with such passion in those gray eyes.

Kelly. It was Kelly! Or someone who looked very much like him.

No. It couldn't be Kelly . . .

A soft, golden haze wrapped around his image, until only his face was visible; the straight jaw, the firm chin, the soft curve of that sensual smile.

But it was growing dim, leaving her, blotting out everything.

Collapsed on the floor of the attic, unable to move for the paralyzing coldness that swept through her, Andy knew she was leaving. She was going somewhere far away. Afraid, unable to comprehend the darkness that slowly closed over her, she reached toward that one last glow of light, the painting, and the young man who smiled down at her with such complete love and joy . . . Coleton.

She was falling. Andy felt it and was powerless to stop it. Still, her hand was outstretched. She had to reach him. If only she could touch . . . him.

Warmth, blessed warmth.

Andy felt it begin slowly; in her fingertips, slipping up her arm, seeping into her achingly cold body, suffusing her with life itself. And then she wasn't falling. She was running; running and laughing, the sound coming to her from very far away and then near . . . very near.

She laughed as she ran across the park, her skirts hitched scandulously high around her knees, her hair pulling loose of its pins and falling down around her shoulders. She didn't care, she'd won. She'd won!

"You cheated!" he accused breathlessly as he caught up to her, his arm slipping around her waist to pull her back from the live oak they'd agreed was the finish line.

"No!" She shrieked with laughter. "Let me go! No fair!" She tried to wriggle out of his embrace only to have him tighten it.

He whirled her around to him, pulling her full against him in the cool shade of the park. "And . . ." he bent low over her, laughing against her forehead, "you cheated. And you tried to trip me." She loved his laughter.

"I did not!" She pulled back indignantly, feeling that momentary flickering sense of loss at breaking the contact. Dear God, she

wondered, how was it possible to love someone so much without losing yourself?

"I won fair and square," she teased back, retreating to the safety of laughter.

"You didn't win." He smiled wickedly, his hair falling across his forehead in the way she so loved.

Unable to resist, she brushed it back, inhaling in surprise at just how that innocent contact could affect her. "I almost won."

"Almost doesn't count." His warm laughter melted to the caress of a whisper.

"You have longer legs," she retaliated with a faint pout, knowing it was hopeless.

"And longer arms." For emphasis he molded her to him, drawing a surprised gasp from her.

"Someone will see us."

"Let them. Let the whole world see us, and know exactly what we feel."

"It isn't proper." She knew the excuse was lame, particularly since she was leaning into his hardened body, luxuriating in the power she had over him, aware of his arousal and feeling her own answering desire. Her gaze fastened on his mouth, wanting him to kiss her.

"Then let's make it proper." His voice was husky as his head lowered, his lips grazing her bottom one.

Her breath caught as her eyes closed, feeling the tantalizing heat of that contact, almost crying out as it was too quickly gone. But even as she looked up at him with such adoring, passionate eyes, he kissed her again, caressing her upper lip with such sweet tenderness that her hands curled into the front of his shirt as she tried to pull him closer and fulfill the kiss.

"Marry me," he whispered the moment his lips slipped over hers.

She clung to him, answering with the language of her tender, young body, his words wrapping around her with aching promise. Yes, her heart cried out. Yes, make me yours. Love me.

He deepened the kiss, stroking her lips apart in a soft, almost plaintive sigh only to slip between them with abandon, to the soft, sweet velvet core of her.

"Marry me," he whispered again and again between soul-robbing kisses that left her weak, breathless, unable to answer except for the language of her own passion.

His hands were in her hair as his lips brushed across her closed eyes, to her temple, and down to the shell of her ear, leaving a silken-wet path where he invaded her senses.

"Be my wife." His mouth lingered over hers, teasing, promising. He kissed the faint indentation at the corner.

"I love you. Be my wife in all ways," he whispered again.

She wanted to cry out, she wanted his kisses so desperately. Why was he denying her? Her eyes fluttered open to stare up into the mesmerizing heat of molten gray.

"Look at me," he commanded gently, and she did.

"Marry me." His hands pressed into the sides of her head, forcing back the passion just enough so that he knew she listened.

"I want you to marry me," He spoke slowly, deliberately. "I'm very serious."

She stared up at him, knowing he was, also knowing a sweeping sense of panic. She loved him. Dear God, more than life itself, but what he was saying was impossible.

"We can't," she breathed through her passion-roughened lips.

"Yes, we can."

"No." Her hands came up over his as if she could try to make him see by sheer force of will.

"I'm only fifteen. You're sixteen. My father would never allow it. You know he's sworn I'm to marry Phillipe."

"Never! You're mine. You know that. You love me." His hands tightened.

She bit at her lower lip as she saw the passion ebb to cold fury.

"Yes!" She whispered with equal passion that was sharpened by fear. "I love you. I've never loved anyone else. I will never love anyone else. I promise you that. But my father—"

"Cannot stop us," he assured her with a finger against her lips to silence her objections. "I've made arrangements."

"What are you talking about?" she gasped, fear and excitement rippling through her.

"I have money. I've made all the plans. We'll go away."

She hesitated, looking away from him.

"Sunny? What is it?" His hands slipped to her arms, forcing

her to meet his gaze.

"My father is to speak to Phillipe's father on Saturday. Mother says it has all been arranged."

His fingers bit into her arms, but she didn't cry out. She understood his pain and anger, for it was her own.

"Do you love me?"

"You know I do."

"Enough to go away with me?"

"I . . ." Her eyes fastened on his and she felt again all the desire and passion and love she'd always known she felt for him surge through her. It obliterated any fear.

"Yes," she whispered from her soul.

He pulled her against him, stroking her hair as his lips caressed her forehead. "You're my life. I love you. I would never ask you to do anything that would hurt you."

"I know that."

"It would have to be soon, before Saturday, before your father speaks to Phillipe's."

She nodded, breathing in the tangy, masculine scent of him, feeling all the love in the world wiping away fear and uncertainty.

He held her gently at arm's length. "You're not afraid?" His gray eyes softened, as if he were trying to see the truth behind the answer she would give him.

"Yes." She answered with heartfelt honesty. "But only that my father will find some way to keep us apart."

"Never. I promise you that. He will never keep us apart."

It was dark and cool inside the small chapel. The only light came from the candles that glowed at the altar, gleaming golden light off the statue of the Holy Mother and the carved figure of Christ at the cross.

Her head was bowed, her hand clasped tightly in his as they spoke the vows that would bind them together for all eternity.

The ancient ceremony was repeated first in Latin and then in French as was the custom. The aged priest blessed the small gold ring that was then placed on her finger.

She had no white gown, no flowing veil. The only flowers were

179

the white rosebuds he'd brought for her.

Slowly he turned to her as the priest finalized their vows. His fingers caressed her cheek, lifting the single tear that left a wet path to her lips.

"Why are you crying?" he whispered with such aching tenderness, pain filling his eyes.

Her fingers twined with his. "It's just that I am so happy."

"I love you," he whispered, sealing the vows with a tender kiss.

"I love you," she answered against his lips.

They rose and thanked the priest. Their horses were waiting outside; a carriage would have been too conspicuous.

They spent their wedding night at Home Farm. It had been empty for so many years, dust and spiderwebs filling the corners. A lizard scampered across the bare floor as the light of their lantern pooled into the main room.

She never saw the dust, or the spiderwebs, or the barren emptiness. She saw only this magnificent young man she loved so desperately.

He built a fire. There were blankets in the corner, and food for morning. He'd brought them earlier that day. She could feel his eyes on her as he came to her and slowly began undressing her in the light of the lantern.

Her breath caught at the light pressure of his hands resting on her hips. She stood only in the lace pantalettes and the camisole, her hands trembling. This was not the first time between them. He had made love to her before, even though she had been raised to believe it wasn't right unless a man and woman were married.

But she'd known from the first moment she saw him, when she was nine and he was ten, that she loved him. She knew it then and every day afterward. And when he finally seemed to notice that the child had become a young woman, she'd known then that when the time came, she would make love with him. It had come, those brief months ago, in the gazebo at Ombre Rose. And she gave herself to him body and soul, and in return knew she'd gained his love.

His hands trembled against her cool skin, stroking her shoulders and arms with feather-light caresses until she burned beneath his fingers.

He reached behind her to loosen her hair as he had a hundred times. Each movement was slow, deliberate, savored, until her hair tumbled over his hands and wrists.

Then his fingers grazed the skin above the bodice of the camisole, slipping into the satin laces. With equal care, he drew out the bow and then carefully unlaced it, until the sheer silk gaped open across her thrusting breasts.

"Dear God, I love you." His arm slipped around her bare waist, pulling her to him, igniting a violent need in her young body.

Her mouth sought his, her hands plunging into the silken waves of his hair. A raw energy of excitement, fear, and desire shimmered through her and she pressed even closer.

They fell to their bed on the floor, clothes stripped away in a flood of passion, their hands moving heat on heat until they lay naked together.

There was no gentleness in him now, but a wild, seething desperation to make her his, really his in all ways.

Her slender body opened to his, willingly, hungrily, arching to take him to the innermost depths of her in one sheathing motion that was wildly frightening in its intensity.

Love moved his hands across her skin to her tautened breasts. Promises molded her lips to his. Need fused their bodies in liquid heat that spiraled out of control until neither of them cared if it ever returned.

"God! How I love you!" he cried out as he felt the quickening spasms of her body clasping his.

"I love you," she cried out frantically, as reality exploded into a shattering realm of light and fire and wind.

"I will always love you." He plunged deep into the welcoming heat of her body.

"Promise me . . ."

"Aways," he breathed against her lips.

"Promise me it will be forever."

"I promise," he cried against her throat. "Forever."

They had no desire to sleep. Long afterward they lay entwined before the fire, letting need warm their naked bodies. Her hair spread beneath them like golden silk. At dawn they made love once more and then dressed. It was time to leave.

They rode along the bayou at Ombre Rose, through bald cypress and past ancient oaks dripping with Spanish moss like so many old women draped in rags.

He rode ahead of her, leading the way. The plan was to reach New Orleans, and from there they would take a packet to Nassau in the Bahamas. He knew someone there who could help them get away, perhaps to England, or north to New York.

They came at them from all sides, the path ahead clearly blocked, their shapes ghostly, threatening.

It was then she saw one, more threatening than the others, and familiar.

"Stop where you are!" The command sliced through the morning mist.

He pulled his horse to a stop ahead of her. "You can't stop us."

"Can't I?" Her father swept down off his horse, gun pointed.

"I warned you what I would do if I ever caught you near her again."

"Yes, you warned me. But as you can see, I chose to ignore it."

She tossed her cape aside, jumping down from her saddle, her skirt catching in her haste to reach her father.

"Please no! Father, you mustn't!" she begged him, placing herself between her father and her husband.

"It was all arranged. I planned for you to marry Phillipe. You knew that," her father exploded at her, fury pulsing the veins hard at his temples.

"Yes!" she cried out passionately. "You planned it! But what of my feelings?"

Her husband had swung out of the saddle and now joined her, placing a protective arm about her.

"There is nothing you can do to stop us."

Was it threat or promise? She didn't know. All she knew was the fear inside her and the comforting strength of his arm. This is where she belonged, where she would stay.

"What is he talking about?" her father screamed. "Of course I can stop you. I will stop you."

"Father, please," she implored. "He's right Father, you can't stop us. There's nothing you can do now." She inhaled slowly, her voice

softening.

"We were married last night, before a priest."

As the full impact of her words stung at him, she heard the fury hiss out of her father, saw the wildness in his eyes.

"Take him!" he ordered, the words echoing back from the fog that seemed to swirl the glade to ominous gray.

She cried out as two men stepped forward to seize her husband. "No! You can't do this, Father! He's my husband!" She watched horrified as her young husband lunged for the pistol in his saddle-bag. He moved a moment too slowly as the two men lunged for him, dragging him back across the clearing. The pistol fell to the ground with a dull thud.

"Father, please!"

"By God, I told you what I would do if you ever came near her again. I warned you!" he shouted across the glade, his eyes wild.

Fear congealed in her throat. She started across the glade to her husband, only to find herself drawn backward. Her head came up, staring into the nameless faces of her father's hired men.

She was dragged across the glade and thrust at the feet of another woman. Comforting arms closed around her. She looked up, her eyes widening at the horrible sight of the raised welts across the woman's dark-skinned face, the split in her lip, and the black bruise that all but closed one eye.

"My God, Angeline! He beat you?" she whispered with aching heart.

"He said he already knew you were goin'. He tricked me into sayin' it, and then beat me like this for keepin' it from him."

Dear God, her father was mad! She was released momentarily as one man went to retrieve her husband's pistol. She clung to the older woman, trying to offer comfort, one guard remaining, his hand grasping at her elbow.

She watched the ghastly scene unfold as her father, only a few feet away, turned to face across the glade.

"Give him his pistol!" came the hoarsely barked command.

She stared, disbelieving. This couldn't be happening! It wasn't possible! Her father was challenging him to a duel!

"Father! He's my husband! I love him! Don't do this!"

"I'll end this now, as I should have ended it months ago. You'll be a very young widow. Perhaps Phillipe will still have you," her father spat out, his voice cold with death.

"Stand back," her husband commanded her softly. "This has to be settled once and for all." His dear, handsome mouth was set in a hard line.

She cried out and ran toward her father, clutching at his arm to stop him.

"Hold her!"

She was dragged backward and held. There was soft weeping beside her.

The cold gray dawn spilled into the glade. Then shadows lengthened and separated as the two men stood shoulder to shoulder, one bent with age, the other lean and tall.

The mist swirled angrily around their legs, their taut bodies ghostlike as each clutched a gleaming pistol in a viselike grip.

Death hovered at the edge of the glade, taunting, luring them on to that precise moment when life and death would meet in a burst of gunfire.

No! This couldn't be happening. She loved them both, and yet unless she stopped it, one of them would surely die. She watched horrified as they slowly turned. Each raised their arm, aim taken. She wanted to cry out, but she couldn't. No sound would come as she watched her father's finger squeeze back on the trigger.

She struggled free, running between them. The roar of gunfire shattered through the still morning air.

"Coleton!"

Her cry echoed through the mist, shattering the silence in the cold gray dawn. Birds startled from the trees, thrusting into a frenzied mass of wings.

She saw the pistol drop from her husband's fingers, the stunned look on his handsome face that went suddenly ashen, the pain that flashed in his gray eyes.

And then it was as if she were once more seeing everything through that long dark tunnel, with only faint light at the end. It was dark, and so very, very cold. But he was pulling her back, holding on to her with the warmth of his arms and tender words.

"I love you," he whispered against her hair, cradling her in his

184

arms.

He was all right! He was alive! She'd stopped them!

She reached up, confusion clouding her eyes as her fingers brushed the tears from her young husband's cheek. Why was he crying?

"I love you," she whispered, and even she could barely hear it. She shivered from the cold. It wouldn't go away.

"Take my hand." His fingers twined with hers. "Hold on to me."

"Promise me." She breathed trying to hold on, but her fingers refused to obey. Even though she could still feel his hand over hers and his arms holding her, his face seemed so very far away.

"I promise! Anything!"

"Love me. Always," she whispered, reaching to cradle his face so that she could feel him if she could no longer see him.

"I will always love you." His voice broke as she felt the heat of his cheek against hers, his tears dampening her skin.

"Promise . . . it will be forever." She brushed his lips with hers, sealing their wedding vows once more.

"I promise," he sobbed. "I will love you forever."

She could feel the brush of his lips, taste the saltiness of his tears.

"Promise me . . . Coleton."

"Promise me . . . promise . . . me." Curled into a small ball on the floor of the attic, Andy whispered the words over and over.

"Please promise me, Coleton." She wept between painful sobs as the light disappeared completely and there was only darkness.

"Miss Amanda? Dear Lord in heaven! Miss Amanda!"

Obie Bledsoe was a part-time gambler, part-time hustler, former riverfront roustabout, and full-time thief.

He had as many aliases as there were days in the week.

Before and during the war, he'd bartered, traded, or sold everything from contraband whiskey to women. He liked five-dollar cigars and fifty-cent whores down on Basin Street.

He had two trademarks—the first, a vile, unpredictable temper some said was the result of being not quite right between the ears after being dumped on his head by a prostitute mother, and the other, the missing last joint of his left pinky finger, supposedly bitten off during an amorous encounter with his favorite mistress.

He'd lived high when the times were good, just as high when they weren't, and through the years it showed as his body went from portly to obese.

When he washed up, bumping among the pilings at the New Orleans riverfront at pier fourteen, he resembled a great white whale, swollen and bloated beyond recognition except for that stubbed-off finger.

Obie Bledsoe was dead. And so was the trail Coleton had followed for more than a week.

When Phoenix had given him the name of the possible connection to the last shipment of stolen arms, there had been a spark of hope all this might be quickly resolved. He'd recognized Bledsoe's name, he'd dealt with him during the war. Not that he liked the man, but times being what they were, you did business with whomever could deliver what it was you wanted. Bledsoe had been that man.

"Damn!" Coleton swore as he turned away from the jellied body rolled in the canvas tarp. Whatever Bledsoe might have known about Gray Fox died with him. There was nothing on him when he was found; not one of his famous extravagant cigars, nor his clothes. Not unless something might have been concealed in the numerous rolls of fat that it appeared someone had tried to carve off him.

He turned away in disgust, the last shred of hope for getting this entire mess over with quickly disappearing as the police wrapped what was left of Obie like a three-hundred-pound flounder. The one officer had mentioned something about questions, but when he turned back around Coleton had already slipped into the shadows.

Bledsoe's trail was cold, dead cold, and Phoenix had been unable to give him anything else to go on except for those newspaper articles about the raids led by the Gray Fox.

What the hell was he going to do now?

Chapter Ten

"Well, well," came the soothing, gentle voice, "so you decided to join us after all. Such a sleepyhead."

"Angeline?" She questioned the shadows beside her bed, her voice thickened with sleep.

"Yes, sweet child. I'm right here."

The mosquito netting was pulled aside, Angeline clearly outlined in the rocking chair beside the bed as Andy lay back against the pillows.

Angeline took her hand, stroking it gently. Andy felt safe and loved, and for those few minutes she simply gave in to it, letting the familiar emotions and tenderness wash over her.

A memory came to her, clear and distinct, like a kaleidoscope, the colors making a brilliant picture, then shifting to make another, equally as colorful, and just as real: Angeline, younger, her voice heavy with concern as she bent over the bed, holding the cup of fragrant, steaming liquid to her lips, her sweet words offering love as she pressed her cool hand against Andy's fevered skin.

"I just made some of my special tea." Angeline spoke softly, or was it from the memory.

"Tea?" Andy tried to remember more, but it slipped away. "Yes, I'd like that."

She drank slowly, closing her eyes as the sweet, fragrant brew worked its loving magic.

"It *is* magic," she whispered. Then her somber eyes met Angeline's over the rim of the cup and she knew this moment was old, and familiar between them. Still, Angeline simply watched her, rocking slowly back and forth.

When she finished the tea and felt stronger, Andy slipped out of bed. She pulled on the light batiste dressing gown and walked to the windows, opening the shutters. The oil painting she'd been working on for weeks stood nearby. She pushed back the cotton cover.

The paint was dried now. She ran her fingers over the varied textures, almost as if they were real, as if she could touch . . .

Her fingers curled. It wasn't possible.

"How long was I asleep?"

"Almost fourteen hours. I had Cairo bring you down to your room."

So, Andy thought, she'd seen the painting in the attic as well.

"You recognized the painting." She spoke softly as Angeline's rocking chair creaked slowly back and forth.

The creaking stopped, but there was no answer.

"They're exactly alike," Andy went on slowly. She breathed in, fighting back uncertainty.

"You know who he is, don't you." She was almost afraid to ask, and her breath caught painfully in her aching lungs.

"He's the old master's son" came the whispered reply so faint Andy turned around to make certain she heard correctly.

"Coleton James." Andy's voice was heavy with emotion, causing Angeline to look up as she repeated the name she remembered from that morning in the gazebo, and just yesterday in the attic.

She didn't really want to ask the next question, but

189

knew she would.

"The other portrait is very old, isn't it."

"It was painted almost twenty years ago." Angeline whispered.

I'm fifteen, you're only sixteen. The words were flung at her from the shadows of memory.

Sixteen. Coleton James was the young man she'd seen in that dream!

No, it wasn't a dream. It was something she . . . remembered. Andy let out a shaky breath, fighting it.

Almost twenty years ago! It seemed he was that very same age when she'd dreamed . . .

She pushed it back, desperate to forget what had happened and at the same time compelled to remember by something she couldn't control.

Her fingers constricted over the edge of the canvas. "Who painted the other portrait, Angeline?"

I painted it! her tortured thoughts cried out. No two paintings are ever exactly alike! Unless . . . they're painted by the same person!

Yes, she knew! Dear God! But to accept that would mean . . .

No! That wasn't possible! It was a crazy notion!

Andy turned. "Angeline! I have to know!"

"His wife painted it," Angeline answered simply, her voice trembling with emotion as she sat stoically in the chair.

Images of the altar, a single white rose and two young people kneeling before a priest pressed in on her, and she felt as if her legs would go out from beneath her. She clutched the window ledge. Other images crowded back at her.

The misty glade in the ominous predawn gray. Two men standing shoulder-to-shoulder. They paced evenly matched steps and turned, their arms raised.

Andy clenched her eyes tightly shut to block out the images, but they followed her there.

"Sunny," she whispered, as certain of the name as she had been of his. She turned agonized eyes to Angeline. "What happened to her?"

"There's no need to go in there," Angeline protested in an agonized whisper as Andy turned the lock in the elaborate wrought-iron gate to the James family mausoleum.

It was located on a knoll, sheltered by pine trees and looking down over all of Ombre Rose. How many times had she passed nearby and never seen it? Perhaps that was why it was undisturbed through all the years of the war. Only those who knew of its existence would even know it was here.

There were four sealed, polished granite tombs inside. The crypts of Patrick James, his first wife; a smaller tomb between them of an infant son who lived less than a year, were sealed with polished black marble.

Against the far wall, stood a single tomb with space for another beside it. It was sealed in white marble, exactly like that of the gazebo. The inscription read:

Sunny R. James
May 17, 1831–September 20, 1846

There are no rules to guide the soul,
no earthly bonds; not life nor death,
but an eternal passion that is forever.

Andy slowly traced the letters with her fingers. The words were somehow familiar.

"You knew her, didn't you?"

Angeline answered softly, "She was my mistress. I cared for her from the time she was a baby."

Andy's fingers curled, remembering the gentleness in the woman's soothing touch. After all that she'd confronted, fear was the last thing she expected now. But she was inexplicably afraid to ask her next question.

"How did she die?"

It was several long moments before Angeline spoke.

"He killed her."

"*Who* killed her? What are you talking about?"

Angeline shook her head as if she thought she'd already said too much. "It's part of the past now—best forgotten." She turned and walked back to the big house, and Andy knew it would be pointless to question the woman further.

Andy closed the gate to the mausoleum. What had Angeline meant, *he* killed her? Had there been an accident? Sunny James had been so young. She felt an overwhelming sense of loss and sadness, something that slipped just out of reach.

At least now she knew one thing—Kelly was actually Coleton James.

That explained a great many things. He'd bid against her at the auction because he'd been intent on having his home back. And when she outbid him, he'd hired on as manager—almost hiring himself, as she thought back on it now, insinuating himself, persuading her to trust him, taking advantage . . .

Oh, God! She'd fall apart if she let herself dwell on what that meant.

But being manager of Ombre Rose was never his intention.

Somehow Kelly-Coleton planned to have Ombre Rose back. And everything he'd done the last weeks was to that end. When she thought back over everything, it all fell into place.

Oh, yes, he'd done his job as manager very well. That explained all the expenses for repairs and equipment, their countless arguments over what she considered necessary and he considered important.

And each time she gave in to his better judgment and

expertise. After all, what did she know about raising sugarcane or running a plantation?

And she was nothing but a damn Yankee!

That was just as big a part of it. When she thought back on it, it all fit like the first pieces of an enormous puzzle. He'd hated her from the beginning because of who she was, but more important, for what he felt she'd taken from him. If she'd only listened, everything he'd said had conveyed that. Everything he'd done . . . including the night of the storm when he'd pulled her into the gazebo.

Dear God! How could she have been such a fool?

And what part had Cairo played in all of this? He'd been with the James family for years. It was only natural to assume his loyalties lay with Coleton James.

She closed herself in the study and buried herself in the plantation records. She ignored everyone around her, spending hours going over journals, crop records from before the war, annual farmers' almanacs, lists of expenses, current crop prices, and the costs projected to take her first crop to market.

It was all there. Coleton James had been very clever. He'd managed to finance the rebuilding of Ombre Rose with her money. And then what?

According to the figures there would be only a mimimal profit after all processing expenses, which included the new wheel for over three thousand dollars that was on order from the Bahamas.

In the meantime the expenses of the new fields would be ongoing. She had her suspicions . . .

She rose from the desk and slowly paced the study, stretching her back against the stiffness of sitting long hours in the chair. And that new wheel still hadn't arrived. Something was wrong, very wrong.

She stared down at the bill of lading for the grinding wheel and knew what she had to do. She rang for Mary. When the woman finally appeared she said simply,

"Pack my things. I'm going to New Orleans."

Obie Bledsoe wasn't the sort of man who had friends. He had acquaintances, contacts, people he passed in the shadows of the underworld of New Orleans, like rats moving through slime-filled gutters and darkened alleys. But even rats left a trail. It was just a matter of finding it. Coleton knew that. He also knew that in order to find it he would have to slip into that underworld.

Still the questions nagged at him. What was Obie's connection to the stolen weapons? And why had he been killed? God knows, lots of people undoubtedly had their reasons, such as those "acquaintances" Obie always dealt with. But if Obie was anything, he'd been clever. He had survived a long time in a world where the only rule was survival. The war and occupation by the Union Army hadn't made a difference to Obie. It simply opened up new opportunities.

Coleton thought of an old saying: Dead men tell no tales. But he knew better. Somewhere, somehow Obie had a connection to someone that had finally gotten him killed. He had to find that connection. It was time to spend a little of the the money Phoenix had so generously made available to him. Money could buy anything, even a blood oath — the only honor among thieves like Obie.

He started by searching the warehouse where the last shipment of Federal weapons had been stolen. On the surface, it was one of Obie's legitimate business enterprises. But as Coleton knew, nothing ever turned out to be what it first appeared with someone like Obie, which meant the warehouse was obviously cover for other illegitimate activities, such as the theft of the weapons. But that was only one of the raids. There had been a half dozen others, and from what Coleton could see, none of them were connected to Obie. That raised another question.

Was Obie involved in just the one shipment?

The warehouse was just like so many others that lined the waterfront: wood structure, wood-planked floor, with loading bays and a frontage out onto the wharf for easy access to boats.

It was clean, in fact immaculate, as if someone had come through with a broom and mop and scrubbed every last speck of dirt. And that nagged at him. Warehouses simply weren't that clean. Had someone come in and cleaned it out trying to cover something up? Maybe something that would tie Obie to them? Or were they trying to find something? But what?

Crouched on the middle of the warehouse floor, Coleton tossed down a wooden match he'd been chewing on. This was getting him nowhere. There was absolutely nothing here.

What next? The most logical man to turn to was Obie Bledsoe himself. He had to get his information from someone. Was that someone Gray Fox? But whoever it was, there had to be conversations, plans made, contacts with other individuals. And Coleton had to find out who those people were. In order to do that he had to become Obie, submerge himself in the man's existence, live the way he lived . . . If he could stand it.

As he walked out of the warehouse he knew there were certain qualities about men like Obie. They usually drank a lot, good cheap whiskey or whatever was brought in the latest contraband cargo. And they liked the ladies. Not the Amanda Spensers of this world, with impeccable family lineage, precise manners, and cool disdain, but women without families, with manners worn on the bedposts in countless shadowed rooms, who were warm and agreeable because that's what the money on the table paid for.

A young black kid down at the riverfront had watched

wide-eyed as Obie's body was fished out of the water. If it was possible, his eyes widened even further at the gaping slash marks on the obese body. Kids like that moved in the shadows, as if they were the shadows. They saw just about everything that went on and heard just as much. From what Coleton saw, the kid knew Obie.

For a twenty-dollar gold piece he had the name of a tavern Obie frequented—the Blue Oyster, run by somebody called Sadie. For another, he had the name of one of Obie's ladies—Ellie.

The Blue Oyster wasn't exactly the drinking room of the Fifth Avenue Hotel in New York, and Sadie, the owner, was no lady. Unless of course, she'd grown a beard, wore a seaman's cap over a balding dome of head, wore just one gold earring, with a knife stuck in the belt girding a protruding belly.

It was the middle of the day, and though the place hadn't really opened for business yet, there were three or four customers. They had either come in early or perhaps stayed over from the night before, slouched over their bottle.

Coleton leaned up against the long bar. The wood was scarred with gouges and filth. Sadie, the bartender, as one drunk pointed out, passed a filthy rag across the bar before him.

"Whiskey," Coleton ordered, taking a quick assessment of his surroundings. There was the main entrance off the street, one door to the right of the bar, probably leading to a storeroom or perhaps a way out the back. He'd noticed an alley backing up to the small wood-and-brick hovel.

There were a half dozen round tables scattered about the room, supporting half-empty bottles and the few numb patrons. One drunk staggered up to the bar and demanded another cup of ale. Sadie poured him a glass and he drank noisily.

A bottle, the cap already cracked open, the contents conspicuously light in color, was thumped down on the bar in front of him. Sadie spat into a smeared tumbler, wiped it with the crusted rag, and slid it across the bar toward Coleton.

"Twenty dollars for the bottle," grunted sweet Sadie.

Coleton's eyes never left Sadie's as he ignored the glass, grabbed the bottle, and tossed back a healthy draught. Just as he thought—watered down.

He reached inside his vest pocket and plunked down a twenty-dollar gold piece beside the tumbler.

"I want some information."

Sadie's watchful eyes narrowed as he wiped several more glasses in stony silence.

"About Obie Bledsoe. I know he used to come here a lot."

The wiping stopped briefly, then started again. "Don't recall nobody by that name."

Coleton shrugged. "Obie liked whiskey and a woman named Ellie." He watched for some response in Sadie's dark, beady eyes.

"I told you, I don't know nobody by that name."

The drunk at the bar staggered over. "Sure you do, Sadie." He hiccuped. "Obie always sits at that table." He pointed an unsteady finger toward a darkened corner.

Sadie slammed a tumbler down hard on the bar. "I told you I don't know nobody by that name!" He turned on the drunk. "That's the last pint of ale. Get outta my place!"

The drunk grinned foolishly. "Ah, Sadie, you wouldn't go throwin' out a good, payin' customer? Would ya?"

Sadie moved behind the bar toward him. "Ye're drunk. And you owe me for the last three tankards of ale. Get outta here while you can still walk."

The drunk leaned back, his weight braced on hands spread against the bar. His lopsided gaze turned toward the far end of the bar where the door opened.

197

A young woman dressed in a blue satin dress had just come in. Coleton watched as Sadie stopped her, whispering something that brought her wide-eyed gaze up briefly. She was quadroon by the looks of her and younger than she wanted to appear. She nodded, her gaze shifted away, and she turned back to the door.

The drunk beside Coleton jabbed a finger at him. "You was askin' about Ellie?" At Coleton's nod, the man looked longingly at the watered-down whiskey.

"It's yours." Coleton assured him.

The drunk passed a tongue over his dry lips. "That . . ." he jerked his head in the direction of the door, "was Ellie."

Coleton shot past the drunk, sidestepped Sadie as he tried to block his path, and charged out into the back alley.

A cat hissed and yeowled, scurrying out of his way. Another drunk, probably one of Sadie's patrons, sat slumped against the back of the tavern. Other than that the alley was deserted. He ran to the street at the end. Nothing, absolutely nothing. She'd only had a few seconds at the most, but Ellie had vanished.

"Damn!" Coleton cursed, then turned toward the Blue Oyster with cold eyes.

Sadie was just reaching for the gold piece. The broad steel blade hissed down, embedding in the wood bar between his first and second fingers. His head jerked up, his other hand going for the blade at his belly.

"In the time it'll take for you to do that, you'll be missing three fingers." Coleton's warning hissed just as deadly.

Sadie wisely brought his hand back to rest on the flat surface of the bar, his fingers twitching nervously.

Beside Coleton, the drunk watched with wide-eyed amazement.

"The whiskey is watered down, and I don't like liars." Coleton flexed his fingers around the handle of his knife. He and Sadie both knew men died for less.

He shoved the gold piece in front of the drunk. "Drink up, my friend, and after this, take your business elsewhere."

"I think I'll do just that." The drunk wrapped a protective arm around the bottle of whiskey. Coleton resheathed his knife and followed him out onto the street.

"Where can I find Ellie?" Coleton held up another gold piece.

"Eh?" The drunk squinted as sunlight glinted off more money than he'd seen in the last several months. He shrugged.

"Don't rightly know. She used to work the Blue Oyster real regular till Obie came along. After that, she was with him mostly."

"What about anybody else he used to meet at the tavern?"

The drunk shrugged his shoulders. "Obie was always workin' some kind of deal. He came, he went. I never paid much attention."

"What about a name you might have overheard?" Coleton was grabbing at straws and he knew it.

The old man's eyes were fastened on the gold piece. That much money would mean several bottles of the finest whiskey, all a drunk could ask for. But he was either already too drunk or too honest.

"Sorry, mister. I don't remember anything. I was always busy myself." He lovingly patted the bottle in the crook of his arm.

Coleton was convinced he was telling the truth. A man who lived in a bottle would tell you everything you wanted to know for another drink. He thrust the coin into the man's hand.

"Buy yourself something to eat."

"Right ye are, mister." The drunk waved, staggered across the street, and practically fell into another tavern.

Coleton fixed the memory of Ellie's thin face in his

Chapter Eleven

The trip downriver took only one day. Lacey had forgiven Andy all transgressions and eagerly accompanied her. August Kittridge acted as chaperone and escort as he had business downriver. A pleasant surprise was to find Parker Rawlins aboard as well. He became Andy's unofficial escort while aboard.

New Orleans was new and it was old, and more European than American. It was new in a sense that it was large, bustling, and growing with the appetite of a city that had survived war and occupation by some of the most powerful nations of the world; old with a history that dated to 1716; European by its very nature as one of the most important seaports in the world and the fact that during its colorful history it had been ruled by the kings of France and Spain, laid siege by the English, purchased by the Americans.

Wherever Andy went, everything she saw was a colorful blending of it all in one magnificent city wrapped like a crescent moon of land at the mouth of the Mississippi River. And for that it was appropriately called the Crescent City.

There was the Vieux Carré, the original New Orleans, a rectangle bounded by the river, Iberville Street, Esplanade and Rampart Avenues. Only the Ursuline Convent remained of the original French structures, the others destroyed by earlier fires. Still the French influence prevailed.

Houses were constructed flush with the sidewalks, built around inner courtyards and gardens. Elaborate ornamental ironwork that reminded her of Ombre Rose, graced upper story balconies overlooking the streets. From the outside they all looked much the same, clustered in austere, plain blocks.

The first day after their arrival in New Orleans, Andy tried to contact the shipping firm of Bright and Son. All her inquiries in the business district met with the same response—no one could tell her anything about the West Indies firm. August Kittridge assured he would make his own inquiries and they would soon have their information. Until then, all she could do was wait.

During their stay in New Orleans they were the guests of Melanie Marchand, a longtime friend of August Kittridge. She was a gracious hostess and had arranged a schedule of soirees and shopping for her younger guests.

On this particular day, Melanie had taken them to a small coffeehouse on Decatur Street. In spite of the war it had opened only two years earlier. The owners served tantalizing concoctions of shrimp and crayfish omelettes, small single-portion soufflés, fresh seafood bisque, and spoon-sized desserts. It was impossible to have just one.

But by far the most unusual thing Andy discovered was the separate ladies' room, where women were seated in a different part of the coffeehouse from men. She pondered that strange fact over an omlette.

"But why shouldn't men and women dine together?" she asked insistently.

Melanie smiled indulgently. Lacey rolled her eyes and gave Andy the feeling this was yet another gaping difference between the North and the South.

"My dear, it simply is not done," Melanie explained graciously.

"But why?"

Pressed for a specific answer, it was clear Melanie had

to ponder that for a while.

"I suppose it is because there is so little in common for men and women to discuss over a meal. Surely you see that men have their interests, and women have theirs, and each would be quite bored hearing little details about the other."

"Andy doesn't think so. After all, she owns a plantation now. At least temporarily." Lacey confided, taking another tantalizing bite of her shrimp soufflé.

Andy flashed her a look of exasperation. She'd made this trip specifically to see about the equipment for the mill. It was her only hope for processing her cane. She explained that all to Lacey, knowing her friend had no head for figures or details. She certainly didn't expect her to understand, but she did expect Lacey to accept her right to do everything she could to hold on to Ombre Rose. It fell somewhere under the topic of friendship and devotion.

"Many women own property, left to them by their families or husbands. That is not so unusual." Melanie smiled softly.

"You don't understand. Andy owns all of it, lock, stock, and bayou. She actually goes out into the fields and helps plant the sugarcane."

"*Mon Dieu!* Surely you're not serious about this, Lacey."

"Of course, I am. Just ask her."

It was clear Andy was in for a great deal of explaining. Melanie Marchand was quite suitably shocked and staring at her with the oddest expression.

"I simply don't see what all the fuss is about. There's work to be done. What does it matter who does it?"

"But that is men's work. It simply is not proper for a lady to do such things." Melanie was appropriately aghast.

"It is, if the lady expects to keep her property and have enough food on the table to survive," Andy stated emphatically, and loud enough for several other ladies seated about the coffeehouse to glance with open disapproval in her direction.

Good God! Andy fumed. What was she supposed to do? Sit in a corner and crochet lace doilies?

"You can't mean that you actually do the work of a field hand?" Melanie was incredulous, but more than stunned she was curious.

"Not every day," Andy conceded. "But I do visit the fields to make certain work is progressing as it should. And there is no one else to go over the expenses and pay the bills. Besides, I've always been good at figures and organizing things." She smiled as an idea occurred. "It's no different than organizing a household. I just happen to find that all very boring." She thought of all the countless details she preferred to leave to Maya or Angeline.

"There's nothing worse than trying to organize jams, jellies, or counting jars of pickled pig's feet, or arranging flowers just so in a vase. After all, how much mental exercise does that take?"

"Bravo!" Melanie announced to both their astonishment. "I couldn't agree with you more, Mademoiselle Amanda. I've simply never had the courage to say it, and certainly not to my husband, as much as I loved him." She smiled with genuine enthusiasm. "After my husband died, I was left a widow with no family. We were never blessed with children, and my parents and brother were long dead. I had a sizable estate and various business affairs left to me. Of course, the natural choice was to retain a lawyer to handle those affairs. I dispensed of my husband's lawyer. He was quite displeased. But then I hired Monsieur D'Nahcram."

"D'Nahcram?" Lacey turned the name over and over. "I think Daddy mentioned him. Did he help you a great deal?" she asked with wide-eyed innocence.

D'Nahcram? Andy's brows came together thoughtfully. It certainly didn't sound French. Then her eyes widened with enormous respect at what she suspected.

D'Nahcram. Of course that was it!

"It spells Marchand backward," she announced with a glowing smile.

"Ah, Amanda, you are very clever. Yes, that is so. And what better way to accomplish something that is opposite from a woman's traditional role?" She spread her hands wide in an innocent gesture.

"What on earth are you two talkin' about? I don't understand a thing you're sayin'," Lacey protested, completely bewildered.

Andy laughed delightedly. "What Melanie is saying is that she didn't actually hire a lawyer at all. She merely gave the appearance of doing so, because it was easier than explaining the truth when everyone would expect her to do no more than arrange flowers and elegant furnishings and give exquisite parties."

"Precisely so." Melanie joined in the laughter.

"Daddy swears that Monsieur D'Nahcram is an absolute genius at business. You can't be him!"

"And why not, Lacey? Is it because that is not what is expected?" Melanie suggested.

"Well, I suppose so." Lacey answered hesitantly. "But it's just so unladylike." She said it almost with disdain.

"Do you consider me unladylike?"

Andy watched her friend, knowing her dilemma. As usual, Lacey had managed to talk herself into a corner. Melanie Marchand was one of the most admired and sought after women in all New Orleans. She was respected as a lady and hostess, spoken of with perhaps a touch of jealousy that came from envy. She was beautiful, gracious, and utterly feminine. It just so happened, as they'd just learned, she was one of the most astute "businessmen" in New Orleans as well. That was obvious by what August Kittridge said of D'Nahcram.

All in all, Andy thought it was outrageously hilarious. If only the proper, dignified men and ladies of New Orleans knew the truth.

"No, of course I don't think that," Lacey assured her.

"It's just that I never thought of a woman doin' those things."

"Ah, dear Lacey, you must learn to challenge the traditional roles and expectations. That is the spice of life. Can you honestly say you enjoy the endless details of managing a house; deciding on which day of the month the rugs must be removed and beaten; how often the crystal vases must be rotated with the ceramic ones so that the room will always appear different; going over the prices of fish and lard at the market; arranging flowers so that the color schemes match perfectly the rugs that you've had cleaned and complement the courses of the meal you've planned?"

Andy giggled. "Lacey can't answer that, because she refuses to do those things. She has Cassie take care of it all," she added, pulling her lower lip between her teeth to force back laughter.

"Those things are borin'!" Lacey protested.

"Precisely, my dear." Melanie smiled, having made exactly her intended point.

"And now I must be on my way. I have a last fitting at the seamstress for the costume I am to wear this evening." She rose from the table, collecting the purchases she'd made that day. They were all invited to a masked ball and formal dinner being given by one of Melanie's very dear friends.

"Do you have your costumes?" she asked brightly.

Lacey's eyes glittered excitedly. "We're to pick them up later. Right now we're to meet Daddy at his offices. He has word for Amanda about some equipment she purchased."

They had just stepped outside the Dutrey's coffeehouse. Melanie had her own driver; Lacey and Andy waited for a public carriage.

"Isn't that Marilee James?" Andy's gaze swept across Decatur Street.

Melanie looked up as she pulled on a lace glove. "I do believe it is. She comes to New Orleans quite often.

Baton Rouge is too provincial for her tastes. But surely you've met?"

"Oh, yes, they've met." Lacey joined in. "You see, Andy is the new owner of Ombre Rose."

"Mon Dieu!" Melanie turned to her with an expression of even keener appreciation. "So you are the new owner of Ombre Rose Plantation. I had heard she put it up for auction. Such a shame."

"I'm afraid sympathy might be more in order," Andy answered truthfully.

Lacey nodded. "You see, Andy's had some setbacks, and the local mill owners simply refuse to process her cane. They're just bein' mean and vindictive."

"On top of all that, you'll just never guess who bid against her at the auction, tryin' to get Ombre Rose for himself, and then had the audacity to hire on as manager usin' a ridiculous, phony name?"

Melanie's carriage had arrived, but she waved for her driver to wait.

"You cannot keep me in suspense Lacey," she scolded. "Please, tell me!"

"Well, it was just none other than Coleton James himself." Lacey nodded, her copper curls bouncing emphatically.

"Sacrebleu! Coleton James! But I thought . . ."

"Well, of course, all of us thought the same thing." Lacey agreed. "But he's not dead at all."

"Does Marilee know this?" Melanie Marchand turned to Andy.

"I just found out myself," Andy admitted, not going into details of how she'd found out about it. She didn't want to get Lacey started on that. She had an absolutely insatiable curiosity about everything. If Lacey had so much as a clue about what had really happened between herself and Coleton James, there would be no end of it. She would wheedle, pry, and badger until she had all the intimate details.

And then there were the twin paintings . . . No, she didn't want to think about that at all. And so far, Angeline hadn't spoken of it again, either.

"Oh, this is very exciting." Melanie let her driver assist her into the carriage. "You see, Marilee James is also a very close acquaintance of our hostess for this evening. In all probability she will be at the ball."

"Only Louise Montfort would invite members of the oldest families in New Orleans and sit them all down to supper at the same table with General Sheridan and his staff. Oh, to be a little mouse, privy to all the conversations and gossip that will take place tonight." She fluttered excitedly as she closed the door to her carriage and waved to them.

"*Au revoir,* dear girls. I shall see you later."

Andy sat in the cluttered office at the riverfront warehouse. August Kittridge sat across from her; Lacey sat to one side. A small, bilious creature who greatly resembled a toad stuffed into a shirt, vest, and suit sat on the other side. His name was Thaddeus Root. Mr. Root was the New Orleans agent for a company by the name of Bright and Sons, located in the Bahamas.

She felt like crying, cursing, and screaming all in the same breath. Mr. Root sat well back in his chair as far away as he could possibly get as she paced toward him. Good, she thought. She was glad he sensed just how angry she was. But it was nothing compared to what she felt at that moment for Coleton James.

So! He'd managed to steal at least another three thousand dollars of her money by writing up a phony receipt for equipment that didn't exist!

What on earth was she going to going to do now? Silence weighed heavily in the office. Finally she turned to the little toad of a man.

"Place the order for the parts and give the invoice to

Mr. Kittridge. I want them delivered one month from today."

"One month? Oh, no, no, no." Mr. Root laughed excitedly. "That just is not possible. Our ship doesn't even leave until the end of the week. It's a three-day voyage to the Bahamas, and that is providing the equipment is in the warehouse there. If not, it has to come all the way from England. Our northern sources are still quite unreliable," he added with a smirk of satisfaction.

Andy came at him from across the corner of the desk, bracing her body on her outspread hands.

"Mr. Root, you *will* have that cargo in Baton Rouge one month from today, at a cost of two thousand nine hundred and forty-three dollars. I don't care where it comes from. I don't care if you have to sit up nights making the parts yourself or have to hire fifty extra people to get it done."

"But I promise you, if those parts are not there, General Sherman's march through Atlanta will look like a garden party compared to what I intend." One delicate hand came down on the desktop with a determined thud. "Is that perfectly clear?"

As she knew he would, Mr. Thaddeus Root crumbled. He didn't like intimidation. She could almost envision his wife, if he had one. She was probably six feet tall and six feet across.

"Yes, ma'am . . . I mean Miss Spenser," Mr. Root stuttered. "I mean, yes, of course, we'll do our best."

"Just make certain that equipment is here on time. And . . ." she straightened to her full height, standing over the man who seemed to shrink into himself with every passing moment, "if you should see Mr. Coleton James, please inform him I'm filing a complaint for his arrest, over the matter of three thousand dollars!" With that, she snatched the original receipt from his grasping little fingers and whirled out of the office.

"But what about payment?" he called after her.

"Take that up with Coleton James as well!" She

209

slammed the door so hard it bounced back open.

The last thing she heard was August Kittridge's assurance the man would have his payment — half when the order was placed and half upon delivery, just like everyone else they dealt with.

"I really don't feel like going tonight," Andy told Lacey when they went to pick up their costumes for the masked ball that night. "Why don't you go without me?"

"Nonsense!" Lacey declared. "It'll do you good to get your mind off your problems."

Carriages blocked the street in front of the store. It was almost impossible to walk inside because of the crowds as party guests or servants came to pick up costumes. It took almost twenty minutes to locate both Andy and Lacey's costumes, then there was a delay concerning the boxes, which were all alike with the store's trademark initial "L" in the corner, for Louis the owner.

On the way out, another carriage stopped in front of the store.

Lacey nudged Andy. "It seems Melanie was right about Marilee attending the ball tonight."

"I wonder who she'll go as," Andy speculated of the lovely, dark-haired woman, remembering how they'd agonized over their own decisions, trying to find costumes portraying some wickedly outrageous or notorious person in history.

"Probably herself," Lacey suggested pointedly.

Andy turned to her with a surprised smile. "Why, Lacey Kittridge, you can be positively vindictive."

"Can I help it the woman's a witch and a traitor? She should go dressed as Benedict Arnold!"

Andy's hand was on the latch to the glass-paned door. Several ladies were crowded inside, while several more waited impatiently behind her. Passersby jostled for position on the sidewalk. She was gently nudged by a tall man in a long coat with a hat pulled low over his eyes.

"Beg pardon, ma'am," he murmured.

She looked up and caught the brief flash of gray eyes as he glanced her way, then disappeared once more in the crowd.

Her immediate thought was that she knew those eyes and the deep timbre of that voice. She stared after him. "It couldn't be."

"Did you say something, Andy?"

She turned back to Lacey. "No, I must have been mistaken. After all, I don't know anyone here in New Orleans." But those eyes continued to haunt her long after the man had disappeared.

Coleton James ducked around the corner. He wondered what the odds were that he and Amanda Spenser would meet on a street in New Orleans. Damn! he thought. What the devil was she doing here? His gaze fastened on the name of the shop as she disappeared inside.

All that day he'd searched the New Orleans riverfront. He asked questions—about Obie, anyone he might have been seen talking to the last days before he died, and about a young quadroon girl in a blue satin dress who fit the description of a hundred girls.

He spread enough of Phoenix's money around to loosen a dozen tongues, and still came up with nothing. Either no one knew anything about Obie or they weren't talking. And Ellie, whoever she was, had vanished.

More than once through the remainder of that day and into the next, he considered going straight to the Hotel Carillon as Phoenix instructed, asking for a man by the name of Deauville, also as Phoenix instructed, and informing him to tell Phoenix exactly what he could do with this whole plan! He'd take his chances without the pardon, and to hell with whomever was pretending to be the Gray Fox.

After all, what did he care about a few stolen weapons? As far as he was concerned, it was simple retribution on the part of a few die-hard Confederates.

But each time he considered it, a voice inside reminded him it wasn't quite that simple. He wasn't following orders given by a commanding officer but only a request from a man he respected. He didn't give a damn about Phoenix, but he'd made a promise to General Lee.

But more than the promise, there was Ombre Rose. It was his home, all he had left in this world that was truly his, an inextricable part of his life he could never let go. It was the one thing he thought of all those years in England and then during the war—that one day he would go home again. And of course there was Sunny.

And there was Amanda, someone he wanted to forget and couldn't.

When he agreed to this scheme, he'd insisted Ombre Rose be part of the bargain. If he were able to expose Gray Fox, his home would be returned to him. It seemed simple enough at the time; fair recompense that what had been taken from him should be returned.

But more and more, every time he thought of it, it was all tangled up with thoughts of Amanda Spenser, with all her ideals, stubbornness, and passion for Ombre Rose. He'd always believed no one could ever love it as he did.

After seeing her fight to restore it as it once was, after realizing she didn't care in the least the amount of time and work it would take, he'd been forced to accept the possibility that she loved Ombre Rose. But she was still just a Yankee. It didn't matter what she felt, or pretended to feel. Ombre Rose was *his* home. And that was why he continued to search for anyone who knew something about Obie Bledsoe.

Tired, frustrated, and more than a little angry, Coleton found himself returning to the riverfront, and the warehouse where that last shipment had been stolen. There had to be a link, something that had been overlooked.

He crouched in the muted light from that one

smudged window and wiped his fingers across the planked wood flooring. The warehouse was spotless, as if someone had come in and methodically cleaned it, right down to the floor, so clean a person could eat off it.

A faint scratching reminded him of the noise rats make, but it came persistently, from one of the large doors that opened out onto the loading dock. The door groaned and creaked, grating open just enough to allow a faint sliver of light and the small figure of a man. He slipped inside and the light immediately disappeared as the door grated shut. Coleton slipped into the darkness along the wall and waited.

Measured footsteps whispered across the floor of the warehouse several yards from where he was hidden. His eyes narrowed trying to make out the man.

In the gray shadows he was small, his body obscured by baggy pants and a heavy jacket. His face was hidden except where the knit cap pulled down practically to the jacket collar. He blended into an indiscernible shape.

But more than his size, Coleton focused on what the man was doing. He walked unerringly across the warehouse, looking back over his shoulder every so often as if watching for something, or someone. He hesitated, cocking his head to listen. Then apparently satisfied nothing was amiss, he moved to the far wall beneath the window, dropped to his knees, and began counting off the boards in the floor. What the hell was going on?

Coleton watched in amazement as a large, rolled bundle was retrieved from beneath the floorboard. Just as the man was replacing it, Coleton stepped from the shadows, his revolver clutched tightly in his hand.

"Drop the knife and turn around slowly."

The little man froze.

Before Coleton realized what was happening, he turned, threw the knife carelessly, and bolted across the warehouse for the door.

Thrusting his revolver into the belt of his pants, Coleton lunged after him. The little man had shorter strides and he caught him easily, throwing him to the floor. He heard the air grunt out of the little man's lungs, but he was in for a surprise.

His small captive wriggled, kicked, and clawed toward the door. Exactly what a woman might have done . . .

Coleton cursed, grabbing his intruder by the shoulders and jerking him around. Surprise was equal on both sides. Coleton stared, while the little man's jaw dropped open. The little man wasn't a man at all.

Coleton sprang to his feet, dragging his captive with him. He pulled her around and flung her against the wall. Large almond-shaped eyes the color of whiskey stared back at him in complete terror.

"Please let me go! Please!" the young girl cried frantically. "I'll give it all back! I swear I will! I don't know nothin'! Nothin'!"

It was Ellie, Obie's mistress, and scared half to death as she hung suspended in his grasp.

"I won't hurt you!" Coleton shouted as loud as he dared, trying to break through her hysteria.

If he let her go, he knew she would run. Coleton pinned her against the wall. "Listen to me, dammit! I'm not going to hurt you!" He shook her until her head snapped back, dislodging the knit cap and somehow piercing through the fear. She stared back at him with wide, frantic eyes.

Her breathing was ragged. She swallowed convulsively, her eyes never leaving his. He could feel the wariness in her stiff body as she strained away from him, the wall bringing her up short. Coleton loosened his grasp just a little.

"I just want to ask you some questions! I need information about Obie Bledsoe. You're the only one who knows anything!"

She started to say, "I don't know nothin'—"

Coleton cut her off, tightening his grasp. "You know a great deal, or you wouldn't be so scared."

"No . . . !"

"If I wanted you dead, you already would be," he whispered menacingly low from between clenched teeth.

For the first time she seemed to actually consider that he might be telling her the truth. She slowly nodded her head.

"Then you'll let me go?"

Coleton nodded. Again that slow consideration.

"All right." She was hesitant; he could hear the uncertainty behind the tentative reply.

Coleton slowly relaxed his grip on her shoulders. When she didn't fight or lash out, he released her.

"Why did you run from the Blue Oyster?"

Ellie rubbed the sore spot where her shoulders had been bruised through the thick jacket. She gave him a tentative sideways glance, then looked away.

"I thought you might be one of them."

"Who?"

"The ones who killed Obie come back to get me."

"Who did kill him?"

She shrugged. "There's nothin' to tell."

"Or that you want to tell?" he suggested.

"They might still come back."

"Maybe," Coleton agreed. "And maybe you should tell me what you know. I'd like to catch up with whoever killed Obie."

"Why?"

Now he had her full attention. It was hard to tell how she felt about the fact that Obie was dead. One thing was certain—she wasn't surprised.

"Because they've got something I want," he answered honestly. She considered that, watching him warily.

"What was in the package you took from that compartment under the floor?"

Her eyes widened innocently. "I don't know what ye're talkin' about." She denied stubbornly.

Coleton grabbed one wrist, tore open the jacket, and jerked the thick package tucked inside her pants. She screamed indignantly, clawing as she lunged at him. He

215

sidestepped, leaving her crumpled on the floor at his feet.

"Someone really should teach you some manners, Ellie." He spoke softly. "First of all, don't lie when someone asks you something. Second of all, don't take on somebody twice your size, and . . ." as she shot to her feet and made a move to lunge at him again, he drew his revolver, clicking back the hammer, "don't take on somebody who has a gun." He aimed it straight at her.

Ellie seemed to dissolve right on the floor.

"It's mine!" She wept into her hands. "Five hundred dollars, just what Obie promised!" She turned tear-filled eyes up at him. "I earned every penny of it, since I was eleven. That's all I want. Just my five hundred dollars."

"How old are you now, Ellie?" He gentled his voice.

She sniffled, wiping her coat sleeve beneath her nose in a childlike gesture.

"Fifteen, come October. I don't know the day."

Fifteen. Sweet Jesus! Coleton thought. And if she'd been with Obie the last years, she'd left the innocence of childhood far behind. He remembered someone else at fifteen . . . Then he opened the package. It was thick, and by the looks of the first few bills he fanned through, there must be several thousand dollars.

"Where did Obie get this kind of money?"

"I told you before, I don't know nothin'."

"You might know more than you think," Coleton informed her. "Tell me about what went on here." He gestured to the warehouse surrounding them.

Ellie shrugged her shoulders. "Obie bought and sold things."

"What kind of things?"

"Cotton, rum, machinery, food, fabrics, coffee." Again that noncommittal shrug.

"Weapons?" Coleton suggested, and was immediately rewarded by the widening of her eyes.

He released the hammer on his revolver, but kept his eyes on her.

216

"Three weeks ago, a shipment of guns was seized outside New Orleans," Coleton explained. "It was traced to here. But before they could be recovered, they disappeared. Then, just a few days ago, Obie turns up dead." He paused. "That wasn't too surprising. After all, a man like Obie doesn't make a lot of friends."

Ellie was silent.

"No one knew anything, and no one cared," he concluded. "But you know something, don't you, Ellie?"

Looking to the bulge in his jacket, she bit at her lower lip. Then after several long moments, she nodded.

"Tell me about it."

She took a deep breath. "Obie said this deal was goin' to make him rich. That's when he promised to pay me the money he owed me." She twisted her hands together to keep them from shaking.

"What kind of deal?"

"He said it was something real dangerous. There was a shipment he was to pick up, bring here, and hold until the buyers came for it." She swallowed hard. "The next mornin' talk all over town was about them stolen guns. I was real scared. Obie got angry, said I should mind my own business." She wiped her nose again. "One night Obie was drinkin' real heavy and I sneaked in here and took a look at those crates. I saw them guns and I knew it was real big trouble if we got caught."

"Go on."

She sniffled. "Obie met with this fella who paid for every last one of them crates."

"Did you see who the man was?"

She shook her head. "Obie went off someplace to meet him. I don't know where, but he was sure struttin' happy with himself when he come back. He sent me down to the Blue Oyster to work 'cause that fella was comin' for the crates. He didn't want me around. When I got back that night everything was gone."

"Like it is now."

Ellie nodded. "Except not like this. It was never this clean. That happened after Obie was found . . . dead," she finished in a small voice.

"What about the money?"

"He put it in that place under the floor. But he showed me first, braggin' on how he cheated that man what bought the guns. You see, Obie was supposed to get a certain price for them guns, but he sold 'em for a whole lot more. I knew when he told me that, he was in real bad trouble. But he just smiled and said it was about time he made his fortune."

"He kept the difference for himself," Coleton concluded. And got killed for it.

Ellie nodded. "I begged him to give it all to the people who brought the crates here, but he said no one would ever find out 'cause he was the man doin' the dealin' in the middle. He was supposed to handle another shipment. He said he already had his instructions."

Coleton scanned the gaping darkness of the warehouse as if he were trying to see those crates. But at the mention of another shipment, his head came up. There hadn't been anything in the newspaper about it, which could only mean it hadn't taken place yet. Obie had been eliminated. That meant someone else would be contacted to move the stolen armaments.

"Did he say anything about the man who gave him his instructions?"

Ellie shook her head.

Coleton took Ellie by the shoulders. "Try to remember."

She shook her head slowly, nibbling on her lower lip. "There was a name, French-soundin'. Obie said the fella used to be the ruler of France."

Ruler of France? Coleton thrust his fingers through his hair. How the hell was he supposed to make any sense of this?

"Obie got a big laugh outta that." She went on. "Said the fella was real poor, common folk, and then he became the ruler of France. Obie said he was goin' to be just as important as that fella Napoleon after this next deal . . . Napoleon! That's it! I remembered!" Ellie beamed excitedly. "Does that help?"

Damn! Coleton thought. The one lead he had was someone calling himself Napoleon. More illusion and deception.

"You did just fine, Ellie. Can you remember when Obie was supposed to meet with Napoleon?"

Ellie's eyes widened. "Oh, he wasn't going to meet Napoleon, he was supposed to *be* Napoleon. And it was supposed to happen tonight."

Obie was supposed to be Napoleon? Tonight?

Something Coleton heard on the streets crystallized—there was to be a fancy costume ball tonight. It would be the perfect opportunity for two people to meet without being discovered. Especially if they were dressed in costumes.

New Orleans had once been a city famous for its society parties and balls. But that was before the war. The citizens had even given up their annual Mardi Gras celebration. There had been no costume balls since. This promised to be quite an event, and it shouldn't be too difficult to find out where it was being held.

"Thank you." Coleton smiled, but his thoughts were racing. Obie was dead. The plan was already in motion for another stolen shipment to be delivered. Someone would attempt to pass information regarding that shipment to a man dressed as Napoleon Bonaparte. Whoever passed that information was connected to the man disguising himself as Gray Fox.

He had dozens of questions. What was the next shipment to be stolen? Who was posing as Gray Fox? Was he simply a former Confederate officer like himself trying to rally the Confederate cause?

Whoever the man was, he was clever. He'd set up a system where none of the people involved knew the identity of his contact. If nobody knew any names they

219

couldn't expose any of the other people involved.

Coleton tied the thick roll of bills with a piece of cord and handed it back to Ellie.

"Take it."

Her eyes widened in obvious surprise. Clearly she hadn't considered he'd even let her have any of the five hundred dollars, much less the entire amount.

"Why you doin' this?" She watched him with open suspicion.

"Because everybody needs a chance to find some happiness, Ellie. That money could buy a new beginning for you, far away from here." He smiled gently, thinking she was so untrusting, so afraid, and so damn young. "Have you got any family?"

She shook her head. "Not nobody that's still alive."

"Well, you can't stay here." He spoke softly, not wanting to frighten her any more than she already was. "The people who came after Obie may come back for that money."

She nodded, her face somber, fear making her gnaw at her lower lip.

Coleton patted her shoulder. "I know someone you can go to in Baton Rouge. He lives at a place called Ombre Rose, just outside of town. You'll be safe there. Tell him I sent you. He'll give you a place to stay until you decide what you want to do. You can trust him. And don't go showing that money around," Coleton warned. "Just use what you need to get there."

"It don't make no sense, you helpin' me and then givin' me all this money. Ain't nobody ever done me no kindness," Ellie said, obviously suspicious of such generosity.

"You helped me. That's reason enough," Coleton answered simply, and realized it probably was the first real kindness she'd known in her brief life.

Two hours later Ellie was on her way to Cairo, and Coleton had learned the location of the masked ball.

In his notorious past, he'd masqueraded as a Union

officer, a physician, a bumbling old drunk, even disguised himself as an old woman once, complete with stuffing in the front of a high-necked dress, in order to get behind enemy lines. Add to that list Confederate, spy, and most recently fugitive.

Now he had to find a costume of Napolean, Emperor of France, attend a fancy costume ball, and catch another imposter.

Chapter Twelve

The Château de Montfort of the New Orleans Montfort du Villiers family resembled a great French country manor house, as it should. The Montfort family, all quite eccentric Lacey had informed Andy, had it built, stone by stone, beam by carved wooden beam, as an exact duplicate of the family estate in the Loire Valley of France.

Louise Montfort was the matriarch of this proud family. She was the daughter of another influential New Orleans family, the Robillards. When war broke out between the North and South she simply packed up her two daughters and three sons and sailed for France.

She had returned early in June, and in the three months since then, she had reopened the house known by all New Orleans as the Château. The masque ball being given this evening was in honor of the return of the Montfort family. In a city that had known little cause to celebrate the last four years, it promised to be the social event of the season.

Lacey was beside herself with excitement. After all, Phillipe and Jean Paul Montfort would be the official hosts, along with their mother. And as Lacey promptly informed her, they were both fabulously wealthy, handsome, and both carried some sort of title, neither of which she could remember.

By five o'clock that afternoon as Angeline was pressing their costumes, Lacey had broken out in a rash so undone was she by the entire event.

Angeline mixed a clear, flower-scented balm, and the rash had almost completely disappeared when August Kittridge and Parker Rawlins arrived at Melanie's house shortly after eight o'clock to escort the three of them to the ball.

The Château was located just at the edge of the city. The drive took almost an hour. Lacey chatted excitedly, oblivious to the infatuated glances that passed between her father and Melanie. Parker Rawlins wore a faintly bemused expression as he quickly slipped in a question to Andy as Lacey paused to take a deep breath.

August Kittridge finally leaned forward, a tolerant expression on his face.

"Lacey, perhaps you had better save your strength. There is to be dancin' this evenin', and it will probably last long into the night."

"Oh, I'm not at all tired!" She smiled radiantly. "Just imagine, a real masque ball. I can't believe it!" She grabbed Andy's hand excitedly. "This is just like the spring cotillion that last year we were in school together."

"Not exactly like it." Andy smiled. "You pushed Carrie Jerome into the piracantha bush at the edge of the terrace."

"Amanda Spenser, you're dreadful, remindin' me of that hateful girl on such a glorious evenin'. But you must admit, she deserved it." She grinned mischievously. "I'll just bet she was pickin' piracantha out of her bustle for the next two weeks." She scratched with wicked satisfaction, then leaned forward excitedly as the motion of the carriage changed.

"We're here! I just can't believe it. Where did the time go?" Lacey laughed gloriously.

"It was probably talked to death," her father grumbled good-naturedly from across the carriage.

"Oh, pooh! I'm not even goin' to pay any attention to that remark. I absolutely refuse to allow you to ruin my evenin'."

"I would say, darlin' daughter, that would be impossible."

"Isn't this just the most excitin' thing ever?" Lacey bubbled as she grabbed Andy's hand excitedly and squeezed it.

"And I must say, Daddy, you do look very distinguished this evenin'," she complimented her father across the space that separated them.

"Damned skirt!" August Kittridge complained about the folly of allowing Lacey and Melanie to select his costume.

"It is not a skirt," Lacey corrected him. "It is proper attire for Henry VIII, King of England."

And that from the king's own very rebellious firstborn daughter, Mary Queen of Scots. Which, of course, was who Lacey decided she must be this evening, considering her red hair and Scots heritage.

They were all to portray someone who was somehow involved with King Henry. Of course, with his flaming red hair, broadshouldered stance, and the addition of a false beard, August Kittridge bore an uncanny resemblance to the monarch. His velvet surcoat with ermine trim and several imitation jewels sewn into the hem completed the illusion.

Melanie had been torn with indecision as to her own costume. As Henry had six wives, she certainly had a wide range of choices. She'd considered going as Henry's last wife, Catherine Parr, but preferred the headstrong character of the willful Anne Boleyn.

"Well, I think you look very regal," Melanie complimented August Kittridge with a little smile.

"Careful now, my dear. Don't lose your head over it all." He teased her back, with a straight face, bringing a groan of despair from everyone in the carriage.

Parker Rawlins chuckled at the ridiculous exchange. Befitting his profession, it was decided he would go as King Henry's confidant and adviser, Cardinal Woolsey.

The carriage rolled to a stop before the sweeping entrance to the Château. Everyone affixed their masks, August Kittridge making some remark about not having the sort of knees one went around exposing in public and absolutely certain his hose were slipping.

It took several moments of careful maneuvering before Lacey could step down. She moved sideways through the door of the carriage.

"Lord Almighty, I almost lost half my underpinnings gettin' outta that carriage. This dress is the most cumbersome thing I ever wore. And I thought hoop skirts were awkward." She readjusted her bodice and her hair, still scratching an occasional itch.

Andy stepped down easily, assisted by Parker Rawlins. She had no such difficulties. "At least you have the costume you ordered." She adjusted the simple fall of her straight-lined, empire gown.

"You look absolutely breathtakin'." Lacey patted her arm. "Besides . . ." She smiled consolingly as they started up the steps. "everyone knows Elizabeth was just the saddest, most dreadful woman. She was called the Virgin Queen, for heaven's sakes. That couldn't have been any fun at all," she declared flatly. "Josephine Bonaparte is much better, even if it was given to you by mistake. She was so much more daring and vibrant. Just think, some poor woman will have to come as Queen Elizabeth." Her eyes widened with a new thought. "What if a man ended up with your costume?"

"Lacey!"

"Well, anyway, this one is much better. You can be absolutely wicked tonight, and with Phillipe and Jean Louis here it will be great fun. With that dark wig and that mask no one will ever know who you really are. Unless, of course, you want them to." Lacey gave Andy a devilish wink.

Inside the main entrance to the Château, Louise Montfort stood like a regal queen greeting her guests. And, indeed a queen was exactly who she was dressed to be. Beside her, in all their finery, stood two young French noblemen.

Phillipe and Jean Louis Montfort were dressed as French royalty of a century earlier, while their mother was dressed as Marie Antoinette, Queen of France.

Greetings were exchanged, laughter rippling on the warm night air as Louise Montfort recognized Melanie's voice. She complimented them on their costumes, welcoming them to her home. Her eyes sparkled behind her silver mask as she greeted Andy.

"Ah, my dear, how exquisite . . . And we have a great deal in common. My compliments to you on your selection. It is a most wicked portrayal."

Andy laughed at the pretensions that accompanied the costumes, as if they had all assumed different identities for the evening. Maybe the mistake in costumes wasn't so tragic after all. In keeping with her identity for the evening, she smiled behind her mask and dropped into a small curtsy.

"Thank you, Your Majesty."

The Château was decorated in the manner of the grand French country home. The main ballroom opened onto a large pavilion that led to gardens, ponds, and waterfalls. The exotic fragrance of jasmine and honeysuckle filled the air. Laughter and conversation floated with the music. There was a breathtakingly beautiful large, indoor marble pool with a fountain bubbling up from the center sprinkling water over a floating garden of gardenias, camellias, and magnolia.

Andy saw pirates, Greek gods and goddesses, a Gypsy, and someone dressed as a Colonial soldier. There were at least three French country girls, a toothless beggar, various lords and ladies, and one knight in shining armor who moved very carefully through the crowd of guests.

She recognized many of the well-known people from history. There was a man who bore uncanny resemblance to George Washington, with a white powdered wig and green tailcoat of the first Continental Army.

She stared, fascinated by one very imaginative costume of a dragon, escorted by a lovely damsel in distress.

Every so often the dragon would spout a puff of smoke that smelled suspiciously like a cigar. It was all done in great fun and none of the ladies seemed distressed by that breach in etiquette. Tonight was obviously a night when rules were hidden behind the masks, along with a person's identity.

But by far the most outrageous costume had to be that of Hannibal. He was a tall man, dressed in wrapped fur leggings and a long fur vest, belted at the waist, with a fur hat, long hair, and a full beard. He carried a wicked sword in one hand, carved of wood, and in the other he held a rope.

In keeping with history, the rope was attached to an elephant. Not a real one of course. This one was only about two feet high, made of papier mâché and sculpted into the perfect form of an elephant, complete with trunk, large ears and tusks. He rolled along across the floor of the pavillion on small wheels hidden under his large, round legs.

It was fascinating, thought Andy. A person could be as outrageous as he chose and no one would ever know the difference. At least not until midnight when Louise Montfort insisted all must remove their masks.

"Would you honor me with the first dance, my lady?" Beside her, Parker Rawlins extended his arm.

"I would be honored, sir. That is, if you're not offended to be seen in the company of a Frenchwoman." She teased about her costume.

"Not the least, especially when the lady is so very lovely." He guided her out onto the floor of the pavilion.

"It's been years since I danced, and of course there wasn't much cause or opportunity during the war."

Everyone passed in a blur of color and bright costumes. She danced several waltzes with Parker Rawlins, twice with August Kittridge, who proceeded to point out people he recognized in spite of their costumes, and several times each with Phillipe and Jean Louis Montfort.

All about the grand pavilion, Louise Montfort's guests

danced and conversed. The knight in shining armor spoke with a lady. The dragon brought a burst of laughter as his tail caught beneath Hannibal's elephant.

Mary Queen of Scots finally appeared at her side, breathless from dancing as a robed Arabian sheik escorted her from the dance floor.

"A masque ball is just the most fascinatin' thing. All this mystery about who everyone is. It's just the most excitin' thing," Lacey sighed with enthusiasm.

"That Arabian sheik seemed very attentive to you," Andy observed casually, watching the guests as they filled the pavilion.

"I think the excitement is all in the disguise," Lacey observed with great wisdom. "I'd probably be dreadfully disappointed if I knew who he really was. But in those robes and mask, well, I can just imagine to my little ole heart's content. By the way, have you seen my daddy?" She looked around the ballroom.

"I saw him earlier. He and Melanie seemed to be enjoying themselves."

"Well, I just don't want him to enjoy himself too much," Lacey replied coolly. "After all, he is a grown man. Honestly, I never would have thought I would have to chaperone my own father. He's gettin' positively googly-eyed over Melanie."

"You're just envious." Andy announced with a subtle shift in the angle of her head as she tried to ease the stiffness in her neck from supporting the heavy wig.

"Envious?" Lacey stared at her aghast.

"Yes," Andy informed her, "as you would say 'pea-green' with envy. You've been absolutely waspish ever since Rafe Kelly left Baton Rouge."

"Rafe Kelly? Waspish?! Why, Amanda Spenser, I am nothin' of the sort!" Lacey sputtered with indignation. The color rose in her cheeks a shade just slightly less flaming than her brilliant hair.

"Tell me . . ." Andy went on, not letting her friend catch her breath, "what did you think about Rafe Kelly?"

228

"Think about him?" Lacey's voice rose noticeably. "I don't think about him at all!" she announced, and snapped her mouth shut while she made great ceremony of arranging her skirts.

Andy pretended to be surprised. "That is very interesting. The man is devilishly handsome, he's the one man I know you haven't managed to wrap around your little finger, and you don't think about him." She smiled wickedly. "Lacey Kittridge, you're are a very poor liar."

Lacey gave her a long look from behind her mask. "It means the man simply doesn't mean anything to me. Now, can we talk about something else besides Rafe Kelly?" She picked at an invisible piece of lint on her tartan. Then her hand shot out and she grabbed Andy's wrist.

"As I live and breathe, that man has absolutely the most nerve of any soul alive!"

"Who? What are you talking about?" Balancing the wig on her head, Andy dared not turn around too quickly.

"Captain Chandler Durant," Lacey announced, inclining her head toward the main entrance to the pavilion. "Only Louise Montfort would be bold enough to invite General Sheridan and his entire senior staff to this party. At least they had the decency to wear costumes like everyone else."

That is, everyone *except* Captain Durant, Andy noticed when she finally turned around. He'd worn a mask across his eyes, but it did little to disguise his identity. As it had before, the blue of his uniform set distance between himself and everyone else in that enormous ballroom. He was the center of attention and authority, just as he'd intended.

The general and his staff moved easily among the other guests, and Andy was relieved for her disguise. Her last encounter with Captain Durant had been anything but pleasant. This evening she had the advantage.

Louise Montfort laughed gaily as she escorted her latest guests about, and Andy was struck by the almost theatrical atmosphere the pavilion had taken on, as if they were all so many players in some sort of theatrical or charade.

The feelings dividing northerners and southerners ran deep, perhaps more so here in New Orleans, a city that had felt the crushing boot of military domination the last three years and then defeat.

"Well . . ." Lacey announced with quiet indignation, "I certainly don't intend to allow the general and his staff to ruin my evenin'." She looked about the pavilion. "I wonder where Phillipe Montfort might have gone off to."

Andy turned to her friend with a bemused smile. "I think I saw him leaving in the direction of the gardens. He was following Helen of Troy."

"Helen of Troy!? And after he promised me the next waltz!" Indignation hissed to quiet fury. "Of all the nerve! Casting aside a queen for a mere Greek legend."

"Actually I believe she was a queen as well. And she was from Troy," Andy pointed out.

"Now you're going to point out to me that is why she was called Helen of Troy. Amanda, please do not be smug. I simply cannot abide it when you are smug about that sort of thing. Now where is Phillipe, I have plans for him."

"I think you'd better discuss this with Phillipe. He seems to have far different ideas." Andy glanced meaningfully toward the double doors that opened out onto the gardens.

"Well, everyone knows you have to plant the idea in their heads so they're convinced they thought of it. What about you? Surely you've met some exciting young men this evenin'. And now that the general's staff is here . . ." She hinted broadly.

"It's a little difficult to tell who's behind the masks. Actually, I'm having a very pleasant evening."

"You've hardly danced with anyone but Mr. Rawlins," Lacey pointed out.

"I like him, Lacey. He's a very kind man. I get the impression he had a family once, but that they're gone

230

now." Andy spoke her thoughts aloud.

Lacey's head came up. "I would have thought Angeline would have told you."

"Told me what?"

Lacey seized her gently by the arm and pulled her toward the edge of the pavilion near the gardens where they would find more privacy.

"I didn't mention anythin' about it, 'cause it all happened so long ago. I was just a baby, but all the old families know about it."

"Lacey! For heaven's sake! Will you explain what you're talking about?"

"All right. You don't have to go gettin' yourself all worked up. And you must promise not to say anythin' to Mr. Rawlins about it. His health is not the best, and well, the poor man has certainly had his share of grief." Lacey pulled her into the spreading shelter of a huge potted fern. "Mr. Rawlins was originally from Virginia. His wife was one of the Junots, from Baton Rouge. After they were married, they settled there and took over the family plantation, Grove Farm. It's not that far from Ombre Rose. He and Patrick James used to be close friends." Lacey stopped and looked around to make certain no one was standing nearby. "They had two children, a boy and a girl. His wife and the son died durin' one of those dreadful yellow fever epidemics. Well, that just about broke the poor man. He sold Grove Farm and moved his daughter into town. I don't know most of the details, and of course a lot of it could be rumor, but a lot of folks think part of the reason Parker Rawlins sold Grove Farm back then was because of Coleton James."

"Coleton James?" Andy's startled gaze met Lacey's through their ornate masks. An unexpected shiver slipped down her spine, causing her to tremble violently. "Why?"

"He was only sixteen. She was a year younger, and well . . ."

Andy's breath caught in her throat. Mental images flashed through her thoughts, images that had first come to her in the attic when she found the painting. It was almost as if she knew what Lacey would say next, and she was afraid of it. Because she knew and didn't understand, she didn't want to hear it. She tried to block it out, wanted to turn and walk away, but some invisible bond compelled her to stay.

Andy held out her hand to stop her. She didn't want to hear anymore. But Lacey misunderstood, obviously thinking she was impatient to hear more.

"Well, the rumor is they were lovers."

Andy closed her eyes, trying to block it out, but the images found her there; images of a young man and girl running across the park at Ombre Rose, then slipping silently into the cool shadows of the gazebo.

Lacey shrugged her shoulders. "But instead of bein' pleased about the whole thing, Mr. Rawlins was furious, absolutely beside himself. He forbade them to see each other, even went so far as to go to Patrick James and demand he keep his son from seein' her. Said he would have him arrested if he so much as tried to see her. That didn't stop them, not even when Mr. Rawlins sent her away to her cousins in Virginia, hoping to marry her off to one of the sons of a friend of his. She refused 'em all, and got so lonely to come home, she supposedly got downright sick. Finally her father brought her back to Baton Rouge. He probably hoped the time apart might have changed their feelins' for one another. But it didn't. They ran away together." Lacey's voice became faint, as a distant buzzing sound filled Andy's senses.

They ran away.

She shivered, remembering the cool night air off the bayou, dark shadows that seemed to follow them, the welcoming glow of light in the window of the chapel, and the simple marriage ceremony. It all came winging back to her on whispers of memories.

"Somehow Mr. Rawlins found out about it and went after them."

Andy reached out to support herself. An almost physi-

232

cal pain poured through her, unleashing thousands of images like fragmented pieces of glass — splintering, shattering, cutting away innocence.

She grasped the stone railing with such desperation that her knuckles strained white. She saw it, all of it — exactly the way it happened. He had found them!

"I don't think anyone knows what really happened. Mr. Rawlins ordered her to return home with him. Coleton James had a gun. Supposedly he just went wild when Rawlins tried to take her away from him."

Andy's fingers gripped the stone so tight they ached.

"It was just so awful," Lacey whispered softly. "I mean after losin' his wife and son."

Andy leaned her forehead against the cool stone column. She felt light-headed, weak, and that buzzing sound . . . It was happening again just like before.

She stared into the pavilion and watched as the lights seemed to fade. She was going away again.

Lacey took her by the arm. "Are you all right? Good heavens! I wouldn't have told you any of this except I was certain you already knew about it."

"What happened when he found them?" Andy clung to Lacey's voice, trying to hold on to the present.

"Well, some folks said it was an accident. Others said he was in a fit of rage."

"Who? Tell me!"

Lacey bit at her lower lip. "Coleton James, of course. Supposedly he killed her."

Those three words, *he killed her*, shattered through Andy. Her grasp on Lacey's wrist constricted. Angeline had said those same words the day she went to the mausoleum at Ombre Rose.

Sunny.

The name slipped softly from dreams and some long-ago morning in the gazebo, the same name on the marble stone in the James's family mausoleum.

"Her name was Sunny, wasn't it."

"Yes, but I thought you didn't know anything about

her."

Because she didn't want to explain, she simply asked, "What happened after that?"

"Supposedly Coleton James was wild with grief after it happened. He refused to let Mr. Rawlins take her back to Baton Rouge. He kept sayin' over and over that he'd never let him take her, that he had no right 'cause they were married. He kept sayin' she was his wife and he would take her back to Ombre Rose 'cause that's where she belonged."

Andy's fingers loosened. She leaned heavily against a support column, letting the cool stone ease the pain in her temples as Lacey went on.

"There was a dreadful scandal. Parker Rawlins took the constable out to Ombre Rose. He insisted he wanted Sunny buried in Baton Rouge, and that he was goin' to bring charges against Coleton for murder."

"By the time the constable got out to Ombre Rose, Coleton was gone. Patrick James had sent him off to London for an extended period of time, if you get my meanin'. Well, there was absolutely nothin' the constable could do."

"And he never returned?"

"Not until just before the war. Patrick James wasn't well. He had a bad heart. And of course Coleton and Marilee never got along. There were more rumors of course—that he joined up with the Confederacy and that he came back once during the war. But his father was dead by then and Marilee had opened up the place to the Yanks. Then he just disappeared. When the war ended, he didn't come back. Everyone just sorta figured he'd been killed in the war. You could have knocked me over with a feather when I found out your Mr. Kelly was Coleton James.

"Angeline was with the Rawlins family for years. She practically raised Sunny after Mrs. Rawlins died. There are some folks say Angeline saw what happened that night. Whatever happened, she never returned to the

Rawlins house in Baton Rouge. Parker Rawlins gave her and her family their papers."

"Papers?" Andy's thoughts moved slowly.

"Givin' them their freedom," Lacey explained. "They were slaves. After that, Angeline lived here in New Orleans for a long time. That's where she learned all that fine sewin'. She only went back to Baton Rouge after her son and daughter died, to raise her grandchildren and opened that little shop in town. To this day, I believe that woman has not spoken one word to Parker Rawlins. You noticed, of course, she was nowhere to be seen when he called for you this evenin'. And I can't imagine why she went out to Ombre Rose, since the place can only hold sad memories for her."

Without thinking, Andy found herself saying, "I think she just wanted to be close to Sunny."

Lacey shrugged. "Well, colored folks do have strange notions about such things. But still, it is kinda strange."

"Oh, look!" Lacey grabbed her arm and pointed out the wide expanse of lawn beyond the gardens of the Château. "They're gettin' ready to set off the fireworks. Oh, Andy, you've never seen anything like it! It's been ever so long since we had fireworks. Since the war started, everyone's always afraid the military might think its an uprisin' or somethin'. Before the war, during Mardi Gras, they used to have huge floats anchored out in the river and they used to set off all kinds of fireworks. The sky used to just light up with it, it was so beautiful." She leaned out over the stone wall, searching the gardens below with a determined gleam shining in her eyes from behind the mask. "Phillipe promised to stand with me when they lit the fireworks. Now, where is that rascal?" She turned to Andy. "Will you be all right?"

Andy smiled. "I'll be fine. I'll just watch from here." She reassured her friend.

"You sure? I can stay here. Phillipe is probably tryin' to lay siege to Helen of Troy," she bit off sarcastically.

"Or he might just be waiting for you," Andy suggested.

235

"That is a possibility. And if I can't have Rafe Kelly, I might as well lead Phillipe on a little bit."

Andy waved her on. "Be sure to let me know how he comes out on your list."

Lacey giggled excitedly as she ran down the steps leading into the gardens. "Why, I wouldn't give that man very high marks at all. He's a dreadful flirt." The darkness in the gardens was only momentary as the first of the fireworks were lit out on the lawn.

They shot into the night sky, bursting into a multihued array of whites, blues, greens and reds. Lacey was momentarily illuminated at the edge of the garden, then faded in the waning crescent of light, only to appear again as a new burst of color filled the sky.

It was magnificent. Andy hadn't seen fireworks since she was a child and Stephen had taken her for a July Fourth celebration down at the harbor in New York City. That seemed so far away now.

She glanced about at the other groups of guests clustered along the terrace of the pavilion watching the fireworks display. She looked for Parker Rawlins, but couldn't find him. It was difficult to understand what she felt for him. He was dying, she knew that. And he'd lost everyone he'd ever loved. It would have been natural to pity a man who'd suffered so much pain and loss. But because she understood that pain, or maybe in spite of it, she felt a genuine affection for him. They had a great deal in common.

Other guests came out onto the terrace overlooking the gardens, their masks illuminated as another round of fireworks burst in the sky overhead. Then they were plunged into soft shadows once more cast from the lights inside the pavilion.

She hoped Lacey had found Phillipe. It was obvious August Kittridge was impatient for his daughter to be settled with a family of her own. She suspected his impatience just might have something to do with Melanie Marchand.

It seemed odd to think of Lacey as married. Stranger still for those thoughts to seem so strong for herself. Certainly she'd considered that she would probably marry one day. But so many things had happened. First the war and now Ombre Rose.

The plantation was the only certainty in her life. It was a haven in a world where it seemed there were few; she felt connected to it in ways she couldn't explain, and she was determined not to lose it.

Everything had always seemed so much simpler when she and Lacey were children. Their biggest concern had been their latest scheme against Carrie Jerome, or Miss Van der Poole.

Andy leaned against the carved stone balustrade wanting very much to be that child again, watching the fireworks with her hand tucked safely inside Stephen's. There were times, more frequently now, when she found herself wanting to go back to another time that was simpler, safer, when there was no war or death.

The pressure at her elbow came lightly at first so that she thought someone had merely bumped against her. She paid no attention. It came again, more insistently, and she thought Lacey might have come back to join her.

"Don't turn around." A voice, very definitely not Lacey's, cautioned her. "Watch the fireworks and listen very carefully."

Andy smiled. Someone was being very mysterious, obviously playing out some charade to go along with the evening. She started to turn around to see who was taking such delight in the masquerade, but a hand tightened over her upper arm with bruising strength.

"Don't be foolish. And don't ask questions. Shut up and listen!" The terse command bit off sharply.

This was going a bit too far. Andy tried to pull her arm away and found it firmly imprisoned. She willed herself to relax. There were several people about. She was perfectly safe.

"That's better," came the muffled reply.

When the next burst of fireworks lit up the sky, Andy turned her head as if concentrating on that arc of light.

So, her mysterious companion was dressed as some sort of nobleman with an elaborate brocade coat. In one sweeping glance she noticed the elaborate wig and a full face mask in the design of a giant golden sunburst. He reminded her of portraits she'd seen of the French kings.

She glanced down, catching sight of his hand locked around her elbow. His hands were fine-boned, almost delicate, with an extravagant jeweled ring, undoubtedly fake, worn on the small finger of his left hand.

He was standing behind and to her left, and the trailing ringlets of his wig brushed her shoulder as he leaned forward to whisper discreetly. "Tell her ladyship to inform her client the package will be delivered according to plan."

"What?" Andy started to turn again, only to feel that grasp tighten.

"Do not turn around!" came the hissed warning, with almost silken threat so that Andy remained where she was, staring straight ahead and watching the brilliant display of fireworks.

She felt the subtle loosening of the grasp at her arm and then the welcoming flow of warmth as blood seeped back into her hand and fingers. He'd released her. Of all the . . . !

Andy whirled around, several well-chosen comments on the tip of her tongue only to be stunned to silence. He was gone, vanished, as if he'd never been there.

Several groups of people stood about her, but none wore the costume of the man with the sunburst mask.

Andy rubbed the bruised skin on her arm, her gaze searching the spectators, but it was useless. He was gone.

Behind the brilliant blue mask, Coleton watched the colorfully costumed guests as they trailed back into the pavilion. Others lingered, couples perhaps, although some

238

of the costumes made that doubtful. They slipped among the fragrant shadows in the gardens where soft laughter mingled with more urgent whispers.

The last of the brilliant fireworks display glowed in the sky, growing smaller like myriad fireflies until they disappeared completely. A man dressed in furred skins strode past, a toy elephant trailing in one hand, a long-legged Egyptian princess in another.

A brilliantly liveried footman greeted the guests as they drifted back inside, announcing one final waltz before the buffet supper was to be served at midnight.

He lit a cigarette, inclining his head and smiling faintly at the appreciative stare from a gaily dressed Gypsy girl. Her smile from behind the mask promised a great deal. Tonight was perfect for deceptions. Tonight, he was Napoleon Bonaparte, Emperor of France.

The information Ellie had given him kept going through his head. Obie was to be Napoleon, probably at this very ball.

And like before, undoubtedly he was to receive information about another shipment. It wasn't much, but it was more than he had before he talked to Ellie. The only question now was, who? Who among all the guests in their varied costumes was the contact?

Obviously the ball was the perfect distraction for someone to pass vital information about stolen armaments to someone else. With everyone in full costume, no one would be the wiser. The information would be passed on and Obie would never know the identity of his contact.

Coleton kept pushing back one nagging thought. Of course, when Obie was eliminated, there was every possibility the costumes and instructions had been changed. Maybe it wasn't to happen this evening.

Still, on the other hand, it was the perfect opportunity. And Obie had been killed only two days earlier. Maybe, just maybe, with all the players in position, the contact was to remain the same, with only Obie's part in the game changed.

If his first suspicions were correct, it was a hopeless situation. He could wander around all evening, hoping to eavesdrop on the right conversation. But if, as he hoped, nothing was changed, there was a chance, just a slim one, that he might still be able to get the information originally intended for Bledsoe.

The only problem was, of course, who among all the guests would have been the natural contact for Obie Bledsoe?

A pirate passed by, whispering to the young lady he escorted out onto the floor of the pavilion. Their costumes were oddly mismatched. She was dressed as a French country lass with a white lace apron over a pale-yellow dress and her hair falling over her shoulders in twin braids. Her identity was hidden behind a cloth mask.

Who? Coleton thought, idly watching the pirate and the country girl. Then his gaze wandered through the milling guests, trailing out through the opened doors to the veranda.

A whisper of a smile quirked the corners of his mouth as he watched the subtle exchange. The lady in question seemed somewhat annoyed with the gentleman standing directly behind her. Their silhouettes were all that he saw as they watched the burst of fireworks. She should have been smiling at such a brilliant display. She wasn't.

Another volley of fireworks burst overhead, and for one brief moment as the starburst of color hung suspended in the midnight-black sky, he saw her costume clearly—the intricate dark curls, the elaborate regal crown, the empire style of her draped gown that clung to every slender line and gently rounded curve, a gown only a queen would wear and every other woman would adopt when fashion dictated otherwise. It was velvet and the same brilliant blue of the military jacket worn by the Emperor of France, with white satin trim about the capped sleeves and daringly low neckline. A mask covered all of her face except for the temptingly curved mouth.

240

Who would wear such a gown? Who, but Josephine Bonaparte, Empress of France and wife of Napoleon. Her costume was unmistakable.

With a self-satisfied smile tipping his mouth, Coleton watched and waited until the exchange was complete. What were they discussing? He saw the faint movement of her lips. An acknowledgment? Hardly genial conversation.

The gentleman was elaborately dressed with jewels, a crown and a golden sunburst mask. The Sun King, no doubt. King Louis XIV of France. How very clever.

As the fireworks at last subsided and the music began within the pavilion, Coleton slipped through the shadows out onto the veranda. The lovely Josephine was still standing there, alone now. If Louis XIV were her escort or husband he would not have abandoned her.

"Good evening, Madame Bonaparte." He seized her by the arm. "You will, of course, honor me with this next waltz."

Chapter Thirteen

Andy might have stepped back, or she might have pulled free, but reaction came a moment too slowly as her hand was trapped by strong fingers. Her head came up and she almost laughed. First Louis XIV with his strangely mumbled message, undoubtedly the result of too much brandy or fine whiskey. And now a man who bore uncanny resemblance to another equally illustrious Frenchman, Napoleón Bonaparte. The costume was an exact replica of one she'd seen in a painting. Except for his height, it was an accurate portrayal. This man exuded that same quiet sense of power and strength the artist had caught in the portrait of Napoleon.

Yes, she almost laughed at the notion that her costume seemed to have such maddening effect to draw first a king and now an emperor. Almost.

The first encounter happened so quickly, with such a strange conversation, actually no conversation at all, but a few hastily whispered words, that she thought it an accident. Surely Louis XIV had intended his strange message for someone else. And yet the bruises on her arm said differently. And now Napoleon.

"You have made a mistake, monsieur," she explained as politely as possible, waiting for him to release her arm.

"I think not," came the husky reply from behind the mask, his hand tightening as Andy was drawn out onto the pavilion floor.

Whoever Napoleon was, he was certainly an excellent partner. His movements were fluid, almost graceful as he executed the steps of the waltz with perfect precision. It wasn't dancing, it was floating. There was barely time for her feet to touch the floor before he'd whirled her effortlessly into the next movement, and the next, until the pavilion with its brilliant lanterns and winking candles was a breathless blur of color.

Andy had danced with other men before. But Napoleon's movements were far different. There was a wild energy in each turn, an animal restlessness that would have been reckless in any other man. With him, it was a barely controlled excitement that seemed to hover on the brink of danger. And yet his form and precision were perfect.

Twice, as he whirled her at the edge of the dance floor she tried to extricate herself from his arm, and each time his arm tightened, drawing her closer, closer than was wisely discreet. She was breathless. Still he persisted. The masks and costumes of the other dancers floated past her like the characters of some child's dream; a Gypsy, a pirate, a king, whirling before her and then spinning away again. And still he refused to release her.

The summer heat, the heady floral fragrance, the scent of candles, the laughter, the music, all wrapped around her.

If there was one exact moment when she no longer strained against his arm, or fought the painful strength in his fingers, Andy was not aware of it. She only knew the pain in her side eased along with her breathing.

It was like sleeping and slowly awakening, images about the pavilion whirling with images of the past. Masks, costumes, the music, it was all the same as an awareness stole over her. It was that instinctive understanding that she'd been here before, seen the masks and gaily costumed couples, experienced that same wild rush of anticipation that tingled across her skin,

felt those strong arms that held her and promised to never let go

A wild panic poured through her as the pace of the waltz increased. She understood now. That morning in the ballroom at Ombre Rose when it seemed she remembered what it must have been like . . . She had remembered!

She hadn't been able to see any of the faces because they were all covered! It had been a masked ball. That was what she had tried to remember and couldn't!

Now it all came whirling back to her, spinning through her thoughts, like the music, the masks and costumes that blurred into a riot of color and sound at the edge of the pavilion. But that was impossible. That had been only her imagination and this man had no part in it. But oddly he did.

If she closed her eyes and thought of it all again the way it had been that day, she could see him again. He was tall, broad-shouldered, with a youthful intensity that was raw, almost hungry. And his laugh . . .

Andy's eyes flew open. That laughter was rich, vibrant, wrapped with a wildly sensual huskiness. It was Napoleon's laughter! It was the same, and not. Now there was a dangerous, threatening edge to it.

And like the man he'd chosen to portray, he was relentless. His movements were powerful as his arm at her waist imprisoned her. She dared not falter for fear he'd simply let her fall, and yet she couldn't keep up this maddening pace.

As the waltz at last seemed to mercifully end, Andy stepped back from her mysterious partner, determined to put an end to the strange encounter. She sidestepped Napoleon, at the same time jerking her wrist up hard in an attempt to twist from his grasp. She only succeeded in acquiring more bruises.

"Please release me, monsieur," she insisted stiffly. "My friends are waiting." She glanced toward the gathering guests who filtered out of the pavilion.

When he refused, she fought to remain calm. Instinctively she understood this man would only be angered by weakness. The fool had undoubtedly had too much to drink. As she whirled to face him, caught by those lean, intense fingers, her gaze fell on Chandler Durant.

Coleton's eyes narrowed behind the mask as they followed the direction of her attention. Durant, he thought derisively. It seemed they were forever running into each other. It was a subtle reminder that confrontation was yet to come. Old debts had to be paid. But not tonight. Now it was far more important that he learn the message that had been passed this evening.

"Don't even think about it," he warned with a low hiss that belied the smile meant for everyone else but her. "You may demand whatever you like, but it will do you no good. I want something from you and I intend to have it, lovely . . . Josephine."

The name was almost spat out as his fingers tightened around her wrist. In one fluid motion that must have looked almost like a lover's caress, he wrenched her arm behind her back and swept her in the direction opposite the one the other guests followed.

Her arm was pinned at such a sharp angle, Andy was certain it would break. She started to cry out only to have it angled more sharply in painful warning as she was propelled from the pavilion out into the shadows that filled the gardens.

He pushed her before him and she almost went down twice, but he forced her to her feet with another twist of her imprisoned arm. When they were some distance from the pavilion and sight of the other guests, he stopped and whirled her around, still holding on her wrist.

"You're hurting me," she cried out softly, trying to loosen his grasp with her other hand.

"I'll do a great deal more than that, dear Josephine, if you don't cooperate."

Fear shimmered through Andy and she fought it back. Who was he? What did he want?

He laughed again as he seemed to read her thoughts. "Don't flatter yourself, my dear. I want information. I believe you have a message for me."

She stopped struggling, flashing him an incredulous

look. Information? A message? What was he talking about?

"As I said before, you . . . have . . . made . . . a . . . mistake!" She enunciated each word very carefully.

"And as I explained, I have made no mistake. I'm fully aware of your conversation with Louis."

Louis? What in heaven's name was he talking about?

Andy jerked around at the sound of voices, softly muted conversation, passing very close by. She saw the soft shimmer of an elaborate gown through the sculpted bushes and deep arbor, heard a woman's provocative laughter and a man's murmured response. They were coming this way! If she just called out to them . . .

The woman's gown was illuminated in the moonlight as the couple walked within a few feet of them on their way to the pavilion. But once again Napoleon anticipated her. Before Andy could even think to call out, before she so much as took a breath, she was pulled into those arms with brutal strength.

He seized her other wrist—both were drawn behind her back—and easily held her in the stronger grasp of his one hand. She was pulled into the hard wall of his chest, his eyes glittering with dangerous warning from behind his silk mask.

"Not a word! Not one!" he whispered against her cheek as his free hand slipped beneath her chin and jerked her face up to meet his. And then to complete the deception of seduction as the other couple happened upon them, his fingers slipped along her jaw with a bruising tenderness that left its mark on her pale skin.

Andy tried to jerk her face away and winced at the painful pressure of those long fingers.

"I don't know who you are, but you will regret this, monsieur!" she hissed as his mouth hovered over hers, those fingers tightening.

His white teeth flashed a wicked smile, made all the more dangerous in the moonlight.

"Don't you remember, lovely Josephine?" He continued

the ridiculous charade. "I am your lover, your devoted husband and emperor." He paused, giving his next words deadly meaning. "I am the man who has the power of life or death over you. You will give me the information I want if you wish to live. It is that simple."

The man was incredible! She almost laughed as she struggled foolishly and earned a reminder of just how much power he did have over her. With one effortless move, he jerked her coupled wrists up with his one hand, sending pain shooting into her cramped shoulders. She gasped. Had the couple heard it?

She had no time to speculate further as that smile deepened with cruel delight and was then nothing more than a flashing blur as his face lowered to hers and those brutal fingers tilted her mouth for his.

His kiss was as punishing as those hands, and meant, she knew, to bruise her to submission. Her mind screamed out as her cry was silenced by his lips. If the couple passing by held any doubt of their apparent trysting, it ended with that kiss.

To all outward appearances they must have seemed like any other couple taking advantage of the warm summer evening and the deeply shadowed gardens.

Having obviously caught sight of them, the couple hesitated, softly laughed their understanding, and slipped discreetly past. The kiss could have ended there. It should have, but it didn't.

It was a perfect disguise as the other couple passed by, and it brought his lovely captive under momentary control. And he knew she was lovely, even behind the mask that covered everything but that sensual curve of mouth.

Her skin was flawless, her face delicately shaped, and the soft wings of brows above, a much lighter shade than her hair, revealing that her elaborate coiffure was, like the rest of her costume, part of the deception. But it was her eyes that intrigued him. They were blue; brilliant, unforgettable blue.

Perhaps it was her eyes, the kiss, or both; not only was

the lovely captive in Coleton's arms treacherous, she was very skillful in the art of seduction. It was there in that kiss and the subtle yielding of her body when she pretended to be indignant. She'd practiced the intoxicating blend of desire and innocence to perfection.

Like the woman she was dressed to portray, she was undoubtedly an accomplished whore. Knowing that should have made him angry.

Andy could have cried out, could have screamed and brought every man into those gardens. Everything in her cried out that she do exactly that, but she couldn't find the will to push away as his fingers released her imprisoned wrists then slipped down her back.

Her breath caught with desire as his other hand remained at her throat, those lean fingers splayed across her jaw as he brought her mouth once more up to his.

Whatever the questions were, they were now gone as his lips slowly began another far more dangerous assault. They slipped over hers with beguiling heat, possessing with excruciating tenderness.

What began as a battle of wills became something far different. His first kiss had been sheer strength, punishment meant to silence her. This kiss, completely unnecessary, completely unnerving, was meant to prove something far different.

He *was* in control, Coleton's thoughts echoed over and over as he felt the subtle shift of resistance in her slender body. And he was lying to himself, completely unaware that his hands cradled her face, until he deepened the kiss and tasted the heated surrender.

Andy's fingers strained to pull his away, to end what she could no longer understand or resist. But instead they twined with his as his tongue invaded her mouth, wrapping around hers in heated battle that demanded more.

He stroked her, enticed her until he lured the velvet wetness of her tongue between his lips, gently pulling it deeper and deeper into his mouth.

She should have resisted when those hands slipped

down her neck, molded with lingering heat over the bodice of her gown, his thumbs stroking back and forth over the hardened nipples beneath the velvet gown. Her breasts swelled into his hands, aching for him to touch her completely, bare skin against bare skin. Dear God, what was happening?

And then those hands slipped lower still, encircling her waist where the gown fell unhindered. They fanned across the curve of her bottom, pulling her hard against his hips, the arousal complete.

His lips caressed her bruised mouth, gently pulling her lower lip between his teeth, before plunging his tongue hard between her lips in an arousal of the senses as well as the body. It was frightening and hauntingly familiar.

"Amanda?"

The woman's voice shattered the spell that engulfed them.

Reason returned, sharp, bitter, and humiliating. In that one moment between madness and reality, Andy jerked away. Bewilderment gave way to sanity, then wounded indignation and anger.

Coleton didn't even see her hand coming, her palm cracking soundly against his cheek. The contact stunned as it was intended, but her surprise was equally great as his silk mask came away with the force of the blow and Andy stared up into that cruelly handsome face, his gray eyes hard and cold.

"You!" Andy choked, wide-eyed from behind her mask as anger sharpened to blind fury. For one long moment all she could do was stand there staring at him.

"Damn you to hell, Coleton James!" With all her strength, she drew her hand back and struck him again. Not waiting to see his reaction, or caring, Andy gathered her skirt in her hand and fled the garden before he could come after her.

He stared after her. Her slender silhouette was joined by another and the two quickly made their way back to the pavilion.

Amanda? The name had been clear, unmistakable. Still he could be wrong.

But he wasn't wrong about that kiss. He remembered it from the gazebo, wet with droplets of rain that left him thirsting for more, much more as they fell across that same flawless skin. He remembered those eyes that had stared up at him with awakening desire as he pressed her naked body back against the cool marble. And he remembered the moment their bodies entwined and then joined in a mindless fury and passion that seemed to bring the storm within.

Amanda Spenser! Yankee . . . owner of Ombre Rose! Bitterness rose like bile in his throat.

Was she thief, murderer, or spy? Or a little of all three?

The important thing was, he was certain she'd received some kind of message this evening. King Louis had made only one appearance this entire evening and that to speak in private with Josephine. And as he'd seen, their conversation was brief, guarded, taken in the shadows where no one else could hear them. It was hardly the intimate exchange of acquaintants or lovers.

He might have followed Louis and had the information of that message, but Louis was only a pawn, someone in the middle passing that information on to someone else. Coleton wanted more. He wanted to know the identity of Josephine's contact, and he wanted to know about the next raid. Eventually it would all lead to Gray Fox, and Josephine was his connection.

"What were you doing out there alone?" Lacey frowned slightly as they stepped up into the lighted pavilion.

"I . . . was just getting some fresh air. That's all," Andy explained hastily, walking quickly on ahead when Lacey held back.

"By yourself? Unescorted? Andy, wait up." Lacey caught up with her and gently tugged at her arm.

"Lacey, please." Andy averted her eyes, thankful for the mask that was still in place.

"Good heavens! Look at your arm." Lacey held on, refusing to release her.

"It's nothing."

"Nothin'? Just look at those bruises! Amanda Spenser, what happened out there in that garden? Did someone try to take advantage of you?"

For the life of her Andy could've sworn there was just a trace of excitement in Lacey's voice.

"No, it was nothing like that," she quickly explained. "I just happened to meet someone . . . a stranger. It's all right. He just frightened me. I wasn't expecting . . ."

Dear God, Andy thought, she was babbling, and sounded ridiculous even to herself. No wonder Lacey was looking at her like that.

"It's really been a very long evening and I've developed a dreadful headache. Do you think we could go back to Melanie's?" Andy suggested, knowing it was unthinkable. The Montfort ball was the social event of the year, probably the only event of the year. Lacey had talked of nothing else for days. Now she was suggesting leaving before the midnight buffet was served.

Parker Rawlins met them just outside the main dining hall, his face lined with concern. "I was looking for you, Amanda."

One look at her disheveled appearance, the paleness of her cheeks, and he immediately took her hand and guided her to one of the many chairs that were arranged along the back wall of the pavilion.

"Are you all right?"

His tone was caring, edged with genuine concern. She forced a smile. "Yes, it's just that I'm tired. Could we possibly leave?" She held on to his hand for strength, feeling oddly safe with him so near. It was that same safe feeling she had always known with Stephen, and undoubtedly with her father when she was very young.

"It has been a rather long evening. Of course we can leave. I'll escort you back to Melanie's." Parker stroked her hand gently. "Lacey, stay with her, I'll see about a

251

carriage."

Lacey waited until he left the pavilion.

"Are you goin' to tell me what happened? Who did you see out there, for heaven's sakes?"

"It was just some stranger." Andy tried to make light of the encounter. "It was nothing, really."

"In a pig's eye." Lacey's mouth twisted in a determined frown. "You're lyin' to me, and we both know you've never been any good at it, no matter how I tried to teach you."

"Lacey, please! I don't want to discuss it now. It's just the heat, and I really do have a dreadful headache."

"Ummm," Lacey remarked, which meant she didn't believe it for one minute.

"That's usually my excuse. You and I both know, Amanda Spenser, you are too straightforward to be connivin' about anythin'. But . . ." she gave Andy one of those terribly wounded expressions that never failed with her father, "I will try to understand if you choose not to speak of it. However," she pouted, her drawl thickening, "I do believe I have the right to know if you were out in the gardens with Phillipe Montfort."

So that was it. "Lacey, I assure you I was not in the gardens with Phillipe." If only it were that simple.

Parker Rawlins returned, bearing a clear crystal tumbler of amber-colored liquid. "I don't usually suggest this, but you look a bit faint. Sip it very carefully." His manner was that of an indulgent father. "It will help calm you. I've located a carriage. A friend from the city graciously loaned me the use of his. He will return with his cousin. I'll go make our excuses to our hostess."

Andy cradled the brandy in both hands. Her meeting with Coleton James had left her shaking badly.

The arrogance of the man! she thought with slow-rising fury. To come here and assault her, all with the pretense of wanting information!

Parker told her to sip carefully. If she were calm she would have been cautious and done just that, unaccus-

252

tomed as she was to the stronger drink. But she was neither calm nor cautious and drank the brandy as carelessly as if it were champagne.

Andy gasped as it burned all the way to her stomach, pooling there like liquid fire, then glowing through her arms and legs, sending a delicious tingling sensation into her fingers and toes. It did seem to have a certain calming effect.

"I think I need another brandy." She held her glass aloft to Lacey, receiving a look of pure dismay.

"That must have been some stranger!" Lacey retorted as she crossed to the damask-covered table nearby and reached to retrieve a bottle hidden beneath the folds of draping cloth.

She shrugged as she came back and answered Andy's surprised look. "They always keep the strong stuff hidden away for the men." She gave Andy a dubious look. "Are you certain you can handle this?"

Andy nodded, holding her glass aloft as Lacey poured the tumbler half full.

"If you're not careful, you'll become tipsy."

"I would like to get tipsy," Andy bit off, the anger only slightly tempered by that first glass of brandy. Damn Coleton James! What was he doing here? Did it have something to do with Ombre Rose?

Of course it did, Andy thought as that faint glow spread even further to warm all the cold places left aching deep inside from her encounter with Coleton James. As long as she lived she would never forget the expression of loathing in his eyes.

What was it he'd said about a message? And why had he been so angry with her? He was the one who'd cheated and stolen from her! He'd lied to her, made her trust him, and then taken advantage of her! No, that wasn't quite right, she hadn't really trusted him. But he had taken advantage of her.

Oh, yes, he'd taken advantage of her all right!

As the memory of that night in the gazebo returned to

taunt her, Andy took another fortifying drink of brandy. It didn't burn so much now, but just sort of warmed its way to her stomach. Dear God, she didn't want to think about that now.

Ombre Rose. It was the only thing that mattered to her. She'd fight to keep it! It was her home! And Coleton James had no right . . . !

"I've made our apologies, and one of the maids brought your wrap," Parker Rawlins had returned.

Andy looked up and smiled faintly, unaware she'd completely emptied the second tumbler of brandy.

"She is not herself," Lacey allowed. "I think it's a good idea you're takin' her home, and be careful. She's not too steady on her feet."

Andy gave her a dark look, just waiting for her to make some comment about the two brandies, but she didn't.

Lacey walked with them to the front entrance of the Château.

"We will talk about this in the mornin', Amanda."

Amanda, not Andy, which only meant Lacey wasn't about to forget what had happened this evening. Knowing her friend, she would simply keep at her until Andy told her everything.

Coleton watched as Amanda Spenser and another young lady entered the pavilion. He recognized Lacey Kittridge; that flaming red hair was unmistakable.

"It's not ended, Miss Spenser!" he vowed from the shadows, his eyes narrowing as a man, dressed in flowing crimson robes, joined them.

Parker Rawlins! Was he somehow involved in the conspiracy?

As much as he would like to have believed it, it seemed unlikely. It would be foolish to make an accusation so openly when everyone had gone inside and they could be seen so easily.

No, Coleton rather doubted Rawlins was involved, although he wouldn't deny the disappointment. He'd like nothing better than to hand Rawlins over to Phoenix.

But if not Rawlins, then who was Amanda Spenser's contact?

He continued watching, knowing he dare not follow into the pavilion. His eyes narrowed with speculation as Rawlins left, only to return a few minutes later to escort Amanda through to the inside of the Château.

As Coleton carefully threaded his way through the gardens to gain better view he heard the unmistakable crunch of carriage wheels in the gravel drive. He followed the shadows around the corner of the Château, stopping as his suspicions were confirmed.

So, he thought with cold calculation, Miss Amanda Spenser was leaving. Was she going to meet her contact? There was only one way to find out.

Captain Chandler Durant stepped from the shadows. He watched as Parker Rawlins escorted Amanda Spenser from the pavilion. He'd known she was in New Orleans, just as he knew where everyone he considered to be important was. Knowing she was invited, he looked for her all evening, trying to guess her costume. His eyes narrowed as he finally understood why he hadn't discovered her earlier. She was Josephine Bonaparte—a most revealing disguise.

But with that very significant fact he'd learned something else as well: Coleton James, the man he now knew to be the infamous Gray Fox, was here as well. And his choice of costumes had been most interesting. He wondered what they had discussed?

Durant turned to his adjutant. "Have my horse brought around front, and inform the general I have been called away on an important matter."

"Yessir!"

Louis XIV made casual note of the guests who departed, swallowing back more champagne. Josephine Bonaparte turned and spoke to the older gentleman at her side as they made their way to the front entrance of the Château. Her mask was clutched in her hand, and he briefly glimpsed her face.

Good God! he thought as the champagne clogged halfway down, and he choked in a loud gasp from behind the sunburst mask. There must be some mistake!

But as he circled around one ornate pilaster column for a better view, he realized it was no mistake. Desperately he searched among the guests for that particular costume. Catching sight of the elaborate satin, he cut through the crowd of guests who slowly made their way into the large dining room. He wedged his way through, slipping discreetly to the side of Marie Antoinette.

"We have a problem!" he hissed from behind the mask.

As the carriage rolled along the darkened road to New Orleans, the brandy and emotional exhaustion lulled Andy into a half-sleep. But memories and images found her there. The last weeks came winging back in fragments, pieces that teased at her, all disjointed, as if someone had thrown pieces of paper into the wind.

But one came back at her again and again, something Lacey had told her. Coleton James was a murderer! He'd killed Sunny Rawlins in a fit of fury and then ran away. Dear God, the man was dangerous . . . so very dangerous.

Andy roused slowly as the carriage rolled to a stop. Somewhere on the road back to New Orleans she had dozed against Parker Rawlins's shoulder.

"Come along, my dear." He took her hand, assisting her from the carriage. Asking the driver to wait, he walked with her to the front door of Melanie's house.

"I'm sorry I spoiled the evening for you." Andy turned as they reached the front door.

"Not at all." Parker Rawlins patted her hand affection-

The Publishers of Zebra Books Make This Special Offer to Zebra Romance Readers...

AFTER YOU HAVE READ THIS BOOK WE'D LIKE TO SEND YOU
4 MORE FOR *FREE*
AN $18.00 VALUE

NO OBLIGATION!

4 FREE BOOKS

TO GET YOUR 4 FREE BOOKS WORTH $18.00 — MAIL IN THE FREE BOOK CERTIFICATE T O D A Y

Fill in the Free Book Certificate below, and we'll send your FREE BOOKS to you as soon as we receive it.

If the certificate is missing below, write to: Zebra Home Subscription Service, Inc., P.O. Box 5214, 120 Brighton Road, Clifton, New Jersey 07015-5214.

FREE BOOK CERTIFICATE

4 FREE BOOKS
ZEBRA HOME SUBSCRIPTION SERVICE, INC.

YES! Please start my subscription to Zebra Historical Romances and send me my first 4 books absolutely FREE. I understand that each month I may preview four new Zebra Historical Romances free for 10 days. If I'm not satisfied with them, I may return the four books within 10 days and owe nothing. Otherwise, I will pay the low preferred subscriber's price of just $3.75 each; a total of $15.00, *a savings off the publisher's price of $3.00.* I may return any shipment and I may cancel this subscription at any time. There is no obligation to buy any shipment and there are no shipping, handling or other hidden charges. Regardless of what I decide, the four free books are mine to keep.

NAME

ADDRESS _____ APT

CITY _____ STATE ____ ZIP

TELEPHONE
( )

SIGNATURE _____ (if under 18, parent or guardian must sign)

ately. "To be very honest with you, my dear, I was quite relieved. I don't have much stamina for those sort of things. You rescued me from falling asleep in some corner and embarrassing myself."

Andy smiled. He was such a gentleman—calm, reassuring, offering his shoulder for the ride home.

"Thank you for bringing me home."

"You're certain you're all right?"

"Yes, of course. I'm just tired."

Parker reached around her, knocking lightly for Melanie's butler. He appeared quickly, equally surprised to find them home this early, even though it was almost one o'clock in the morning.

"Now that I've seen you safely to your door, I shall bid you good evenin', or rather good mornin'." He squeezed her hand gently as guided her into the house. He looked up at her. "If you're indisposed or not feeling up to it, just send round word to my hotel and we will plan the opera for another evening," he suggested of their plans for that coming evening.

"I'll feel fine after a good night's sleep," Andy reassured. She wouldn't have missed going for anything. "Thank you."

"For what, dear girl?" He was genuinely surprised.

"For being my friend. Not many people would be seen with a Yankee these days."

He held on to her hand, gently smoothing her fingers as if he didn't know quite what to say. He cleared his throat as he stared down at her hand in his.

"I've been alone a great many years, Amanda. With my grieving and my regrets. They weren't very happy years, and there were times I just wanted it to be over. But you've given me something very special, my dear. Something I once thought lost to me forever, just by your simple caring." He looked up at her then, and his eyes were filled with tears.

"God knows, I deserve to be alone." He waved her aside when she started to protest that he didn't have to say anything.

"I don't have a great deal of time, Amanda, but you've made what time I have left a gift—something wonderful and rare to be treasured. Rest assured, young lady, I should be thanking you." Then, as if he felt he'd probably said too much, he leaned forward and quickly kissed her on the cheek.

"Up to bed with you now, muffin."

Andy's head came up in surprise at the casual endearment. But he'd already turned to retrace his steps back to the carriage, calling out to the driver. She shook her head, as something vague slipped away from her. She was just tired.

She bid Melanie's butler good night and walked slowly up the stairs to the room she and Lacey shared.

Up to bed with you now, muffin. Andy laughed softly, oddly comforted as the words echoed around her.

Sleep tight and don't let the bedbugs bite. She stopped and turned on the stair, certain he must have forgotten something and returned to the house, now calling that childhood saying after her.

But there was only the single glow of the one lantern left for Melanie and Lacey. The butler had returned to his room at the back of the kitchen. The house was silent. She must have imagined it.

Angeline stirred in the chair beside the window where she'd dozed.

"You are back so soon?"

Andy slipped off the cape, rubbing the muscles of her neck, sore from supporting the heavy wig all evening. Thank heavens women no longer found them fashionable. She didn't want to mention the matter of Coleton James to Angeline, not knowing what the woman's reaction would be.

"It wasn't necessary for you to wait up."

"I always wait up." Angeline spoke softly, coming out of the chair to take the cape.

"How was your evening?"

Andy sat at the dressing table, removing the fake jewels and the ornate, equally fake crown from atop her head.

"There were a great many people. The costumes were very colorful. The Château Montfort is beautiful," she answered simply, catching Angeline's questioning stare reflected in the mirror before her. Then she concentrated on helping to remove the burdensome wig.

Andy shook out the fall of her own waist-length hair, massaging her temples. As she had gotten into the habit of doing, Angeline unfastened the closures at the back of the gown. Her hands lingered as her fingers lightly brushed Andy's back.

Andy was tired, emotionally spent out from her encounter first with the mysterious Louis XIV, and then with Coleton James. But tired as she was, she was more than aware of the woman's careful watchfulness. It was always there, whenever Angeline was around her. Usually she ignored it. The woman was kind, loving, and absolutely giving of herself, for reasons Andy couldn't begin to understand. But somehow tonight it grated against her already sensitive nerves.

"I'll finish undressing." She fought the pounding in her temples as she reached to struggle with the last closure at her waist. Finally unfastening it, she shrugged out of the gown.

It was hot, her skin damp from the humidity. She reached for a cloth to soak in the bowl of refreshing herbal water Angeline had placed on her dressing table.

Her movements were slow, lethargic, and she tipped the bowl. Too late, she reached to save the crystal decanter that contained the perfume she'd bought only days earlier.

It toppled and broke, drenching her chemise in the fragrant mixture.

Andy jerked back, blood dripping from a cut on her finger.

"Damn! Now look what I've done!"

259

"Here . . ." Angeline took her hand gently and wiped away the blood with a handkerchief. "You're a might fidgety tonight."

Andy laughed softly. "I'll reek of lemon and verbena for days." She watched as Angeline inspected the cut. Her touch was so gentle.

"Will I live?" Faint amusement pulled at Andy's mouth.

It was a simple question, but it brought Angeline's head up sharply, her dark eyes filled with a strange light.

"It's just a small cut." Angeline frowned with her own thoughts as she tied the handkerchief about the wounded finger.

Andy reached for her hairbrush, drawing it through the long waves of her hair.

"You'll have to fix me one of your special nutmeg poultices."

Angeline stared back at Andy from her reflection in the mirror. "Why'd you say somethin' like that?"

Andy looked up, her hand stopping in midair. "Say what?"

Her voice was hardly more than a whisper. "About my nutmeg poultice."

"I don't know." She shrugged. "It does sound rather odd, doesn't it? I probably read about it, or maybe it's one of Lacey's strange concoctions."

Angeline shook her head. "Miss Lacey wouldn't know about somethin' like that."

"Then I probably read about it somewhere."

Angeline's eyes were dark and troubled. "That nutmeg poultice is somethin' my mama taught me, and her mama before her. There's no way nobody would know somethin' like that."

Andy laid down her hairbrush. "You must have mentioned it to me."

Angeline said nothing. Instead, she picked up the hairbrush from Andy and began stroking her hair.

"Why'd you come back from that party without Miss Lacey and Miss Melanie?"

260

"I was tired. Something happened . . ." Andy turned away from the scrutiny of Angeline's dark eyes. There were times she felt they saw too much. And she didn't want to discuss Coleton James with anyone. Then she looked up, disguising her uneven mood with a smile.

"You don't need to brush my hair. I can do it." She spoke softly.

Angeline continued as if she hadn't heard her, drawing the brush out the full length, working through the tangles. She smiled at Andy's reflection as she continued brushing.

"I always used to brush Miss Sunny's hair for her. She'd come home from a party or a ball, all dressed in her finest gown. And she'd be so excited about what happened that evenin', goin' on and on about who wore what dress and which young lady danced with a certain young man. After I helped her out of her gown, she'd sit down at her dressin' table, jes like you are now. I'd take all the pins outta her hair and let it down long. It was all pale and golden, and hung right to her waist." She hesitated. "She had hair jes like yours."

"Angeline, please . . ." Andy swallowed back the emotion that choked in her throat. But Angeline wouldn't stop.

"I'd brush it and brush it until it shone like spun gold. And do you know what she used to say to me? She used to say, 'Angeline, you don't need to brush my hair. I can do it.'"

Andy sat completely still, stunned by the exact words she'd spoken only moments before.

"She was always like that, seein' no reason to have someone do somethin' for her when she knew she was jes as capable. 'Course that made folks want to do for her all the more. I suppose that's why I loved her the way I did. That and the fact she never once made me feel I was any less a person than she was." Angeline's dark eyes locked with Andy's in the mirror. She went on brushing as she spoke. "She would share all her secrets with me. I knew

261

who her best friend was. I knew about the time she put pine pitch in her tutor's chair. He was pickin' pitch outta his pants for weeks, insistin' to her daddy that she was hopeless in her studies. But she was just high-spirited. I knew that. And I knew when she first met him."

Andy had no doubts who she meant.

"She was only twelve at the time, still a child in so many ways, but there was something different about her from that day on. She had her heart set on Coleton James."

It was the first time either of them had mentioned his name, and it was as if it came from very far away, instead of in this same room. Andy reached for Angeline's hand to stop her, hoping as well to stop her from saying more. She wanted to believe she didn't need to hear more. But she was lying to herself.

Angeline slowly continued. "She saw him against her daddy's wishes, and I knew it would cause her heartache. But she was always so happy when she rode off to be with him, tellin' Mr. Rawlins she was with friends."

"He found out about it," Andy whispered.

Angeline nodded sadly. "It was bound to happen. He was so afraid of losin' her. He forbid her to ever see Coleton James again. But she would have none of it, sayin' over and over how she loved that boy. Then she came home one evenin' when she was supposed to be out with one of her young lady friends. There was a look about her, her eyes all alight and sparklin', all excited, like she knew somethin' and was dyin' to tell it, but was afraid to. I knew she'd been with him. It was a special look, as if Coleton James was life and breath to her." Her fathomless eyes met Andy's as if she could see deep inside her.

Andy rose abruptly, tearing her gaze away from Angeline's.

"I'm really very tired," she explained hastily, crossing the room and quickly crawling into the large four-poster bed.

Angeline set the hairbrush down. She picked up the costume Andy had worn that evening and placed it in the wardrobe, to be returned to the costumers in the morning. Then she came to turn down the lantern beside the bed.

She hesitated, and then as if on impulse, leaned over and tucked the sheet in around Andy.

"I'll make that poultice for your hand in the mornin'." Angeline smiled softly, then reached to drop the insect netting into place.

Andy caught her hand. "Thank you."

Angeline looked as if she might say something else, then hesitated and said simply, "Good night . . . Miss Amanda."

Andy tossed and turned restlessly. The night heat was like a smothering blanket in spite of a faint breeze coming through the opened window.

Unable to sleep, she stared through heavy-lidded eyes as the curtains billowed like a cloud over the shadows at the window. Drowsiness finally came, but it was more a drugged lethargy from champagne and brandy and Coleton James.

Andy dreamed of brilliant ball gowns, costumes, and masks. They whirled through her imagination, the masks suddenly pulled away to reveal faces, and then the faces whirled away for they were masks, too, until she couldn't tell which was real and which was the disguise.

But one remained; a young man's face.

His smile was intoxicating, the lips sensual. The jaw was strong and angled, his nose straight between faintly arched brows as if he were surprised, or amused.

His hair was soft brown, tipped with gold from the sun, waving lazily off his forehead and about his neck. Then she saw his eyes, and realized it wasn't surprise or amusement at all but some hidden promise as they compelled her to him.

They were gray, like storm clouds or the mist off the bayou, banded with soft gold that melted the coldness. It was the heat that was hidden in those cool depths.

Standing so close their bodies could have touched, she pressed her hand against his cheek, closing her eyes with the thrill of sensation that pulsed through her at the simple contact as he turned and kissed the palm of her hand.

So long . . . Dear God . . . it had been so long.

She watched him, his eyes, every emotion that slipped across his lean, handsome face. She traced every feature with her fingertips, remembering.

Then his smile somehow saddened. His hand closed over her hand, his fingers twining through hers.

With his other hand, he reached up and slowly began peeling away the features of his face.

Andy stared horrified, then twisted away, refusing to watch this macabre scene. But his hand was clamped over hers, his lean fingers preventing escape. She was jerked around to face him, forced to watch. Andy scratched and clawed at his hand, fighting to free herself. She couldn't watch this! She just couldn't!

Then he pulled the last of it away, and slowly looked up.

Dear God! It had been a mask! And now she was even more frightened. She didn't want to see his face!

Chapter Fourteen

Andy gasped, trying to claw away the hand that suffocated across her mouth. She was certain she screamed, only there was no sound, only the wild screaming in her head. She struggled against a weight across her shoulders, pinning her back into the bedclothes that tangled around her legs. She stared, wide-eyed with terror, into the shadows of darkness, straining to see, but at the same time horrified of what she would find.

"Stop!" The command hissed very near her ear, making her realize the weight that pinned her was an arm. A man's arm! But instead of obeying, she renewed her struggling.

"The choice is yours, Miss Spenser!" The comment was punctuated by a grunt as she freed her arm, her elbow striking someplace vulnerable.

The pressure across her shoulders shifted. Andy almost thought her assailant might have decided to let her go. In the next instant, as she felt the cool smoothness of steel against her throat, she knew he hadn't. Dear God! A knife! There was no choice at all, and Andy immediately ceased struggling.

"Very good, Miss Spenser. I wouldn't have given you credit for being that smart."

That smart! Of all the . . . !

Fear shifted to indignation. Just let her get a hand free and she'd show him smart, Andy thought with a vengeance.

Of course the only thing preventing that at the moment was the undeniable fact that his one hand was firmly clamped over her mouth while his other restrained her with uncanny ease, almost as easily as Coleton James . . .

Andy's eyes narrowed in the dark as she strained to turn her head even a fraction of an inch to get a better look at her "guest." Even if he hadn't flashed her that aggravating smile, she would have known him by those eyes that glinted silver in the moonlit room.

"And a very good evening to you, Miss Spenser."

That brought another round of struggling that was much more quickly subdued with only the lightest pressure from the blade. She groaned, she screamed, she must have shouted every curse in the English language. It was all muffled behind his hand.

"And of course it's very nice to see you once more, as well. You'll forgive me if I came in unannounced."

Andy growled, trying to inch away from the length of his body sprawled across the bed beside her.

"And no, I really can't stay very long," he responded inanely. "I'm sure you'll understand that I only have a few minutes."

Andy rolled her eyes in exasperation and blind fury. The unmitigated gall of the man! Coming here in the middle of the night! God's nightgown! What the devil did he want? If she only had a gun! She could think of no less than a half dozen reasons to shoot the man, beginning with stealing her money.

But she didn't have a gun, and even if she had, it would have been extremely difficult to shoot him under the circumstances. However, if she could just open her mouth a little.

"Ouch! Sonofa—!"

Andy had no doubt what the rest of the comment would have been as she clamped her teeth down over one of his fingers.

Before she could so much as inhale to let out a scream, Coleton James had jerked her out of the covers and buried her facedown in the feather mattress of the bed, at the same time wrestling her arms behind her back.

Andy tried to struggle against his hands, but she was having a difficult enough time simply trying to keep from suffocating to death, never mind the undignified position she now occupied in the thin chemise, with the silk yanked halfway up her legs and her bottom poised in a very unladylike position.

She was dying. Andy knew it. She was smothering to death. This madman, this fiend, had come here to kill her.

Oh, God! Lacey's words came slamming back through her befuddled brain. "They say he killed her." He was capable of it. Andy believed that absolutely as she was roughly bound with the satin cording ties from the bed hangings. He jerked the knot tightly, pinching the soft skin at her wrists. Andy cried out, but the sound was lost somewhere in all that feather ticking.

Then just as roughly as she was slammed facedown into the mattress, she was hauled back out of it and thrown down on her back. She inhaled, a deep, ragged sound, struggling just to draw air, but the madman must have thought otherwise. Instead of the welcomed gulp of air, Andy was choked by the wadded handkerchief that was thrust into her mouth.

Without the least care for bruises or her state of undress, she was dragged into a sitting position, hands bound behind her, feet dangling over the edge of the bed. Breasts heaving, choking on the dry cotton that clogged in her throat, Andy glared up at the silhouette of the man who towered over her.

"Very good, Miss Spenser! You can be most cooperative once you know the rules."

Andy pinned him with a murderous expression in her eyes, quite simply because it was the only thing she was capable of doing at the moment. It wasn't much, but it gave her a little satisfaction. She mumbled through the gag.

"Yes, yes, I quite understand your opinion of me. It matches mine of you." Coleton stood over her, fighting to bring his own breathing back under control. She'd put up a better fight than he thought. He should have remembered that damned Yankee determination.

He resheathed the knife, smiling as she watched every movement with large, round eyes. God, even trussed up like a Christmas goose, she was beautiful. Beautiful and treacherous. He would have to remember that.

"I want just one thing from you." Coleton dropped down into a crouched position on the rug beside the bed. He laughed bitterly as she cringed away at that comment.

"As I said earlier, 'Madame Bonaparte' . . ." he added meaningfully, "don't flatter yourself. What you have to offer in that regard simply is not that good."

That brought on another fit of choking as her eyes flashed blue fire at him. He reached up, a smile teasing at his lips as he lightly stroked beneath her chin. It had the desired effect, and she jerked away from him.

But Coleton was a master of eloquent torture. He'd learned it well during the war. There were ways to get the information he wanted. And he wanted this information badly.

His fingers closed around her slender throat, making certain she understood the subtle pressure. She quit straining away from him and he immediately lightened his touch.

"Very good. We understand each other. And it isn't even necessary for you to speak," he informed her coldly. "At least, not yet." As his fingers eased down the column of her neck, he felt the wild racing of her pulse. Then they traced over the angle of her collarbone. His thumb lowered deliberately down into the valley between her breasts exposed above the gown. That brought renewed choking.

He deliberately fanned his hand across the frantic rise

and fall of her right breast. His fingers locked over the narrow strip of bodice, jerking her up to him.

"But you have my guarantee, Miss Spenser. You will give me the information I want."

He towered over her. His authority was complete and Andy knew it. Dear God, what was he raving about? What information? What was it he was so certain she knew? She could only stare up at him defiantly in answer.

Her hair tumbled down over her shoulders in a golden torrent. Even with little light in the room he could see it, feel the silken heat of it twisted around his hands. It was almost his undoing. He remembered it from that night in the gazebo; wet and wild like a live thing clinging to him, and then hours later as it tangled about their naked bodies. He shoved those memories to the farthest corners of his mind.

He didn't want to remember anything about Amanda Spenser, except this moment right now and the information she could give him.

"If you're ready?" he asked mockingly, then shoved her back down onto the bed.

Ready? For what? Dear God, what was wrong with the man? Couldn't he understand? She hadn't the faintest idea what he was talking about. And as for wanting something from somebody, she wanted something very much. She wanted her money back, and she wanted Coleton James out of her life and away from Ombre Rose for good!

"We'll start very simply," he instructed her in a low voice. "I'll ask you a question, and you'll give me the correct answer. Now listen very carefully; I want to know the name of your contact. And . . ." he warned her again, "don't give me any trouble, or try to lie to me. Because if you do, you'll be punished. Is that clear?" To emphasize that particular point, he reached around her and jerked her bound hands up at an excruciating angle.

Andy gasped at the sharp, wrenching pain. The pigheaded buffoon! The pompous ass! The—!"

She croaked with a mixture of raw fury and indignation as the gag was roughly jerked out of her mouth.

She tried to swallow, she tried to move her tongue, anything to bring moisture to her mouth.

"Damn you!" she half whispered. The rest was lost as her parched voice failed her.

"The answer, Amanda," he reminded her coldly.

"I don't know what you're . . . talking about," she rasped through dry lips.

Coleton reached to the nightstand and poured a cup of water. He thrust it against her mouth, spilling most in the process. It molded her already revealing gown to her breasts.

Silently fuming, Andy considered telling him exactly what she thought of him for that as well, but held her tongue. She swallowed slowly, savoring the relief from the water.

"That's not good enough, Amanda."

She cringed inside at the way he said her name, as if it were something vile and loathsome.

"I don't know anything!" she whispered, feeling a good deal of frustration along with fear and anger. Why did he keep asking her that?

"I don't know what you're talking about."

"I saw your little conversation with Louis this evening. What was the message he gave you?"

Andy shook her head, at the same time wondering if she could make it to the door. Even if she could, there was no way she could open it with her arms bound behind her. She could always cry out, but only Angeline and Melanie's butler were in the house. Dear God, why had she insisted on coming home early?

"I don't know." She shook her head wearily. "Why do you keep asking me?" She glared up at him. "I . . . don't . . . know!"

Coleton refused to accept that. He'd seen her talking to Louis. "Dammit! You know something, and you're going to tell me," he insisted, his eyes narrowing. "But if you're not concerned what will happen if you don't cooperate, then maybe you should be concerned for Rawlins."

Andy's eyes widened. "You wouldn't!" She was incredulous. The man was mad.

"You seemed fond enough of the old man," Coleton pointed out, "but he's nothing to me." Less than nothing, Coleton thought bitterly.

"Please don't hurt him," Andy begged frantically, biting at her lower lip as she glanced wildly about. Dear God! He was mad to threaten Parker Rawlins after what he'd done to his daughter. Her frantic gaze froze on the nightstand. She snaked out her right foot, hooking it around the leg of the small table and pulling with all her strength.

The nightstand toppled, taking the bowl of water with it. Both crashed loudly to the floor. At the same time, Andy pushed to her feet and bolted for the door.

He was on her before she'd crossed half the distance, throwing her to the floor and pinning her with his long body.

Silence echoed through the big house. How could they have not heard, Andy thought frantically.

Coleton James's hand was clamped firmly down over her mouth.

"Not a sound," he warned, his breath brushing her cheek, sending a shiver of cold fear down her spine. They waited and listened. Andy twisted at the sound of the butler calling to Angeline from the bottom of the stairs, followed by the woman's muffled response just outside the door.

"Damn!" Coleton cursed. With his hand still over her mouth, he came to his feet in one fluid movement, dragging Andy with him.

The sound of footsteps was distinct now from the hallway beyond her door.

Andy's eyes gleamed with wicked satisfaction. She would take great delight in bringing charges against Coleton James for assaulting her.

But she quickly realized she wasn't to have that satisfaction. She cried out indignantly as the wad of material was quickly shoved back into her mouth, firmly held in place by a silk cloth tied at the back of her neck. She was thrown helplessly back into the voluminous depths of the mattress. She silently swore. As long as she lived she'd never sleep on one again; depending, of course, on just how long that proved to be.

All her groaned protests didn't so much as draw Coleton James's attention. He crossed the room and threw back heavy drapes, sheer undercurtains, and opened the louvered doors out onto the narrow balcony.

Good! She thought with a vengeance. He was leaving. Then Coleton James turned back to her.

"Please believe me, Miss Spenser, I regret this more than you do." He spoke solemnly, reaching inside his coat pocket.

Andy's eyes widened. Dear Father in heaven, he was going to kill her with a . . . handkerchief?

She stared wide-eyed as he pulled out a long silk handkerchief and slowly came toward her.

She panicked. Of course! He'd decided the knife would be too messy, he was merely going to strangle her to death!

As he bent over her, Andy tried frantically to twist away from him. When she realized it was impossible, she clamped her eyes shut against the nauseating fear that congealed in her stomach. She tried to imagine what death was like, but her mind went completely blank. She waited for that constricting tightness, and gasped . . .

He was tying her ankles together!

Andy tried to kick at him. It was hopeless. He seemed to have twice as many hands as any normal man. If she thought she felt helpless before, it was nothing compared to now. Nor was her earlier surprise anything to what came next.

She heard Angeline call from the other side of the

door, and tried to groan loudly enough to draw the woman's attention. There wasn't an opportunity for more as Coleton James lifted her off the bed and tossed her over his left shoulder. The force of it drove what little air she could breathe out of her lungs. Andy dangled helplessly down the length of his well-muscled back, her face buried somewhere in the jacket at the back of his waist.

She heard Angeline's concerned voice once more as he hooked one leg over the ornate wrought-iron railing, carefully turned, and then began a quick descent. As Andy was jostled and bumped against that rock-hard back, the ground came up at her at alarming speed. She was torn between blind panic and engulfing nausea. Escaping second-story windows, she decided, was best accomplished when not dangling upside down.

God's nightgown! she thought with a vengeance. It would serve him right if she got sick.

However, if she thought the trip out that window was dangerous, it was nothing compared to being tossed across a saddle and jostled for God only knew how many miles.

She was going to die like this, Andy was absolutely certain. How absolutely mortifying to be flung over the back of a horse and carried off to heaven knew where, for reasons only a madman could understand. And with her dead, Coleton James would simply return to Ombre Rose and claim his home.

Dear God, how she hated Coleton James!

Somewhere on that wild ride through the streets of New Orleans she fainted.

When Andy came to, she was slowly aware of three things: a garish purple-and-red satin bedcover beneath her, the nauseating muskiness of stale, cheap perfume, and a loud pounding somewhere close by.

None of it was familiar, all of it was increasingly confusing as her senses cleared. And then she remembered

. . . Coleton James!

She sat up in the bed and was aware of something more. Her wrists were still bound, but the gag she remembered at her mouth was gone. Her gaze focused on Coleton as he jerked open the door to the outlandishly decorated room, answering that frantic knocking.

"What is it?" he whispered impatiently, and was answered by a softly feminine voice.

"We have visitors."

The voice was urgent and suggested these visitors might be unwanted. Andy strained to listen as the woman she couldn't see went on to explain. "A group of men are searching every house in the district."

House? Andy looked about the room, trying to make sense of everything. Where was she? Where had he taken her? Her eyes widened at the satin-and-lace lady's undergarments draped across the doors of the armoire. They were in every brilliant color imaginable. An impossible thought flashed into her mind. It couldn't be.

"Stall them," Coleton ordered the woman.

"It will look suspicious," she answered.

"Do your best. Give me five minutes." He shut the door and whirled back to her.

"Glad to see you decided to wake up from your little nap," he remarked.

Andy ignored the gibe. "Where are we?" she asked with a throat still dry from the gag.

"There's no time to explain. I brought you here to get some answers out of you. But it seems we have company—unwanted company."

"What is this place?"

"Amanda . . ." His voice had a warning edge to it. "I don't have time for this." His cold gray eyes scanned the room, then fastened back to her, scrutinizing her. "Get out of that nightgown!"

She stared at him, her thoughts slow and dulled from just awakening. All she remembered was being thrown over his shoulder, bound and gagged, and then hoisted out the window of her window at Melanie's as if she were a sack of grain. There was some memory of cold night air and that jarring ride on a horse. Then nothing more, certainly no memory of this place with its heavy green velvet drapes, gold tasseled canopy bed, and gaudy pink crystal bed lamp.

"I will not. I want some answers." She jerked her chin up with all the defiance she could manage dressed only in her nightgown. "Where are we?" she demanded again.

Coleton crossed the room. "At a friend's . . . You might say she's a businesswoman," he added with a leering smile.

Andy's gaze took in the bed, the clothes, the feather-trimmed dressing gown and man's shirt across the foot of the bed, indicating someone—or two someones—might have left quickly and comprehension dawned.

"This is a . . . whorehouse!"

"Very good, Amanda. You're very perceptive." He raised his pistol. "Now, get out of that gown and into that bed."

Andy stared at the pistol. Considering everything else he'd done in the past, she believed he would use it.

She turned her back for what little privacy that might offer and swallowed hard as she slipped the dressing gown off her shoulders.

Andy heard sounds of movement around the room when she finally turned around and brushed her hair back over one shoulder. Her eyes widened at the sight of Coleton James's bare chest, widening further as he reached for the button closures of the pants he'd worn as Napoleon Bonaparte.

"What are you doing!?" she whispered frantically, immediately regretting it as his cold gray eyes came up and regarded her evenly.

"Come now, dear Amanda," he replied mockingly, "you certainly can't be shy after all that we've shared."

His tone was deliberately cruel, and Andy fought back the tears that stung at her eyes. If it was the last thing she did, she wouldn't let him see her cry. She wouldn't allow him the satisfaction of knowing how humiliated and degraded she felt. She hitched her chin up a notch, meeting him glare for glare.

"You said you weren't interested in . . . in that sort of thing."

"I'm not. As I told you, my dear Amanda, you don't hold the least fascination for me. However, staying alive does. I didn't survive the war just to end up a target for some private citizen eager to make a name for himself by turning me in. But appearances can be deceiving. And that's just what I intend when those men search this room," he informed her coolly, slipping the pants down over his lean hips, revealing that he wore absolutely nothing underneath.

"They're going to find a man and woman in the throes of passion: Love for a price." He thought of what he'd seen pass between her and the man disguised as Louis XIV. "A whore exchanging favors for payment."

How could he be so cruel? She should have turned away. But no matter how hard she tried, no matter how hateful his words were, she couldn't tear her eyes away from him. She was fascinated by his body. He was lean and darkly tanned to where his pants rode on those hips. He was used to hard physical labor. The corded muscles along his shoulders and neck were sharply defined, as were the several scars of paler skin. One thick scar marred the skin just below his collarbone. Another, smaller scar patched the skin just beneath the ribs on his left side. But it was the crisscrossed pattern of scars across his back that took her breath away.

They formed a stark, cruel pattern over the heavy muscles. Andy cringed. He'd been beaten, and beaten badly.

He looked up, a slow, deadly smile curving beneath his mustache as he saw the direction of her gaze. "A token from a Union officer during the war so that I wouldn't forget the true and just cause of the war. Knowing your sympathies, Miss Spenser, I know you can appreciate his handiwork."

"No, I didn't . . . That is, I'm sorry." She fumbled badly with the excuse and knew it. As it was, she didn't know what to say, and she couldn't stop staring. That night in the gazebo it was impossible to see anything. There were only sensations, textures, and instinct. She was fascinated at how truly exquisite he was. The scars weren't frightening, only the reason for them was. In truth, they made him seem that much more powerful and dangerous. And there was more.

As she stood watching him strip away the elegant general's costume and fling it atop the billowed canopy overhead to hide it, it seemed the light in the room grew dim, as if someone had turned down the single lantern at the table. The shadows slipped across the carpet toward the bed, engulfing them, transforming them, taking her back, back . . . to another time and place.

No, it wasn't possible! Not him!

The man she saw walking toward her was softly muted in the shadows of some vague memory. He moved with a lean animal intensity that was vaguely frightening and completely familiar. Andy swallowed hard, trying to think of a way out of this. The last thing on this earth she wanted was to be in bed with Coleton James, clothed or otherwise.

Coleton heard the tread of heavy boots farther down the hallway followed by a woman's indignant voice and the slamming of a door. He tore back the covers on the bed and turned to her.

"Get into that bed!"

Perhaps it was the way she simply stood there, her pale skin exposed in the soft light. Or perhaps it was the look in her eyes—that wide-eyed, questioning expression of uncertainty when he expected anger.

Maybe it was the slight parting of her lips as if she were about to say something. It was all so completely opposite of what he expected of her that it set Coleton back for a moment and broke down the wall of anger. He recognized something in those brilliant blue eyes. It was like looking through a window with the sun glinting off the glass, reflecting back yet allowing him to see vague images hidden on the other side; images . . . and memories.

His right hand slipped beneath the fall of her hair, his fingers caressing her cheek. And in that simple touch, that breath of a moment in time, a deep longing ache shimmered through Andy. She closed her eyes, trying to fight back the images that leaped at her through the shadows in the room, only to find them waiting in the darkness behind her eyes.

Coleton bent and picked her up, expecting resistance. There was only a subtle tensing in her body. He deposited her on the bed and slipped in beside her, drawing the satin sheet over her shoulders. He felt a faint shiver slip over her pale skin at that brief contact.

Andy scooted as far away as possible, but the shock of cold steel against her skin brought her up short. Coleton James's gun was tucked just beneath the sheet, the barrel aimed right at her throat.

"Now, my dear, you're going to give the performance of a lifetime. After what I saw this evening, that shouldn't be all that difficult."

"I don't know what you're talking about." Andy's voice caught in her throat as her eyes fastened on that deadly revolver.

He tilted the barrel of the revolver up, forcing her chin up at an odd angle. "You will act the part of a very beautiful, very attentive whore. Is that clear?"

Coleton was lying on his left side, propped up on his elbow. The bed was shrouded in shadows; he didn't want anyone to see his face. Amanda lay facing him, straining as far away as possible from any contact. Only the bodice of her green costume was exposed. But that was too much for believability. He transferred the revolver to his left hand, bringing his right up to slowly untie the black lace closure. Her hand immediately closed over his to stop him.

"You wouldn't!" Andy gasped.

Coleton merely cocked a golden brow at her with maddening authority. "You know I would." He raised the revolver just enough to make his point. "Now, Amanda, either you unlace it or I will."

Her eyes sparked liquid fire. Not surprising, Coleton thought. Everything he'd done to her this evening undoubtedly ruffled all her fine Yankee sensibilities. But he suspected the part of whore would come to her very easily.

For reasons she didn't fully understand, Andy knew she couldn't bear the thought of his touching her. Biting back embarrassment and humiliation, she slowly unlaced the front of the costume. A door slamming down the hall outside the room startled her. She looked up wide-eyed at the door, thoughts of escape churning through her mind.

"Don't even think of it," he warned her. "Not a word, not one look or gesture to even make them suspect anything." The last part hissed out at her as voices came to them through the door. Brilliant color stained across her cheeks.

"Amanda!" His voice was low, intense, warning her attention away from the door.

He knew she was humiliated beyond description. Whatever her part was in the conspiracy, it obviously had not included something like this. And that was surprising. He brought his hand up beneath her chin, his fingers lightly stroking her skin.

"Look at me."

Her eyes flew open, filled with an almost pleading desperation.

"That won't save you, Amanda." He smiled softly, with almost a trace of regret. "Do exactly as I say."

"Put your arm around me," he commanded, giving only the slightest indication he was even aware of the sound of heavy footsteps passing just outside the door. It was an order, just like everything else he said or did, and meant to be obeyed.

Andy curved her left arm over his right shoulder and immediately felt the heat that seemed to leap from his skin to hers at that simple contact. She wanted desperately to pull her arm away but didn't dare. Her gaze fastened on the revolver.

"Like this?" she whispered from between clenched lips.

"Exactly. You learn quickly." His smile was maddening.

"They'll be coming in here any second now, Amanda. Make them believe this is the only place you want to be." His eyes held hers as she looked up. "Be convincing . . . darling," he whispered threateningly, his voice silken and deadly. He shifted the pistol down only an inch or two as his right arm slipped around her waist, pulling her full against the naked length of his body.

Surprise came, not so much at the fact that he took her into his arms—she'd already guessed what he intended—but at the intensity of that contact. Skin against skin was like fire igniting, then spreading down the entire length of their bodies everywhere they touched.

"Kiss me, Amanda." It was so simply spoken, a whisper that shocked her senses. She brought her hand up over his bare shoulder, determined to do exactly as he ordered her, no more. Still her fingers trembled at that contact with his heated skin. She'd never taken the initiative with a kiss before. There was something awkward and at the same time thrilling about it.

She tried to remember times before when one of her beaux had kissed her, but every memory focused on Coleton James, and that made her even more uncertain and angry.

"I hate you, of course," Andy reminded him as her fingers slipped through the thick waves of hair at his temple.

"I wouldn't have it any other way," he assured her in a low, husky voice.

There was something in the way he said it . . . Andy stared into the infinite gray of his eyes, seeing something there from some long-ago awareness. It was frightening and compelling at the same time. More frightening was the realization that she wanted to kiss him.

In her tangled thoughts she convinced herself it was to prove she could do just that; she could perform as he wanted her to and it would mean nothing, absolutely nothing at all.

She slipped her hand behind his neck, drawing him down to her. Like a whisper, she brushed her mouth against his, tentative at first, hesitant in something she'd never been in control of before.

It was like a dare, someone taunting her. She accepted it, tilting her face slightly, and then touching his bottom lip briefly with hers, once, twice, then moving to the corner of his mouth and the soft brush of his mustache.

Yes, I'll prove it means nothing, Andy silently vowed as she breathed against his mouth. She angled her smaller mouth against his, tracing the full curve of his lower lip with her tongue, then thrusting below his mustache to explore the softness of his upper lip.

Is that what you wanted, Mr. Coleton James? she thought with a vengeance, parting his lips as he'd showed her in the garden, her tongue slipping inside to alternately caress and tangle with his.

Dear God, Andy thought. He tasted sweet, wild, and hot. Desire ached through her.

It wasn't supposed to be like this. "Damn you!" Coleton groaned, thrusting his hand into the thick mane of her hair, his fingers stroking the taut cords of her neck as he ___ control away from her.

___ beginning something with her delicately ___ he knew she hadn't the least intention of finishing. *He* would finish it!

His right hand stroked her neck, his thumb caressing the erratic beating that drummed beneath her skin. He felt the wild torrent of emotions that pulsed through her. He tilted her chin, forcing her to meet his gaze.

His kiss, when it came, cruelly obliterated everything else about them. She was oblivious to the men who boldly walked into the room. She was stunned beyond knowing whether or not they glanced to the bed or stood and watched. But it didn't end there. It didn't end even after the door thumped shut behind them.

Coleton stroked her, caressed her, boldly made love to her with his mouth. Then he teased and tormented, brushing her sensitized lips, building the fire then banking it, pulling away to stroke lightly, maddeningly, until she cried out softly.

Andy strained away from him, her hand flattened against his bare chest. Then she shuddered as he plunged full into her mouth, but it was a shudder of slow-building desire. He robbed her of breath or even the will to breathe, controlling the passion with blinding pleasure. Her fingers curled, wanting to draw him closer.

It began as it had in the gazebo, that unleashing of desire that flashed out of control. It was something primal, instinctive . . . familiar . . . and frightening.

Coleton had wanted her that night. He'd felt that same desire earlier this evening. Now he felt it again, teasing, tormenting. Instead of the anger and bitterness of only moments before, he now felt an overwhelming need to protect her. He bent over her, brushing her lips with his, tasting again the aching sweetness. He kissed her cheek, her eyes, and the salty tears at her lashes, recapturing something he'd thought lost so long ago.

Promise me . . . promise me you will always love me.

Andy had no idea whether she thought the words or spoke them. Suddenly they were there, wrapping around them both, transporting them beyond this dark and the danger that seemed to fill every cor ish crimson carpet, the elaborate velvet bed hangings all disappeared in the mist that seemed to surround them, taking them to another time and place, to a barren room where there were only the few blankets beneath them and the warmth of the crackling fire at the hearth, the heat stealing across their naked skin and burning into their equally naked souls.

The door was thrown open and Andy instinctively

tensed, reality jarring back sharply. Coleton's fingers bruised against her skin, painfully stripping away the desire.

"Not a word," he warned. His back was to the door, a perfect target. His legs were entwined with hers beneath the satin coverlet, his hips intimately pressing her back into the sheets.

For one brief second he saw everything focus back into her vivid eyes, heard her sharp intake of breath, felt the subtle tensing in her body, and knew exactly what she was thinking. If she was going to cry out, it would be now.

Chapter Fifteen

A man growled orders to another at the doorway. The light from a lantern was thrust through the doorway and pooled on the bed, catching the silvery glow of her pale hair. Whatever passed between them seemed to disappear with that invasion of light. Without understanding why, Coleton felt unexpectedly angry. He wanted to shout at them to get out; he wanted to hold onto that elusive moment when it almost seemed he held something in his hands that had slipped from his life so long ago.

Andy felt the lean muscles of his body grow rigid, like a snake preparing to strike. She saw the coolness return to penetrating eyes, and something seemed to curl and die inside her.

It had happened again. For those few brief moments somehow she'd slipped away from the nightmare of this place and his anger, to another place . . . and this time he'd gone there with her.

She breathed out a soft sob, feeling a deep, lonely ache, seep back inside her. She wanted to hold on to those moments that seemed to exist only in some far corner of her imagination.

Dear God! What was it? What did it mean?

Now, when Coleton kissed her again, forcing her head back, it was a perfect performance and cruelly different from those first kisses. He stroked her shoulders, turning her onto her back, knowing those men watched. Revulsion coiled deep inside her. There was none of the desire or need she'd felt only moments before. It was all gone, replaced by bruising indifference. Dear God, how she hated him!

And then they were gone, the door thumping closed. Coleton jerked away from her, tearing back the sheet as if he couldn't stand to look at her, much less touch her. Andy shuddered, raw emotions churning through her. She did hate him! She did! She bit back a quiet sob, gathering the sheet over the gaping bodice of the costume. Her skin still burned where he'd touched her. Her head came up as the door was thrust open unexpectedly.

Coleton instinctively rolled from Andy's side, raising the pistol he'd concealed beneath the heavy coverlet. Stark naked, landing in a crouched position on the floor, he placed himself between the bed and the door, at the same time taking deadly aim at the silhouette outlined in the doorway.

"Good God, Coleton! Don't shoot!" the woman who had been there before whispered frantically from the doorway as the steel barrel of the revolver glinted in the light.

Coleton relaxed his aim, slowly coming upright. "Are they gone, Valentine?" His voice was faintly husky.

"For now." The woman cast a quick glance to the bed, then looked away.

"Perez will keep watch downstairs."

Coleton stalked across the room, retrieving the clothes brought earlier. He quickly slipped into his pants.

"Do you have any other clothes that might fit her. Something a little less conspicuous."

"What are you doing?"

He looked up briefly. "Leaving."

"But you cannot leave now!" Valentine protested. "These men are searching the entire district. If you try to leave, you will be caught."

"If we stay, we'll be caught. You know as well as I do they'll be back when they don't find what they're looking for."

"But here you have a chance," she argued helplessly.

Coleton quickly buttoned the worn gray Confederate shirt with the mended patches that matched those scars Andy had seen earlier. He quickly pulled on his boots, pausing only once to look up at Valentine.

"If I stay here, I endanger you." He said it simply, and left unsaid what he meant; that he would never do that. He cut a quick glance to Andy.

"About those clothes?"

"One of the other girls sometimes dresses up as a boy . . . One of her customers . . ."

Andy stared incredulously. Certainly the woman didn't mean that one of the men who frequented this place liked to pretend one of the girls was actually a boy!

"Please get them, Valentine. We haven't much time."

"Colton James, one of these days you will take one too many risks and die for it."

He looked up at her, flashing a rare, quick smile. "Dear Valentine, we all die someday. Some of us merely get to choose the place. Now get those clothes."

"I'm not going anywhere with you," Andy announced, crawling to the far side of the bed.

"You'd prefer to stay here?" Coleton suggested, knowing full well she would do exactly as he said so long as he had the gun. And there was still the matter of that information he wanted.

"I'll find my way back to Melanie's house. Since you obviously have men after you, you won't want me slowing you down," she rationalized.

"You're right about that," he agreed, turning to her as he belted the revolver into the holster at his waist. "I fully intend to be rid of you just as soon as you give me the information I want."

"That again?" Andy gritted her teeth.

"Yes, that again." He slipped the gun from the holster and slowly walked toward her. "Now, I want the truth. What exactly did your friend Louis XIV say to you tonight?"

Andy winced painfully as he reached out, twisting his hand in her hair and jerking her up to her knees on the bed. She tried to loosen his grasp.

"I already told you. It was nothing . . . nothing that made any sense. I thought he was drunk!" she spat out.

"I don't care what you thought. Try to remember! Your life depends on it."

Andy closed her eyes, trying desperately to remember. God's nightgown! What was so damned important about some foolish gibberish.

"It was something about a lady," she cried out as he jerked her head back hard.

"You'll have to do better than that." He leaned over her, pressing the barrel of the revolver into her neck.

"He said something about a package . . ."

"What package?"

"I don't know!

"Think! There has to be more!"

"I'm trying! It's a little difficult when you're pulling my hair out!"

His hold relaxed slightly. "Amanda!"

He'd meant it as a threat, she was certain of that. But there was something about the way he said her name; low and husky, rough and silken at the same time, that made shivers of remembered desire slip like fire over her skin, and she hated him for that as well. She gave him a murderous look.

"He said, 'Tell her ladyship . . . to inform . . . someone.'" She closed her eyes, trying to remember.

"Who?"

"I think he said 'client.' He said to tell her ladyship to tell her client that the package would be delivered according to plan."

"According to plan? What plan? What about a time or place?"

Andy shook her head, as much as his grasp would allow. "There was nothing more! That's all he said. Just that it would be according to plan."

"What the hell is that all supposed to mean?" Coleton glared down at her.

"How should I know?"

"Who was Louis XIV?"

Andy doubled her fist in frustration, wanting to punch him right in that arrogant nose. "He was wearing a mask! I don't know who he was!"

"You expect me to believe that? He gave you a message."

"I don't know who he was!"

"What about his voice?"

Andy shook her head. "I didn't recognize him."

"Who were you to give the message to?"

Andy clawed at his hand, at the same time shifting her weight and twisting away from him. She was certain she lost several strands of hair, but she also gained her freedom, coming around to glare at him, cold fury sparking in her eyes.

"Damn you! I told you I don't know who he was! The message doesn't mean anything to me. I don't know who it was meant for. I don't know anything about any of this. This man dressed as Louis XIV walked up to me and started mumbling something about a package. I don't know anything more!" And with that she whirled around and started around the far side of the bed.

"Amanda!" He tore after her, stopping only as Valentine rushed through the door.

"They're coming back. Perez saw them leave the house down the street. I brought the clothes."

Coleton seized them in one hand, Andy in the other. He thrust the clothes into her arms. "You'll have to change later."

"But I told you what you wanted to know."

"Right." He jammed a long, wicked-looking knife into his left boot. "Now I just have to decide how much of it is the truth."

"Oh no you don't, Coleton James! I'm not going with

you!"

There was mutiny in those lovely blue eyes. Actually she was quite a sight, with her thick golden hair streaming over her shoulders—bare shoulders—at that. As it was, she was wearing very little, just the scanty green satin costume Valentine had first given her. She'd managed to lace the bodice closed, but it covered very little.

Coleton grabbed the satin dressing gown and threw it over her shoulders. "You'd better cover up, it could be quite cool out this evening."

"You're not listening! I'm not going with you!"

"You *are* going with me, Amanda. It's merely a matter of how it's to be done. You can walk out of here with me and cooperate, or you can be carried out the way you came in. The choice is yours."

Choice? The man was insane! He wasn't giving her any choice at all and they both knew it.

"Coleton! Quickly! You must go now if you're to get away from them!" Valentine urged frantically from the hallway.

It was all settled very quickly. He merely grabbed Andy by the arm, twisted it painfully behind her back, and emphasized that he wouldn't hesitate to use the gun if she so much as let out a peep. She believed him.

He shoved her out into the hallway. They descended the stairs, turning toward the back entrance where they'd come in only a few hours earlier. Perez stood guard at the door. The long hall was cast into complete darkness as Valentine doused the lantern she carried.

Andy came up behind Perez's wide back. Coleton was right behind her, his fingers locked over her wrist pulled behind her back.

"Perez has hidden your horses. I will keep them until you return. It is better if you go on foot—less obvious."

"Thank you, Valentine." Coleton kissed her quickly.

"I wish I could offer you more."

Coleton hesitated only a moment before shoving Andy out into the alley. "Perhaps you can. You know just about everyone in New Orleans. What would someone mean if they were trying to get a message to 'her ladyship'?"

Andy jerked around. Was it possible he believed her?

"Her ladyship? It could be someone with a title, perhaps someone of the old French nobility. Years ago there were many émigrés. But most of them have dropped their fancy titles." Valentine hesitated. "There is a possibility, but it is very remote."

"What is it?"

"Who gave you this message?"

As Coleton's gaze shifted to Andy, Valentine shook her head. "One such as she would not know of it."

"I need something, Val, anything. It could well be a link to whomever is posing as Gray Fox."

That name again, Andy thought. Who the devil was Gray Fox, and what did any of this have to do with her and that ridiculous message?

"There is a slim possibility . . . There is someone, but this person is very dangerous. This person is connected to many bad things—opium that comes in on the ships since the war . . ." she hesitated. "White slavery—women and men. This is not the sort of person you should seek out unless you have something to offer in return."

"I've heard of just about everyone in the business in New Orleans. Who the devil are you talking about? Is it someone new?"

"You have heard of this person. I am referring to the Duchess." Valentine laid her hand on his arm. "Be very careful, Coleton James. Many men have gone to the Duchess. Few return."

"Christ! I thought the Duchess left for San Francisco."

"For a while. But someone like that one always goes where there is a great deal of money to be made. And there is a lot of it in New Orleans since the occupation and now with Reconstruction. The Duchess knows a great many people in high places of the new government. Be very careful, Coleton," she warned again.

"Where can I find our 'friend?' " The way he said it

made Andy sincerely doubt the word. "The usual place?"

Valentine shook her head. "Not since the war. It is too dangerous, and as I said, the Duchess is very careful. They have taken over the fort on the Isle Au Pitre out beyond Bay Boudreau. They have their own little harbor, and it is well armed. I have heard it said they are using the old cannons left by the French to defend the island. Even the Bluebellies wouldn't go near it. Now they leave the Duchess alone."

Coleton grew thoughtful. "It would be easy enough to smuggle cargoes in and out of that chain of islands."

"Yes, very easy."

He looked up. "Thanks again, Valentine. I owe you."

"You owe me nothing."

They slipped silently out into the darkened alley. The door whispered shut behind them, lost in the inky blackness of all those buildings that were exactly alike. The moon had started a downward arc, reminding Andy of how achingly tired she was. It cast a silvery pool at the end of the alley.

Coleton stopped, pressing them both back into the shadows behind a building.

"What is it . . . ?" Anything more was quickly muffled beneath his hand. Andy saw a streak of steel glinting in the muted light as he brought the revolver up. He pulled her along the rear of the building, staying in the shadows. Andy clung to the clothes Valentine had given her. Otherwise she felt practically naked. The dressing gown gaped open over the scant costume. Cool night air brushed against her bare legs and equally bare feet.

Somewhere nearby a cat squawled. Something clattered on the cobbled alleyway and Coleton flattened her against the building with his own body, practically smothering her. Andy struggled against the sweaty saltiness of his hand only to have him press against her until she thought her shoulderblades would melt into the brick.

Coleton nodded toward the end of the alley. "We'll make a run for the main street. There should be people still about."

"But . . ." She had time to catch her breath and not much more. She was about to say the street seemed the worst possible choice if he was trying to avoid someone. However, it promised possibilities for her own escape, so she merely nodded in response.

Coleton seized her hand and pulled her along behind him. He set a murderous pace, running among the shadows. Shouts broke out behind them. Andy glanced back once briefly and caught the silhouette of a large man as he charged into the alley. Orders were shouted and several more men poured in behind him. Coleton's hand was locked around hers; she had no choice but to keep up or fall. She had no doubt what his reaction would be to that. He'd simply leave her to those men, or promptly shoot her.

She was briefly contemplating her choice when the first shots were fired. Rather than taking time to return the gunfire, Coleton chose to put as much distance between them as possible while keeping out of sight of those men. The darkness of the alley broke as the moon shone brightly over the roofline of a one-story building, plunging the entire alley into bright light just ahead.

Quickly making his decision, Coleton pushed Andy in front of him, shoved her on ahead to the far side of the alley as he swung around, and returned gunfire with the men following them.

Andy screamed as several shots popped in front of her. Driven by fear and the certainty that Coleton James might change his mind and leave her at any minute, she hitched the long dressing gown up around her knees and ran for the far side of the alley and the safety of shadows. They were almost to the street at the end. If they could just make it.

Coleton jerked around, catching a quick glance as she ran ahead of him. For one brief moment they were both fully exposed in the silvery light of the moon pouring into the alley. Her pale hair whipping out behind her was like a silvery beacon. Several shots were fired. Some sparked off the cobblestones, others clinked against brick buildings; not one of those shots came even remotely close to him.

Several gunshots zipped through the air before her. They were close, too close. Another volley sparked in front of her. Andy gasped at the sudden pain that stung her right shoulder, but there was no time to think, much less worry about it.

Coleton dove after Andy, catching her about the waist and plunging her out of the brightly lit alley into the shadows at the far side. He shielded her with his own body, not giving either of them time to rest as he pulled her to the safety of the street.

They rounded the corner, ran down one side, and slipped into the recessed doorway of a tavern. Coleton was right. There were still a great many people out on the streets at this ungodly hour of the night. Couples strolled by, the women keeping a secure arm on less steady gentlemen as they guided them to some discreet location. An occasional drunk staggered out into the street. Music filled the night air from several well-lit locations where a red beacon was continuously lit, signaling the business of the establishment.

Andy was certain she would collapse if he didn't stop. She gasped great gulps of air as he finally ducked across another alley, stopping briefly in front of an ornately decorated place with etched-glass windows and red velvet portières with a name emblazoned in foot-high gold letters proclaiming it to be Belle's Place. Several carriages and closed coaches were tied out front, the drivers dozing in their seats.

Coleton jerked open the door to one coach and shoved Andy inside. Then he roughly awakened the driver and quickly gave him instructions. He vaulted inside, slamming the door behind him. Without a word, he leaned across the inside of the coach, jerking down the window shades. As the coach lunged into motion he lit the one lantern inside.

"Damn!" Coleton moved across the coach, jerking the green dressing gown aside. Good God! She'd been shot. For a fragment of a moment, he was taken back to another time and place. Images flashed through his frozen thoughts as he stared down at the stark contrast of crimson blood against pale skin.

For a brief moment a feeling of overwhelming helplessness twisted deep inside him. That time before, it was exactly like this . . . and he'd lost her . . .

Dear God, she'd been shot . . . her blood was running through his fingers . . . he couldn't stop it! Dear God! He couldn't stop it!

With sheer force of will he pushed the painful memories back. Slowly, he brought back the control. Only his voice betrayed any emotion. It was deep and husky, and broke softly.

"You're bleeding." His fingers closed around her arm with surprising tenderness.

Alarmed at his sudden closeness, it was only then that Andy looked down at the blood trickling down her shoulder. It was as if all energy seemed to drain out of her, and she felt the pain that pulsed through her skin. Her eyes widened at the sight of the creased flesh. She'd seen gunshot wounds before, at the hospital during the war. But it was something entirely different to see her own skin raw and bleeding.

She swallowed back the wave of faintness, jerking her arm from his grasp.

"It'll be all right. It's just a scratch." She scooted as far away from Coleton James as possible. She didn't want his help or concern. Undoubtedly the only thing he was truly worried about was his damned information!

Andy seized the hem of the dressing gown and tore off a strip of green satin. She felt that contemplative gaze on her and looked up.

For a fleeting moment she saw something behind that wall of indifference that was always so perfectly in place.

She saw pain so deep and anguished that it tore apart all her tightly controlled anger of this man. And then it was gone, the emotions deliberately hidden away behind that careful facade.

He simply stared at her for several long moments, as if he were trying to find an answer to something. Then his gaze slowly wandered the length of her scantily clad body. Andy grabbed the remnants of the dressing gown about her, struggling to tie the bandage with her left hand. She wasn't doing a very good job of it.

Coleton grabbed the satin bandage and gently seized her arm. "Do you know what you're doing?"

"I can manage very well, thank you," she replied tartly, trying to jerk her arm away and wincing at the pain it caused.

"I can see that," he remarked tightly as he applied light pressure to the wound, expertly wrapping the bandage around her upper arm, crossing it, and tying it over her shoulder.

"You're very good at that," she remarked with equal venom. His expertise obviously came from being shot at so much.

"When you see a friend with an arm shot off or his guts hanging out from being blasted by a mortar, you learn to improvise, do whatever it takes to save his life." He gave her a long look. "Sometimes that's all that matters in war; that and what's waiting for you back home." Those gray eyes pinned her back, his meaning all too clear. He was speaking of Ombre Rose.

When he spoke of home, his voice had softened, opening up a slight crack in the armor of that cold facade. Just as quickly it closed, shutting her out.

"But that doesn't mean much to Yanks, does it?"

When he released her arm it was as if he couldn't bear the touch of her, as if he were pushing aside something that was loathsome.

Andy swallowed back the stinging comment she would have preferred. This man was far too dangerous to provoke. And so she simply asked, "Where are you taking me?"

Again that long, slow perusal. "I'm taking you somewhere where you'll be safe. Then I have to find someone."

Andy tried to draw a deep breath. It felt as if her heart had lodged in her throat, she could still feel it pounding wildly from their race down that alley. And she felt more than a little shaky from the wound.

She finished tying the bandage. "I told you everything I know. I demand that you allow me to return to my friend's home immediately." The minute she said it, Andy realized just how ridiculous that sounded. She was in no position to demand anything. Still, she lifted her chin slightly.

Dear God, she was tired. And she felt battered and bruised. By now, everyone at Melanie's house would know about her disappearance and would be frantic with worry. How was she ever going to explain any of this, beginning with Louis XIV in the gardens at the Château Montfort and that damned message Coleton James was so absolutely certain meant something? She rubbed her temple, feeling the first twinges of a headache. She looked up at him. He was still staring at her in that strange way.

"As much as I would like to do just that, I can't," he informed her coldly.

"What do you mean, you can't? It's really very simple. You just direct the driver to take me home. Or is it that you don't believe me about the message?"

Again that long perusal. Of course that was it. Andy collapsed against the back of the seat, closing her eyes as exhaustion seeped into every part of her body. "It's what Louis told me. That's all I know. I don't know who 'her ladyship' is!"

For several long moments, as the coach jostled through the streets, rounded several corners, and clattered over a wooden bridge, there was only silence between them.

She slowly opened her eyes to find him watching her with those unreadable gray eyes. "You still don't believe me, do you?"

"At the moment it doesn't matter what I believe. Those men who chased us believe you know a great deal."

"What are you talking about? I don't know any of them."

"Perhaps not," Coleton allowed. "But they know you, and they were trying to kill you."

"That's ridiculous." Her voice was shaky. "They were shooting at both of us. You're the one who's running from someone," she rationalized, her confused thoughts refusing to accept what he was saying and what she knew in her heart to be true.

"Maybe, but those shots were meant for you." He watched her evenly. "If they'd wanted to kill me, they had plenty of opportunity and you know it."

Andy drew in a deep breath, fighting to keep herself from going over the edge. What she wanted right now was to give in to the hysteria, to just let herself go and have a good screaming fit and then a good long cry. But if she did give in to that urge she wasn't at all certain she could stop . . . and then there was Coleton James.

She'd rather run stark naked through the streets of New Orleans before she'd let him see how all this was affecting her. She wasn't about to give him the satisfaction of seeing her break down in tears. And then there was the nagging thought that he was absolutely right about all of this.

Someone trying to kill her? She wanted to deny it, but the pain that throbbed through her arm said something entirely different. She knew beyond a doubt those men had clear aim at both of them as they crossed the alley. But only one of them had been shot.

Damn! She hated to admit he was right, about anything. Double damn!

Coleton watched her for any signs of unusual weakness, but all he saw was fatigue and a grim acceptance of at least part of what he was saying. He felt a kindling of respect for her. She'd been through a lot this evening and hadn't cried, fainted, or complained.

"You can't go back to your friends, Amanda. I'm taking you to someone who'll take care of that arm and keep you safe." *And out of my way,* he thought to himself.

It would be very easy. If she was telling the truth about the message, with those men after her there was really only one place she would be safe. And if she wasn't telling the truth, it was still the best place for her—in the hands of the man who'd gotten him into this in the first place.

There it was again, that faint tingling of heat that rippled over her aching skin like a soothing balm at the way he said her name. It was like a caress of the body as well as the soul. And at that precise moment, she needed it badly, but didn't believe Coleton James was capable of it. In the past, he'd proven just what a bastard he could be. She didn't trust anything about him.

"Why should you care what happens to me now that you have the information you want?"

His gray eyes narrowed to dangerous slits as he watched her through the dim light of the coach.

"Contrary to what you want to believe, Amanda, I don't want you dead. I simply want you gone from Ombre Rose."

"And you've done everything to make certain of that, haven't you!" she choked out, pain and fatigue goading her emotions.

"Yes, everything," he admitted without the least attempt at a lie.

"Then how do I know those men weren't hired by you?"

When Andy allowed herself to think back on those frantic minutes in the alley, she remembered with sickening reality the fear as the bullets whizzed past her head or skittered along the cobbled stones only inches from her feet. Someone had wanted her dead, wanted it badly, and very nearly succeeded. Was it Coleton James?

"If I wanted you dead, dear Amanda, I would have

done it long ago. I've had plenty of opportunities," he replied coldly.

"Oh, God," she whispered brokenly, knowing he was right and hating it. It was true. If he'd wanted her dead, she would be. Her voice was hardly more than a whisper.

"What happens now?"

"Get dressed. You're too much of a target running around in that satin underwear, although the view is very tempting."

He sat back, a faint smile curving his sensual lips. It was the first he'd smiled at her all evening and it warmed her straight down inside in spite of the way she felt about him.

Andy slipped farther back into the shadows of the coach, drawing the dressing gown with her. She started to turn down the lantern for more privacy while she changed into the borrowed pants and shirt, and then thought better of it. Coleton James was far too familiar with darkness. She left the lantern lit so she could keep an eye on him, using the dressing gown as a shield.

"Then we're going to see a friend."

Once more, the way he said the word made a shiver of apprehension slip across her skin. A man as dangerous as Coleton James would only have dangerous friends, she was certain of it. She was equally certain that everyone else was considered an enemy. She had no doubts which he considered her to be.

Andy clumsily buttoned the shirt and tucked it inside the pants. She threaded a band of green satin through the belt loops as the coach jolted to a stop. Without waiting for the driver, Coleton sprang out the door and pulled her after him.

She caught a brief glimpse of the gold letters in the sign over those elaborate doors before she was pulled through the ornate lobby. He'd taken her to the Hotel Carillon.

Chapter Sixteen

Andy stared about her as they entered the hotel. After Valentine's and that wild chase through a part of town that obviously enjoyed a lurid reputation, she was stunned at the subtle elegance of richly understated carpets, soft woods, lush ferns, and gleaming brass.

The Carillon was as fine as any hotel in New York, and if she hadn't felt as if she were about to collapse any minute from complete exhaustion, Andy would have been embarrassed at her disheveled appearance and Coleton's cast-off clothes. But at the moment it was about all she could manage just to stay on her feet, bare as they were.

She slumped wearily into a loveseat tucked behind a large potted fern and buried her face in her hands. God only knew what time it was. She felt as if she hadn't slept in days, and found it hard to believe she had been at the Montfort masquerade ball only a few hours earlier.

Coleton immediately went to the front desk. There was no one about, so he rang the service bell. When there was no response, he rounded the elegant, carved mahogany front desk and went into the office, discreetly hidden behind panels of frosted glass. He immediately found the night clerk.

"I'm sorry . . . sir," the deep nasal twang immediately revealed the clerk was a northerner, "we have no rooms available."

He gave Coleton a narrow look down the length of his thin nose, one eyebrow cocked with self-important authority. He was a long man, with long hands, long fingers, and a long stare. His expression was cold, closed. It was obvious he took one look at the gray military shirt and made an accurate but hasty assumption.

Coleton leaned across the desk. He'd been shot at, chased, and followed one impossible lead after another the last few days. He was dead tired and the last thing he wanted was some fool reciting some phrase obviously prepared for undesirable clientele. To top it off the man was a Yank.

He reached over the desk, grabbed the man by his silk cravat and hauled him across the desk in little more effort than it would have taken to sign the guest register. At the same time he eased his revolver from the holster.

"Now listen, and listen very carefully. I want to see Duvalier and I want to see him now." He brought the end of the barrel of the revolver up beside the man's right eye so that it was within full, close view.

"Duvalier?" The clerk's voice broke as his eyes rolled nervously and focused on the revolver. "I don't think—"

He was cut off as Coleton pressed it against the man's right temple. "I don't want you to think. I want a room and then I want Duvalier!" His voice hissed deadly as he continued. "Do not contact anyone else. Do not call the authorities. If you do, you're a dead man. Is that clear?"

The clerk was white as a sheet. Eyes closed, sweating profusely, he swallowed hard and nodded. "Perfectly . . . clear."

"Good!" Coleton thrust the clerk away from him. "Now, I want a room, hot water, fresh linens, and food. Steak rare, potatoes, peach pie, and a bottle of whiskey. And don't send someone to tell me you can't find any of it. Is that clear?"

"Yes-s- . . ." the man stuttered, wiping the beads of

301

perspiration off his forehead.

"Yes, what?" Coleton demanded.

The man looked at him incredulously and then his eyes widened in comprehension. "Yes . . . sir," he responded, his frightened gaze trained on the revolver in Coleton's hand.

"And I'll need the key for that room," Coleton reminded him, impatience edging his words.

"Yes sir. Number two-fourteen, one of our finest suites. And everything you've requested will be sent up immediately."

Coleton gave him a long, hard look before slipping the revolver back into the holster. "You do good work, boy." He smiled that deadly smile once more.

"Amanda . . ." He nudged her gently. Her head jerked up, soft eyes registering sleepy confusion.

"I got us a room." That got exactly the response he thought it would. Her blue eyes widened, the dark bands thickening with anger.

"I will not . . ."

He was careful to take her by the left arm and pulled her out of the loveseat.

"I'm not going to argue with you. We both need a few hours' sleep." And with that he pulled her up the stairs to the second-floor suite of rooms.

If she wasn't so tired, Andy might have admired the room. As it was, she simply slumped onto the settee, thinking she could make a very nice bed of that. She heard voices, bits of brief conversation, and was vaguely aware someone moved about the room. She opened her eyes just as the uniformed hotel attendant whisked past her, nodded to Coleton, and closed the door behind him. She might have been interested to know of their brief exchange if her weary gaze hadn't fastened on the tub in the adjoining room.

"A bath," she whispered with slightly more enthusiasm than anyone should have who had been awake practically the entire night. That is of course, unless one had been dragged through every back alley, whorehouse, and street in New Orleans! At that moment she would have killed anyone who tried to stand between her and that tub. She didn't even care if she drowned from exhaustion just so long as she made it to the tub.

"Go right ahead," Coleton remarked with wry amusement as he saw the direction of her gaze. "I can wait my turn." His only answer was the slamming of the door to the bathing chamber. No thank you's, no gratitude, no acknowledgment whatsoever.

"You're welcome," he whispered to no one but himself, and then turned to the door of the suite. This would be a good time to send off that telegram he'd been considering. Phoenix had promised him all the help and support he needed to find whoever was impersonating the Gray Fox.

He'd made a deal with Phoenix, but he didn't trust him. After all, he was a Yank, and just a little less than five months ago, he was killing Yankees. Since it seemed finding Gray Fox was turning out to be just a little more difficult than he originally bargained for, he wanted to call in some help of his own.

Given the telegram went out first thing in the morning, Rafe Kelly could be back in New Orleans in just a few days if he came by way of the gulf. Right now, Rafe was the only person he trusted.

Coleton slipped out the door, locked it so that Miss Amanda Spenser couldn't just walk out of the hotel, and went downstairs to the front desk. He wanted to make arrangements for that telegram and he wanted to see Duvalier—now.

Andy waited until she heard the click of the latch at the door to the outside room. She opened the door and quickly crossed the room, silently damning Coleton James as she tried the latch. No good there, she thought turning back into the room.

A quick survey of the windows that opened out onto the street convinced her she didn't want to try that escape. It was a clear drop to the street below with nothing to break her fall except the cobbled street. It wasn't very promising. She paced the room.

Again and again her weary gaze came back to that bathtub. She could stay out here until he got back or she could be enjoying a much needed bath. Andy was nothing if not practical. In the end, practicality won out.

She tried the door one more time just to make certain it was locked, then returned to the bathing room. At the turn of a brass lever, hot water hissed through the pipes and splashed into the porcelain, claw-foot tub.

Thank God for modern conveniences, she thought with a luxuriant sigh as she trailed her hand through the water to test the temperature. She'd fully prepared herself for whatever was offered, so long as it was wet and soap went along with it, and was pleased to see there were several fragrances of soap. It was absolutely amazing what small luxuries could be had now that the war was ended and one had enough money. She wondered if Coleton James had enough. At Lacey's they'd been lucky to have strong lye soap. It took off the dirt and a fair amount of skin with it. The wife of one of the field hands made lye soap at Ombre Rose, but when Angeline came, she taught the woman how to make soap from a special blend of ash and animal fats that was boiled, mixed, drained off, and boiled again over a period of several days, producing finer soap that was blended with camomile and rose scent. It was a luxury compared to the lye soap, and she'd used it sparingly. Now her eyes gleamed with delight as she looked at the selection available.

There were small cakes of soap in three different fragrances of lemon, rose, and lilac. There were glass bottles with a delicate fragrant liquid that looked like oil. She poured a liberal amount into the bathwater.

"That should cost you a small fortune, Coleton James," she murmured, and smiled in spite of the fatigue that pulled at her, adding more. It was amazing what a small dose of revenge could do for sagging spirits.

The liquid burst into bubbles as water poured from the spout, creating a tub of fragrant, foaming liquid. Andy quickly began unbuttoning the shirt, then stopped. She checked the door; no lock.

"Well, there's nothing to be done for that," she sighed, realizing this certainly wasn't the time to start worrying about the threat of lost virtue.

"A little late for that," she whispered shakily to herself as she finished undressing and coiled her hair on top of her head. She stepped into the tub, slipped into the frothy, fragrant water, and immediately thought she would just as soon stay here forever. It was wonderful.

Coleton slipped back into the room. He'd been gone almost an hour. The telegram would go out in the morning to Rafe, and he'd met with Duvalier. He wanted to see Phoenix as soon as possible.

He poured himself a cognac and quickly downed it. Christ, he thought. It'd been years since he'd enjoyed such fine cognac.

He poured another as he surveyed the room and glanced to the door closing off the bathing chamber. She'd been in there almost an hour and would probably stay in there to spite him until she looked like a piece of shriveled fruit. Amanda Spenser was a complication he hadn't counted on. But when Phoenix got here . . . Coleton frowned. There were no sounds coming from behind the door. There was nothing but silence. He knew she was tired and she might have had some shock from that shoulder wound. What if . . .

Eyes closed, bubbles tickling at her chin, Andy leaned her head back against the rim of the tub. It was so peaceful and quiet, she could almost fall asleep. The thought occurred to her it was almost too quiet. A faint breath of cool air brushed across her shoulders.

Andy slowly opened one eye. Then both flashed open, wide pools of vivid blue anger.

"Don't you ever knock?" She sank lower into the foaming bathwater, using the blanket of bubbles for a shield. Coleton James stood, leaning against the doorway, a wry smile easing faint lines from the corners of his eyes and mouth, making him look maddeningly handsome in that pale-gray shirt.

"Do you always go sneaking about where you're not wanted?" she muttered. Beneath the water she snuggled her knees to her chest and wrapped her arms about them. He'd come in so quietly, she hadn't even heard him.

"I didn't hear anything, and I thought . . ." It was a weak excuse and they both knew it.

"That I might have escaped?" she finished for him. "I tried. The door was locked. Unfortunately *this* one doesn't lock." Andy glared at him. "I thought all southern men were supposed to be gentlemen."

"Just like we're all deplorable slave owners who beat our men, rape their women, and sell off their mixed-blood children?" he accused, watching her evenly. Her eyes darkened. He'd struck home. Everyone was entitled to their opinion, but he just didn't like being labeled with a bad lot. "I do have my moments." He held out the tumbler of dark amber liquid.

"What is it?"

"The finest French cognac. That shoulder must hurt a little. It'll help deaden the pain."

Andy's eyes narrowed suspiciously. "Why should you care?"

Coleton tried not to think about how beautiful she was. "Let's just leave it that I feel responsible."

"And coming from someone who threatened to kill me

306

himself no less than three times, that is rather remarkable. But you really mustn't concern yourself. It takes more than a little scratch . . ." she bit off scathingly, huddled beneath her bubbly shroud.

"I suppose that means you don't want this," he responded with maddening softness that had the effect of grating on her nerves. How like him to be kind and considerate just when she was getting used to his threats.

"That is a pity. It's really very good cognac." He shrugged and started to drink it down.

She stopped him, her eyes narrowing. He was goading her, thinking her some simpering, weak-kneed, mealy-mouthed, helpless female. But what if he'd put something in the drink?

She immediately realized how ridiculous that was. As he'd said earlier, if he wanted her dead . . .

She took the tumbler and sipped slowly. Her brother let her sip from his glass occasionally when she was younger, so the taste of it wasn't offensive. Actually the cognac was deceptively smooth, warming a path all the way down her throat. It did seem to ease the ache in her shoulder, but Andy would rather die than admit Coleton James was right about that. Still, she smiled faintly as the heat slipped down to her toes.

Coleton gestured to the water. "Since you insist on sharing my bath, is any of that water still warm."

"Your bath!?" she sputtered, a large swallow of cognac going down too quickly. Her eyes watered, and it was several seconds before she could draw a breath. She glared up at him. "You did say I could use it first! Surely a 'southern gentleman' can be taken at his word," she added sarcastically.

"True, but I didn't mean all night." He leaned forward, bracing his weight on his hands at the edge of the tub.

Andy blinked, trying to focus the room around her as a soft, languorous glow spread into her fingertips and across her cheeks. She took a deep, steadying breath.

"If you'll just give me a minute, I'll get out," she suggested in a voice that was a little too breathless. Then she hiccuped. Embarrassment flamed across her cheeks.

God's nightgown! The man would think she was inebriated after two sips of cognac!

Coleton held the tumbler to her lips. "You'd better have another swallow. It will get rid of those hiccups."

Andy gave him a suspicious look, fairly certain this was probably something else she couldn't trust about him. "I sincerely doubt that."

"But it's true — an old southern remedy," he teased thinking that the more he poured down her, the easier it would be to leave her later, without protest or confrontation. She'd be asleep for hours. Hopefully, by the time she awakened, he would have Gray Fox exposed and Ombre Rose would be his. And after that, he tried to convince himself, he didn't care what happened to Amanda Spenser.

Andy didn't care whose remedy it was. At the moment she was too angry to care. She seized the glass. Fixing Coleton James with a level glare, she drank most of the cognac in one long swallow. She gasped and coughed, cursing him all the more for her embarrassment.

Coleton took the tumbler and set it aside, smothering back a quirk of a smile at her little show of bravado.

"You've had long enough for your bath, Amanda," he announced as he unbuttoned the faded gray military shirt.

Andy's eyes widened. "What are you doing?"

"Unless you want to share my bath, I suggest you get out now," he replied evenly, meaning every word. He dropped the shirt to the floor and reached for the belt buckle at his pants.

"Don't do that!" she gasped, holding out a hand to try to stop him.

Coleton looked up. "Do what?"

"You can't get undressed!"

"I thought that's what people usually do when they're about to take a bath."

"Well of course they do . . ."

"Good." And he promptly slipped the belt from about his waist and unfastened the top button.

Andy shot up out of the water, determined to get out of the tub, then sank back under the layer of bubbles on the surface of the water just as quickly.

Surely he didn't really expect her to get out of the water with him standing right there!

Her eyes narrowed. The swine! Of course he expected it. He'd deliberately placed himself between her and the towel on the hook at the wall.

"I see you changed your mind." A dangerous grin curved his mustache. "You surprise me, Amanda. I would have thought that a young lady with your Yankee sensibility wouldn't be caught dead in a man's bath. Particularly a Reb's bath."

"I did not change my mind! I simply can't get out with you standing there," Andy protested. "The least you can do is . . ."

"What, Amanda?" he asked just a little wickedly.

Color flooded Andy's cheeks. She wanted to say the very least he could do as a *gentleman* was turn around and allow her some measure of privacy in getting out. But as he'd already proven on several occasions, he was certainly no gentleman.

But surely he wouldn't really undress completely! Andy's thoughts focused back on those brief, terrifying moments at Valentine's when he'd done exactly that without the least hesitation. She angled her jaw a notch higher, trying for cool detachment.

"I refuse to sit here while you undress! I . . . I . . ."

Coleton unfastened the last button, looking up at her briefly, as if he couldn't care less what she did. "Then I suggest you get out." He dropped his pants and stepped out of them.

"Damn you . . . !" Andy choked with all the angry indignation she could muster under the circumstances, her eyes widening at the sight of his naked body.

He turned and slowly came toward her in a stalking movement. Andy concentrated on those eyes—anything else was far too dangerous.

"You wouldn't dare," she breathed out slowly, seething with anger.

"Oh, but I would, Amanda. You've had more than enough time for your bath. Now I want one. Besides . . ." he fastened those cool gray eyes on her, "I can't imagine that you're this modest about a simple bath. After all, we have made love. It isn't as if we're strangers."

"Made love!" She was aghast. "I would hardly call what happened, making love," she choked out in shocked dismay, stunned she could even get the words out.

"It was an accident; and I prefer not to think about it. And if you were any kind of gentleman, you wouldn't remind me of it." There they were again, tripping over her expectations about the qualities of his character when they both knew full well he had none.

Her eyes remained fastened on his, widening as he approached the tub in slow, even strides. He was going to do it! She knew it and lunged out of the water, grabbing for the edge of the tub. Being seen naked was small consequence to staying in that tub. Especially when the look in his eyes took on that steely, dangerous glint.

She was about to step out as he stepped in. And she was so intent on doing it quickly, she didn't pay much attention to what she was doing. Her hand missed the edge of the tub as her foot slipped on the slick bottom.

Andy gasped as she went down, water sloshing over the edge, bubbles stinging in her eyes. She sputtered and coughed, trying to sit up as she pulled her wet hair out of her eyes. When she was finally able to pull the sodden mass aside, she glared at him, seated opposite her in the tub, his long legs tangled with hers.

"You did that deliberately!" she choked with humiliation and rising anger.

"If I'd done it deliberately Amanda, I wouldn't have splashed so much water. You've spilled half of it."

"It's just what you deserve for being so . . . so . . ."

"Yes?"

She slapped the water in frustration, exposing a great deal of glistening skin in the process.

"If you'd just waited this would never have happened. Now, let me up!" She struggled to get out of the water, not caring at that moment what he saw. But her legs were hopelessly pinned beneath his stronger ones and she slumped back against the end of the tub, almost going under again. She glared at him with all the cool Yankee aloofness she could muster under the circumstances.

"Please let me up," she insisted with tight-lipped fury.

"Of course. Anything to oblige, Miss Spenser."

He said it with such maddening arrogance that she wanted to take the soap and rub it in his eyes. He shifted his right leg, casually resting it across hers.

"If we're to do this, I suggest you move your foot."

She glared at him as his fingers closed over her ankle, pinned alongside his very naked thigh. Thank God those bubbles obscured just about everything from view. She sank just a little lower beneath the surface. He flashed that maddening grin as he gently shifted her foot. She suspected he was enjoying this very much and jerked back, sending another wave of water over the side. "I can move my own foot!" she informed him with equal coolness. And she did, only to have it once more seized by those strong fingers bruising her flesh.

Her infuriated gaze came up to meet his. Anger was running an equal race with humiliation. She was caught. It was as simple as that. She dare not stay in that tub and she couldn't leave, at least not without suffering the worst embarrassment either way. And there was the matter of her ankle, firmly held in that viselike grasp.

"Not *that* direction!" Coleton warned as he caught her foot and removed it from a very vital area between his legs. He bent his knee, guided her foot underneath, and held it gently aloft.

"This direction." He teased her to complete mortification, still holding on to her ankle.

"Please let go of my foot," she insisted tightly from between thinned lips, trying to pull her knee back.

Coleton cradled her left foot in the palm of his left hand, holding it prisoner. With his right, he gently kneaded the small, high arch.

"This foot?" He smiled in spite of himself, imagining how all this must look. Actually it was very funny when he thought of it. They were enemies. He'd fought Yanks on more battlefields than he wanted to remember and killed a good many as well. Four years of war had blurred right and wrong into a battle just to survive and go home. But the Yanks wouldn't even allow him that. They'd taken his home and his land when it was all that was left that mattered. And this very lovely young lady represented everything he'd fought against those four years.

Amanda Spenser was everything he believed a Yank to be, and more. She was cool, outspoken, and hardminded. She'd bedeviled him for weeks with all her highflung plans for Ombre Rose, and always with that damn practicality behind it all. And Lord, she was stubborn. His Irish ancestors paled in comparison to this little Yankee carpetbagger. The only thing he couldn't figure out was why. Why was she so damned determined to have Ombre Rose?

Not that it mattered now. As soon as he exposed the impersonator of Gray Fox, Ombre Rose would be his. What would Amanda Spenser's reaction be to that? Much the same as now, he suspected, only more so.

He smiled again in spite of himself. He'd shared his

bath with a woman before, but never one quite so reluctant.

He had little doubt what she would do if the tub wasn't so slippery. And he to admit that Amanda Spenser did provide a very fascinating sight with nothing but water glistening over her pale body. He liked the slick contact of her slender legs against his. It recalled those moments they'd shared in the bed at Valentine's, and before, in the gazebo. Only now he wasn't holding a gun on her. If Amanda Spenser were anyone else . . .

"My foot, please!" she reminded him, trying to jerk it out of his grasp. "And please stop that!" Andy ordered when he only tightened his grasp.

"Do you mean this foot?" he asked with maddening calm that had the effect of setting her nerves on edge.

Andy stared as he lifted her other foot and slowly began massaging it. Her knee spasmed back at the delightful sensations his strong fingers sent through her skin and muscles. He stroked up her ankle, along her calf. Andy swallowed slowly.

"If you'll simply release me, I'm certain you'll enjoy your bath much more without me."

Coleton stroked her with his thumb, making small, circling motions as he gently kneaded the muscles in her leg.

"You must learn to relax, Amanda."

"I am relaxed, or at least I *was*," she remarked pointedly, and more than just a little breathless. It was terribly warm in the small room and his fingers were having a terrible effect on her concentration—or was it all the cognac she'd very unwisely consumed?

"Before I came in here?" he suggested with a faint smile as he stroked the back of her knee. She tried to kick out at him, simply getting more water in her hair and eyes.

"Yes," she replied slowly, his fingers massaging her muscles to jelly. Her legs felt heavy and everything about

313

the room had taken on a soft glow.

"Please!" Her throat was dry and there was a faint buzzing somewhere very far away. She couldn't tell where it was coming from.

The way she said it, soft and faintly husky, sent desire spiraling through him in spite of all his iron-willed determination. "Please what, Amanda? Surrender?"

She was stunned by the harshness in his voice. Surrender? What the devil was he talking about? She simply wanted him to release her.

"No, I didn't mean that at all . . . I . . ."

"I think surrender is the right word, Amanda."

His voice was lower, faintly threatening. His eyes narrowed as his fingers bruised into her skin. "A Yank would want that—total and unconditional surrender. Isn't that right, Amanda?"

Andy shivered. There was something behind his words she didn't understand. He was the one who'd burst in here and simply invited himself in. He was the invader for God's sake! And *he* was talking about surrender!? She shook her head as she tried to jerk her foot free. She didn't understand what was going on; she simply wanted to get away from Coleton James.

"Isn't that right?" His words hissed through the warm, damp air in the small room.

"I . . . don't . . . know," she answered uncertainly.

"Don't know! Isn't that unusual, for you, Amanda Spenser, or for any Yank!" He spat the word out as if the very sound of it was loathesome.

She whimpered softly as his fingers closed viselike around the vulnerable arch of her foot.

He leaned toward her, tucking her foot against his chest. "If I refused to surrender to General Grant and the entire Union Army, what makes you think I'll surrender now?"

"I don't think you'll surrender," she whispered with a soft catch in her voice, that contact far too intimate, far

314

too unsettling. Then her gaze came up to meet his evenly. "There's too much hatred in you to ever surrender to anyone."

It was a battle of wills, and Andy already knew that where Coleton James was concerned, she had none of her own. Her lower lip trembled faintly, but she'd be damned if she'd let on how he was hurting her. It's what he wanted; she could see it in his eyes. He'd undoubtedly take some perverse satisfaction in knowing he'd caused her pain.

Coleton saw the subtle darkening in her blue eyes. He knew he was hurting her and knew just as well he could break every bone in her foot and she'd never cry out. There was that kind of strength in her. The catch in her voice came out more as a soft sob, but it was all she'd give him. There was too much pride and stubbornness in her.

"I surrendered only once, Amanda. And vowed it would never happen again."

Instinctively she knew it had nothing to do with the war. "I'm not asking you to surrender anything," she whispered softly, her blue eyes like deep, dark pools.

"But I lose if I surrender."

"You lose nothing, because you have nothing."

"Nothing?"

He slowly bent her leg, his hand sliding up her thigh. With his other hand, he reached up to her face, stroking droplets of water from her cheek. The anger was gone now, replaced by something equally dangerous. The question filled the air about them with a thousand answers.

His fingers fanned across her jaw, his thumb tilting her small chin. He stared down into the languid depths of liquid blue eyes, losing himself to that intense color that seemed to wrap around him. He wanted to hurt her for the feelings she stirred in him.

"Please don't!" There was a hint of desperation as her

lashes fluttered uncertainly. Her hands came up to his hard-muscled shoulders to push him away. Instead, they slipped over slick bronzed skin, igniting fire.

"Don't what?" Drawn by those eyes, Coleton brought his other hand up to cup her face.

"Don't. Stop," she breathed, panic taking hold.

"Don't stop?" Coleton asked as he slowly took a droplet of water from her lower lip with his tongue.

Andy shivered at his touch, so brief and yet so intense. Her eyelids fluttered downward as she felt herself slipping into a deep languid pool of sensation. She should fight him, she wanted to fight him. She wanted to stop him. But she hadn't the strength or the will. Not when he was touching her like this.

"No! I mean . . . *don't!*" she insisted, and then in a less certain whisper as his mouth stroked hers, "don't . . . stop." Desire shimmered through her. Andy's eyes closed as she tasted the sweet heat of his breath, the mixture of man, night air, and danger, far more intoxicating than any drink. God help her, what was happening?

Water and fragrant oil coated them both, making skin slick against skin. His fingers slipped over her, his touch a wild energy.

"Oh, God," she breathed, taking the heat of his breath for her own, "please don't stop." It was an agonizing plea that came from some secret place inside her.

That faint buzzing came from the darkness behind her lids. It was familiar and more than a little frightening. It was pulling at her.

It had come to her before—at Ombre Rose with this man. She didn't understand what it meant any more now than she had before. All she knew was that she couldn't stop it, didn't want to stop it, because it meant she was going away to some other place, some other memory so elusive that it was found only in these moments. And the feelings, sensations, and emotions were so intense she wanted to hold on to them forever. Why or how no longer matter. She knew simply that it would happen again and she wanted it to.

Dear God, Coleton thought, this was madness. And like madness, it was powerful, frightening, and uncontrollable. And because it was, he simply let it happen.

The moment his mouth slipped over hers, she went breathlessly still. He heard her sharp intake of breath, felt surprise at the yielding softness of her lips. With a hoarsely whispered curse, his right hand slipped up the curve of her water-slicked thigh, his thumb tracing over the bone at her hip to the indentation at her waist. His long fingers broke the surface of the water, fanning over the slick fullness of her left breast and he was lost.

Coleton could feel the shock and desire trembling through her. His own body went rigid with the sensation that poured through him as he tasted the parted softness of her mouth, nibbled at the fullness of her lower lip, then returned to taste her fully again. His fingers gently caressed her breast as it filled his hand, soft as water, hot as fire. He stroked his thumb back and forth over the sensitized nipple until it hardened in answer.

Her lungs felt trapped against her ribs. One moment Andy couldn't breathe, the next, she doubted she would ever need to again. It seemed all the bones in her body had melted into the water that surrounded them. The buzzing that had begun faintly had now become a roar in her ears. Behind her eyes was a rush of vivid, brilliant colors and images, like fragments of pictures all spinning at her. They were bits and pieces of some larger picture she couldn't see, much less understand. All she understood was the wild, chaotic sensations that tore through her every time Coleton's hands moved over her body. She should stop him . . . she could never stop him.

She heard a soft, sweet moan and never knew it was her own. Her hands slipped up his arm, her fingers tingling over the hardness of muscles, remembering, remembering . . .

She traced the sharpness of collarbone, her hands slipping behind his neck to wrap around the corded muscles. She slowly opened her eyes, wanting, needing, to see his face. He was all gold and bronze, sunlight and warm earth, mixed with the misty gray of the bayou in those eyes. Those eyes; dearly familiar, and now completely unguarded, the shield of indifference stripped away by naked desire.

"Coleton." She whispered his name, her voice coming both from some long-ago moment and now. It was dear to her and new, so fragile in her imagination she shivered with something very near fear at the truth that slipped toward her from the shadows of her mind.

Her fingers tangled in the shaggy mane of his soft brown hair, remembering how it turned to gold in summer sun.

Andy's lips parted, insistently drawing his tongue inside, the taste sharp, the need sharper. She needed more, so much more.

Was she breathing? She hardly knew.

Was she alive? She had to be, or perhaps she'd slipped into someplace before life, before this moment, into the past, back, back . . .

She could smell him; his scent now mingled with hers in the fragrant water. Her heart began to thunder wildly, feeling as if it would burst beneath her breast within his hand. There was more, instinctively she knew it, and she wanted to find it.

Coleton felt her small teeth nip at his lower lip and fire centered low in his body. With a desperation he hardly understood, he pulled her against him and ravaged her mouth even as it opened beneath his. He'd hated her, raged against her, wanted revenge for everything the North had robbed him of. In that moment, he was more her prisoner than she his. He was drowning in pure sensation and knew it. He knew as well there was no stopping it. He wanted her now—he'd wanted her from the very beginning.

His hand moved down from her breast to the flat plane of her stomach, kneading the pliant muscles that seemed to leap at his touch. All caution, all reason spun out of control.

The water was like a silken womb, closing them together as his hand slipped lower still, finding the softness that waited for him. As his mouth made love to hers, he parted her, shuddering at the wet heat that enveloped him.

This was some new part of loving and Andy arched against his hand, her breath coming in deep, sharp gasps.

"Cole!" she whispered, unaware she'd used that shortened, endearing name. And then her eyelashes swept up, her gaze meeting those startled gray eyes.

The words were only half formed in her imagination, but the truth was there, shimmering between them like the desire that was hot, wild, and undeniable.

Reason told him it was wrong, more wrong than anything he'd ever done in his entire life. Of all the women he'd known, why should the one he desired be her? There were no answers except for the desire that rocked through him. It was bitter betrayal and he was powerless to stop it.

In one fluid motion, Coleton slipped his arm about her waist and locked her to him. He could feel her firm, high breasts crushed against the wall of his chest and he groaned, breathing her in. He stood, taking her with him, their slick bodies sliding together, her slender thighs slipping between his.

He wanted to hate her, and perhaps part of him did, for what she was slowly doing to him. He wanted to take her to the brink of absolute passion and then coolly leave her, but even as he thought it, he knew he couldn't

319

do it. He'd known it in the gazebo. He knew it when he kissed her in the gardens at the Chateau Montfort, and he knew it now . . .

Earlier that night at Valentine's had been prelude to something that had to be fulfilled. He tasted the sweet desire that heated through her and knew that moment was now.

He would take tonight, and in the taking fulfill some small part of the revenge he wanted. And then he would simply leave her with all her Yankee treachery and pride.

There was no care for the rich, thick carpeting scattered with wet footprints as he lifted her glistening body from the tub. Her arms were twined about his neck, her cheek against his shoulder as she drank the drops of water that beaded his neck and chest.

The urgency that coursed through them both made the journey to the bed perilous and so Coleton simply lowered her to that thick carpeting, her damp hair tumbling about her shoulders like molten gold.

One heavily muscled leg skewered between hers, tenderly trapping her. Eyes closed, moving with sheer sensation, her legs caressed his, luxuriating in the coarse hair that roughed her thighs. His hands braceleted hers, slowly drawing them over her head. When his head lowered, his mouth moved deliberately away from hers, finding the exquisite softness beneath her left ear.

Her hair smelled of damp night air and soft flowers, Coleton discovered as he buried his face in it. Earthy, primal, alluring. Beneath him, her body was taut as a young sapling one moment, melting against him like warmed honey the next.

Coleton bit tenderly at the skin below her ear, down her throat, tracing a path to her breast with his tongue.

"I hate you," Andy whispered, as much for what he'd already done as well as what he was now doing.

"Hate me tomorrow," Coleton's voice ached against the

thrusting fullness of that breast, laving the taut nipple with his tongue.

At that first contact, Andy arched convulsively against him, her hips locking against his and she felt his desire pressing hard and hot against her stomach.

Coleton tasted the breath that shuddered through her as he returned to tease the tip of her tongue. He wanted more, so much more . . . needed more. It was the first time in years that he'd given in to the need. He'd thought it dead so long ago. Now it knifed through him, demanding to be fed, new and wild, like the first time. In a way it was surrender.

Andy hadn't known there was so much to feel; not before in the gazebo, when they'd come together in an almost blind, reckless passion that knew no reason or sanity. This was different, far different. He was taking the time to taste and arouse every part of her. And it was as if he knew her; knew every place that ached for the stroke of hand or mouth.

She throbbed with hunger and longing at the scent of him, and she discovered as she traced her tongue along his collarbone the taste of him. And then, far more stirring than his touch, there was the sound of her name murmured thickly against her mouth.

His fingers were strong on her face, tensing, stroking, as if he were trying to commit each feature to memory . . . or remembering. There was the frantic beat of his heart against hers, so that she couldn't know which was which. And there was the maddening heat of those hard, calloused hands caressing her breast, turning the very core of her to liquid.

Passion replaced the languorous heat of desire and she ached with it. Her hands flexed and spasmed, longing to touch him as he was touching her.

She hurt with an overwhelming need that clawed through her, pounding with every beat of her heart until she was certain it would burst from her.

"Cole . . ." she whispered again, as only one had ever whispered it. It was filled with passion, pleading, and an edge of desperation.

He moved slowly with her. Before, he'd made love to her quickly with a sort of madness that seemed to drive them at each other. Now he forced himself to go slowly, to savor every touch, each tremulous sigh that escaped her swollen lips, every stroke of her heated body beneath his. He released her wrists, his hands sliding down her damp body, his mouth following.

Andy twisted beneath the impassioned assault. Every last shred of caution spun away. "I need you," she whispered with a longing that came from her soul. "Love me. Please love me . . . as you once loved me."

He heard, but the words slipped away into the haze of passion to be remembered later.

Her skin was hot and damp wherever Coleton touched. She moved under him, twisting, trembling. He tasted her, all of her. The dark sweetness of her woman's passion filled his mouth, making him think of how it would be when he filled her with his own body.

He breathed in the scent of her skin, damp from the bath and him. No woman since Sunny had ever driven him to madness with desire, simply because no other woman was Sunny. Not until now, this moment. Now the madness spun around him. His thoughts reeled as his senses filled with this woman. It wasn't real. And yet even as he forced it back, there was that aching part of him that wanted to believe.

When his lips came back to hers, Andy tasted the desperation on them. And she understood. Even though every part of him would deny it, his heart could not. Needing to make him believe, she spoke with her heart and her body.

When Coleton slipped inside her, he lost that much more of himself. She surrounded him, enclosed him like a fiery glove.

Andy cried out at the exquisite torture of feeling him move into her, becoming a part of her as he had that night in the gazebo, and as she'd imagined countless times since.

Yes, her anguished thoughts cried out. *Yes,* her heart echoed.

She whispered his name over and over against the fevered column of his throat, loving the sound of it, loving him.

Coleton bent to find her lips, breathing her sigh as he lost a little more of himself to a truth too fantastic to believe. But it was there, just as she was there, her slender body wrapping about his, taking him deeper inside her until they seemed to become one person, one heart, one memory.

Andy arched as he stroked within her. Time and again he took her to the very brink of fulfillment, only to hold her back. She was certain she begged him to stop, just as certain she wanted him never to stop. Each breath seemed her last as it ached in her lungs, and the rush of desire replaced it with a wild exhilaration proving she needed none. If there was a moment between life and death, he took her there, allowing her to dangle precariously before reclaiming her again.

She became a wild thing beneath him. It was a hunger of the senses and could only be sated by this man. His arms trembled about her, his breath came in deep, ragged gasps. His hands buried in her hair, tangling, twisting as his fingers molded about her head.

"Promise me," she whispered against his mouth. "Promise me."

Slowly, those haunted eyes opened, and she knew he understood.

"Sunny?" he whispered brokenly, his voice aching with passion and the need to believe. It was almost like a prayer, disbelieving and yet filled with such desperation.

Tears pooled in Andy's eyes, not from sorrow or regret

but from an ache of longing that had lain sleeping within her so long.

It was madness, but Coleton couldn't stop it. He filled her again and again, trying to drive the truth away. But it was there with every stroke of her body taking his. He knew when it began; heard the sigh become a moan in her throat, felt her body pulse around him as their hands joined, their fingers twining. Her slender body shuddered as she took him deeply, and she gasped, crying out.

Coleton swallowed the cry, following her as he poured himself inside her.

Her body was still sheened with passion as Coleton lifted her and carried her to the bed. His own body was still moist with her sweetness. He laid her down gently, lingering over her, tracing her features, finding no resemblance. All those emotions, the questions and answers were pushed back into that safe little place where he'd locked them away all these years since Sunny.

He stroked her pale-gold hair. It was like silk—lustrous, glistening.

"Dammit!" he cursed softly as desire coursed through him once more at just the sight of her. "You're not Sunny!"

In half-sleep, she turned. Her lips brushed against his roughened fingers and then parted, as if she would say something. It came out as a soft sigh, the crescent of her dark lashes fanned with sleep across her flushed cheeks.

"No surrender," Coleton promised, rubbing the back of his fingers against those faintly bruised lips. He had to touch her, all of her . . . just once more.

He slipped into bed beside her. His long body curved around her slender one, his legs taking possession as they scissored with hers. His fingers closed over the bone at her hip, snuggling her bottom against him. He slipped his right arm about her waist, his fingers curving around the fullness of her left breast.

He buried his face in the soft silk of her hair, inhaling the sweet scent of her body and their lovemaking. He kissed the damp curve of her neck, his lips brushing the small perfect mark at the back of her shoulder.

Chapter Seventeen

Andy stirred slowly. The first streak of morning light filtered into the room. She curled her arm beneath her head, closing her eyes and closing out the light. She wiggled her toes, luxuriating in the smoothness of satin sheets.

Satin sheets!?

Her eyes snapped open and she jerked upright in the huge four-poster bed, the satin sheet slipping away from her bare breasts.

"Oh, God, this must be some kind of dream," she murmured with sleep-thickened voice as she dragged her fingers back through her tangled hair. She clutched the sheet tight against her body as she looked around, blinking against fatigue and the grittiness in her eyes from too little sleep.

This was not her room at Ombre Rose, nor was it the guest room at Melanie's. Nothing was familiar. Not the pale-blue walls, the thick dark-blue carpeting, the damask settee, or the expanse of large bed that surrounded her. However, the man's shirt and pants, scattered across the thick blue carpeting, looked vaguely familiar — too familiar.

"Please let this be a dream," Andy whispered as she threw her legs over the side of the bed and took the sheet with her. But even as she wished it, the events of the last several hours came swimming back to her all too vividly.

"Coleton James!" It came out so violently that Andy jumped at just the sound of his name. Those were his clothes, donated by some whore he'd obviously been living with, and this was his room, or at least one that was generously offered to him for his own private use. But Coleton James was nowhere to be seen.

Andy darted into the bathing chamber, coming to an abrupt halt as she stared down at the porcelain tub. Even now her cheeks flamed at the memory of what had taken place in that tub—or at least begun there.

She quickly left the small room, closing the door emphatically behind her. That brought her back to the middle of the room, damp carpet cool beneath her feet. She closed her eyes, fighting back the embarrassment at what had taken place on that carpeting. But even as heat flooded her cheeks, other less certain emotions washed through her.

"Damn," she softly cursed as she took in the emptiness of the room. Everything of the evening before came back to her in a rush . . .

The Montfort costume party and that strange encounter with a man disguised as King Louis. Coleton James had followed her into the gardens;

Parker Rawlins had escorted her back to Melanie's house. Coleton James had abducted her;

Hiding out in that whorehouse with Coleton James only to be shot at. Andy felt the light bandage at her arm and amended that thought. Not shot at, but *shot!*

Brought to this hotel under the threat of a gun at her back. And then . . .

Well, she didn't want to think of that, but Coleton James was responsible for it just as he was responsible for everything that had happened to her over the last few hours.

Andy took quick survey of the room as she brought her churning thoughts back under control. His clothes were gone. The gun was gone. Coleton James was gone.

So, he'd left! After he'd gotten the information he wanted. But what the devil did it mean? What did any of it mean? Well, she wasn't about to wait around to find out.

Andy snatched the shirt and pants from the floor and quickly pulled them on before she realized she had no shoes. A quick inspection of the closet revealed it was as empty as the

327

room. Andy shut the door, wanting to slam it. But at this un-godly hour of the morning it would only draw attention, and that was the last thing she wanted.

"God's nightgown! Why am I worried about shoes? Every-one will take one look at my clothes and think the absolute worst." Which brought another interesting question: Just how the devil was she going to explain all this to Lacey and her father?

"First things first," she reminded herself as she tucked the long tail of the shirt inside the waist of the pants, then cinched them up. If she didn't get out of here, there wouldn't be any need to worry about what she would tell anyone.

Twisting her long hair and tossing it back over one shoul-der, Andy took a long, slow breath and tried the door. She let out a slow breath of relief as it opened easily, the soft glow from hallway lamps spilling briefly through the opened door-way into the room. She quickly slipped outside and closed the door behind her.

"So far, so good," she quietly congratulated herself as she looked first to one end of the hallway, then the other. The night before, they'd come up the stairway from the right. The hallway to the left turned a corner. There might be a back entrance or a employees' stairway.

The door at the end of that second hallway opened easily, a set of stairs leading up to the floor above, disappearing down into darkness below. She quickly made her choice.

Andy hated narrow, dark places. She always had. It was like walking in a fog, unable to see anything in front of her. It left her completely disoriented until she quit trying to rely on her eyesight and began relying on her other senses to guide her. She breathed in slowly, let her right hand feel along the wall, and found she could actually anticipate the distance of the next step without tumbling head over heels down the stairs. She was just becoming confident when she smashed her nose into a wall.

Extending her arms in front of her, carefully inching her right foot forward, Andy realized she'd obviously come to a stairwell landing. She found the doorknob. The door opened freely into another small hallway. It was dark as well, but her gaze immediately fastened on a narrow strip of light down low at the floor at the other end. Another door. She quietly walked toward that light. Six paces, eight, twelve.

She found the doorknob by aiming straight from her hip. She was getting good at fumbling around in the dark. Taking a deep breath, she turned the knob, praying she'd find someone on the other side who could help her.

The light was painful at first until her eyes adjusted. Slowly the shapes of the room came into focus and Andy's eyes widened at sight of the black stenciled letters that appeared backward on the frosted glass—Hotel Manager. This was the office behind the front desk of the hotel! She couldn't have hoped for better luck.

Andy slipped into the back of the office. It was so quiet at first she thought she was alone. Then she saw the man at the desk. It wasn't the night clerk who'd argued with Coleton. Maybe this man worked daytime hours.

Taking a deep breath, she slowly walked forward. She didn't like sneaking up on anyone and didn't want to frighten the poor man. She could imagine his surprise at suddenly finding someone in his office.

Andy reached out tentatively to touch his shoulder. "Excuse me, sir." There was no immediate response.

"Sir?" He didn't turn around, didn't move or so much as indicate he'd even heard her. Maybe he was asleep. It must be difficult coming to work so early in the morning. She tried again.

"Sir?" Andy prodded him more persistently. She laid her hand on his shoulder as she rounded the chair. "Please, I just . . ."

The chair spun around abruptly and her hand fell away. Andy's eyes widened. The color drained from her face. Her throat closed around a terrified scream as she stared at the blood-splattered body slumped in the chair.

The man's skin was ashen. His eyes stared transfixed, the pupils widened and vacant. Even his lips were that same ghastly color of gray as his mouth hung open. In fact the only thing about him that wasn't gray was the slash at his throat that lay open like a horrible, gaping smile — a smile of death.

Sheer terror locked in her brain. Andy backed away. She had to get out of there. She turned to run, only to find it was too late. A hand clamped down over her mouth.

Scream after soul-shattering scream clawed into her throat only to be trapped there as she was caught by arms that were like steel about her. Andy struggled, fighting those hands that seemed to control her so effortlessly.

She was certain she heard screaming, only no one came. There were only those strong arms and unrelenting hands bruising her to submission. Exhaustion seeped through her and she became painfully aware of the hand across her face and realized the screaming was in her head.

From somewhere beyond the wall of terror, she heard someone calling her.

"Amanda!"

Somehow the sound of her name focused her scattered thoughts. Or perhaps it was the fact that she couldn't breathe beneath the smothering strength of that hand cutting across her mouth. She was pinned back against the hard line of a man's body, struggling to breathe, fighting to free herself. The warmth of his breath against her cheek stopped her, his words slicing through the terror of the grisly scene that followed her behind tightly closed eyes.

"Amanda! For God's sake! I won't hurt you! Be still or you'll bring them all down around us!"

She retreated to some dark void within her brain, mentally closing out the horrible scene that played over and over in her imagination. Dear God, she could almost smell the death in the room. It was the same as during the war when she'd worked at the hospital, but never like this.

Dear God! What was wrong with her? Andy felt as if all the air had been drained from her lungs, as if she'd taken a physical blow. And all the strength seemed to drain out of her, as if it were her blood. No matter how hard she fought them back, images flashed across the back of her eyes . . . and there was pain, so much pain.

Through the swirling mist she saw the bent oaks; streamers of Span-ish moss clung to the branches like a mournful shroud; and the two men, standing back to back; the glint of steel and she was running; the deaf-ening roar of the explosion;

It roared painfully in her ears and Andy clasped her hands over them to close it out.

"Amanda!"

She mentally clung to that harsh voice as if it were a lifeline back to sanity. She knew that voice . . .

It came softer this time—the gentle whisper of her name bringing her slowly back. Slowly the loud roaring subsided until it pulsed through her rhythmically. Only now did she realize it was the frantic beating of her own heart.

And now that voice was like a caress. "Amanda."

She nodded, and the hand across her mouth slowly fell away.

Coleton turned her away with his own body, blocking her view. He was afraid she was about to collapse. His body molded hers, instinctively protecting her, giving her time to calm down. She seemed so small and vulnerable. His hand stroked through her hair, soothing her, his mouth against her ear.

"Are you all right?"

He felt her deep intake of breath and the silent sob that shuddered through her. She nodded faintly, melting into his arms.

One by one, the images slipped back into the shadows until they were nothing but a blur of light and color. Andy clung to him as if she would never let him go. Sobs spasmed in her throat, tears spilled down her cheeks. Her fingers twisted in the fabric at the front of his shirt. She clung to him for dear life.

"Dear God, it's so horrible." Her tears soaked through to his skin.

Coleton's hands spread soothingly across her back, letting her have these few moments to get past the first shock. But he couldn't give her long. Damn! This was a complication he hadn't counted on.

"Who could've done something like that?" she murmured in puzzlement. At first, it didn't occur to her that Coleton might have had something to do with the man's death. Now, sniffling loudly, fighting back another wave of sobs, she pushed back from him, wiping her tears with her shirt sleeve and glaring at him suspiciously.

Coleton saw the question in her darkened eyes.

"He was already dead when I came down. You have my word on it."

Andy swallowed back the sobs she couldn't seem to control. "Your word as a . . . gentleman?"

She sniffed back a fresh wave of tears, deliberately avoiding any glance at the body of the man in the chair as Coleton released her and moved around her.

There was a trace of that endearing wry smile of his. "Of course."

Then he became sober once more, wishing there was any other way. Last night he'd gotten the information he needed about the location of the Duchess from Duvalier. The Duchess was the connection to whomever was impersonating the Gray Fox.

Then he'd very carefully made arrangements for Duvalier to hand Amanda over to Phoenix for safekeeping. But those plans were now changed. Duvalier was dead and his contact with Phoenix was gone.

How much had Duvalier's murderers learned before they cut his throat? Or had that been his reward for his silence?

Were they the same men who'd fired those shots in the alley in back of Valentine's? As he'd pointed out to Amanda at the time, their aim hadn't been off. He'd been exposed in clear range no less than three times in that alley and had escaped uninjured. Obviously Amanda was their target.

He had to assume those same men may very well have followed them here. Those same men were undoubtedly responsible for Duvalier's murder and they were looking for Amanda.

"We've got to get out of here," he announced quietly, removing the gun from his holster and checking the chamber.

Andy sniffled loudly, certain she hadn't heard him correctly. "What do you mean, *we?* When you were gone I thought . . ." She sniffled again, then shrugged.

"You have the information you want. You don't need me." She stated what she thought was rather obvious.

When he looked back up at her, the smile was gone from those eyes, replaced by a familiar coldness.

"No, I don't need you." The words were equally cold. They seemed to freeze right through her. Without saying it, his meaning was obvious. He'd used her.

"But *you* need me," he went on to inform her calmly.

"What!" The body was temporarily forgotten. A last sob caught Andy in indignation. "I most certainly do *not* need *you!*" Was that really a smile? A damn smile? The arrogance of the man. The absolute . . .

He'd gotten just the reaction he intended. If she could get angry, she'd be all right. He gentled his voice, not wanting to draw attention, and not caring to take the time to explain everything right now. So he stated what he knew would slice straight through to the heart of all her anger and indignation.

"The men who killed Duvalier," he gestured to the man slumped in the chair behind her, "will be back."

Andy clenched her teeth together. "You pigheaded, arrogant, bast — !"

He leveled those disconcerting gray eyes at her. "They're after you."

Those three words had the effect of a rug being pulled out from under her. Andy could only stare at him as each word penetrated. She cut a brief glance back over her shoulder, her voice suddenly quiet. She gave a nervous little laugh.

"Surely you don't mean the men who did that . . ."

"I mean exactly that, Amanda. Have you forgotten last night in that alley?"

"I wouldn't have been in that alley if you hadn't abducted me." Those twin vivid pools of blue fastened on him, and Coleton felt something deep inside tighten as the ghost of a memory from the past few hours came winging back at him.

Dear God, she reminded him so much of Sunny. It was the

333

vulnerability that peeked through when that carefully constructed facade of aloof indifference slipped a notch or two. Just like last night, when he'd almost believed for those few hours . . .

He pushed it back with a vengeance. It meant nothing! They'd both been tired, she was scared, the cognac . . .

The muscle in his jaw worked as he fought back emotions he didn't want to confront. He took hold of her arm, pushing her across the office.

"We don't have time to argue about this. You go with me, or you stay here and end up like Duvalier. It's that simple, Amanda. Do you really think they'll let you live?"

She whirled on him. *"They?"* Who are they?"

"I don't know yet. But they're obviously worried about what you know, or what they think you know. They followed us here."

"And they killed Duvalier. Do you want to end up like that?" Coleton had grabbed hold of her. His fingers bit into her upper arms as if he could shake some understanding into her.

Andy swallowed convulsively, refusing to look back at the desk. "No." Her voice was small.

"Then, my dear, we really have no choice." Coleton's voice was low. "Neither one of us." He reached for the doorknob.

"What about . . . him?" Andy pulled back on his arm.

"He'll be found." It was said so coldly, without any emotion.

Andy's fists clenched at her sides. She was perfectly aware of that. It just seemed so dreadful to simply leave the man there like that.

"He's not in a position to care about it, Amanda."

The tone of his voice was surprisingly gentle as if he somehow understood how difficult this was for her. Andy nodded, feeling warmth seep back into her icy veins at just the sound of her name. He always called her Amanda—except for last night when he'd he'd called her that other name. She put that out of her mind. Right now she had to, or she was certain she'd go mad.

"Are you all right now?"

"Yes." She took a deep breath as he slowly pulled the door open. She tugged at his sleeve. "Don't you think it's a bit dangerous, leaving through the hotel lobby? They could be waiting for us."

"They could be, but they're not. At this moment they're searching every room in this hotel."

Andy jerked back on his arm. "Do you mean to tell me that you knew about all this and just left me up there?"

"I was on my way back up to get you after I found Duvalier. I had no way of knowing how much he'd told them. Since those men didn't go straight to our room, I have to assume he didn't tell them what they wanted to know."

Andy's eyes were large as saucers. "Then he died because of me." That horrible thought was just beginning to sink in.

Coleton took hold of her and jerked her out behind the front desk. His eyes narrowed as he scanned the deserted lobby. "It doesn't matter now!" he whispered harshly.

Andy shuddered at the cruelty of his words. God, how she hated him at that moment. How could she possibly ever have let him touch her the way he had last night, or make love to her? There was no compassion in the man, none whatsoever. He was cruel, deliberately so. And somehow he was involved in all this.

Dozens of questions flew through her scattered thoughts with no time to find answers to any of them at the moment. Somehow, someone wanted her dead, because of a ridiculous message that was obviously intended for someone else. Something about the evening before at the Château Montfort nagged at her, but she couldn't quite grasp it. That and the fact that Coleton James wasn't about to give her time to do that.

He pulled her along behind the desk, using the frosted glass partition of windows as a shield.

"I suppose you have a plan to get us out of the hotel," she whispered sarcastically at his back as he kept one hand firmly on her wrist.

"Not really. I'm sort of making this up as we go."

"Oh, God."

Coleton smiled. "Don't worry. I've managed to survive an entire war this way."

"That's what I'm worried about." She took a deep breath. "What are you waiting for?"

He gave her a long look. "The thought occurred to me that these men know what you look like, but they don't know what *I* look like."

The thought occurred to Andy that he might just decide to leave her there. "Aren't you assuming an awful lot? They could just as easily have seen *you* in that alley."

"Maybe. Maybe not." He looked back at her thoughtfully from his crouched position behind the front desk. That glorious mane of golden hair was like a beacon. He remembered the way it spread across the pillow when he made love to her the second time last night. And he remembered the feel of it, thick and silken in his hands, and his memory. He frowned. "We need a disguise for you." Without warning, he reached behind her.

Andy flinched and ducked.

The frown curved upward with amusement. "You don't need to flinch, Amanda. I don't beat helpless women, just slaves. Remember?"

"Helpless!" He really was such a cad sometimes. Any further indignation was muffled under the brim of a bowler hat. It was several sizes too big and easily flopped forward, balancing on the bridge of her nose. Andy shoved it back on her head. It immediately fell forward when she tried to speak to him.

"What . . .?" She shoved it back again, giving him a murderous look. "What do you think you're doing?"

Next came the jacket off the coat stand. Coleton dragged it around her slender shoulders, closing it over the shirt she wore. He took hold of a handful of thick tawny hair, gently twisting and then stuffing it under the edge of the hat at her neck. The thickness of her coiled hair snugged the hat down over her head, but she was still forced to tilt her head way back, looking down the length of her very short nose to see out from under the brim.

"This won't fool anyone," she informed him matter-of-factly.

Coleton gave her a thorough inspection, from the tip of the hat down to her bare feet poking out from the edge of his pant legs. "It'll have to do," he said, trying to assure her.

"What about you?"

Now the smile deepened. "I'm gambling that you're the one they're looking for. Come on." He seized her by the arm and pulled her to her feet.

"That's just great. I'm so very glad to know that I'm the target and you're not really in any danger at all." She anchored the hat on her head with one hand as she tried to look at him. It was easier said than done since he towered over her by at least a foot.

"I suppose we're going to walk right across the front lobby and out the front doors."

Coleton tucked his arm through hers. "I can't think of a better way out of here right at the moment."

"I suppose you know what you're doing."

"It's a cakewalk. I used to do this sort of thing all the time during the war. Nothing to it." He smiled again in spite of himself, knowing it would infuriate her. He liked seeing the anger spark in those magnificent blue eyes. Except right at the moment they were pretty well hidden under the hat.

Andy's eyes widened as Coleton slipped his revolver out of the holster and tucked it into the bend of her arm, his hand covering the handle.

"Just in case," he assured her as he pulled her along with him from behind the front desk.

"I don't think I want to know what that might be," Andy whispered beside him as she tried to match her shorter steps to his longer ones. After all, she was supposed to be a man in a coat and bowler hat.

She mumbled a desperate little prayer as they stepped out into the wide expanse of the front lobby, completely vulnerable. She wanted to bolt and run for the door, or the nearest settee, potted plant — anything to hide behind. But the restraint of Coleton's fingers biting into her arm warned her they couldn't draw attention to themselves. As if a barefoot man in an oversized coat and hat holding hands with another man wasn't obvious enough.

There was no getting around it, she was scared. She cut a quick glance to Coleton from under the hat. He took in the entire lobby in one sweeping glance. She saw, as he, too, obviously had, the two Union soldiers seated across from each other, both apparently absorbed in the morning paper. Something about the way they just sat there made Andy uneasy. One looked up briefly as she and Coleton continued on across the lobby.

A porter came down the stairs and walked toward the front desk. Andy held her breath as he started around the counter toward the office. But he simply turned, replaced a key on the board, and then left. Then she saw the front-desk clerk who had signed them in the night before.

He came out of a large adjacent room. The ornate lettered sign beside the entrance revealed it was the dining room. The desk clerk stopped and spoke to another porter, smiled, and then proceeded to the front desk. They'd just reached the foyer, when they heard the clerk shouting.

"You, there! Hold it right there! Stop! Thief!"

Coleton pulled Andy in front of him and propelled her out the double glass doors of the hotel. The hat came off, her pale hair streaming behind her. Out of the corner of her eye, Andy saw the two officers throw down their newspapers. Without pausing to take a breath, Coleton pushed her down the street, around a corner, across another street, and down a side alley. They ran the length of one block, cut across another street, losing themselves into the congestion of carriages and wagons.

Coleton set a murderous pace, darting down back alleys, side streets, cutting across main avenues. Andy was hopelessly lost. Twice she thought they turned back in the direction they came, only to find she didn't recognize any of the shops on the street. He cut down another street and obviously had no intention of easing the pace.

Andy pulled back on his hand. She was suffocating from

the stifling heat of the wool coat on such a warm, humid morning, she'd stubbed her toe on a cobblestone, she had a horrible stitch in her side from running so hard, and she had to rest. In short, she wasn't going any farther.

Coleton turned on her. "We can't stop here! They could be right behind us!"

Andy's eyes narrowed. "You knew all along those two soldiers were the ones who were after us!"

He continued to pull her along behind him at a modified pace that could best be described as a brisk walk. Andy thought she was going to die.

"Didn't . . . you?!" she growled at him between gasps for air. She dug her bare feet in as best she could and jerked hard.

Coleton whirled around to face her. "Yes, them and their friends upstairs." He read the mutinous expression in her vivid eyes.

"There was no time to explain anything to you. Any minute the others would have been down that stairway. I couldn't take that chance!"

"Is that right?" Andy exploded, finally drawing a deep enough breath to get all the words out at once.

"Yes, that's right! And we're not stopping now. It's fair enough to assume those men are right behind us. And *they* won't slow down." He pulled her on down the street.

Andy clawed at his hand. She tried slowing him down and paid dearly for it with her chapped and blistered feet. They wove through people who passed by. Still she twisted her wrist back and forth trying to loosen his grasp. It was no use. She stumbled along behind him, trying to keep up. If she fell, she knew as she'd known last night that he'd probably leave her there. Logic might have argued that he wouldn't have bothered to bring her along if that was what he intended. But at the moment, Andy wasn't thinking very logically. All she could think of were her poor aching feet.

"Damn you to hell, Coleton James!" she screamed at him. "I'm not going any farther!"

"We're not stopping!"

"Let me go!"

"I give the orders!"

"Not to me you don't!"

They had just cut down an alley behind several shops. Empty barrels, boxes, and crates were stacked against the back walls of the buildings. A black-and-white cat had just finished off a plate of scraps and sat watching them. Its head bobbed back and forth as if it followed their animated conversation.

Andy pulled free of Coleton's grasp and hobbled to one side of the alley. She up-ended a small crate and sat down, in silent declaration that she refused to go any further. She winced as she lifted her right foot and propped in on her left knee. She carefully probed the tender cut, not even looking up as his shadow fell across her.

"Let me look at it." He crouched down in front of her, taking firm hold of her ankle.

Andy tried to jerk her foot back, remembering the night before and the effect those fingers had on her. She didn't want him anywhere near her feet!

"Relax, Amanda. I won't hurt you." With equal determination he refused to let her go. He turned her foot, gently probing the cut skin.

"There doesn't seem to be anything in there," he announced.

Andy gave him a long look. "And I suppose along with your other skills acquired during the war, you learned all about wounds." The comment was meant to be sarcastic, and the moment he looked up, she realized he understood exactly that. She saw it in the faint flicker of response behind the coolness in those gray eyes.

"Among other things," he answered simply, making her wonder what those other things were. "When you live with death all the time, you learn how to hold on to life a little longer. You learn how to sew flesh together or open it up to get out a bullet." He gently prodded her foot, his fingers gentle and caring.

"If you don't have a needle, you use a hot iron to close a wound. If there isn't medicine to take the edge off a man's pain, you put a piece of wood between his teeth and hold on to him until he passes out."

Those gray eyes came up to regard her evenly as he tenderly cradled her foot. "The Yanks had all the medicine and needles and clean bandages. Toward the end my men had so many wounds you couldn't close 'em with a hot iron or a needle. You Yanks won by bleedin' us to death."

There was something so solemn, so poignant in his voice. And then his voice hardened. "But then you wouldn't know about that, would you, Miss Spenser!" His words cut at her. "You sat in your fine Yankee home untouched by the war. And when it was over, you came south to see what it was all about. Just like all the other Yanks—carpetbaggers and thieves, like vultures to steal what was left."

There was so much anger and hatred in him. At last Andy thought she understood his true feelings. It was what had driven him all those weeks at Ombre Rose. It's what drove him now.

"You're wrong." She choked back tears and anger, knowing he probably wouldn't listen to her. "I didn't come for that. I never intended to stay."

"But when I saw Ombre Rose I just knew . . ." She hesitated. How could she possibly explain what was she felt that first time—that feeling in her soul as if she'd somehow come home.

She scrubbed at her eyes with a vengeance as tears threatened again. "I didn't know who you were when I bid against you for it."

"Would it have made any difference?" Those gray eyes impaled her.

"I wish I could say it would have." She had to be honest with him. "But I don't know. All I know is that I belong at Ombre Rose." Her voice was quiet and somber. "And I'll fight to keep it."

Coleton slowly rose to his feet. Such a pretty little speech! What the hell else had he expected? And now he was stuck with little Miss Yankee Carpetbagger. But only for a little while—only as long as it took to expose Gray Fox, turn her

341

over to Phoenix, and collect his reward. He jammed the revolver back into the holster that molded his thigh.

"Stay here and stay out of sight. I'll be back as soon as I can." He jerked the brim of his hat down low over his eyes, wondering if those two blue-bellies had been able to follow them. He was counting on the fact that he knew New Orleans better than they did. He turned and headed toward the end of the alley.

Andy watched him leave, knowing by the hardness in his words she dare not try to follow and wondering if he would come back . . . wondering whether she wanted him to . . .

Was she any worse off taking her chances with those men who'd chased after them? And why had they chased them? Were they they same ones who'd fired at them in that alley behind Valentine's? Were they responsible for Duvalier's death? What did they want with her?

Dear God. So many questions and no answers. And Coleton James thought the grieving and loss were all his, that no one else, especially a Yank, had suffered because of the war.

"You're wrong, you know." Her words stopped Coleton at the end of the alley. Her eyes fastened on the hard set of his shoulders, the tight curl of his fist. He slowly turned around and looked at her, those eyes angry and cold, silently daring her to say anything more. She swallowed the knot of emotion that choked at her.

"We bled, too, Coleton. We all bled, and died just a little." She took a deep breath, needing to say this and knowing just as well it probably wouldn't have any effect on him.

She willed her voice not to shake. "My brother was killed in an ambush three days *after* the surrender. He's buried somewhere in Virginia. Nobody really knows where." She stared down at her hands clenched in her lap.

When she looked up, she saw something different in those gray eyes. And then Coleton simply turned and left the alley.

Andy moved the crate back into the shadows at the side of the alley. Boxes and crates surrounded her, shielding her from view.

It was cool in the shadows. She slumped back against the

brick wall of a building and wearily closed her eyes. Mentally retracing the events of the last several hours, she counted two hours of sleep. She was bone-tired.

"Just a little while longer, Coleton James. Then I don't care who's out there, I'm leaving."

"That won't be necessary."

Andy's eyes flew open. She squinted up into the sun high overhead and saw two shadows looming over her. Their billed military hats shielded their faces. Before she could move, before she could even yell, one hamlike fist closed over the front of her shirt and she was hauled off the top of the crate.

She gasped, striking out at the man in the blue uniform. "Let me go!"

"Aw, come on, Riley. It ain't nothin' but a skinny kid. The lieutenant said we was lookin' for a woman."

The first man was younger, hardly more than a boy. He held back, uncertain. It was the one called Riley, she had good reason to fear. His fingers twisted in the shirt, choking off her air as she swung back and forth in his grasp, feet dangling just off the ground.

"What the hell is a kid doin' in an alley?" he grunted.

"Take a look around, Riley. They're everywhere. This town is crawlin' with 'em. Come on, we gotta keep lookin' or the lieutenant is goin' to be real angry."

"That's jes' what I'm thinkin'." Riley leered into her face. His eyes were close set above a large nose that was badly scarred and flattened across his face. Another scar began high on one cheek and descended to an upper lip distorted by more scars. They thinned into a pale maze as they spread wide in a gaping expression across his uneven teeth. Some were rotted back to the gums, others were missing completely. Andy cringed away from the stench of his hot breath.

"The lieutenant won't like it if she tricks one of us and gets away again." The man called Riley shook Andy back and forth.

"He said she wasn't dressed like a woman." He pulled her close, leering into her face.

Andy practically gagged. She clawed at his hands, trying

343

desperately to loosen his grasp on her shirt. She couldn't breathe. Tiny pin dots of light sparkled behind her eyes and she felt faint. He shook her again, hard, then reached for the hat perched precariously on her head. He yanked it off and tossed it to the ground, whistling low as her hair tumbled to her shoulders.

"Oooeee! Lookee what we got here!" Riley exclaimed as he stared down into her face. "This ain't no boy at all!"

The young soldier came forward for closer inspection. "Reckon it's her?" His breath sucked back between his lips. "Must be. Can't see no other reason why she'd be hidin' out here in this back alley. Although . . ." And with that, Riley hooked his fingers at the V of the shirt where the buttons closed almost to Andy's neck and yanked viciously downward.

Andy gasped as she fell from Riley's grasp, the shirt separating as the buttons scattered across the ground. She fell to her knees, her arms wrapped across her bare breasts.

"Sweet Jesus, Riley! The lieutenant jes' said to bring her back. He didn't say nothin' about hurtin' her." The young corporal was clearly upset. He rushed forward to try and help her.

"Get back! She ain't hurt! The lieutenant also said she was a whore and a *spy.*"

Andy grabbed for the torn shirt, clutching it to the front of her body as she fought back revulsion. Her head snapped up, her eyes locked on the man called Riley. "Get away from me!" she hissed. "Get away!" She drew in a ragged breath.

Dear God! Where was Coleton? Had he truly abandoned her?

"Get back!" she shrieked at the top of her lungs, not caring who heard. It sounded as if her voice echoed back to her from very far away. Dizziness overwhelmed her and she fought it back, swallowing convulsively, inching herself away from the huge man.

"If you touch me again . . .!" She clenched her teeth, knowing her voice shook and hating herself for that sign of weakness, especially now when she was completely alone and vulnerable.

"I swear I'll kill you!" She was backed up against a crate, any further retreat blocked.

Riley knew she was cornered and laughed, a sick, nauseating sound that began low in his wide body and rumbled through his chest as he slowly came toward her, closing the distance.

"Riley, don't," the young corporal pleaded. "We're jes' supposed to bring her in, so's they just want to ask her some questions."

"They can ask 'em . . . later. Right now I want to teach the little lady some manners. Beginnin' with proper clothes for a lady to wear. I don't care much for them pants, any more than I cared for that shirt."

He advanced several steps closer until he was once more bending over her. He ran his tongue over his lips, thinking how that lustrous gold hair would feel in his hands, how that gleaming, pale body would feel moving under him. He reached for her long hair, curling the fat ham of his fist in the lustrous satin length.

Andy clenched her teeth tightly together, mentally willing herself to remain calm as her right hand closed over a piece of broken barrel stave. Then Riley hauled her to her feet.

"If you want to live, you'd better listen to the boy, Riley!"

Three sets of eyes jerked to the end of the alley. A man, his shadow tall and lean against the bright sunlight in the street beyond, stood casually. His stance was relaxed, one foot slightly ahead of the other, his lean hips cocked to the side. His arms hung easily at his sides. The wide-brimmed hat was worn low over his eyes. His pants were a pale, faded gray. The shirt was the same color, with a double row of gleaming buttons across his chest, left open on one side. Coleton James exuded a lean animal intensity that made the corporal hesitate.

"Riley?" The corporal swallowed hard, his eyes widening in alarm.

The man called Riley followed his gaze. "Well, I'll be damned! Back off, Johnny Reb! This ain't none of your concern!" he warned the stranger.

"You're wrong. The young lady is my sister."

"Damn!" the young soldier swore under his breath.

"Relax, boy. He's bluffin'. Prob'ly jes wants her for himself." Riley's eyes narrowed as he tightened his fist in Andy's hair.

She winced. It felt as if he were pulling it out. She gritted her teeth against the pain, keeping her eyes fastened on the stranger.

"Either that, or could be he's the one who helped her escape." Riley speculated, running his tongue back over his lips. "We could have that reward all to ourselves, boy," he grunted in appreciation as he whirled Andy around in front of him.

"This what you want, mister?" he taunted, dragging Andy in front of him, his thick fingers biting cruelly into the soft, bare flesh of her shoulder. Andy clutched the torn shirt across her breasts with one hand.

"Hurt her and you're a dead man," came the solemn promise.

The corporal shifted uncomfortably, his frightened gaze darting back and forth between Riley and the stranger. Riley tried to make out the man's features more clearly. Andy could only stare, certain she hadn't heard correctly.

"Riley, maybe we ought to let her go. The man says she's his sister," the corporal suggested.

"Like hell!" Riley spat out as he jerked Andy painfully back against his side. "You want her, mister? You come and get her!"

"Oh, God!" Andy whispered, fighting back the hysteria that clawed into her throat. Everything that came afterward blurred into a horror of nightmarish screams, exploding gunfire, the burn of acrid smoke filling her lungs, and Riley's cruel laughter.

Coleton stepped from the shadows. His hand moved back from his left hip, revealing the holster neither man had seen. He pulled another gun from behind his back with his right hand. It was heavier than the revolver although the barrel was only slightly longer.

"Sweet Jesus!" The young corporal screamed the warning as he dove for the far side of the alley and pulled his revolver from his own holster. A trail of bullets followed him, popping at his feet just as intended.

"Goddamn you!" Riley roared, jerking Andy upright like a human shield as bullets came close — too close. He screamed as a bullet caught him in the shoulder. Cursing, his hand twisted in Andy's hair.

Pain tore white-hot as Andy's head was yanked back. Everything passed before her in a blur; the young corporal running, the roar of gunfire all around them, the look of fury in Riley's crimson face as he leaned over her reaching for his own gun. It gleamed as he pulled it from the holster.

All thoughts of modesty temporarily forgotten, Andy brought the barrel stave up from behind her back and grasped it in both hands. Swinging with all her strength, she brought it up fast and hard, rounding on Riley with a blow that would have crushed the skull of a lesser man.

Riley staggered, momentarily off balance, surprise registering across his florid features. Before he could find his footing, Andy swung on him again, bringing the stave up alongside his head.

Her hair streamed over her shoulders and tumbled into her eyes. The force of the first blow practically sent her to her knees. She tripped, fell, and drove herself back to her feet as she went after Riley again.

"Don't do it!" Coleton warned the young corporal as he stood over him.

"Throw it!" he commanded, and the young soldier did exactly that. The revolver landed at Coleton's feet. He kicked it into the stack of crates and boxes at the far side.

When Coleton turned to help Amanda, the corporal bolted for the end of the alley, never looking back as he disappeared into the street beyond.

Riley refused to go down. Blood poured from the gash at the side of his head, and still he stood. He roared a curse as he raised his pistol and aimed.

Andy crumpled to her knees. She hadn't the strength to strike him again. He towered over her, and for one terrifying moment seemed to hang suspended above her.

It was over now, he would kill her. She knew it. His face began to fade before her—the light in the alley grew dim. If she was about to die, she didn't want to know or feel anything.

Andy was going away again—to that faraway place she'd gone to before. Only this time she knew there would be no coming back. It would all end here; the journey was over and she would have failed. She would never she see Ombre Rose again. And she would lose Coleton . . .

In her heart she knew it would be forever this time. There wouldn't be another chance . . .

Please, no! her heart cried out.

A single shot roared through the alley.

Riley staggered backward and collapsed.

Coleton ran to Amanda. With the cool precision that came from having killed before, he thrust the revolver back into his holster and the sawed-off shotgun into the scabbard at his back. Yet, his hands shook when he reached for her.

Her shoulders were bare, the wild torrent of her tangled hair shielding her to the waist. Still, a wild, possessive anger tore through Coleton at just the thought of that man touching her. His hands shook uncontrollably when he touched her.

"Are you all right?" His voice ached in his throat as he gently lifted her face. "Amanda?"

Tears streaked her pale cheeks. Her vivid blue eyes were dark and wide with terror. She breathed convulsively, her bottom lip trembling. She was staring at him but seemed to look straight through him.

"Amanda!" He shook her gently. "It's over, Amanda." He shook her again.

Dear God, don't go away from me, he thought desperately. He'd heard of it before, a shock so severe that the mind simply snapped. Desperation seeped ice-cold into his veins. "Amanda!"

She blinked uncertainly, coming back from that deep, dark void—back into the warm light.

"Cole?" He was here. "Cole!"

It was all she said, but it shattered another part of the wall he'd built around his emotions. He pulled her into his arms.

"I thought you weren't coming back." She wept into the curve of his neck beneath his chin. Her arms slipped beneath his and around his back, clinging to him as if she'd never let him go. She was oblivious to her lack of clothing.

Coleton closed his eyes as he stroked his chin over her silken head. He slowly released the breath that ached in his lungs. She was all right.

"I told you I would," he answered simply, wanting to reassure her, needing it for himself as well. "I gave you my word," he whispered against the silk of her hair.

She nodded beneath his chin and he smiled at the thought of how very small she seemed now. His arms tightened around her. He found it difficult to believe that this slender young woman was the very same person who'd tried to take off Riley's head with a barrel stave. By the looks of the Union soldier, she'd done a fair job of it. He kept her turned away from Riley's body.

"I know," she answered softly, when she could manage to put at least two words together. And then as if just remembering that the shirt Coleton had given her lay in shreds several feet away, she pulled back, embarrassment staining her cheeks as she clasped her arms across her body.

"Your word as a gentleman?" She smiled tremulously.

This time Coleton smiled back. "Absolutely, Miss Spenser." Then he slowly released her. He looked down at her folded arms. "I think you'll be needing the clothes I brought," he observed. "And then we have to get out of here. That corporal was scared, but he'll be back with more men. And those bluebellies don't take kindly to having one of their men killed, even if he did deserve it. Remind me not to make you angry." It was meant to lighten the moment, but Coleton could see it had the exact opposite effect.

Andy started to turn around. "My God! Is he dead?"

Coleton gently prevented her from seeing Riley's body. "Yes, Amanda. He was an animal, he deserved to die."

Andy shuddered. "Did I kill him?" she asked weakly.

"Do you have so little faith in my aim?" He answered her with a question, wanting to protect her from the truth. There was no need for her to know that he was undoubtedly dead before Coleton ever fired that second shot.

"No, I didn't mean . . ."

"Come on . . ." Coleton wrapped the remnants of the torn shirt around her, closing it discreetly across her breasts. "Like it or not, it looks like I'm stuck with you. I can't leave you here to tell the blue-bellies I killed one of their soldiers."

"I didn't mean . . ." I would never tell them that." Her eyes were wide blue pools, swimming with fresh tears that threatened.

"After all, you saved my life."

"Do I have your word on that, Miss Spenser?" He smiled at her, his mouth curving upward under the soft brush of his dark mustache.

She managed a tremulous smile and gestured to her pants with a shaking hand. "You have my word as a 'gentleman.' "

"Good." He smiled briefly, then became more serious. "I brought you some other clothes." He gestured to a neatly tied bundle that had been thrown to the ground.

The ghost of his smile returned. "You'll catch your death, dressed like that." He pulled the front of her shirt together. There was a warmth and gentleness she'd only glimpsed before.

Then he looked up. "By the way," the smile gone now, "can you handle a gun?"

Chapter Eighteen

"It won't bite you, Amanda." Coleton gave her a faintly bemused look. He leaned back against a large rock, crusted with bracken and the abandoned shells of crustaceans, and took another bite of the French bread and cheese he'd brought back from an earlier foray at the waterfront.

"Guns are dangerous," she answered simply, trying to hand it back to him. She would much rather eat. She'd had only a few nibbles of the food he'd brought back after venturing forth earlier from their latest hiding place.

Coleton shook his head. "They're only dangerous to people who don't know how to use them."

"Guns kill people." Andy fastened him with a stubborn glare.

"You're wrong, Amanda. People kill people, and anything can become a weapon in the hands of the wrong person."

"I don't see why it's necessary for me to know how to use a gun," she persisted.

Coleton gave her a thoughtful look. His gaze broke from hers as he cut another piece of bread and cheese, as if he was considering what she'd said. He handed the small sandwich to her, his gray gaze boring into hers.

"It's necessary, because at the moment there are two of us and a great many more of *them*." He chewed in silence, his eyes never leaving hers. "*They* all have guns, and *they*

351

want you dead."

Andy swallowed convulsively and once more went through the motions of unloading and reloading the revolver as he'd shown her. When she'd reloaded the revolver three times, she looked up with a faintly mutinous expression to see if he was satisfied.

Apparently he was. He nodded, taking the revolver from her. "The only question is, can you aim it and fire it?"

He took out a small pouch of tobacco and paper, and rolled a cigarette. The sounds of the waterfront were muffled by the heavy timbers overhead. They would wait until dark and then make their move. Besides, he knew Amanda was exhausted.

"What are they after?" she asked softly.

She'd been so quiet he was certain she must have dozed off.

"Obviously they think you know something," he answered quietly.

So, they were back to that. Andy smothered back another yawn. "I told you everything I know. There was just that message about the Duchess. I don't know *any more* . . . If it just hadn't been for that mistake about the costume . . ." she muttered sleepily as she finally gave in to fatigue and closed her eyes.

"What did you say?" Coleton jerked her upright, his fingers biting into her upper arms. "What did you say about the costume? Amanda! What about the costume?"

Now she was certain of it—Coleton James was mad as well as dangerous. She was tired, scared, and in no mood for his high-handedness. She finally managed to remove two fingers and jerked her arm free.

"It was the wrong costume!" she explained, unable to see what all the excitement was about.

"Which one was the wrong one?"

Now she was certain he was one brick shy of a full load. Or maybe several bricks. It was as if they were having two distinctly separate conversations.

"My costume for the Montfort ball," she continued through thin lips. "It was the wrong one. I was supposed to go as Queen Elizabeth. But the costumers gave me the wrong one." She gave him a withering glare. "It was too late when I found out the mistake. All I could do was go as—"

"Josephine," Coleton finished for her as a few more pieces to the puzzle fell into place.

He went on, talking to himself as if she weren't even there. "And with the mask, Louis had no way of knowing there had been a switch. He was simply following instructions passing that message on to you." He looked up as if suddenly remembering her and bringing her into the conversation. "But how would he have discovered the mistake? You wore the mask the entire evening, except—"

"Except in the garden," Andy bit off with more than just a little anger.

"And you left right after that. Who saw you leaving?"

Andy pushed her fingers back through her hair. She was achingly tired. At that moment she wasn't interested in who might have seen her.

"I can't remember."

"Think, Amanda."

"I'm trying," she growled, thinking that all her aggravation over the last couple of months centered around this one man, and he wasn't letting up now. Well, if he wasn't about to let her get any sleep, then she could at least eat. While trying to remember the details of the night before, she seized the bundle of bread and cheese, neatly wrapped in a newspaper. She picked through the pieces, sandwiching the slices together and munching thoughtfully. Her gaze fixed on the glaring print of the newspaper headlines. She brought it slowly into focus, Coleton momentarily forgotten. But only for a moment. Then he was the complete focus of her attention.

"This is about Duvalier! This article says he was mur-

353

dered and several thousand dollars in gold taken from the hotel safe." She raised questioning eyes. "The military knows the identity of the murderer. The Gray Fox?"

"Amanda! That's not important now. Try to remember last evening. Who saw you leaving the Château?"

Confusion clouded her eyes. The Gray Fox? Money stolen? But that wasn't true. There was no money taken.

"Amanda?"

Andy had heard of the Gray Fox. Practically everyone had. He was a Confederate spy, supposedly responsible for the North losing many key battles during the war. He'd gained an almost mystical reputation, his exploits recounted in the New York newspapers.

She remembered Stephen saying on one of his leaves home that if they could stop the Gray Fox, they could no doubt end the war more quickly. But whenever they thought they had him, he always seemed to escape, like the creature he was named for—quick, sly, elusive. And then at the end of the war, she read he was supposedly killed somewhere in North Carolina. She also knew that recently there had been several incidents of attacks on military shipments that were somehow attributed to the Gray Fox.

"I thought the Gray Fox died at the end of the war," Amanda suggested.

Coleton leaned his head back and closed his eyes. There was a weary ache behind his eyes he hadn't experienced in a long time. He tried to ignore it and then simply gave in to it, knowing the cause. He recognized that stubborn, inquisitive tone in her voice. He'd heard it often enough at Ombre Rose. She wouldn't be satisfied until she had an answer. And from where he sat, there was really no reason to lie to her.

"That's exactly what everyone was supposed to think." His voice was low, reflecting a fatigue that came from more than just the last several hours.

His words slowly sank in. *Exactly what everyone was sup-*

posed to think. Her eyes widened. He hadn't explained anything. Not really. It was the way he said it. And she knew.

"You're the Gray Fox."

"I *was* the Gray Fox," he allowed, with deliberate emphasis on the word *was*.

Andy took a deep breath and tried to hold back the fear that vibrated along every nerve ending.

"Did you do all those things they said you did?" Andy thought of the stories that had made him almost a legend.

"We all did a lot of things during the war that we're not happy about, or proud of," Coleton replied so low she strained to hear him. There was a huskiness in his voice she'd never heard before. Then his eyes came up to meet hers, clear like crystal, brilliant with secrets. And she knew then he would never tell her everything.

"I did what I had to do. But I didn't murder Duvalier."

"What about all the robberies, those stolen military shipments, and raids against Federal military posts? There were people killed."

His eyes changed, turning dark as smoke and equally dangerous. But the fire was banked.

"There's no reason for you to believe me." His voice was soft, almost a whisper; the look in his eyes went to slate. "For me, when the war ended, the Gray Fox was truly dead."

Andy's fingers curled against the desire to smooth away those tiny lines, to tenderly kiss the crease until it turned into one of those rare smiles, to erase the shadows of painful memories from those gray eyes. But that wasn't possible, she cautioned herself.

"What about last night?" His words jolted her back to the present and their unresolved conversation.

She drove her fingers back through her disheveled hair as frustration returned. What did he hope to learn? "Lacey Kittridge saw me leave. And Louise Montfort, her butler, the driver and—"

"Parker Rawlins?" he suggested.

"And *you*. She gave him a narrow look.

"Rawlins knew where you were staying. It would have been easy enough for him slip back there and follow us from Melanie's house."

"That's ridiculous. He's not a well man."

"He could have sent someone or hired those men," his eyes glinted, "and sent those blue-bellies after us."

"So could you for that matter," she pointed out, her eyes sparking vivid blue anger. "I only have your word that you found Duvalier already dead."

"It doesn't make sense for me to kill the man who was supposed to help me."

"And that raises another very fascinating question." Fatigue was stripped away by rising anger. Those blue eyes bore into him. "Just what is your part in all this? How are you involved?"

His gaze fell away. "I'm looking for someone. The woman who should have gone dressed as Josephine Bonaparte had the information I needed to find that person."

Now she understood at least part of what was going on. "You thought I had that information," she speculated, then her eyes widened.

"Of course! You went dressed as Napoleon hoping to get information from Josephine! Only I was the wrong Josephine."

"So it seems." He nodded, a curl of smoke drifting lazily above his head.

Andy quickly realized she had only one answer, and it raised dozens of new questions.

"What about Duvalier?"

"I didn't kill him," Coleton answered flatly, finishing the cigarette and flicking the glowing stub down onto the rocks below. He gave her a long look, refusing to give any further explanation. It was as simple as that and she would have to accept it.

Andy swallowed, an uneasy feeling slipping down her spine. "What about those men in the alley this morning?"

"I don't keep company with blue-bellies," he answered flatly. Then his somber expression curved into a cold smile. "We have different opinions about . . . things."

She shook her head. This was getting nowhere, which was precisely what she suspected Coleton James wanted. "But what about—?"

He cut her off. "Get some sleep, Amanda. When it gets dark, we'll go for a swim."

"I am *not* going in that water! It's dark, and there might be sharks!" Andy wrenched her arm free of Coleton James's fingers.

"Can't you swim?"

Even in the dim light that filtered through from lanterns on the docks above, she could see the glint of challenge in those gray eyes as he calmly assessed her.

"Of course I can swim," she replied with slightly ruffled dignity. "Actually, I'm a very good swimmer. My brother taught me. But that is beside the point."

"That, Amanda, is precisely the point." He finished shoving the remainder of their simple meal back inside a canvas bag. His revolver followed, along with the short-barreled shotgun. It was tightly rolled, then rolled again in another square of canvas, and tightly bound.

"That," he announced, "should keep it dry while we're in the water."

"Wait just a minute! I'm not going in there," Andy announced with equal determination.

Coleton looked up. There it was again. A flash of that indefinable something about her, as if he were looking into the eyes of someone he knew. It lingered now, as she sat there, perched on a rock only inches away, all her uncertainty and questions wrapped up in a neat little bundle of stubbornness.

"All right," he answered evenly. "Then stay here until I get back. Or go back to Melanie's house and see just how long it takes those men to find you. I figure you'll be safe until daybreak, noon tomorrow at best. They'll be searching this side of the docks then. But who knows?" He shrugged as if he couldn't have cared less. "Maybe you'll get lucky and they won't find you."

"That means you'll be at the mercy of the roustabouts, riffraff, and dockside vendors. I understand they do a thriving business in the underground white slavery trade."

"White slavery?" Andy echoed as she swallowed back the loathsome words. Surely he was joking again, but then, he hadn't been joking about going for a swim.

He gave her a long look. "The carpetbaggers and some of the new freedmen have established quite a nice, profitable business. They acquire women, young boys, and girls for the captains of outgoing vessels bound for San Francisco. They end up in some of the professional houses there."

"Houses?" She didn't really want to ask; she already had a suspicion what he meant.

"Like Valentine's, only worse," Coleton explained. "Val takes care of her girls. They have a home, nice clothes, and a share in the take. Most others don't even have that. They just get the clothes on their backs, only they don't have much use for those when they're working."

"You are being ill-mannered and crass." At that moment, she wanted to strangle him for trying to scare her. Surely it wasn't dangerous if she just kept quiet and hid until he came back.

"I'm being honest with you, Amanda. That is the reality of what you're facing if you stay here alone."

"And if I go with you?"

"The worst that can happen is that you'll get wet, and I think we could both use a bath." That cool implacability slipped into a raffish smile as he fingered the front of her shirt. She knew exactly what he was thinking of, but she refused to give him the satisfaction of revealing that their previous bath together held any fascination for her.

358

Still she frowned. At this point she considered Coleton James to be about as trustworthy as a lizard. She still wasn't certain what he had to gain from all this. He certainly wasn't doing it to help her out. In spite of what had passed between them, he'd made his feelings more than clear about that.

"Are there sharks?" she asked in a small voice, silently shuddering at just the thought as she looked out at the inkiness of water lapping around the pilings. She vividly remembered tales of great white sharks off the New England coast when Stephen used to take her sailing. They'd seen one once. They were huge, horrible creatures capable of capsizing smaller craft. And of course, there were countless stories of fishermen and sailors who'd been victims of shark attacks.

"Not that I know of."

Andy swallowed hard. If he was lying . . . Her eyes narrowed at the humor in his voice. He was laughing at her! Damn him, anyway! Well, she absolutely refused to let him know how she hated the idea of going in that water.

"All right. Where are we going?"

Admiration shaded Coleton's eyes. He could tell just by the set of her slender shoulders that she'd probably rather take a beating than put one toe in that water. But as he knew it would, Yankee hard-headedness won out. And in this instance he had to admit begrudgingly that he was glad she was a true Yank.

He stepped down onto the rock beside her and gestured out through the upright pilings toward a double row of glistening lights, out over the water. "That is the *Natchez*, from up north near Ohio. She makes port here in New Orleans every ten days, takes on supplies and passengers."

"Does she carry cargo?"

"The passengers *are* her cargo." Coleton smiled when he saw the faint glimmer of confusion in those soft eyes.

"She carries a very special sort of passenger — gamblers. They're professionals, and they go aboard for just one reason. She came into port yesterday and she's been taking on supplies most of the day for the return trip upriver. They anchor her out there to keep unwanted people from coming aboard to bother the clients. The reservations are by special invitation only. The *Natchez* stops at every port up and down the Mississippi. She'll leave first thing in the morning. And we leave with her."

"You seem to know a great deal about her."

"A little. A friend of mine spent some time on her."

"A friend, or yourself?" Again there was that closed expression, and she knew he wouldn't tell her more about that part of his past.

"Is the Duchess in one of those ports upriver?"

"The Duchess is aboard the *Natchez*."

Andy's gaze fastened back on that distant glow of lights stretching several hundred yards out across that murky darkness. The *Natchez* was bigger than the *Iron Queen,* an impressive sight with both decks aglow with lanterns. Music drifted to them from over the water. It seemed business was good aboard the *Natchez* tonight.

She swallowed back her doubts of Coleton James and that water. She really had no choice. "When do we go?"

"Right now." He took her hand and led her down the rock-strewn barrier below the docks.

Andy removed the boots he'd brought back for her and stuffed them inside her shirt as he instructed. She tied the shirttails tight about her waist. Relying on the cover of darkness, she unbuttoned the pants and pulled them off.

Coleton caught the glimmer of the pale satin camisole as the overhead lights filtered down through the heavy timbers of the dock. "What are you doing?"

Andy looked up, swallowing back embarrassment. There was little need of it. Coleton James had seen her in far less clothing. "I'm taking off as much clothing as

360

ossible. I don't want to drown wearing these heavy clothes."

Coleton let out an appreciative chuckle. She was practicality to the core.

"If you're laughing at me, so help me I'll . . ."

He couldn't resist the contrast of defiance and vulnerability that lit up her eyes. It reminded him of . . ." Without thinking, Coleton bent over and brushed his lips across hers.

His fingers lingered against her throat, feeling the leap of her pulse. "I'm not laughing at you." His voice was husky. When had everything between them become less clearly defined? When had it become so difficult to remember she was his enemy, the person who was responsible for taking Ombre Rose away from him? When had he begun to *feel* again?

Coleton cleared his voice and jerked his hand away. The tide's going out. We need to go now." He moved down toward the water, his legs bare to his thighs where his pants were tightly rolled, his shirt removed. The bundle with the guns was tightly strapped to his waist.

Andy followed slowly, still recovering from that inexplicable tenderness. She sucked in her lower lip as she watched him wade ankle-deep into the water.

He turned back to her. "Amanda?" His hand was outstretched to her.

She bit at her lip, images of all sorts of sea creatures filling her head. She clenched her fists and forced herself into the water up to her ankles. Her lack of clothing was forgotten.

"I hate this," she muttered to herself.

"Amanda!"

"I'm coming! I'm coming!" She walked in knee-deep. The water was surprisingly warm. Did sharks like such warm water? Coleton's arm slipped around her waist, eliminating the chance for retreat.

"If I drown, or something swallows me, I swear I'll use

361

that gun on you, Coleton James," she solemnly vowed a
water slipped to her waist, then her shoulders, the bottor
falling away completely beneath her feet.

He laughed softly, a deep, resonant sound that wa
comforting. "Somehow I believe you would, Amand
Spenser." He stroked easily through the water just ahea
of her, his body leaving a rippling wake on the glistenin
surface. Andy concentrated on that wake and the glean
of his muscular shoulders breaking the water ahead c
her. She didn't want to think of what was below her i
the murky depths. There was every possibility that Cole
ton James had lied about that.

They made the swim easily. Soft pools of light fron
compartments lining the lower deck of the *Natchez* dance
on the water, exposing them briefly. Coleton slipped be
neath the surface, reappearing at the stern of the rive
boat. His head and shoulders were an inky form agains
the stark white of the shallow draft wooden hull. And
followed, feeling the water stream through her long hai
She broke the surface just a few feet away, tired an
breathless. Coleton's warm fingers closed over her arm
pulling her to him.

He supported her in the water until her breathin
eased. She could feel the brush of his strong legs agains
hers as he tread water. In the languid, warm water, thei
bodies entwined in a subtly sensual movement that quick
ened her pulse and made her breath come all the mor
rapid.

"I'm all right now." She kept her voice quiet as sh
wedged her hands between Coleton and herself. She coul
feel the tautening of muscles across his chest, the heav
thudding of his heart beneath her fingers. If anythin
that simple contact made her more breathless and sh
gently pushed herself a safe distance away.

Coleton motioned silently to the towering machinery c
the huge wheel at the stern. It sat idle in the water, be
tween the long thrusting arms of framework. The bottor

paddle lay a few feet beneath the surface. He stroked quietly through the water, disappearing around the shallow stern.

It couldn't have been more than a couple of minutes, but it seemed like an eternity before she saw him again. He pulled himself up on the outside frame of the huge wheel, climbed the paddlewheel like the rungs of a large ladder, then swung easily down onto the deck.

A door opened as two men emerged from the boathouse only a few feet above Andy. They were momentarily illuminated by the glow of a lantern, then there was nothing more than shadows as the light was closed behind the door. Andy quickly slipped through the water, flattening herself to the hull of the boat. She heard the tread of footsteps so close. She held her breath and prayed they hadn't seen her. Then she thought of Coleton and offered a second prayer that he was safely hidden.

The voices of the two men drifted down on the warm night air.

"Did you check on the cargo?"

"Yeah. Everything's quiet."

"Any of the passengers make any complaints about those staterooms being closed off?"

"There were a few from the regular customers. Seems they didn't like bein' put out of their usual accommodations." The second man's laugh came low in his throat. "The Duchess took care of 'em. Gave 'em deluxe rooms on the second level and treated 'em to a private dinner with all the fancy trimmin's and some of that fine Kentucky bourbon we took last trip downriver. They won't be complainin' anymore."

"I don't care about complaints," the first man responded. "I just don't want anyone wanderin' around aft."

"Relax. Like I told you, I took care of everythin'. Besides, I got Hoskins down there. You know how he is, he plain don't like nobody. He won't let anyone go snoopin' around."

Andy was afraid to breathe, much less move. But movement was necessary or she'd simply sink. Mercifully, any sound was lost in the slapping motion of water against the hull of the *Natchez*. She watched the flaming arc of a cigarette tossed from the deck above her. It flared briefly in the night air, then extinguished with a brief hiss as it hit the water only inches from where she treaded water.

"Don't forget to check on Hoskins at midnight. We don't want any more problems. There have been enough already with this shipment. And the Duchess don't like problems."

There was no response, and Andy could only guess the second man had silently agreed. She wondered if Coleton were close enough to hear the conversation.

"I'm going to get some sleep. If there are any problems, let me know. Don't bother the Duchess with them."

"Right ye are, boss. I'll take care of it."

The conversation continued briefly, but became muffled by the sounds of water, the creaking riverboat, and receding footsteps. Andy let out a long sigh of relief, then slowly began to make her way back to the stern where Coleton had gone aboard.

She began to panic when there was no sign of him. Surely he wouldn't simply leave her there. Relief flooded through her as she saw a shadow move darkly against the side railing of the deck.

"Are you coming aboard or do you want to swim around with the fish all night?" He spoke softly and with faint amusement as he leaned out over the railing, extending his arm.

Cad! Andy thought. He was enjoying this, as if it were nothing but a Sunday stroll in the park. As his fingers closed firmly over her wrist and she leveraged her foot against the submerged framework of the paddlewheel, she thought briefly of pulling him into the water. It's what he deserved of course, but there was the possibility her little

ct of revenge would bring the entire crew down on
hem. And by the sounds of the conversation she'd over-
eard, they didn't want that.

She hestitated briefly, thinking of how he'd treated her
he last twenty-four hours. It would be thoroughly enjoy-
ble tossing him into the gulf.

"Don't try it" came the faintly amused warning from
bove her. Andy's startled gaze met his as he swung her
asily free of her foothold, dangling her briefly out over
he open expanse of water.

"You wouldn't!" Indignation hissed out of her lungs.

Soft laughter lit up the depths of those gray eyes as
Coleton thoroughly enjoyed her dilemma.

"No more than you would, Amanda."

His words were husky with a suppressed warmth that
ingled through her. But in spite of that warmth and the
urve of that maddeningly handsome smile, she knew he
vould do it. It was a smile of promise.

She dared a quick look down at the water below her.
he'd been too busy on the swim out here and avoiding
eing seen to worry too much about what was down
here. Now she had time to consider it once more, and
he really didn't want to go back in. Damn him, anyway.

"Aren't you afraid we'll be seen?" she gasped as his
rasp on her slipped deliberately.

"I like taking chances, Amanda."

Well, I don't, she silently fumed, knowing there was re-
lly only one way out of this. Everything in her practical
Yankee background argued that he wouldn't bring her
ut here to simply dump her back into the gulf. But the
motional side of her argued he would do precisely that
inless she gave in first.

"Coleton!" It was a pleading request without actually
ising the word he wanted to hear. He had a feeling it
vas all he would get out of her. She did have that
lamned streak of stubbornness.

She would have gasped if there'd been time. But as

quickly and easily as he'd dangled her over the side of the deck, Coleton swung her up beside him, his other arm encircling her waist and pulling her against him.

"What?" he asked, that maddening smile on his lips only inches away from hers. Their wet bodies were molded together. In spite of the evening breeze that cooled over the water, heat shimmered between them. The hand that had so effortlessly held her out over the water now slipped beneath her chin.

Andy's lips parted, but if she intended some biting comment, it was forgotten at the feel of his fingers gentling against her skin.

"I . . ." she faltered, her gaze locked by his.

"You've forgotten how to ask for something," he reminded her with a whisper, having the distinct feeling that Miss Amanda Spenser rarely asked for anything. She was strong, deceptively so, both physically and emotionally. She'd shown it to him countless times at Ombre Rose. What she'd endured would have broken any other woman and several men he could name.

Sunny. His tortured thoughts filled with the memories. This is what the girl on the verge of womanhood would have been like. The strength, the courage, the passion— they were all there, unfolding like the petals of a delicate flower, releasing the beauty and fragrance of what the flower was destined to be.

What was it about Amanda? His thoughts fragmented back to her. Was it Yankee ingenuity? That flagrant practicality of hers that could drive a man to distraction? Or was it the muleheadedness? Or some magical combination of all three? She certainly wasn't calculating, cruel or ruthless, as he'd first thought all those weeks ago. And God knows he'd wanted to believe that of her. It would have made everything he was doing so much easier. But she wasn't that at all.

Quite simply, she didn't fit all his notions about Yanks. Except, of course, for that streak of stubbornness. It was a mile wide and deep, running from the top of her head to the tips of her toes.

"You forgot . . ." He couldn't resist, and touched his lips to her cheek, taking several droplets of water on his tongue with deliberate slowness, tasting her, prolonging the memories of Sunny even if he knew it was wrong. "You forgot to say 'please'."

At the brush of his open mouth on her skin, Andy's fingers curled against the bare skin of his chest. Low, turbulent waves of sensation swept through her, making her tense. This was dangerous—standing here on the deck of the riverboat, when anyone might come along and find them, more dangerous still for what that simple contact was doing to her. Something seemed to ripple along her skin, though he never touched her, except for his arm about her waist, his lips against her cheek.

"I . . . hadn't we be better get out of sight?"

"Afraid of being seen?" Watching her stunned eyes, Coleton slowly journeyed to her other cheek, brushing her skin with that same feather-lightness, tasting wet heat.

Andy felt the waves rise until there was a familiar echoing roar in her head. She heard a soft moan, unaware it was her own. As hunger swept through her, she turned her mouth toward his. It was madness, and thoroughly dangerous, and she wanted more. But he glided up her skin, whispering over her eyelids so that they fluttered down. As if intoxicated, she allowed him to roam over her face, leaving her lips unfulfilled and trembling with anticipation. She tasted his breath on them, felt the warm flutter as they passed close, but his mouth dropped to her chin to give her only a teasing touch of his tongue.

Her fingers flattened against the muscled wall of his chest, only to curl inward with the tightening knot of sensations that poured through her.

Coleton's body was throbbing, aching to press hers and

feel the yielding softness that came only from her. The wet fabric that separated them clung like skin. It hid nothing and almost felt like flesh against flesh. Almost.

Against his cheek her hair was like wet silk. He'd begun wanting to punish her. Now *he* was punished by the sweet betrayal of his own body, desiring her as he'd desired only one other woman. It took every ounce of control to prevent his hands from diving into her wet hair, to keep himself from plundering the mouth that waited, warm and naked, for his. He traced her ear with his tongue, sipping the salty droplets from her skin, and felt her shudder. So, she felt it, too.

Slowly, he brushed kisses up her temple and over her brow on his way to her other ear. He nibbled gently, letting his tongue slide over her skin until he heard her moan again. She would stubbornly deny the desire, but her body couldn't.

Still he avoided her mouth, pressing his lips to the pulse at her throat, fighting the urge to move lower, to feel, to taste the subtle sweep of her breast above the satin camisole. Her pulse was erratic, like the sound of her breathing. And it had nothing to do with the swim.

He could have her now—instinctively he knew it, as he'd known it last night, and before in the gazebo. There was that inexplicable pull between them that kept her lingering in the shadows of his mind even when they were apart and made him now almost regret that he would ultimately betray her. And, dear God, how he wanted her. In a brief flash of recognition he knew he wanted all of her—the stubbornness, the stiff Yankee pride, the relentless determination. But he wanted Ombre Rose as well, and in taking it he would lose her. Her passion for Ombre Rose was genuine. In his soul he knew that. When she realized what he was after, she would hate him.

"Cole." Not Coleton as before, but Cole, the way Sunny had said his name so many years ago. It came

368

throatily through her lips, arousing him further and at the same time sharpening the regret. Gently he pressed his lips against her neck.

Andy's lips felt as though they were on fire. She had thought she understood hunger, but she'd never known hunger like this. God help her, she wanted him.

He drew far enough away to see her eyes. There was no light in them now, only the opaque shadows of desire. Her lips were parted, her breath shuddering through them. He bent close but kept his lips an aching whisper from hers.

"This is too dangerous," he said with far more meaning than the risk of the two men returning and finding them there. Then he turned and left her stunned, wanting, and furious.

Andy swallowed back disbelief. Her cheeks flamed. She wanted to scream her anger and frustration at his departing back but had just enough control to realize that would be not only foolish but disastrous considering their current situation.

She stared after him, struggling with the fury, clamping down the string of curses she'd never known herself capable of thinking, much less using, and silently contemplating her alternatives. The problem was, the only alternative was a long swim back to the waterfront. And with a quick glance into that murky darkness surrounding the riverboat, she realized it was no alternative at all.

"Damn!" she choked out, but it was as much for herself and her own lack of control. What was wrong with her anyway? She shivered as the night air breathed against her bare legs reminding her of her nakedness. She pulled the rolled pants from inside her shirt. As Coleton disappeared into the darkness on the port side, she struggled to pull them on. She wasn't about to be caught in less than her underwear, but the cambric pants were soaked and heavy, and simply refused to pull on.

"God's nightgown! I must be mad," she swore under

her breath, shoving the pants under one arm and padding softly across the wood deck in the direction Coleton had disappeared. It was completely dark in the compartments on this side of the riverboat. She felt her way along the railing, cursing herself and Coleton James. The nerve of the man. He'd actually left her . . .

Andy gasped, her eyes widening as she came up hard against a muscular shoulder. A scream churned into her throat and was immediately smothered beneath a warm hand.

"For God's sake, are you trying to alert the entire crew?" Coleton growled against her ear as he pressed her back against the wall of the passageway that lined the deck. Slowly he took his hand away.

"As if they didn't have enough time to find that out already!" She glared up at him through the darkness, her voice hissing out anger.

"Come on." He seized her hand and jerked her behind him.

"Do you know where you're going?"

"We need a place to hide. Then I need to talk to the Duchess about that message you were given."

"Why don't you just go up and ask her," Andy suggested, slipping through the shadows with him. She could see the bemused expression that glinted in his gray eyes.

"Let's just say the Duchess and I didn't part on the best of terms the last time we met. I could just as easily get my throat cut as get that information. And I don't care much for that. I need to get the Duchess alone."

Andy tried to ignore the tightening knot of resentment deep inside. After having met Valentine, she could just imagine the relationship Coleton might have had with the Duchess. The name itself brought all sorts of things to mind. Obviously the woman was very enterprising. The *Natchez* was hers, a sort of floating gambling palace from what Coleton had said. And with a regal title like that, she was undoubtedly not only beautiful but worldly as

370

well.

"What about an empty compartment?" Andy suggested archly.

"There aren't any aboard the *Natchez*," Coleton remarked with cool certainty. "The passenger list is always full. Even during the war."

"There's an entire section of empty compartments," Andy announced, gaining more than just a little satisfaction when he turned and looked at her with a bemused expression, as if to suggest he didn't know whether she was joking or guessing.

"Lower deck, just aft of the pilot house."

"And I suppose you know the difference between fore and aft." His mouth twitched with faint amusement, thinking he'd caught her.

"If this thing had sails, Coleton James, I'd show you just what I do know. I learned to sail on the Atlantic Ocean. I know fore from aft, the bow from the stern. And . . ." she planted her bare feet firmly, "I just happen to know there are empty compartments aboard this boat."

"And just how would you know that?"

She took a step closer, thinking she'd like to take a jab at the arrogant angle of his chin. She'd punched Stephen once when he'd teased her unmercifully, and she was willing to wager she could at least surprise Coleton James. But for now, satisfaction at knowing she was right was enough. She'd save the punch for later.

"While you were busy climbing all over the stern I overheard two men talking. There are several empty compartments on this trip."

He frowned. "That's against the Duchess's greedy nature. Why would several compartments be empty?"

Andy shook her head as if the answer were too simple. "To carry cargo, of course."

"The *Natchez* doesn't carry cargo, just passengers."

She flipped her damp hair back over her shoulder. "This trip, she's carrying cargo."

Coleton jerked around, his eyes narrowing as he contemplated the row of blacked-out cabin windows just down the deck. He started toward the nearby companionway that led to the inside companionway. Andy's hand caught him as she whispered a warning.

"It's guarded."

He whirled on her. "I suppose you overheard that, too." The cool smugness in her eyes was answer enough.

"They'll be checking the guard again at midnight."

"Then we wait until midnight to make our move."

Our move. She had almost laughed when he said that. She wasn't laughing now as Coleton slipped down the dimly lit companionway. She waited in the shadows, heard a dull thud, and held her breath.

"Amanda."

She almost jumped out of her skin.

"Come on," Coleton whispered, returning to lead her down the companionway. The guard was nowhere to be seen. They slipped inside one of the darkened staterooms. Andy almost tripped over the man's prostrate body.

"Oh, God!" It rushed out of her. "You didn't . . ."

"He'll have one helluva headache in the morning."

She let out a slow sigh of relief. Coleton quickly closed the door behind them and turned the bolt. A quick inspection revealed the windows were not only closed but sealed around the edges to prevent anyone from seeing inside and also blocked every bit of light from inside. Coleton stripped the guard of his jacket and stuffed it up against the bottom of the door. He struck a match, lighting the single lantern that sat atop a long box. Light pooled in the small compartment.

Unlike the staterooms aboard the *Iron Queen,* this one had no bed, no chair, not even a small table. It had been stripped of all furnishings. In their place were several wooden crates of varied sizes. Andy ran her hands over the rough wood.

"You said the *Natchez* didn't carry cargo. What is this?"

"That's a very good question." Coleton inspected the boxes. There was no name stenciled in paint, no identification whatsoever. "I think I'll just take a look." He slipped a knife from the sheath at his belt and pried the lid off the nearest box. It creaked loudly in the still cabin as the nails gradually gave way. He lifted the wooden lid. Andy peeked over his shoulder.

"Oh, my God."

Chapter Nineteen

"What is all of this?" Andy gasped, her stunned gaze lifting to scan at least a half dozen other crates the exact same size as the opened box, along with several more of varying sizes.

Coleton's expression was grim. "Rifles and armaments."

Confusion drew her soft golden brows together. "But this isn't a military vessel," she protested. "I thought it was against the law for anyone to have weapons except for the military."

"It is." He nodded grimly.

"Then that means . . ." She hesitated, moistening her suddenly dry lips.

". . . these are stolen weapons," he finished for her.

Her eyes fastened on him. "You expected to find this, didn't you?" she asked.

Andy barely had time to pull her fingers back as he dropped the lid down on the crate, gently tapping the nails back into place. Silence drew out in the small compartment. "You knew these rifles would be here, didn't you?" she repeated insistently.

His gaze met hers briefly. "Let's just say it doesn't come as a surprise," he answered. He could see the doubt in her eyes, the silent questions in the frown.

He retrieved the canvas bundle he'd brought aboard and untied it. "We know from the message accidentally passed to you at the Montfort party that the shipment is to be delivered 'according to plan'. And we know what the shipment is." Dropping into a crouched position, he unwrapped the revolver and the short-barreled shotgun. He carefully inspected each. Obviously satisfied they'd survived the swim from shore, he flipped the chamber of the revolver back into place.

"Then the Duchess is the one you're after," Andy concluded. "She must have hired someone to pretend to be the Gray Fox."

Coleton's expression was slightly bemused. "Maybe." It was an easy solution — maybe too easy. He was already thinking beyond that possibility.

Several people were already dead because of these stolen shipments, and the Duchess wasn't the sort who liked to soil her lily-white hands with blood. There was a great deal of risk involved, and while undeniably greedy, the Duchess had never been one to take chances. Then there was the fact that the entire web of information leading back to the Duchess had been an intricate one, cleverly thought out to protect the key person. And the plain and simple truth was, the Duchess had never been overly bright.

On the surface it all seemed to fit. Aboard the *Natchez* the Duchess had access to every port up and down the Mississippi, without fear of question by the military authorities. In exchange, the provisional government undoubtedly required some sort of payment in return. It was called protection money, and it all worked very nicely.

The *Natchez* could go anywhere without question, even unload a small, inconspicuous cargo. And the payment for that cargo could easily make up the difference for money paid to the blue-bellies. It all came very neatly back to the Duchess. And because it did, there was something that kept nagging at him.

Andy's frown deepened. He didn't seem convinced, but

she didn't have the energy to ask him what puzzled him. Fatigue pulled at her.

"What are you going to do now?" she managed.

Coleton grabbed the rope he'd tied around the bundle for their swim from the docks. "I'm going to make certain our friend over there doesn't walk in his sleep." He went to the prostrate guard who was sprawled on the floor just inside the doorway of the compartment. In quick, efficient steps he removed the man's coat, then he bound his wrists behind his back and anchored them to his bound ankles. He tore a strip of the man's shirt and stuffed a wad in his mouth. With another strip he secured the gag.

He shoved the bound guard into the far corner behind the stacked crates. "That should keep him quiet." he observed.

Andy could only stare at the huddled mass that had been the guard only moments before. She shivered involuntarily, her fingers rubbing across the flesh at her other wrist as she thought how painful those ropes would be when he regained consciousness.

Coleton saw the involuntary gesture. "He would have killed *you*, Amanda."

Her eyes were wide, the irises an inky wide band. There were deep circles of fatigue smudged underneath, and she shivered again. He crossed the compartment, taking the lantern with him. She was cold when his hands brushed the wet shirt that encased her arms.

"What do we do now?" she asked from between chattering teeth.

"You're getting out of those wet clothes," he ordered, starting to unbutton the shirt.

She slapped his hands away. "We're both wet," she pointed out, not trusting the change of expression in his eyes or his nearness. That kiss had been dangerous, far too dangerous.

One brow cocked slightly in that maddening expression

she'd come to know very well. It meant there would be no compromise.

"That may be, Amanda. But I'm used to it and you're not. Down here on the gulf, it's damp even when it's hot. People who aren't used to it sometimes catch fever. And the plain truth is, I won't have time to play nurse-maid to you when I decide to move. Unless, of course, you've decided you'd like to stay here until his friends come back for him."

"Is that right?!" Indignation replaced the fatigue, hissing out in a low whisper. "Well, you needn't worry about me. I'm healthy as can be." Lack of sleep, fear, anger, and humiliation of the past two days pushed her. She picked up the bundle of her wet pants and boots, her movements animated, infuriated.

"Where are you going?"

She stalked barefoot across the compartment. The crates filled half the compartment, stacked to the low ceiling in two corners. The guard lay slumped in the third. The sight of his bound body brought her up short.

"Amanda!" It was more a warning this time.

She turned on him, every last shred of control dissolving. "If I can survive all night in a downpour, I'm certain I can survive this!"

The moment she said it, she regretted her words. She knew by the look on Coleton James's face that he remembered everything about that night at Ombre Rose.

"I'm certain you can." His voice came low, soothing, with more hidden meaning than she wanted to hear. And then it was as if he were speaking to a child who'd misbehaved. "Come here, Amanda."

She hesitated, uncertain exactly what she should do.

"Amanda?"

Still she hesitated.

He sighed when he saw she would come no closer. "I was simply going to offer you my shirt. It's dry." He pulled it from the rolled canvas bundle and held it out to her.

She took it reluctantly. "When mine is dry you can have it back."

"Fair enough."

Andy stepped behind the stacked crates and slowly peeled away the wet shirt and satin costume. They plopped into a sodden pile at her feet as she pulled on the dry shirt. She reluctantly had to admit it felt much better. She draped the garments, along with her pants, over one of the crates and stepped slowly from the shadows.

When she looked up he was watching her with a strange, contemplative expression.

"Thank you," she whispered grudgingly, hating to be obligated to Coleton James in any way. It was too dangerous, and it seemed she was continuously obligated to him for something.

She glanced about the small compartment. There was only one vacant wall, and Coleton James sat back against it. One knee was bent, his arm resting atop it. The other leg stretched out before him. His calmness was deceptive. The revolver lay only inches from his left hand.

He motioned beside him, offering the guard's heavy coat. "You go ahead and try to get some sleep."

"What about you?"

"I'll sleep between blinks." He smiled faintly when she stared at him. "I don't need much. I'll just rest. I don't want any surprises from the rest of the crew." He indicated the bolted door.

Andy nodded. She supposed there wasn't any harm in resting for just a few minutes. She was exhausted.

"Do you have a plan?" She was almost afraid to ask.

He smiled this time. "More or less. But it will have to wait until the guests have retired for the night. And that could be hours. The Duchess always stays until the last card game is finished. I want to talk to *her* alone."

She had that nagging feeling, he was doing it again—making this up as he went along. "Which is it, more or less?"

"Get some rest, Amanda." He avoided answering her. "Or I just might be tempted to make you take the first watch."

She gave him a dubious look. "You trust me with the gun?"

"No." He said it simply, never opening his eyes, but a hint of that smile returned. "But I suppose the worst you could do is shoot yourself."

Her eyes narrowed as she silently fumed.

"Sit, Amanda," he commanded softly, without opening his eyes.

"Just for a little while," she agreed, slipping down beside him, but careful to put some distance between them. After all, she was wearing only his shirt, even if it did come to her knees.

Andy curled on her side, folding her arm beneath her head for a pillow. She tucked her knees to her chest, and pulled the wide shirttails over her bottom.

Coleton couldn't resist stealing a glance or two. A smile pulled at the corners of his mouth. She was trying to be so modest and dignified, and had strategically turned on her right side, toward him, as though facing the enemy.

"It could get a little cool tonight." He started to pull the coat up over her.

"I'm fine. *You* use it." She gave him a long look, then closed her eyes. "Just give me a few minutes, then you can rest."

"I'll try to remember." His smile deepened. He was willing to bet she'd be asleep in less than two minutes.

He turned the lantern down low and leaned back against the wall, his hand resting over the revolver.

"Coleton?"

"Hmmm?"

"What will happen when you catch the person pretending to be the Gray Fox?"

He heard the soft sigh of a yawn. "I'll turn him in to the authorities."

"What will you do then?" she murmured sleepily, hardly able to get out the words.

Coleton stared through the pale darkness. Slivers of moonlight framed the windows on the starboard side. The wick of the lantern glowed soft gold. It pooled on her thick hair as it tumbled over her shoulder, turning soft as satin as it dried. He was close enough to touch it and took several tawny strands between his fingers. She never stirred as they curled about his hand.

What would he do? The question was easier than the answer. The words cut at him simply because he knew exactly what he would do, and knew it would hurt her.

He could hear her deep, even breathing and knew he could be honest because she would never hear him.

"Then it's time to collect payment, Amanda."

The light at the window shifted to the soft gray of dawn. Coleton stood beside it. It was impossible to see out, but he knew it was morning. Noises had roused him—subtle noises. The change of the water lapping against the hull, a distant shifting of steel mechanisms, the whooshing of water as it was plunged beneath the huge paddlewheel, then reversed and churned forward. The pilot of the *Natchez* carefully maneuvered the huge sternwheeler about in the channel in preparation for the trip upriver. He was familiar with riverboats. It was still early. The night crew wouldn't be relieved for another hour yet. He had at least that much time. The guard was still unconscious in the corner.

Coleton gently roused Amanda. She came awake slowly, at first resisting and trying to curl back into a tight ball.

"Amanda."

"No. It's too early," she murmured, not asleep, not awake, but drifting somewhere in between. "Please, Cole, say we don't have to leave yet."

At first he thought she was awake, but she simply nestled her head deeper into the curve of her arm, and sighed deeply. Her words stunned, coming back from a long time ago with whispers of painful memories from the past.

He reached out to shake her shoulder gently, but his fingers curled with that elusive desire to touch more. He stroked the satin softness of her cheek, feeling her coolness and the heat. He watched fascinated as dreams fluttered the closed crescents of her long dark lashes.

Morning. It had been the one time he could never have with Sunny—until that last morning. They'd shared the night and themselves—young, impassioned, and in many ways naive. But for those hours of the night and into the dawn, she was his.

It became more than a memory as he leaned over her, watching sleep play across her exquisite features. He smiled at her faint frown as his thumb stroked her bottom lip. She sighed, the frown softly parting her lips.

It was more than he dared, and not near what he wanted. Lost in the memories, feeling them blend with reality, Coleton bent over her, tentatively touching his mouth to hers.

It began as a caress, a whisper, something stolen before she awakened completely. But it became so much more. It came from the past to the here and now, washing over him as he felt her sleep-filled response. Yesterday disappeared in this moment as she filled him—the sweet scent of her, the dark woman-taste of her mouth, the satin-soft skin over the curve of slender jaw. His fingers trembled, curling into damp palms, cursing himself, cursing her as he was powerless to do anything but deepen the kiss.

Sleep had stripped away her defenses, the dreams had

made her vulnerable. And now they became reality, stirring images of the past into sensations that she felt, tasted, and needed.

It was like making a journey back into the past while still aware of the present, and she responded to that need until it became desire.

Her breath sighed and mingled with his until it became his breath. Her skin heated beneath his fingers until it became his heat. He found himself wanting those stolen moments to go on forever, yet knowing they were already gone as her lashes fluttered upward, revealing the smokiness of passion and darker shadows of confusion. The dreams faded, lingering only in the brush of his mouth, and then it, too, was gone. And there were only his eyes, so close, like windows to the soul and then carefully shuttered as he pulled back from her.

"You're leaving?"

Was there regret as well as concern? He didn't know. He only knew everything was less easily defined now. She pushed back the thick tangles of her long hair and sat up as sleep receded completely. All the barriers were firmly back in place.

"It's time."

He rolled silently away from her and sprang to his feet with the ease and stealth of a man who'd lived at the edge of danger and death too long. He crossed the compartment, taking the shirt she'd worn the day before. It was dry now. He quickly pulled it on, ignoring the buttons as he impatiently shoved the tails into the waist of his pants.

"What happens now?"

He looked up only briefly as he pulled on his boots, then seized the coat and cap the guard had worn.

"Now, I pay a visit to the Duchess and find out about this." He gestured to the stacked crates. Andy rose and crossed the cabin, seizing her pants and the satin costume. They were almost dry. Coleton's hand stopped her.

"I go alone."

"Oh, no—"

He cut her off. "I need you to stay here and watch him." He gestured to the motionless guard. "One of his friends came by a short while ago. I think I convinced him everything was all right."

"And just how did you do that? Hit him over the head, too?"

He smiled. Miss Amanda Spenser, damned Yankee, was amazing. She could go from soft and yielding, filled with passion, to indignant and determined in less time than it took for him to think about it.

"We had a very brief conversation through the door. He asked if everything was all right and I assured him it was."

"And he believed you?"

His smile deepened. He loved the expressions that transformed her lovely face. Right now it was disbelief.

"Let's just say he didn't shoot his way in here, and he hasn't come back with a few dozen more men. I'd say we have a fifty-fifty chance that he believed it."

"And I say you're crazy."

She stood, feet planted, hands on her hips, and made an altogether very fetching sight, dressed only in his shirt.

"That may be, but it's worth it. The stakes are very high."

"Just what are the stakes?"

He ignored her and slipped across the room, picking up the shotgun. "I've left you the revolver. Do you think you can use it?"

"I ought to use it on you," she replied through thin lips, deciding to try another tactic. "You need me, Coleton James."

Need. It focused everything that had passed between them moments before. Yes, it was there, for the first time in nineteen years. He'd thought it dead, buried, gone, a part of him he could never get back, or want to get back. But he'd felt it with her, when he'd never felt it with anyone since Sunny. It was like the first time — wonderful and frightening.

Not for her! his thoughts cried out. He didn't want to feel the need, but he had.

"Stay here. I'll be back." His voice had a hard edge that hadn't been there before as he turned toward the door, slowly scraping the bolt back from the lock.

"Will you?"

He looked back, only once, and read the myriad questions that were all wrapped up in that one small question. He wondered if she was even aware of everything she asked, and decided she wasn't.

"I may be a lot of things, Amanda. But I'm not a liar. I always keep my promises. Lock this behind me." And then he was gone, the door whispering shut behind him.

At that moment, Andy hated Coleton James — again.

The *Natchez* moved through the water of the gulf into the mouth of the Mississippi, leaving New Orleans behind in the predawn light.

It was quiet, with only the motion of the water or the muffled rasp of drunken snoring behind closed doors to break the early-morning stillness. An occasional voice called orders from the upper deck and was answered somewhere up ahead. But except for those few diligent crew members, the *Natchez* slept.

Coleton carefully threaded his way down companion-ways, ducking behind a post, slipping into a darkened corner. He made his way forward where he knew the larger compartments were. The Duchess would have only the largest and finest. Encountering a crew member, he shrugged the coat he'd taken from the guard up higher around his neck and pulled the man's cap down low to hide his face. A gruff greeting was met with only a nodded response.

Then he heard the faint clink of silver and china. He

followed it, ducking into an adjacent passageway as a young cabin boy emerged from one compartment, pushing an empty serving cart. There were equally empty bottles of champagne, the finest money could buy before the war, and the Duchess's favorite.

Coleton's eyes gleamed with dark satisfaction from beneath the cap as the boy moved past him, obviously in the direction of the galley. He checked both ends of the passageway, then quietly slipped to the door and knocked. The sultry, faintly weary voice from within beckoned him in.

Andy counted—sixty seconds to every minute. She'd dressed. She'd eaten. Now she paced the small cabin. By her calculations Coleton had been gone at least fifteen minutes. She chewed at her bottom lip, biting down hard as a low, muffled moan came from the corner.

God's nightgown! The guard was regaining consciousness! Now what was she supposed to do? Her hand closed over the revolver. The coldness of the steel barrel had frightened her before. Now it was oddly comforting. She leaned against the far wall and continued to count. The moaning ceased and she relaxed, but only for a short while. Soon the tension built again.

Was it twenty minutes or longer? She'd lost count, and started again at twenty. Then she paced, the restlessness driving at her.

What if someone came to relieve the guard? Coleton was fortunate enough to pull off a bluff the first time. She knew she'd never be as lucky.

Would she then have to use the gun? Great balls of fire! She'd never even fired one! She shoved the infuriating wisps of hair that tickled back from her face. It wasn't hot in the cabin, but her skin was damp.

How many bullets were there? Could she aim the revolver at someone and pull the trigger? Could she kill?

"Damn you, Coleton James!" She cursed softly, wishing he were there at that moment so she could tell him exactly what she thought of him face-to-face. She stalked to the end of the cabin and turned.

"Twenty two."

At twenty five minutes—more or less, as Coleton would say—she refused to wait any longer. Something must be wrong. And in that case, this was the wrong place to be. She tucked the revolver into the waist of her pants and opened the door slowly.

Andy checked the passageway. It was dark, with light only at the end. Since there were no passengers in this section, there was no need of the overhead lanterns. She closed the door softly behind her and made her way down the passage.

Out on the open deck, Andy flattened herself against the wall of cabins. She encountered only one crewman and ducked down an adjacent passage. She stopped in the cool morning shadows that filled this side of the riverboat. Damn! How was she ever going to find Coleton?

This was madness. She should never have left the cabin. He could be anywhere. She peeked slowly around the corner, the breeze off the water stirring wisps of hair at her temples. Perhaps she should go back. She whirled back around, intent on just that, and gasped at the hands that caught her.

"Amanda!"

Her eyes widened, her breath caught in her throat, she felt all color drain from her face. It was several very long moments before she recovered, air seeping slowly back into her lungs.

"Captain Durant."

"Good God, Amanda!" His fingers bit into her upper arms. "What the devil are you doing here? Are you all right? Do you realize how many people are looking for you?"

All his questions came at her at once.

"Where is he?"

"He?" It didn't register at first. Everything was moving too fast. She was still trying to recover from the fact that Chandler Durant was aboard the *Natchez*.

"Coleton James. My God! Did he hurt you? My men have been looking for you for two days."

"Where is he?"

She pulled back as his fingers tightened, and tried to loosen his grasp. "You're hurting me."

His hold loosened slightly, but still he refused to release her. "He's a dangerous man, Amanda. Father in heaven! When I heard you'd been abducted, I imagined all sorts of dreadful things. He's a killer, Amanda. I don't know what he's told you, but he's a criminal. You've got to tell me where he is."

"Captain!"

It was hoarsely barked, the voice excited and drawing the attention of both. The sergeant motioned his men forward. Coleton James hung between them, his weight supported as his head slumped limply forward.

Chandler Durant released Andy in a movement almost as brutal as his grasp. Blood seeped back into her bruised arms. Going to his men, he grabbed Coleton by the hair and jerked his head back viciously. Blood trickled from Coleton's lips, mingling as more trailed from a head wound.

Andy's stomach knotted, her heart twisting as if someone had reached deep inside her and seized it.

"No," she whispered desperately and started forward, only to be once more restrained, this time by one of Durant's men.

"He's not dead, my dear." His voice was silken with the threat. "At least not yet." He looked up to his men. "And I don't want him to suddenly end up that way. Is that understood?" It wasn't a question at all, but a very explicit order.

Andy's stricken gaze jerked back to Chandler Durant's. Surely that meant this was all some sort of mistake.

Then the rasping voice pulled her gaze back to Coleton as he hung, beaten and battered between the two men, all but dead.

"How long did you wait, Amanda, before you told them?"

"No! I didn't tell. You don't understand." She struggled to reach him. Dear God, he thought she'd told them where he was. She saw Durant give the silent command.

"No! Wait, please!" She tried frantically to reach Coleton, but she was restrained. Andy could only watch helplessly.

"How long, Amanda?" his swollen and cut lips whispered as he was dragged away. The words tore at her.

"Come along, my dear." Chandler Durant's words grated across her raw nerves as his arm firmly guided her, his men only a few paces behind them. "I know this had been a dreadful ordeal for you. You must tell me everything."

"Captain, please, you must believe me."

"Amanda, please call me Chandler. After all that we've meant to each other . . ." And . . ." he took the revolver from her, "you certainly won't be needing this. You're safe now."

That brought her gaze up sharply to his as he escorted her to a nearby cabin.

"He saved my life." She pleaded for what had to be the hundredth time in the past hour.

And for at least that many times, Captain Chandler Durant ignored her. "Coleton James is a war criminal. He was a spy, responsible for countless murders." He massaged the dull ache at his temples. It was over. It was finally over. He'd vowed to trap the Gray Fox. Now he had him. It was the perfect ending to an almost perfect military career.

As he thought of that one flaw on an otherwise unblemished military record, his fingers constricted. But now he had the man responsible for that unfortunate bit of misinformation. He rose, giving the outward appearance of the elite West Point officer he was supposed to be.

"You will listen to me, Amanda," he said, his voice calm. "When the surrender was signed, he refused to accept it. We have proof . . . he simply fled the country." His eyes gleamed with enormous satisfaction.

"And we have proof that he is responsible for numerous crimes against the military occupation government since the war. We have even uncovered a conspiracy to assassinate General Sheridan, as well as several other Union army generals. It's all part of an elaborate plot to undermine the Federal government, resurrect the Glorious Cause and plunge this country back into war."

Andy sat down on the narrow bed. She rubbed her fingers across her forehead as if she could physically remove the confusion and fatigue.

"All I know is that he saved my life."

"After he abducted you," Chandler Durant quickly pointed out. "Dear God, Amanda. Think! The man is utterly ruthless. He's killed any number of people. And to think he was with you at Ombre Rose all those weeks. It's clear what he wanted."

Her startled gaze came up to his.

"He wanted his home. Bitterness is like a disease, Amanda." He knelt before her, none more familiar than he with that emotion.

"He never forgave the fact that Union forces occupied the plantation. He was determined to have it back, no matter what the cost," the light in his changed to something dangerous, "to perpetuate the sort of system your brother died trying to end."

His gloved hands had once more closed around her arms, biting into the soft flesh. Durant's words pounded at her, twisting everything around. The air seemed to compress in her lungs. Her thoughts churned back to the conversation they'd had earlier. Coleton James had seen

389

King Louis pass that message to her at the Montfort ball; Coleton James had followed her to Melanie's house and abducted her — all because of that message. They had barely escaped capture at Valentine's. Duvalier was murdered, and once more, they barely escaped. Then those two soldiers had attacked her in the alley.

The way Durant explained everything she could almost believe it was true. "But there were people after us. He said someone else was responsible for those raids and stolen armaments — someone else posing as the Gray Fox. He was trying to find that person when I was given that message at the Montfort party."

Durant's hands covered hers. "Of course that is what he would say, Amanda. He had to make you believe in his innocence, to get your cooperation. He was after the shipment aboard the *Natchez* all along."

He saw by the instant response in her eyes that he was right. James had come aboard to find that shipment. "You intercepted that message, a message he vitally needed. But once you were given that message he couldn't risk your telling someone else. Abducting you was a guarantee of his safety. The man is very clever." *But no longer.* Durant's smile deepened.

"But what about Duvalier?"

"A very unfortunate incident. He was one of my men, of course. Coleton James murdered him."

Andy came up off the bed. "I just don't know . . ."

Durant came to his feet and gently took her hand. When she tried to remove it, his fingers closed over hers insistently.

"You're tired, of course. This entire matter has been a dreadful ordeal. I'll have one of my men bring you clothes and something to eat. You may stay here, of course, until we reach Baton Rouge. Your friends will be quite anxious to hear that you've been safely found." He turned toward the door.

Andy followed him. "What will happen when we get to

390

Baton Rouge?" she asked.

Durant hesitated, his hand coming up to stroke her cheek. "There will be a small inquest, of course. You'll be asked to give your side of the story."

Andy felt relief pour through her.

"And then Coleton James will be put to death before a firing squad." He inclined his head faintly and started out the door.

She stared after him. A firing squad? But just before he'd mentioned an inquest. Surely . . . She started out the door after him, almost colliding with one of Durant's soldiers. Her questioning gaze met Durant's.

"Merely for your safety, Amanda. Coleton James is under heavy guard, but I don't want to take chances. After all, he has escaped before."

She pushed her way around the guard. "You said there would be an inquest."

Durant stopped and slowly turned about, taking her hand and placing a kiss against the back of her fingers: "Merely a formality, my dear. Coleton James's fate was sealed the day the war ended." He smiled over her hand. Then his expression grew somber.

"It's unfortunate there are some who simply can never accept defeat. Now, please, Sergeant Meachum will escort you back to your cabin. You'll have plenty of time to rest." He inclined his head, his bearing perfect, his eyes cool.

"I've waited a long time for this, Amanda."

She had no choice. She saw it in Chandler Durant's eyes and those of the sergeant as their gazes met briefly. The sergeant was an older man with streaks of gray shot through his black hair. His nose was bent, and he had a habit of shifting his eyes. For a moment she thought she recognized him, but he gave no outward sign that he knew her.

The door closed behind her, and Andy slumped on the bed. Everything Chandler Durant had said was all

391

twisted inside her head. And there was the image of Coleton James and the way he looked, beaten and bloodied, betrayal and accusation hard in his eyes. She drove her hands frantically back through her hair, trying to sort everything out.

The hard rasp of metal against metal brought her startled gaze up. She leaped from the bed and quickly crossed the cabin. She tried the latch. It held fast. Was she being held prisoner as well?

There was no clock, no timepiece whatsoever in the cabin, making it impossible to know the time. But she was aware the sun had been high overhead for quite some time when the brisk knock sounded at her door. She almost laughed at the thought of someone expecting her to answer it.

She swung off the bed. She'd tried to take a nap, but found herself too restless. She smoothed her hair and her wrinkled shirt and waited while the bolt was slipped back. Sergeant Meachum swung the door as a man pushed a wood serving cart through the doorway. He was dressed in a long white apron tied over an enormous belly, white shirt rolled back over beefy arms.

"I'd like to see Captain Durant." Andy informed them both. There was nothing but silence as the stocky man removed a plate, bowl, and eating utensils from the top of the tray.

"It's very important," she insisted, though neither man acknowledged her. "I have information about Coleton James."

That brought only the tiniest flicker of interest from the man with the apron. It was quickly hidden away as he finished removing everything to the small bedside table. Meachum motioned him from the room.

"Please! It's very important. Captain Durant would want to know about it."

A rolled bundle was thrust into her arms. "The captain said to give you this." And then the door was slammed in her face, the bolt thrust once more into its place.

"Damn!" Andy tossed the bundle into the far corner of the bed. Why wouldn't anyone listen to her?

She felt guilty about being hungry. Time and again her thoughts focused on Coleton. Were they feeding him? Had they bound his head wound? Durant's orders were explicit that he was not to be allowed to die. Surely that meant they would . . .

It surely meant nothing.

"God's nightgown! What am I going to do?" she muttered in confusion.

She ate, though she hardly tasted anything. She took a sponge bath from the water and soap provided in the shallow basin across the room. She even managed to wash her hair. She tried to sleep, and tossed restlessly, listening for that bolt to be unlocked, for voices or footsteps, anything.

The afternoon sun trapped long shadows in her room. It was warm, the only air coming through that one guarded window. She adjusted the louvers down, closing out Captain Durant, closing out the guards. Were they protecting her, or preventing her escape? Andy sat on the edge of the bed. A dull ache began at the back of her head, down low at her neck. It spread as everything Chandler Durant said came back to her:

Coleton James was the Gray Fox . . . All the arguments and accusations screamed back in her imagination.

Andy clasped her hands over her ears as if she could block out the voices. But still they persisted, louder and louder, until they became a roaring in her ears, humming along her nerve endings, burning in her blood.

She knew the moment it started, and the next moment when she began to leave. The images whirled past her; all the images of her life. She saw Lacey and her father, Parker Rawlins, and Eunalee Whitherspoon. Then they were gone and she was going back farther still. She saw the loving faces of her parents, but they were soon gone. They faded away from her, leaving a momentary sadness that was quickly swept away in the whirlpool. All the moments of her childhood spun at her, then spun away just as quickly. It was as if someone had strung together pictures of each moment in sequence and then ran them past her.

Some lingered; she caught only brief glimpses of others. Then everything moved faster and faster, in a blur of sight, sound, and textures.

It was only a pin-dot of light at first, indistinct, distant, like a star. But as she traveled back farther, the light became brighter and brighter, until it was the entire focus of everything she felt or saw. It was like traveling through a tunnel of darkness and emerging into the light:

Cool, gray. Morning mist, dawn's first light. At first she only felt them. Streamers of Spanish moss dripped from the gnarled branches of a massive oak.

And then she saw them; shadows that lengthened and separated as the two men stood shoulder to shoulder. The mist swirled angrily about their legs, ghostlike, as each clutched a gleaming pistol in their hand.

No! This couldn't be happening. She tried to call out, but the words wouldn't come. She struggled to reach them, but invisible bonds restrained her.

She broke free. She was running. She stumbled, fell and drove herself to her feet. Fear congealed in her stomach, the scream was trapped in her aching lungs. She had to stop them . . .

She ran between them as gunfire roared through the glade. She could see his face now; lean and handsome, and young, so very young. He cried out, his face contorting in a terrified expression.

The ground seemed to fall away beneath her, and still she fought to reach him. Then his hands were on hers, his arms pulling her against him. And the soft gray of those eyes blurred as he bent his head to hers.

"You're safe. You're all right," she gasped. "I had to stop you.

I had to . . . please understand. I love you. I couldn't bear it if anything happened to you."

"It's all right." His voice trembled against her ear. *"I know."*

She could feel the thundering of his heart as he held her against him. His fingers trembled as they stroked her cheek. His breath shuddered against her lips.

"It will be all right. I'll never let you go."

She clung to him. *"Promise me . . ."*

"I promise . . . anything." There was anguish in his voice.

"Promise . . . you will always love me."

His eyes closed in agony. *"I swear I will always love you."* It came out as a harsh whisper, filled with passion and aching desperation.

"Promise . . ."

His fingers laced with hers as he cradled her in his arms. *"Forever,"* he whispered as he kissed each finger. She tried to hold on to his warmth.

She tried to touch his cheek, but her fingers wouldn't obey. She could see the soft gold streaks in his brown hair, the sweet, sad curve of his mouth, and the one dimple that creased his left cheek. His eyes were that soft, tender shade of gray, and they were filled with tears. And then everything was slipping into the mist.

"Coleton," she called to him. *"Please don't go away . . . Please! I can't lose you! I can't!"*

"I can't lose you again."

"Coleton!" Andy sobbed his name as she jerked upright on the small bed.

It was like a dream. No, a nightmare, she thought. But she knew she hadn't slept.

"Oh, God," she whispered.

Like those times before when she'd had the experience, she felt physically worn out, drained. And she ached, deep inside, with a hollow emptiness, a deeper longing and hunger than anything she'd ever known before.

She had no reason to believe Coleton innocent of the

crimes he was accused of. No reason at all, except for the past—their past . . . together.

Andy propped her forehead on her bent knees. She closed her eyes, holding on to the truth this time. Each time she remembered a little bit more. It was like the layers of her paintings, colors carefully applied, adding more and more depth and texture to the picture.

Now she understood the painting she'd felt compelled to finish. It had been a portrait of Coleton, not as she knew him now, but as she'd known him before—in that other life, before when she had been Sunny Rawlins. In her heart and soul, she knew it was true.

She didn't remember all of it. She hoped that would come in time. And she had no idea how she could possibly make him understand, or anyone else for that matter. It was too incredible, too impossible.

Was it a miracle? She'd always believed they were possible.

Or some twist of fate that had brought her out of one life and into another?

The one constant before and now had been her love for Coleton. She accepted it and knew it was true. She would never understand all the twists and turns of this life that had ultimately led her back. It had begun that day she first saw Ombre Rose—again. Ombre Rose had been the link back to Coleton.

"He'll never believe me," she whispered, her throat aching. "He's so bitter about so many things. He hates me because I'm a Yankee, because he thinks I've taken Ombre Rose away from him." She laughed, a sad, bittersweet laugh.

Dear God! How could he have changed so much? Or *had* he changed? Andy fought the feeling of helplessness.

"Why?" She pounded the bed with her fist. "What am I supposed to do? How can I make him understand?"

The answers were there deep inside her. Instinctively she knew that. Just as she knew she couldn't bear to lose him again, for then she truly would be lost. She looked up, drying the tears, finally accepting.

"I have to stop them. Somehow I'll stop them. I won't let them kill him."

Chapter Twenty

Because Captain Chandler Durant was so predictably efficient, a by-the-book officer, Andy knew he would send for her.

He was also amazingly thorough, another trait she made note not to forget. The bundle of clothes he sent for her was aggravatingly complete.

The blue satin gown was obviously intended for evening wear, but fit remarkably well. It was delivered, along with most of the accessories a lady would wear; camisole, corset, stockings, bustle, petticoats, and shoes. She questioned where an officer might come by such garments under the present circumstances and immediately thought of the Duchess. Of course, these must have come from her.

Andy's first impulse had been to toss them all aside, something deep inside her stubbornly refusing to dance on a string like a witless puppet for Chandler Durant. But then she calmly reminded herself, for the moment Chandler Durant controlled all the strings. And so she dressed and waited.

Each hour took them closer to Baton Rouge and the moment when Durant would hand Coleton over to the military authorities for the "inquest," a situation and an outcome Durant would also control. So, she paced and waited, and paced again.

Still, when the knock came at the cabin door, she jumped, her nerves drawn taut. She fought to hold on to some shred of calmness. Fear congealed in her stomach, but determination won out. The knock sounded again, this time with more impatience.

"Just a moment," Andy called out. Then she took a deep breath, her gaze coming back to the now-empty tray that had been delivered earlier in the day. She had no appetite, but she had forced herself to eat. Now, only the silver service and an empty plate remained.

Her fingers closed over the knife. Lifting her skirt, she slipped the implement through the delicate satin garter that secured her stocking. She felt like a pirate. Smoothing her skirts back into place, she offered up a prayer that no one would notice the missing knife.

She smiled faintly as she opened the louvered door to the cabin. "Thank you for waiting, Sergeant. I'm ready now."

As they stepped out into the companionway, Andy's attention fastened on the two heavily armed guards several doors down. The door to a cabin was unlocked from the outside, and one of the men carried a tray of food inside. He immediately returned, the heavy lock was slipped back into place, and the two guards took their positions, one on either side of the door. As far as she knew, there was only one prisoner aboard the *Natchez*.

Andy acted as if she'd only taken casual notice of it, then turned and fastened a beguiling smile on her face.

"I'm absolutely starved. I thought supper would never be served." She saw the immediate confusion in the sergeant's eyes at her change of attitude. Much as she hated flirting with the detestable man, it was necessary. He hadn't seemed to notice her curiosity about that locked cabin.

Andy had hoped the evening meal would be the customary military affair, with Durant's junior officers present. But as she was shown into the small but elegantly furnished cabin, her gaze fastened on the two place settings. Durant turned, inclining his head in greeting. He then silently dismissed Sergeant Meachum.

She watched the man leave, feeling a deep twinge of regret that no one else would be joining them. The thought occurred for the second time that day that she had seen the sergeant somewhere before. But at the moment, just where or when escaped her.

"Amanda?"

Her attention abruptly came back to Chandler Durant, and she murmured the requisite apology when she realized he had called her name twice. "I'm sorry."

"That's quite all right. It's understandable considering what you've been through." He rounded the small, linen-draped table and assisted her to a chair.

"Amanda, I feel we have become quite comfortable with one another. I know the past two days have been a terrible ordeal for you," he went on with that solicitous smile of his that she'd begun to recognize was used very effectively, "I was hoping perhaps you'd like to tell me about it."

So you can have more evidence against Coleton James? So you can follow your orders—by the book, and hand him over for execution? Andy thought with a vengeance behind a faintly tremulous smile that disguised her true feelings.

"You're right of course. It was dreadful. I find it difficult to believe it all." She deepened the smile. "It absolutely grieves me to think of what Miss Kittridge and her father have had to endure, not knowing my whereabouts."

"Of course."

He'd reached across the table and covered her left hand with his. "I was hoping perhaps you might be able to reveal something of Coleton James's intentions concerning the weapons."

Andy subtly removed her fingers from his grasp. "I was his prisoner. He didn't tell me anything about his plans."

"I had no idea there were weapons aboard this boat."

"Yes, well, because of these raids and attacks by the Gray Fox, the military has been forced to seek other less conspicuous methods of transporting supplies and armaments. I've personally been assigned to see that the shipments arrive at their destinations safely, and that the Gray Fox is stopped." There was something in his voice that slipped cold fingers across Andy's skin—something deadly.

400

Andy ground her teeth, her cheeks beginning to ache behind the ridiculous smile she was forced to wear.

"I suppose this will mean a promotion for you, Captain."

"Yes, and please, call me Chandler. I had hoped that after this amount of time, you might come to regard me as a friend . . . and possibly a suitor."

Andy would like to have appeared surprised, but there was actually no surprise at all. Captain Chandler Durant's intentions had been obvious from their first meeting in St. Louis. Just as her intentions had been equally clear, and hadn't changed.

She swallowed back the bile that rose, along with the lie. "Actually, Captain, I am still mourning the loss of my brother."

"Yes, of course. I understand."

His expression indicated he understood completely, but that it hardly mattered.

"And naturally I respect your grief. But we have been acquainted for some time now, and my feelings for you can't have gone completely unnoticed."

"Please, Captain. This is hardly the time or place."

"Then when we have returned to Baton Rouge, perhaps you will allow me to call on you. I will be leaving the military shortly and I was thinking of making my home in the South. There is no reason why that couldn't be Baton Rouge. Naturally I wouldn't expect you to give up the Ombre Rose plantation."

Andy's surprise must have been obvious at the announcement of his retirement. He took it as obvious encouragement. "Actually, Amanda . . ." he took her hand once more, this time insistently, refusing to release it when she pulled back, "my feelings run very deep. Times being what they are, what with the war just ended, it's a time to move forward, a time of healing and prosperity. I was hoping I might have your answer when we returned."

It was obvious he hoped for a great deal! "I don't know what to say."

He smiled, but it wasn't quite a smile. It was more an

401

expression of immense pleasure and self-assurance. His gaze traveled from her face to the daringly low neckline of the gown and lingered.

"You see, Amanda, my name could protect you from the rumor, scandal, even suspicion of the last two days." At her obvious confusion, he simply went on. "People will talk, there will be speculation as to why you didn't attempt to escape from Coleton James. My superiors might even question that you had a part in some elaborate scheme involving Coleton James."

She felt as if his eyes had undressed her and shuddered. "That's ridiculous." She couldn't believe what she was hearing. Why on earth would he suggest such a thing?

"However, Amanda, as my wife," his gaze came back to hers with delicious anticipation, "you would be beyond all reproach. It would simply be an unfortunate set of circumstances and you would have my protection. No one would dare question you."

Or run the risk of ending up before a firing squad? Andy's blood ran cold in her veins. Because this was the last thing she'd expected, any response was slow to come. She simply sat there and listened.

"Therefore, I would like this matter resolved as soon as possible. With your consent, we could be married aboard the *Natchez* at the next stop. That would eliminate embarrassing questions and speculation of your character as well as your reputation."

Speculation? Reputation? God's nightgown! This was no marriage proposal. It was a threat! She was being blackmailed into marriage. Why? She refused to believe it was out of his undying love for her, and she certainly had no such feelings for him.

Andy folded her hands in her lap to keep them from shaking with suppressed anger. The nerve of the man! The absolute unmitigated gall! For him to think that she was simple-minded enough to cringe at the possibility of a soiled reputation and seek protection from him! She almost laughed. If Captain Chandler Durant only knew . . .

But she didn't laugh. She laced her fingers together tightly and squeezed back the desire to claw that arrogant, self-assured expression from his face. Inhaling slowly, she kept her voice calm. "I'm very flattered by your concern, Captain. But after everything that's happened, I simply can't think of all this right now." She swept her lashes up, fixing him with an imploring gaze. Her lower lip trembled faintly in what she hoped would be taken as feminine fluster. It was a performance to make Lacey Kittridge envious.

"I do hope you understand. I'm just weary to the bone. But I am grateful for your solicitous concern . . ." she almost choked on this next part, "and your affection. I do understand the situation and you're quite right. I know you'll understand when I ask if we can speak of this again in the morning, when I'm rested and can think more clearly."

Andy was intimating that her answer would be "yes"—an answer she had no intention of giving him.

He rose solicitously, the perfect gentleman. His uniform was perfect, his manners were perfect. "Of course. It was inconsiderate of me to extend the evening so long." He escorted her to the door and opened it. Sergeant Meachum stood at his post.

Durant restrained her hand, his fingers faintly bruising. "As long as we understand each other, Amanda." He left the meaning behind the words unspoken, but she understood nevertheless. He efficiently handed her over to Meachum.

"I will see you at breakfast, Amanda. We will reach our first stop shortly before noon."

She understood only too well.

"Escort Miss Spenser back to her cabin." He gave Meachum his orders as he lifted her hand and lingered with a kiss at the back of her fingers.

"Until tomorrow, Amanda."

"Good night," she whispered, her throat tight with strained fury and more than a little desperation. She had to do something and it had to be tonight.

She walked stiffly before the sergeant, glancing only briefly as they passed the two armed guards. Her thoughts

403

raced. She had to do something and quickly, for she had no doubt she would once more be locked in her own cabin. And once that lock was slipped into place, it would be difficult if not impossible to escape.

The lower deck was almost completely deserted. Laughter, voices and the distinctive sounds of bottles clinking against glasses came from the open windows of the top deck where she surmised a rousing evening of gambling was already in progress. Lanterns decorated the rail above, swinging gently with the motion of the riverboat. She thought she heard a woman's raucous burst of laughter—the Duchess no doubt. There was the lively tinkling of music as a piano player went through a rousing rendition of Dixie.

What must Chandler Durant think of that? The piano player would no doubt be put before a firing squad, she thought darkly.

Andy hesitated at the door, waiting for the sergeant to open it for her. When he did, she smiled sweetly and stepped inside.

"Oh, Sergeant, could you help me with this window? I tried earlier and it just wouldn't open. I think it might be stuck. And it is dreadfully warm in here." This time, she smiled at him radiantly with just the right amount of uncertainty and helplessness reflected in her eyes.

As he nodded and moved past her to the window on the opposite side of the cabin, Andy carefully pushed the door closed with the toe of her shoe. As she knew it would, the window opened easily. Andy picked up the empty water pitcher.

The crash of broken porcelain was followed by the dull thud of Sergeant Meachum's body hitting the floor.

"God's nightgown! I've killed him!" Andy swore softly under her breath as she looked for signs of movement. She breathed with relief when she finally found the faint pulse. She must have knocked him out cold. Seizing the knife from her garter and brandishing it like a sword, she kicked at his foot. Nothing. Andy bit at her lower lip. Something that Coleton had said came briefly to mind. She had no plan, she was just making this up as she went along. What the devil was she supposed to do now?

"His gun!" Andy whispered to herself as she looked down at the knife. She might not know how to fire a gun, but at least she knew how to load one, and she didn't like knives, especially after seeing what had happened to Duvalier.

And damned if Meachum wasn't practically lying on his military revolver. It took a great deal of effort but Andy managed to roll him over onto his back. She quickly seized the pistol.

Now what? Andy stripped the sheets from the narrow bed and tied the sergeant as best she could. Then she gagged him. She had no idea how long he would be out, but she didn't want him coming around too quickly. Stepping back, Andy felt only a faint twinge of remorse.

"This is no time for regrets, my dear," she quietly scolded herself as she replaced the blade beneath her garter and carefully changed the revolver into her right hand. She held it down at her side, concealed in the fold of her skirts as she opened the door of the cabin and stepped outside.

"My, what a lovely evening," she declared just loud enough for the two guards to hear her, hoping it appeared she'd merely stepped outside to get a breath of fresh air.

One guard looked up as she approached. "Where's Sergeant Meachum?"

"The sergeant? Oh, he left. He said he was needed up on the deck."

She saw the question in the man's eyes as he glanced first at her, then at the closed door to her cabin.

"Just hold on right there, miss," he ordered curtly, moving away from his post.

Andy pulled the pistol from the folds of her skirt and aimed it directly at the two men. "Please don't move, Corporal," she informed him quietly. "I'm not very good with this and I wouldn't want to hurt anyone."

Both men's eyes widened in surprise. It was obvious, whatever they expected, it hadn't been this. Andy could imagine what Lacey would have said.

"Now hold on, miss. Just take it easy." The first soldier held his hand up. He started to step away from his companion, trying to widen the distance between them so that she could concentrate on only one at this short distance.

"Please, Corporal, I don't want to shoot you, but I will if you take just one more step."

He stopped dead in his tracks.

"Now, please put down your guns and push them over here."

Slowly their belts and holsters came away, followed by a rifle. The weapons were shoved toward her.

"Thank you. Now please unlock that door."

The two men exchanged a brief look, then the first one turned to her. "We don't have the key. Only the captain has that."

The revolver was heavy. Andy tightened her grip and brought it up level with the man's head. "You are a liar. I saw you open it earlier. Open it now, or I will shoot you." Whether or not she would do it, not even Andy herself knew. All she did know was that she intended to have that door opened.

Shaking his head, the corporal reached inside his pocket and took out the keys. The door was easily opened. Andy motioned both men inside. She picked up the discarded guns, keeping the pistol aimed at the corporal.

There was a single lantern burning inside the cabin. It was dim, but it lit the small cabin. Coleton James was nowhere to be seen.

"Step inside, Amanda!"

Andy whirled around just inside the open doorway. Coleton stood to her left and slightly behind her, shielded by the open door. His hands were unbound and he clutched a sturdy chair leg in his hands.

"Coleton . . ." she gasped, as much from surprise as from the horrible sight of his face. He'd been beaten and beaten badly. One cheek was bruised purple with a long cut where someone had become too enthusiastic with the punishment. A scrape colored the skin across his chin, and he moved stiffly as if every bone in his body ached. So much for Captain Durant's orders that he was to be well treated.

He shoved her roughly aside, quietly closing the door behind her and the two guards as he took the revolver from her.

"What are you doing here? Don't tell me that damned Yankee conscience began to bother you?"

Andy stiffened at the cruel words. It was no more than she should have expected.

"I know what you must think . . ."

"Do you really?" he spat out at her in a whisper so violent, so lethal it sliced the warm air of the cabin. He jerked his head in the direction of the two guards.

"Tie them. You'll find the ropes on the floor over there at the end of the bed."

He was angry. From his way of thinking she understood it. Still, he hadn't even given her a chance to explain. She found the ropes where they'd fallen after he'd worked himself free. Dear God, they'd bound him to the stationary legs of the bed.

Andy almost dropped the ropes as her fingers felt something damp and sticky. She opened her hand. The bloodied rope made a snaking pattern across the palm of her hand. He'd paid the price of blood for his freedom.

"Amanda!"

He'd shoved the two guards against the far wall and ordered them to place their hands at their backs. He motioned to her with the pistol.

"Tie them tight. I don't want them escaping and bringing Durant down on our necks."

Andy tied their wrists and then their ankles as Coleton instructed. They were gagged as well and then separated, each tied at opposite ends of the bed where they couldn't help each other.

Coleton opened the window and tossed the rifle and one of the pistols into the night air. They landed with a faint plop in the water; the sound quickly churned under the relentless beat of the paddlewheel. He turned and thrust a revolver at Amanda.

"If either one of them moves, shoot 'em. Just make certain you don't shoot yourself."

"Coleton . . ."

"Save it!" he bit off angrily.

"I didn't have to come here!" she spat out, equally as angry. After all she'd been through, he didn't even have the decency to listen to her. He looked at her for a long moment, those gray eyes she remembered so vividly from the past now filled with emotions she'd never known in him.

"I'd have made it without you."

No, not without me — not again. She wanted to shout it at him, but she dare not. He'd think her mad. Right now there was only his anger. He couldn't comprehend anything else.

"Perhaps, or you might have only gotten as far as the first guard. They had guns, you didn't," she flung back at him.

"Why did you come back here? Why did you take the chance?"

Because I love you. She wanted to scream it at him.

"Because it was important that you know I didn't betray you. And this was the only way I could prove it to you." She could feel the tears pooling in her eyes and hated herself for that weakness. Now of all times, she wanted to be strong and stubborn and unbending. And the damned tears were making it impossible.

Something twisted deep inside Coleton as he saw those vivid blue eyes fill. Tears. Christ! He'd never been able to handle a woman's tears. Not since . . . Sunny. That last day came back to him vividly and he could almost feel the wetness on his fingers. Tears are the blood of the soul, a priest had once said.

And now, more than the pain of his bruised and battered body, more than the harsh reality that he probably wouldn't get out of this alive, Amanda's tears caused him the greatest anguish. His jaw worked, his lips thinned into a hard line. He wanted to be angry. God knows he'd had hours to work on it. And she was the natural choice for that anger, he'd been certain she'd betrayed him to Durant. But underneath the certainty was doubt.

"Stay here!" He brushed past her and headed for the door.

Andy blinked, certain she hadn't heard him correctly. He couldn't, he wouldn't simply leave her there!

"Where are you going?"

Coleton turned back briefly at the door, the hard core of anger dissolving inside him. The look in her eyes was shock mingled with disbelief and more than a little fear. Any other woman would have pleaded with him not to leave her. Not Amanda. She simply demanded to know where he was going with all the stubborn Yankee straightforwardness he'd come to expect. A man would always know exactly where he stood with her. She was honest without pretensions or airs. And she was tough.

The hard line of his mouth softened into a brief smile that was gone as quickly as it came.

"I have a little unfinished business. If they give you any trouble, or if anyone comes near that door, shoot first and ask questions later." He opened the door a crack, glanced down both directions of the passageway, and stepped outside.

"Coleton." Her hand stopped him. It was the gentlest pressure; the restraint was in the soft, vulnerable look in her eyes.

He brushed her cheek briefly with the back of his bruised knuckles. "I'll be back." And then he was gone, slipping into the darkness at the end of the passage. Andy closed the door behind him and sat down to wait. For the second time in a matter of hours she began counting off the minutes.

She had to believe he would come back.

Andy was becoming more anxious by the moment. She kept the revolver aimed first at one guard, then at the other. She went to the door twice and checked down the passage, but there was no sign of Coleton. Fear knotted her stomach

409

—the fear that he might have been seen and caught. When the faint rapping sounded at the door, she almost jumped out of her skin. She adjusted the louvers, letting out a sigh of relief when she saw Coleton.

"You were gone so long," she whispered as she opened the door.

"There was just one small detail I had to take care of. By morning, when they make their first stop, this riverboat will be crawling with Federal troops. We have to get out of here." He rechecked the ropes on the two guards.

Andy pulled her lower lip between her teeth. He was still so angry with her, she could hear it in the edge of his voice and the curt words that conveyed only what was absolutely necessary. This was hardly the time to try to explain her feelings.

"Coleton, I . . ."

He cut her a brief glance. "What is it?" He bit off sharply.

It stopped her cold, and she ran her fingers back through her hair, struggling to find the words. There was so much to tell him, so much that she knew he would never believe—would never want to believe. If he would even listen.

"I . . ." She hesitated and then took a deep breath. Perhaps the best words were the simplest ones, ones that had been spoken between them so long ago. "I once made a promise . . ." Again she hesitated. This time when he looked at her, he didn't break his gaze away so quickly.

Perhaps it was fancy, maybe some trick of the imagination, but there was something about the breathless, almost painful quality in her voice that caught at him. The word "promise" held him. His brows came together as he watched Amanda Spenser struggle with something she obviously wanted very much to say. And for some inexplicable reason he found himself wanting very much to hear it.

Her lower lip trembled, her eyes glistening with emotion as she remembered the words that had been their vows to each other all those years ago. But the expression on his face was so intense, those eyes closed and hard, and she was suddenly frightened that he would laugh at her, throw it all

410

back in her face. She couldn't bear that, and so she did the only thing she could. She forced a laugh, more at herself.

"I made a promise . . . that I would do whatever was necessary to help you." She let out a tremulous breath.

"I know what you think of me, and in many ways I can't blame you. But I know you didn't murder Duvalier, or do any of those other things they've written about in the papers." She wouldn't even begin to try to explain why she felt that way, not right now. "That's why I came here." At least he seemed to accept her explanation, and if she wasn't mistaken, the hard angle of his shoulders had eased.

He rose slowly from checking the two guards.

"That should keep them for a little while." He turned to her. In the dimly lit cabin, her luminous eyes were big as saucers. "Better let me have that revolver." His voice had changed, from anger to something quiet and contemplative.

Her mouth turned in the beginning of a smile, reminding him how long it had been since he'd seen one of her smiles, longer still that he'd looked for it.

"Are you afraid I'll shoot you with it?" Andy was immediately rewarded with the flash of an unguarded smile, a shadow of the smiles she remembered from so long ago.

"I had considered that. I'm surprised you didn't practice on that sergeant."

"I had considered *that*," she informed him saucily, grateful to be able to release some of the tension that throbbed inside her.

"You may still have to use it, if we don't get out of here. Come on."

They left the cabin. Coleton locked it from the outside, then guided Andy ahead of him down the passage toward the starboard deck. They headed for the stern of the *Natchez*, keeping to the shadows. Several times drunken guests staggered out onto the deck above them and looked over the side. Andy prayed they hadn't been seen.

"I suppose you have a plan for getting us off this riverboat," Andy gasped as she was stuffed behind a huge water

411

barrel on deck.

"There are rowboats secured at the stern, to be used in case of an emergency." Coleton motioned to the section of deck that lay ahead. The open companionway led to the top level. Bright light exposed the entire width of deck. Anyone crossing the deck took the risk of being seen. And they needed to cross it. He saw the apprehension in her eyes.

"The guests are far too busy and far too drunk to notice," he encouraged her, and to prove it he slipped across the deck, melting into the darkness beyond.

Andy bit at her lower lip, casting a wary glance up the companionway. Loud, raucous voices bantered back and forth as several guests came to stand at the top of the companionway.

"You took me for everything I had this evening," came one loud, disgruntled male voice.

"No more than you took from me last night," another gentleman replied.

"Amanda!" Coleton whispered from the shadows, motioning her to follow. Gathering her skirts in one hand, Andy started across the brightly lit deck.

"And just what do we have here!?" Strong fingers closed over Andy's wrist, spinning her about. "Someone wandering about where they're not supposed to be? Hmmm?"

Andy stared up into the face of a tall, elegantly gowned woman. She was dressed in a jade green gown edged in black lace. Her hair was titian, the most exotic color Andy had ever seen even in this dim light, and it coiled in a thick mass atop her head, with a long fall extending down the length of her back. She stood at least a full head taller than Andy, towering over her with a bearing that could only be called regal.

Her face was artfully made up, her skin lightened with a thin layer of pancake makeup. Color had been added to her cheeks, but it only dramatized the high cheekbones. She wasn't what Andy would have called a beautiful woman, but she was striking. She winced, bent over almost backward by that strong hand twisting hers behind her.

It all happened in the flash of an instant, yet Andy knew she'd just encountered the Duchess.

Coleton stepped from the shadows, confronting the woman who was almost as tall as he was. "Let her go!"

The Duchess fixed him with a cold glare. "Captain Durant mentioned something about you," the silken voice purred in contradiction to the strength in those fingers.

"Such nasty business, confiscating the *Natchez*. Not at all good for business, if you get my meanin'." She pulled Andy another few steps away. "And Coleton James, also known as the Gray Fox. You've caused me a great deal of trouble. And that makes me very unhappy."

To emphasize just how unhappy she was, she reached up and twisted her hand in Andy's hair, jerking her head back painfully. Andy tried to pry her fingers loose.

"Two birds attempting to flee, or so it would seem. Captain Durant will be very interested to learn about this. It just might be worth all the trouble I've been having lately."

"What trouble would that be?" Coleton followed them, stalking.

"You should know all about that, Coleton, darling. Naughty, naughty, you simply couldn't accept that the South lost the war. You must learn to accept certain things Coleton. I've learned to accept them."

"Is that right?"

"Yes, and you could have been a part of it. I did make you that offer just before the war ended."

Coleton laughed. "It was an offer I simply had to refuse. I'm certain you can understand my reasons."

They might have understood, but Andy didn't understand any of this. She twisted, trying to break free. The Duchess simply tightened her grasp and continued to move backward, taking Andy with her.

"Yes, I suppose," came the smoky reply. "Just as I have my reasons for this." She jerked Andy back another couple of steps.

"Coleton!" Andy cried out, trying desperately not to draw attention from the top deck.

"I'll say it just one more time." Coleton spoke low, but the warning sent shivers down Andy's spine. "Let her go."

"Ah, Coleton. I can't do that. I simply can't let the two of you escape. You have to stand trial. It's as simple as that."

"I don't think so," Coleton informed her evenly, as if they were doing nothing more than simply standing there chatting about the weather.

Andy groaned, certain she was about to lose a great deal of her hair.

"But I have Miss Spenser," the Duchess purred, her grasp on Andy shifting as she reached for something in the pocket of her gown with her right hand. Andy saw the hard gleam of a small pistol no bigger than her fist the second before she felt the press of cold steel against her temple.

"And unless you want to see her shot as well, I suggest you come along. Quietly."

Coleton's fingers twitched just over the pistol stuck in his belt. He dare not reach for it. Damn! He knew the Duchess, and because of it, knew he couldn't bluff his way out of this one. There was more than just himself at risk.

"Don't be a fool," he warned.

"A fool? Not hardly, Coleton darlin'. You're the one who's a fool thinkin' you can get away from Durant. After all, it's his little game."

Coleton knew exactly what the Duchess was talking about. The game was revenge. Durant had been obsessed with it since he'd captured him that time before Vicksburg. When he escaped he only raised the stakes. It didn't matter that Durant had the wrong man this time. He had the man he wanted.

"Duchess? That you?" a slurred voice called down the companionway.

"Yes Tommy darlin'," the Duchess called up to the faceless voice. "I need Captain Durant and his men. Run along like a sweetheart and get him for me, will you?"

"What?"

"Tommy! Get Captain Durant!" the Duchess called up to him in a firmer voice, her eyes never leaving Coleton's.

414

"It is such a pity," she lamented with a wistful sigh, then made the mistake of twisting her hand again in Andy's hair.

Fancy little pistol or not, Andy had had enough. If she was going to die, it was going to be with all her hair intact.

"Let me go!" Shifting, Andy stomped on the woman's right foot. She heard a loud gasp of pain and took advantage of the woman's momentary surprise by bringing her fist up under the Duchess's arm. The pistol was knocked from her fingers, clattering across the wood deck. She saw Coleton reach for the gun.

"Why you little bitch!" the Duchess screeched, grabbing for more hair.

The one and only time Andy had fought with anyone had been at school with Carrie Jerome. She'd split Carrie's lip and was sent home for a week. The appalled horror of her aunt Lenore at her being such a wild hooligan, as she called her, was mild punishment compared to Miss Van der Poole's switch. But as compensation, she did have the rather grand pleasure of knowing she'd punched Carrie Jerome right in the mouth.

Andy twisted to her right and came up under the Duchess's left arm. As she did so, she grabbed for that gleaming titian hair, sinking her fingers in deep.

"I said *let go!*" Andy jerked back, intent on repaying some of that pain and stared horrified as that entire, elegantly coiled titian mass came away in her hand.

The Duchess screamed a miserable sound, turning on Andy as she let go of her. For several long moments they just stared at each other.

At first Andy couldn't comprehend what had happened. She simply stood there staring first at the elaborate hair that dangled from her fingers, and then back at the Duchess. Her eyes widened.

"You're not a woman at all! *You're a man!*"

The Duchess snarled as she lunged for Andy. "I'll get you for this." She grabbed for Andy. "You're coming with me."

A man! God's nightgown! And that had been a man calling down to her, er . . . er him. Did that mean . . .?

Her thoughts went no further. As the Duchess's hand closed over her arm, Andy doubled up her right fist and pulled it back. In less time than it took to think about Carrie Jerome, she punched the Duchess right in the nose as hard as she could.

The Duchess reeled back, blood trickling down her—his—upper lip, an expression of complete surprise registering in his eyes a moment before they rolled back in his head and he keeled over backward.

"Amanda! Are you all right?" Coleton took her gently by the arms.

"I could have used a little help."

Amusement glinted in his gray eyes. "You seemed to have everything pretty well under control all by yourself. And I make it a rule to never interrupt a good fight."

"Did you know about that?" Andy pointed incredulously at the Duchess.

"A well-kept secret."

Andy turned and stared at him. "Did you . . . I mean she said . . ." She shook her head, clearing the confusion, "he said . . . after all that the two of you had meant to each other . . ."

There was a hint of a smile curving his mustache. "We go back a long way."

"Friends, huh?"

"Something like that. Let's just say I knew the Duchess before he was the Duchess." Coleton looked down at the prostrate man in all his satin finery. "Where did you learn to do that?"

"Girl's school." Andy glanced down at the Duchess with a trace of chagrin. "Let's just say that for a moment, she—he reminded me of someone."

"I trust you weren't the closest of friends with that person."

Andy shrugged as she rubbed her bruised knuckles. "It just seemed the thing to do at the time. I don't like having my hair pulled." Then her soft brows knitted together. "I asked you a question. Did you ever . . . well, what I mean is . . . she's a he, I mean a man, and well she . . . he sounded as if the two of you had . . ."

"Had what, Amanda?"

"Damn you! You know what I mean!" she exploded at him.

"I think I do." He took hold of her arm and pulled her toward the stern of the *Natchez*. "We can talk about it later." He sobered, his expression grim.

"Right now I think we better get off this boat."

Andy's head came up. She looked around, thinking surely that Tommy was on his way back with Chandler Durant. "Everything's all right. We'll make it."

"Everything is not all right, Amanda. Run!"

"What is it? What's wrong? Has something happened?"

A quick shout of orders came from the top deck. Either the guards and Sergeant Meachum had been discovered, or Tommy had found Durant. In either case the alarm was sounded and Andy could see the silhouettes of the armed soldiers as they ran along the top deck toward the companionway. They hadn't taken more than a dozen steps when Andy felt the deck shudder beneath her.

Coleton pulled her along without breaking stride. "Don't stop! Keep going!"

"What is it?" Andy gasped as she ran after him.

Another shudder ran the length of the *Natchez*, catching them mid-deck. Andy was thrown up against the outside wall of one of the lower deck cabins. The heaving motion beneath her feet was followed by a rumbling that began low and then intensified.

"Coleton?"

"Come on," Coleton ordered. "We don't have much time." His fingers tightened over Andy's wrist as he propelled her ahead of him. It could come at any minute and he wanted her as far away from it as possible. He hadn't counted on that little interruption by the Duchess . . . If they could only reach the stern of the boat.

When it came, the explosion tore a hole big enough to walk through in the side of the *Natchez*. Andy screamed and

417

Coleton flattened her against a cabin wall, protecting her with his own body.

"My God! What happened?"

Both their gazes fastened on the giant fireball that sent streaming sparks out into the night. The fire met air and roared to life, blasting searing fingers out across the deck they'd crossed only moments before.

"It's that little emergency I was telling you about," Coleton offered by way of explanation. "Come on. It'll get worse when the fire reaches that shipment of munitions."

Andy couldn't imagine that it could get any worse. The deck of the *Natchez* now rolled at an awkward angle and it increased as they approached the stern.

"The explosion must have ripped a hole into the hull."

"We're sinking?"

"That's a safe guess."

"Sinking! Right now?"

Coleton laughed. "I tried to schedule it at a more convenient time, but there just wasn't one."

Andy's face paled. "How deep is it in this part of the river?"

"It's pretty shallow here." Coleton assured her as they climbed up the deck to the stern which had risen a few feet out of the water as the *Natchez* began to take on water.

"I suppose you had a good reason for doing that." Andy cast a quick look back over one shoulder at the lower deck that was now engulfed in flames.

The huge paddlewheel lurched at an odd angle, the steam engines still driving them in spite of the fire. The *Natchez* was listing at a steep angle, the wheel half in half out of the water. Water churned crazily through the wheel and sprayed down on them both as they pulled themselves around the end cabin and were flattened against the wood wall by the angle of the boat. Water washed over the low side of the deck.

Coleton wiped water from his face and grinned down at her. He seemed to be enjoying this thoroughly.

It seemed the thing to do at the time.

The *Natchez* groaned as she filled with water and slipped another notch into the inky-dark river. Water swirled up around their knees, soaking Andy's skirts and dragging her toward the low side. Coleton caught her, propelling her toward the port side where a rowboat dangled awkwardly.

"Damn!" Coleton swore as another shudder rocked through the *Natchez*.

"What is it?" Andy clung to the railing beside him. Her hair was plastered to her head, the gown soaked through to the skin.

"The lines are tangled. I can't free it."

"What about another boat?"

Coleton gestured across the partially submerged stern. "It's under water."

Overhead, the enormous paddlewheel groaned as it slowed, then finally stopped altogether.

"The boilers must be gone," Coleton surmised as the last of the water cascaded down from the top of the wheel. He jerked around as shouts and the sound of boots along the upper deck came distinctly now that the wheel was silent.

Andy's gaze followed his. For a brief moment she was certain she saw Chandler Durant silhouetted against the light pouring out from an upper level cabin. Other shadows swarmed before him as his men clamored over the deck. She screamed as several bullets popped into the heavy timbers around them.

"It won't break loose!" Coleton cursed again, then he turned and returned the gunfire. Beneath them, the *Natchez* listed more to starboard, the port side heaving at a sharper angle out of the water. Andy was thrown against the armature of the wheel.

Coleton caught her as her leather-soled shoes slipped on the wet deck. All about them the *Natchez* erupted into flame and chaos. He pulled her through the wheel structure, bullets deflecting off metal, others embedding in wood with a dull thump.

"Where are you going?" Andy gasped as she reached for a handhold and pulled herself out onto a low platform that was part of the wheel frame. Usually submerged, it now thrust out of the water.

He was several feet ahead of her, his weight braced against the next flat paddle. He pulled her up beside him. "What do you think of a midnight swim?"

Andy's eyes widened. She took a deep breath, her gaze darting briefly out over the inky expanse of river that surrounded the crippled riverboat.

"Not much," she confessed. It was all she had time for as Coleton thrust his revolver at her.

"Hold this," he ordered as he gave her the gun, his arms slipping beneath hers.

The thought flashed through Andy's head that this wasn't exactly the right time for an embrace. "What are you doing?"

Coleton's fingers closed over the fabric of her gown. He tore it open, scattering dozens of tiny buttons into the Mississippi River.

Andy gasped as he jerked her gown down around her hips. He was equally efficient with the satin ties of her bustle and layers of petticoats. He looked up with a rakish grin when she stood only in her chemise and bloomers.

"What? No corset?"

At that moment Andy gave serious thought to punching *him* right in the nose, but she was too busy holding on to the gun with one hand and clinging to the heavy beam overhead with the other.

"Does this mean what I think it does?" she asked, sincerely hoping it didn't. Several more bullets shot past them. Voices shouting over the roar of the fire were much closer now as well. She was certain she heard Durant cursing.

"Come on, Amanda. It won't be so bad. The shoreline isn't that far, and I know for a fact that you're an excellent swimmer." His arm encircled her waist. He took the revolver and jammed it into his belt.

Andy groaned. "I hate this part of your plan," she shouted over the roar of gunfire.

"Amanda . . .", his mouth whispered against her cheek,

420

"this wasn't in the plan." Then he chuckled softly. "There aren't any sharks this time."

Her head came up, her expression accusing. "I knew you'd lied about that!"

It was muffled into a sharp gasp as she followed Coleton's gaze. There was no time left. Durant and his men had worked their way back to the stern and down onto the lower deck. They were coming right at them.

Coleton jerked almost convulsively and cursed. Her gaze shot back to his momentarily. Then there was no time to think as he lunged, his weight carrying both of them off the back of the riverboat as a shattering explosion tore through the *Natchez*, and they plunged into the dark depths of the Mississippi River.

Chapter Twenty-one

"Shallow!?" Andy accused as she came up gasping for air. Coleton was a short distance away.

"Save your strength for swimming," he countered, and moved ahead of her in what she hoped was the direction of the shoreline.

As they stroked through the water, the deafening roar of an explosion brought them both momentarily back around.

Lights glowed from lanterns on the top deck of the *Natchez,* lending an eerie sight to the crippled riverboat. She was completely still in the water, that huge paddlewheel like a large, angry claw poised to strike as she listed badly to port. She was obviously taking on a great deal of water. It was already pouring over the lower starboard deck, working its way forward as more and more of the riverboat tilted crazily in the water. A huge fireball engulfed the midsection of the *Natchez.* And now, along with the fireball sending eerie fingers into the black night sky, there was a vaporous cloud of steam as water drowned the huge boilers that had once driven that powerful wheel.

Andy looked at Coleton as they both treaded water, each wrestling with their own thoughts. Her brow wrinkled with unspoken questions. Why was it necessary to blow up that shipment of arms?

His eyes met hers briefly. She thought he must see the

422

doubt. Then his gaze cut back to the *Natchez*, aglow in the heavy night air.

"They'll be after us as soon as they cut that boat away."

Andy's attention jerked back to the crippled riverboat. They were close enough to hear the frantic cries of the passengers and crew as they clamored out onto the open decks. Some were dressed, others were clad only in night clothes. One and all, they launched themselves into the river, coming up to grab at some piece of floating debris.

Some of the passengers were angry, others were obviously uproariously drunk as they called back and forth to one another in high spirit at what they considered to be an adventure.

Another explosion lit up the night and illuminated the aft section of the *Natchez*. Andy could see the outline of the remaining rowboat and the half dozen men who struggled to cut it free.

"Oh, God," Andy whispered as she tread water.

"Durant's men" was all Coleton said as he stroked past her.

It was no longer a matter of whether it had been right or wrong to destroy that shipment. Chandler Durant intended to see Coleton put before a firing squad. Now Coleton was an escaped prisoner, and she had gone with him. Andy knew precisely their predicament. She turned in the water and stroked after him.

She had always been a strong swimmer. She'd spent every summer swimming in the surf out on Long Island, much to her aunt Lenore's great displeasure. But that was years ago, and the current of the river dragged at her. It was exhausting. It seemed they would never reach shore and Andy knew her strength was fast disappearing.

Either Coleton had misjudged the distance or he was deliberately taking them to another location. Twice the current almost pulled her under. Each time, Coleton caught her. It was pitch-black, clouds obscuring the moon, yet he always seemed to know exactly where she was. Andy was glad one of them knew; she was completely disoriented.

Now he had stroked ahead of her, disappearing in the inky darkness that surrounded them.

"Amanda!"

She willed strength back into her aching arms and legs, pulling slowly toward him. Coleton's fingers closed over her wrist as he pulled her to him. He'd grabbed onto the heavy snag of a tree thrusting out of the water.

Andy gasped as the current caught her and dragged her under. Coleton's grasp tightened, his arm going around her waist giving her a solid anchor in the swirling current. She came up coughing and choking, pulled against the hard wall of his chest. Her arms went around his neck.

"Are you all right?" His voice was low, urgent against her temple.

She nodded to assure him. "Just let me . . . catch my . . . breath."

"We can't stop. The shore's only another twenty yards or so. Can you make it?"

Her legs felt as if they'd never support her again, her arms were still around his neck, her cheek against his chest. She nodded, not at all certain she could but knowing the danger if they didn't keep moving.

Coleton tilted her face up. She couldn't see his. He was only a dark shadow above her, but she could feel his mouth and the kiss as it missed, finding the corner of her mouth. His lips moved, repositioning over hers in a quick, hard pressure that ended altogether too quickly.

"Come on, Miss Spenser," he teased. "Let's see if a Yank can keep up with a Johnny Reb."

She pushed against the circle of his arm. "I can outswim you any day of the week, Coleton James. But you have an unfair advantage. You know the river and I don't."

His arm tightened about her so briefly it couldn't have

been called a hug. Then he separated from her and stroked on ahead through the water. "Then prove it, Miss Spenser."

She knew he was goading her, teasing her until she had no other choice but to prove she could. Somehow he understood how little strength she had left. A challenge like that couldn't be ignored. They'd been challenging each other from the moment they met.

When her feet first brushed the silty river bottom Andy thought she would burst into tears, she was so grateful. Except she had no strength left for tears.

Here, out of the main current, the river lapped lazily against the shoreline. She simply kept her head above water and let herself gently wash ashore.

Andy lay there, gasping for air, her heart hammering in her veins, her arms and legs refusing to move.

Out in the middle of the river, the *Natchez* lay dying. The glow of the fire flickered back along the shoreline. Coleton was frantic, then he saw the white of Amanda's bloomers and camisole, stark contrast against the dark shore. He crawled to her on hands and knees, fear churning a tight knot in his stomach.

"Amanda!" He turned her roughly. His fingers bit into her arms. Her eyelids fluttered briefly, then swept up.

"Stop shaking me!" she whispered hoarsely, anger sparking in those brilliant eyes that looked like blue flames as they reflected the distant glow of fire aboard the *Natchez*.

For a brief moment, his feelings were unguarded, fully exposed. "I was afraid . . . I thought when I saw you just lying here . . ."

"Well, I'm not!" Andy propped herself up into a sitting position, pushing her wet, tangled hair back over her shoulder.

Then she smiled weakly. "I couldn't let you win that bet."

"I already did." Coleton grinned back at her; then it

faded as shouts were heard out on the water.

"Come on!" He jerked her to her feet.

Andy groaned, as her knees buckled. "Where are we going?"

"Into the bayou."

"What?" There was no time for more. They'd obviously been seen. She gasped as gunfire erupted from out on the water, no more than twenty or thirty yards from shore. Several shots plopped into the water at the river's edge; others thudded into the soft mud of the riverbank—much too close.

"Damn!" Coleton cursed as he pulled her behind him.

They ran up the riverbank and plunged through the sparse cover of trees that lined the water. River oaks and bald cypress were draped with Spanish moss. It caught at Andy's face and hair like spiderwebs laced through the low-hanging branches.

She stumbled, fell, and Coleton dragged her to her feet, hardly breaking stride.

When they stopped it was only to listen for sounds of those who followed. Then Coleton changed their course.

Andy ran past the point when she thought she would collapse. Pain shot through her right side. She wanted to beg him to stop, but she couldn't spare the strength that effort would take. There was no sense of direction, only Coleton pulling her onward, along a course only he seemed to know.

The river had long since disappeared at their backs, or perhaps it was close by and they'd only been running in circles. The trees around them had become dense and they were forced to slow their frantic pace and thread their way among them. Overhead, the treetops were illuminated by a pearlescent moon as it emerged from behind a thick bank of clouds. It was a blessing and a curse. They could now see the direction they fled, but those following could see as well. And they *were* following.

There were times when Coleton stopped that Andy

heard nothing. Other times she heard the faint, distant rustling of leaves underfoot or the snap of an occasional twig broken underfoot as someone closed in very close. The night creatures around them heard it, too. The chorus of bullfrogs would hesitate and there would only be the buzzing insects and the screech of a distant heron.

She was exhausted, Coleton could feel it in the weary sag of her hand in his when he was forced to slow their pace. He knew it was all she could do just to keep going, but she never hesitated and never complained. He knew she never would. It was that damnable Yankee obstinance.

The damp heat plastered their clothes to their bodies. He knew she had no shoes. She had lost them somewhere in those frantic last moments as they left the ship. Now twigs and brambles cut at her feet. But she never complained about that, either.

When neither of them could go any farther, they stopped briefly to rest—both knowing it wasn't for long. It was then he heard voices in the distance, perhaps a hundred yards away but nonetheless distinct. Coleton immediately changed direction again. When he stopped again, there were more voices, coming from an entirely different direction. Andy heard it this time and looked at him questioningly.

"They've split up into two groups. They'll close the gap, hoping to trap us in between," Coleton explained.

"What are we going to do?"

"We're not going to wait for it to happen." He shoved Amanda before him, knowing there was only one choice.

Andy gasped the moment her feet touched water. It was cool and oozed with mud, soothing her raw and blistered feet. But there was no time to enjoy it.

Coleton pulled her against him, his fingers pressing gently against her lips to silence her. Then his hand slipped to hers and he pulled her deeper into the water.

Andy heard the voices again, coming from behind

them and again from slightly to their left. Water lapped around her hips, mud oozing up through her toes. Had they doubled back to the river?

She groaned inwardly. Surely Coleton didn't expect her to swim again . . . ? But that was exactly what he expected.

Andy slipped in up to her shoulders, Coleton firmly guiding her ahead. She didn't hear voices again, but twice she thought she heard something slip into the water behind them. Knowing her white bloomers and camisole could easily be seen, she was grateful for the heavy canopy of trees overhead that blocked the light from the moon as it emerged from behind a bank of clouds.

Her feet touched firm footing. Coleton scrambled out of the water just ahead of her. He extended his hand and pulled her out of the water. Her hands closed over a branch and then another as she scrambled up behind him onto the trunk of a fallen tree.

The roots of the bald cypress were shallow, spreading like the gnarled spokes of a wheel out from the tree. The trunks were massive, growing in twisted and deformed shapes that looked like bent and stooped gnomes.

Coleton had grown up in the bayou. He knew it, respected its mysterious ways, and had learned to survive in it. Now he sought protection in the hollowed-out trunk of the massive cypress that grew in a tangled web. Though they couldn't outrun whoever was following them, they could hide.

Standing upright on a massive, exposed root, Coleton pulled Amanda up beside him and gently wedged them both into the open cavern of the ancient tree trunk. Their bodies were molded together in the tight space that was no bigger than a small closet. He gently pressed his hand against her mouth, warning her to be silent.

Every nerve ending tingled with fear. Andy could feel the blood pounding through her veins, sweat trickling down her skin. She closed her eyes, almost believing that

428

if she couldn't see those men, they wouldn't see her and Coleton. She didn't move, didn't even breathe. For a few desperate moments it seemed as if everything had stopped. There were only those voices, drawing closer, closer . . .

She tried to block them out, but couldn't. Her head came up in alarm, her eyes wide, searching Coleton's, as she heard several men not more than a few steps away.

They had followed them to the water's edge. If either she or Coleton made the tiniest sound it would all be over. Fear was like a living, breathing thing causing sensations Andy had never known before—unbearable coldness with moisture pouring off her at the same time, the frantic need to breathe, yet the inability to draw a single breath, desperation—just wanting it all to be over but determined to remain hidden.

Dear God! How did he do it? Andy wondered. His body was relaxed as he flattened her against the inside of the hollowed-out tree trunk, shielding her from the opening where they'd squeezed inside. Her hands were flattened against his chest. He'd leaned his head back, his eyes were open, watching calmly. His breathing was rapid but measured. The hand that pressed against her mouth never trembled as he drew it away.

Control. How did he do it? Andy felt something very near resentment well up inside her.

At any moment those men might find them. It would mean a firing squad, and he simply watched and waited. As if it were nothing more than a game. And looking at him now, all her nerves stretched to the breaking point, Andy realized that in a way it *was* a game. A deadly game that Coleton James had no intention of losing.

Even now as they stood there, those men not more than two feet away, his hand slipped to the belt at his waist. His fingers closed over the handle of a knife.

Oh, God! Fear closed off her throat, making her feel as if she were smothering. Andy buried her face in Coleton's

429

shoulder and concentrated on the steady beating of his heart as the men came closer. Any moment now . . .

"Amanda?"

Andy opened her eyes. She darted a quick glance up to Coleton. His arm had eased from around her. His head was resting back against the gnarled bark inside the upright tree trunk. His eyes were closed, lines etched deep at the corners.

"They're gone."

Her lungs ached as she took a small breath. "Are you sure?"

"As sure as I can be, stuck in this tree trunk."

She looked past his shoulder. It had gone from dark to gray beyond the hidden shadow of the tree. Now she could actually see the water lapping lazily against the gnarled roots they'd climbed over.

Her eyes widened. They hadn't doubled back to the river at all. The water surrounding them was still and quiet, smooth as glass, and black, unlike the river that was constantly in motion and a muddy brown color.

"My God!" she whispered. "Where are we?"

"We're in the bayou, Amanda." Coleton slowly opened his eyes and took a deep breath as if gathering his strength. He slowly pushed himself upright and pushed out of their hiding place.

"We can't stay here," he observed. "We've got to move on; they'll be back with more men. Durant isn't about to let us escape that easily."

Andy nodded wearily, knowing he was right. He held on to her hand as she squeezed past him. She ran her other hand back through her tangled hair as she looked down at the water that surrounded them. Then her eyes widened at sight of the two gnarled and long-snouted creatures that lay barely submerged along the water's edge where they'd crossed last night. She took several steps back. Alligators!

Andy whirled on Coleton, several well-chosen words on

430

the tip of her tongue about stomping through alligator-infested waters. Then she stopped, her eyes widening. "Oh, my God!" she whispered, horrified, as she stared at him and the spreading crimson stain that had soaked down the length of his left sleeve.

"You're bleeding!"

"It's not bad—just a scratch." Coleton tried to move past her, but even as he said it, the pain and weakness threatened to buckle his knees and he knew it was a lot worse than just a scratch.

Andy scrambled back up the twisted base of the cypress. Dear God! When had that happened? She hadn't thought any of the shots came that close before they hid in the tree. She looked up at him then and knew. It had happened as they'd gone over the side of the *Natchez* and he'd protected her from those gunshots with his own body. She took hold of the front of his shirt and started to unbutton it.

"Let me look at it."

He tried to push her hands away. "It's nothing, just a scratch. There isn't time." Then, fighting the pain and dizziness, he took hold of her shoulders, more to steady himself than to restrain her. "We have to get out of here now, Amanda," he commanded.

Andy felt the weakness in him, the pressure of his hands at her shoulders that was far too light and more than a little unsteady. It was more than just a scratch. A scratch wouldn't have bled that much.

"Be quiet!" she ordered with a whisper. "Do you want to bring them back?"

Andy gently pushed him down against the base of the tree trunk and opened his shirt.

Coleton watched her face as she pushed back the shirt. He knew he was bleeding heavily. He leaned his head back and closed nis eyes.

"Make it quick," he said, fighting back the pain.

Andy swallowed hard. "Just a scratch?"

He smiled faintly and shifted his shoulders, wincing at the pain that small movement caused. "I've had worse."

Andy took a deep breath as she pushed the shirt back off his left shoulder. The fabric was matted into the wound. As she peeled it away, the small trickle of blood opened to a steady flow. Her stomach twisted at the sight of the almost perfect bullet hole, black and gaping in his shoulder, blood streaming freely from the gaping wound.

She let out a shaky breath but said nothing. Dear God, how much blood had he lost? Her thoughts reeled back to the hospital in New York and the countless wounds she'd seen as soldiers kept coming and coming in a never-ending stream of bandages and sores and maimed limbs.

"I take it it's a little worse than a scratch."

She didn't reply, so frightened by what she saw, then laughed unsteadily, trying for humor—anything to take her mind off the ugly wound. "And to think they were aiming at me. If all of them shoot that badly, we have nothing to worry about."

He laughed, closing his eyes. "Seems like somebody's always takin' a shot at you, Yank." God, her fingers were cool against his hot skin. He almost didn't mind the pain, just to be able to feel her hands on him.

Andy yanked away the wide ruffle at the bottom of her bloomers then separated it, taking one long strip and folding it into a thick square pad of bandage.

"Just something temporary, Amanda." Coleton focused on the delicate oval of her face, the halo of disheveled gold hair and those sooty lashes downcast in concentration. Once, a long time ago, during the war when he'd almost died, he'd had just that vision in his head. But now, those brilliant blue eyes with their flecks of gold flashed up at him and he was certain that under any other circumstances she would have given him a piece of her mind. She said nothing but pressed the thick bandage carefully against the wound.

"Hold this in place," she commanded in a tone that said if he even tried to argue with her, she'd probably take his head off.

He really had no idea how frightened she was, Andy thought grimly as she forced herself to concentrate on binding the wound. If she hesitated, if she stopped for one moment, she knew she'd break down and cry like some simpering, weak-kneed, pasty-faced idiot. And she'd be damned if she'd let Coleton James see that.

She wrapped the second strip of fabric up over his shoulder, crossing it over his back, then bringing it around to tie in front.

"You do that very well." His voice was low, heavy with pain.

"Not well enough. I don't know how long it will last, and the bleeding hasn't stopped. The bullet is still in there." She'd discovered that much when she peeled off his shirt. There was no point of exit at the back of his shoulder. That could cause all kinds of problems. If he didn't bleed to death, he would slowly be poisoned to death.

She worked furiously, tying off the bandage as tightly as she dared to still allow for circulation yet staunch the flow of blood.

"Where did you learn to do that so well, Amanda?" he asked.

Pulling his shirt back up over his shoulder, she finally looked up. "In a hospital in New York City, during the war. They needed all the help they could get." She shrugged as if to make light of it. But his eyes pinned her. "There were a lot of wounded . . . both northern and southern. At first, we were just supposed to talk to them, write letters to their families, make things easier while they recovered." She shoved her fingers back through her hair in a gesture he'd come to recognize very well, then took a deep breath. "There were so many and it got so bad, the doctors couldn't keep up with it all. Sometimes we had to . . . help in the surgery. Other times, all we could do was hold their hands, talk to them, try to make the end . . . a little easier." Her throat ached. "So many of them were so young and so far from home. That was the hardest I think; knowing they would never go home to their families again."

"And you were very young, too." Too young, Coleton thought, and too beautiful and innocent to have endured that. It welled up inside him—hatred for this side of war that no one ever spoke of. It was always about glory and winning, never about dying. But Amanda Spenser knew something about dying. He could see it in the shadows behind her eyes. And now she tried to hide the pain, as he had a moment before, simply because he knew sometimes that was all you could do.

"Anyway . . ." she sniffed back the tears, "I've had enough of dying. It's not going to happen again, not here."

She fixed a smile on her face, but he knew she was completely serious. "I swear to God, if you die on me, Coleton James, I'll never forgive you." And she waved a fist at him for emphasis.

His long fingers wrapped around her small fist. He'd learned a little more just then about Amanda Spenser. She'd known pain and suffering and loss. It had been from a different perspective than his, but nonetheless real and unforgettable. And it obviously had a profound and deeply moving effect on her. That was something he would never have expected from Miss High and Mighty Yankee. But then there was a great deal he'd come to know about her that he would never have expected.

Besides, and he smiled faintly, she had a solid right punch and he'd seen what she could do with it. "Thank you, Amanda. I'll try to remember that. Can we go now?" He straightened and pushed to his feet. His face went ashen, the effort costing him a great deal as he stepped down into the water and crossed to the other side of the narrow channel.

"All right. But we'll have to stop if that bleeding starts up again." She started to follow him and then hesitated as her gaze snapped back to those two alligators partially submerged like two stationary logs drifting only a few feet away.

"Coleton! What about *them?*"

"They don't eat much," Coleton called back over his shoulder.

That did it! Of all the pig-brained . . . She didn't have the faintest idea why she had felt sorry for him.

"Don't eat much . . . ! she muttered under her breath, then glanced nervously down at both alligators. One seemed completely oblivious that they were anywhere near, but the one closest opened an eye and stared at her fixedly, as if he were considering her for his next meal. Taking a deep breath, Andy plunged through the water and scrambled up the opposite bank, thinking of several things she'd like to say to Coleton James.

Andy glared at his back and would have told him exactly what she thought except she was too busy worrying whether or not alligators traveled on land.

Coleton chuckled in spite of the gnawing pain that hadn't let up in his shoulder. Then he heard a very distinct and unladylike expletive, followed by her frantic dash through the water behind him.

"Try not to let everyone know where we are, Amanda," he whispered back over his shoulder and received another softly muttered curse.

Andy lost all track of time except to know they'd been walking for a long time. Her feet were tender and cut. It seemed she managed to step on everything that lay in their path, except alligators. She would have been certain they were hopelessly lost, but for the fact that Coleton always seemed to know exactly where he was going.

Exhaustion and hunger pulled at her. Then she felt compassion, thinking how much worse Coleton must feel with that bullet in his shoulder. Still, he refused to allow them any rest. He pushed them on, until the sun was hot overhead, shafting directly down on them, turning the bayou into a steaming pressure cooker. Andy's undergarments were matted to her skin with sweat and grime. Her hair was tangled with leaves and twigs, and she feared something that flew had taken up permanent residence. She prayed it wasn't a bat but just some large insect although she wasn't overly fond of them, either.

She scrambled over yet another downed tree that he stepped over so easily with his long-legged stride and sank in practically up to her knees in loose, shifting peat. She was hot, sticky, and the entire morning had been the meal for everything that flew or crawled. She was covered with bites and welts, and if that wasn't enough, she was stuck. Andy couldn't pull her feet out of the boggy black ooze she'd stepped in. Instead of struggling to free herself, she simply sat back on that fallen tree trunk and folded her arms defiantly across her breasts.

"I'm not going a step farther!" Andy informed him bluntly, and gave him a withering glare when he stopped and turned.

She prepared herself for battle. "I won't go any farther. I refuse. I simply won't do it!"

The battle never came.

"All right, Amanda," he answered simply.

Her determination slipped just a little. It wasn't like him give in so easily. Something was wrong.

She came to her feet, slowly pulling first one then the other from the sucking mud.

"What is it?" Andy approached him slowly.

He looked up at her briefly. "Nothing," he answered slowly. "You're right. We should stop for a while."

"Exactly," she agreed, still uncertain why he had capitulated. "I just didn't think you would give in so easily."

Coleton slumped back against a rotted-out stump. "What makes you think I have?"

"Well, it's just that you always fight me about every-

436

thing . . ." She touched his arm, wanting to check the bandage, and drew back with a soft gasp. "My God! You're burning up with fever!" she observed with horror.

He caught her hand, his fingers hot around her wrist. "It's nothing to worry about."

Andy stared at him incredulously and slowly shook her head. "That bandage has to be changed. It's soaked through."

"Are you always so bossy?" he asked from between dry lips. His color was ashen, the lines about his mouth deep with pain as she opened the shirt.

Andy fought back her fear. He was in pain, a great deal more than he was willing to let on. But the last thing Coleton James would want was sympathy. She dampened another piece of cloth torn from her bloomers. Squeezing water over the bloodied bandage, she was able to loosen it.

His jaw worked as he gritted his teeth against the pain. "Listen Reb, the fact is, I need you. I haven't the slightest idea where we are. As long as you're alive, I have a chance of getting out of here."

Through the fevered haze, Coleton watched her face. It told more than she ever would. *I need you*. He knew how she meant it and wished for more. "Were you this tough with those wounded soldiers in that hospital in New York?" he asked.

"Sometimes." She answered simply, even though it was a lie. There had never been one as stubborn or reckless as Coleton James. The men she'd help bandage in the hospital wanted to live. It was almost as if Coleton James had some kind of death wish. She peeled the last of the bandage away, all color draining from her face. Her hand shook as she threw the dirty bandage aside.

"That bad?" he asked.

"Bad enough," she answered simply.

Andy said nothing more as she carefully cleaned the wound. Even as she felt those hot gray eyes on her, she worked in silence. The wound was already infected, she didn't need a doctor to tell her that. The skin surrounding the bullet hole was swollen and hot, oozing a thick, dark mixture of blood and fluids. She'd seen similar wounds too many times.

She looked at him briefly from under her lashes and saw the flash of pain that distorted his face as she gently probed the wound. They could go no farther, of that she was certain. She was equally certain that if she *asked* him to stop he would refuse.

"Amanda, please don't poke any more holes in me." He seized her fingers. It took all his strength for that one brief smile.

Andy sat back on her heels, knowing there was only one way to handle Coleton James and that was head-on. She took a deep breath and braced herself. "That bullet has to come out. You'll die if we go on." The long, surprisingly steady look he gave her was a bit unsettling.

"And you're an expert on this sort of thing?"

Andy nodded. "I've seen enough wounds like this. You weren't the only one watching men bleed to death, Coleton James."

The fevered look in his eyes sharpened. He made a sweeping gesture with his right hand. "This isn't exactly a New York City hospital and there are men after us."

"I'm well aware of that," she conceded softly. "But if we don't stop now and remove that bullet, then they will have exactly what they want—your death. Except for the small fact that you will have deprived Captain Durant of the pleasure of seeing you die in front of a firing squad."

His eyes narrowed slightly. "You don't mince your words."

"There's no time for pleasantries," she flung back at him, reacting out of fear and doubt; filled with doubts of her ability to handle something like this and acute fear for his life if she didn't. His eyes closed, and for a moment she thought he might have dozed or perhaps passed

438

out. She bit at her lower lip.

"Amanda?"

Her head jerked up in surprise to find him watching her.

"Just how do you propose to get the bullet out?"

She suspected he was only humoring her and had no real intention of allowing her to remove the bullet. She could see it in the hard set to his jaw, which worked with every pulsing of pain through his shoulder.

"You have a knife." She gestured to the one secured in his belt. "We'll need a fire to sterilize the blade, and," she gestured to the rows of now-dry ruffles at the bottom of her bloomers, "in spite of our situation, we have plenty of bandages."

"Just like that?" Coleton speculated from between thinned lips as he gritted against another wave of pain. He closed his eyes as he fought back weakness. He knew she was right about that bullet.

To her surprise, he nodded. "How much time do you need?"

He'd caught her off guard. "At least an hour," she guessed uncertainly, having no way of knowing how deep the bullet had traveled. And he had lost a great deal of blood. He couldn't stand to lose much more. If she didn't find the bullet quickly . . . She refused to think about that possibility. She simply would find it.

Again he nodded, his eyes closed again, his words brief with fresh pain. "One hour, but no fire. It might be seen. And we can't stay here. We're too much out in the open where we are." He opened his eyes and struggled to stand. Andy was immediately beside him, her arm going around his waist.

"All right, one hour," she agreed. "We'll find a more secluded place, but I need that fire," she insisted adamantly. "It's necessary."

"Damned stubborn . . . Yank!" he groaned as he leaned against her. "Can I trust you not to run me

439

through with that knife?"

"You can't afford *not* to trust me," Andy flung back at him. She knew the anger was the only way he could deal with the pain.

Andy found the hollowed-out trunk on higher ground. Some animal had burrowed out, then abandoned a massive fallen oak. The tree had once been nearly six feet in diameter.

"Aren't you the least concerned the former tenant might want it back?" Coleton grunted with pain as he sat down and leaned back against the inside of the trunk. The effort had cost him strength, his face was drawn and ashen.

"We'll discuss it when he comes back." Andy helped ease him into a more comfortable position. He caught her hand, his fingers hot against her warm skin. Still, he smiled in spite of the pain. "Are you any good with a knife?" he asked.

"Are you worried?" she retorted as she made him as comfortable as possible.

"Let's just say you've got sufficient reason to want me out of your life—permanently."

"You're wrong," she blurted out, then bit at her lower lip, wishing she hadn't said the words. Now wasn't the time or place to talk about feelings—not when she was just beginning to understand everything herself.

He brought his fingers to her lips in a tender caress. "That's a bad habit. I once knew someone who . . ." he hesitated, ". . . used to bite her lip, too."

When he smiled faintly, she knew what it was he was remembering. "Really?" She looked away, fighting back the swell of tears that suddenly overwhelmed her as she tried to busy herself with making him more comfortable. She took a steadying breath before asking, "Who was she?"

Coleton's fingers slipped beneath her chin. He slowly tilted her chin up. Even through the fever and pain, he saw it, that elusive something in those brilliant blue eyes that had haunted him from the very first moment he'd laid eyes on her. When her guard was down, when her defenses were completely stripped away, he saw the weakness in that tough, stubborn Yankee facade. And he saw something else behind the mannerisms and clipped speech—a way of holding herself, of walking and talking, that was somehow different from the Amanda he knew— as if there were someone else inside her. It was there now as his fingers traced her cheek, and he took a tear on his finger, just as he had once before, long ago. And she had asked who *she* was.

"She was someone very special," he answered simply.

Andy breathed out a ragged sigh, her hand flattening over his, pressing it against her cheek as she closed her eyes and cherished this moment between them. There was so much more he had to understand and accept. Would he accept it? Could she make him understand?

She pulled away from him, knowing now was not the time or place for amorous attention. "If I've only got an hour, I better get busy."

"You'll need this." He pulled the knife from his belt.

"I don't suppose you have any matches." Andy said teasingly, but her eyes widened as he unscrewed the round disc at the end of the knife handle.

"It's a knife with a compass on the outside," he held up the disc, "and matches on the inside—to keep them dry." At her incredulous expression he went on to explain. "Everything a man needs to survive."

"Did you learn that in the war?" She proceeded to tear the rows of ruffles from her bloomers, wishing she had something cleaner.

"I learned it from Cairo. He knows a great deal about survival."

"Are we going to survive, Coleton?"

"I'll do my damndest to see we do," he promised. "Just get this bullet out of me first."

Andy tore the cloth into strips. "What will you do if we get out of here?"

He gave her a long look. "I have to find out who's been posing as the Gray Fox—the person responsible for the attacks on the Federal arsenals."

"What happens then?"

He couldn't tell her the truth. At least not all of it—that Ombre Rose was the reward for the identity of whomever was posing as the Gray Fox.

"I have to clear my name, and stop Durant."

He said it so simply, yet it made shivers run down her spine, and she knew there was more than he was telling her.

"Why does he hate you?"

"Because of the war."

"There were a lot of people who fought in the war."

"Yes, but only one person who cost him the most important promotion of his career." At her surprised look he went on. "As far as I was concerned, I was simply carrying out my orders and trying to stay alive. Our paths crossed and he lost a promotion because of it. He's never forgotten that and swore he'd see me dead." He let out a long sigh.

"You might say he took the war personally. A lot of men did. For Durant, the war didn't end when it ended."

"He won't give up, then?"

Eyes closed, Coleton slowly shook his head. "No, he won't give up."

It was said so simply, with a vague shrug and yet it frightened her.

"I'm going for firewood," she said, standing abruptly.

"Don't go far," Coleton warned. "They could be anywhere."

Andy was gone only a short while. She found several pieces of dry wood nearby and followed Coleton's instructions for laying the fire. Soon it crackled to life, flames spreading through the dried leaves up into the small twigs, then up through thicker ones until a steady flame burned. Andy laid the blade of the knife in the flames. It was the only method they had of sterilizing the blade. She'd seen it done this way in the hospital when medical supplies were low.

Andy passed it through the flames several more times.

"Are you planning on cauterizing it?" Coleton questioned painfully as he eased down onto his back.

"Perhaps you would like to do this yourself," she suggested archly.

"It wouldn't be the first time."

"Lay back and be quiet," Andy suggested in a tone that hinted it wasn't really a suggestion at all. He'd removed his shirt. She rolled it and placed it under his head. Somehow she believed he might have removed a bullet himself.

"Yes, ma'am," he sighed, and closed his eyes.

It scared her to see him this way. She wanted him angry or teasing. She could deal with that. Seeing him like this frightened her.

"This might hurt a little."

"I know it will hurt, Amanda." His eyes opened slowly and found her. "There's no help for it. Do what you have to do."

Andy tried to remember everything she'd learned at the hospital. She'd helped the doctors countless times, but this was different, and the knife seemed so inadequate. She looked up as Coleton reached for a small piece of wood and placed it between his teeth. Then his hand reached for hers, giving her his confidence and what little strength remained. He nodded, laid his head back, and closed his eyes.

It was worse than anything she imagined. Carefully flattening the flesh around the wound to make it taut, Andy swallowed back nausea as blood seeped through her fingers. But by far the worst was when she probed for the bullet. Her confidence wavered.

443

What if the bullet had shattered a bone? What if it had fragmented? She'd seen the doctors at the hospital spend hours removing tiny bits and pieces of bullets, forced to close the wound before they were through when the patient could endure no more. She didn't have hours to do this—Coleton didn't have hours.

Her hand shook and she broke out in perspiration. She tightened her grasp on the handle of the knife. Coleton jerked spasmodically when she finally located it. The bullet was deep, but it was in one piece and resting against a bone. Sweat poured off him, making his skin slippery, and her chore all the more difficult. He screamed, the horrible sound choked back by the stick.

Removing the bullet required probing the wound with her fingers and trapping it against the blade. When she finally pulled it out and flung it away, she almost collapsed.

"It's out," she breathed, forcing her hands to move to the freshly folded cloth. She had to get the wound bandaged before he lost more blood. She worked quickly, pressing the heavy pad against the flow of fresh blood, binding it in place as she had before

"You have to sit up so that I can wrap this around you . . . Coleton?" She looked up to find he'd passed out. Somehow she improvised, rolling him gently to one side, forcing the wrap beneath him, then rolling him back. At least it was secure.

Andy tucked his shirt around him, cleaned the blade, and laid it aside. She doused the fire, and curled up to wait.

She had no idea how long she'd slept. She hadn't meant to. Now the bayou had slipped into a late-afternoon sultriness that was smothering. The water lazily wound its way around protruding, gnarled knees of cypress roots and trailing tips of dangling moss. The air was still and heavy with heat and mugginess and the slightly fetid odor of decaying vegetation.

Something had awakened her. She sat up, curled her knees beneath her, and listened. It was cooler inside the rotted-out tree trunk, the outside sounds muffled by the heavy wood. Coleton stirred beside her, turning his head, his dry, parched lips mouthing words.

On her earlier exploration for firewood, she'd found the burled knot of a cypress tree and used it for a crude bowl. She'd filled it with water to clean his wound. There was still some left in the bottom. With a square of cloth she trickled water into Coleton's mouth.

He drank it greedily without opening his eyes, then slipped into that dream state of the mind that fever created. His body twitched, his left hand jerked spasmodically, fingers flexing as if he were grasping something. He whispered, but it made no sense to her.

His movements became wildly physical, the words incoherent. He twisted and turned. Andy feared he would open the wound again.

She lay across him, holding him down. Then a greater fear sank in. What if those men who had followed them into the bayou were close by? They would surely hear him.

Andy clamped her hand over his mouth. She had to keep him quiet. But even with the fever burning away his strength, she was no match for him.

Coleton jerked violently away. His fingers dug into her shoulders, bruising as he held onto her. "Anything."

"It's all right," Andy whispered against his cheek as she tried to soothe him.

". . . won't let them . . ." He held her away as fingers bit into the soft skin of her upper arms. His eyes were wide, glazed with pain and fever.

"Coleton! Please!" She reached out to him, trying to break through the delirium of fever as her fingers stroked his cheek, then touched his lips. "It's all right—everything will be all right. You have to rest now." She had to find a way to reach him.

445

"I promised . . ."

"I know," Andy whispered, forcing back panic. If those men were anywhere near . . .

"I tried, but he came after us . . ."

She thought he must be thinking of Durant.

"It's all right. We're safe."

He rambled on feverishly. "No! It will never be over. I couldn't keep my promise . . ."

Andy couldn't be certain what he was talking about, but she went along with it as she tried desperately to press him back down.

"You kept your promise," she comforted him. "Everything will be all right. I promise it will."

"I didn't . . . I couldn't . . . Oh, God, there was so much blood . . ." His eyes were wide, staring straight at her. "So much . . . I couldn't stop it . . ." He held his hands out before him and stared at them. The expression on his face was full of anguish.

Andy fought him with all her strength, pinning his left arm to his side. "Coleton, please! It doesn't matter now." The agony in his voice tore at her. It was then she heard voices.

She jerked around, her gaze scanning the rise above them. Dear God, what if the men came this way? What if they'd heard him!?

"Coleton! You have to be quiet! They're coming. Please!"

He didn't hear her. "Dear God," his voice broke in a sob, "I lost you . . . *I* was to blame! You were all I ever wanted . . ."

Andy stared at him—the voices momentarily forgotten, and she knew. She wrapped her arms him, tears filling her eyes.

"It's all right, Cole," she whispered against his hair. "Everything is all right . . . I'm here now." Somehow she had to reach him—had to make him understand in spite of the fever.

His hands buried in her hair, his fingers pressing into her head as he stared up at her. She felt the wildness seep out of him as he stopped fighting her. His head fell back and she thought he must have passed out again, but when she looked up she found those intense gray eyes watching her, completely lucid for a brief moment.

"Sunny?" His fevered gaze searched hers.

Tears spilled from the tips of her lashes.

"Yes." Her voice broke with a soft sob. She knew the chances were he would never remember what had passed between them when he awakened.

"Sunny." It was no longer a question, but a sigh. "I kept my promise . . ."

She stroked his damp brow, brushing back the soft brown hair. "I know you did, my love. I know."

His eyes closed, the lashes curved downward against his cheeks, no longer trembling with the delirium of fever. His arms closed around her, as if he would never let her go.

"I will always . . . love you, Sunny."

She could barely hear the words as he slipped once more into unconsciousness, but she understood and pressed her mouth to his, tasting her own tears as they fell from her cheek.

Chapter Twenty-two

Coleton slept through the afternoon and night. Twice, the voices she'd heard came alarmingly close but disappeared each time.

The fever rose, then abated. Just before dawn it finally broke, sweat pouring off him. She bathed him from the bowl of water. He opened his eyes and stared back at her weakly but completely lucid.

"How long?"

"Since yesterday."

Coleton shifted, wincing at the pain in his shoulder. "You got the bullet out?"

So, he didn't even remember that. She nodded. "It was deep, but I got all of it."

His gaze traveled to her bloomers and he smiled faintly. "It's a good thing I didn't have any more wounds."

"One was enough," Andy snapped. She was bone-tired, she'd hardly slept, and he had the damned nerve to lie there grinning at her.

"It almost killed you."

Coleton watched her, saw the flash of anger. Could it be little Miss Yankee was disappointed he hadn't died?

"Sorry to disappoint you, Amanda."

Andy's stricken gaze flashed back to his. "You ass! That isn't what I meant!" she blurted out without thinking. Then she mentally berated herself. Dear God, what must he think of her? She began folding a length of ruffle that had been folded and refolded several times as she'd watched him sleep.

Coleton slowly pushed himself to a sitting position with his right arm. His hand stopped her. "What *did* you mean?"

"That bandage should be changed." She avoided an answer and his direct gaze. But he wasn't about to let her off that easily.

"Amanda?" He wanted to know why she was angry.

Her mouth worked into a soft frown as she busied herself checking the bandage at his shoulder.

"Amanda!"

Not a question this time but a demand. Her eyes snapped to his briefly then darted away.

"You had a fever. You said . . . some things," she answered simply.

He grinned, a sort of lopsided, rakish grin with the heavy growth of beard and his hair tousled. It was heart-stopping just how handsome he was in spite of the drawn look about his eyes.

Dear God, she hadn't known, hadn't guessed or even dreamed of the man he would one day be. He had been so very young—they had both been. Now he was older, experienced, worldly, a man who had seen more than he wanted and lost a great deal more. And he was scarred now. She'd seen the unmistakable mark of a bullet hole in his side, the crease of a scar at his cheek, and the deep marks across his back.

Coleton James was different, changed, mature, a man where there had once been just a boy. Dear God, she had loved one and was now falling in love with the other. She almost laughed out loud at how ridiculous it was, for they were the same man.

"You don't have to worry unless I promised something. In that case, I can't be held responsible."

It was said with that same rakish grin. Little did he know how close he came to the truth.

"You talked about the past."

449

The grin faded. "The past is best forgotten." His voice was gruff. "God knows I've tried to forget. I apologize for anything I might have said."

Her hands stopped midair, and the look she fastened on him was so stirring, so filled with pain. Apologize? She didn't want his apologies. She wanted him to remember. Obviously he didn't.

"What is it, Amanda?"

She shook her head and swallowed hard. "Nothing. Let me finish this. Then I think we should go. We had visitors last night."

His fingers clamped over her wrist. "Durant?"

It was all forgotten now. So easily. She shook her head. "I didn't recognize his voice. But there were several of them."

"Which direction were they headed?"

He remembered nothing! Andy tied the bandage tight—very tight, causing him to wince.

"That direction," she indicated with a tight-lipped nod.

Coleton frowned at both the pain and that piece of information. "They're headed deeper into the bayou. How many were there?"

"It was difficult to tell. Maybe a half dozen. There were a lot of voices."

He sat up, the lines deepening between his eyebrows as he forced back the pain. "Six men? There weren't that many in the boat off the *Natchez*."

"They weren't from the *Natchez*," she answered simply.

"How do you know that?"

"They talked about meeting someone from the riverboat. Something about it all being changed now."

"What else?" Coleton pulled on his shirt, wincing painfully.

"There wasn't anything else. They moved on. Who do you think they were?"

"I don't know." He stopped, took a deep breath, and then crawled out of the hollowed-out tree. He stood, immediately reaching to steady himself.

450

Andy was immediately beside him. "What are you trying to do? Open that wound again? You've already lost too much blood."

"Evidently." He grinned up at her weakly. "You have a sharp tongue, Amanda. I don't suppose you could account for some of that blood loss." It was meant as a joke, but it came off badly. He could see it in the stark look in her eyes. And then it was immediately gone and she looked as if she could let more blood. Christ! Had she really been that concerned about his recovery?

Andy wanted to shove him down the embankment. "I did the best I could under the circumstances. But I can see I should have left that bullet right where it was. Blood poisoning takes several days. It might be slow, but it's effective, and far more enjoyable to watch."

He reached out to stop her as she whirled away from him. "Amanda, truce. I'm sorry . . ." He gestured wide with his good arm. "If it was something I said, then I apologize."

Something he said? Yes! She wanted to scream at him. It *was* something you said! Last night, when you had that damned fever, when you remembered, really remembered, and for a moment nothing else mattered.

But she didn't scream. Instead, she folded what was left of the bandages. He would need them later.

He reached out. "Amanda, please." She wouldn't look at him. His hand dropped to his side.

"We can't stay here," he announced, bending to retrieve his knife. He pushed it through his belt. "We've got to keep moving."

"The bleeding could start again . . ." she started to protest, more than a little angry.

At least he had that much from her, it was better than her silence.

"It's dangerous to stay here. Those men may come back. And Durant's men are still after us. We've got to go."

"Where?" She flung it at him like a challenge.

451

Coleton almost laughed. That look he'd seen earlier was gone. There was a trace of the old Amanda in her now. Feet planted, hands on her hips, dressed only in her underwear with that wild torrent of gold hair spilling around her shoulders, eyes flashing fiery blue. She was quite a stirring sight.

"Deeper into the bayou."

She whirled around, staring at the winding watery path. "But those men . . . ?"

"We'll stay behind them. Don't forget, Durant is back there." He gestured in the direction they'd come the day before.

"But couldn't we just follow the river?"

"Durant will have soldiers searching both sides of the river from New Orleans to Baton Rouge."

She swallowed, looking back to the lazy-moving stream of water, remembering the alligators.

"I hope you know what you're doing." She fell into step behind him as he moved through knee-high ferns and twisting vines, following some invisible trail.

"I do, too." Coleton murmured as he broke the path ahead of them.

It was slow, agonizingly slow. Coleton was weak from loss of blood and fever. That first day they found black-berries and gallberries in thickets on the high bank as they followed the inland channel. Coleton pointed out the black fruit of the saw palmetto. Andy knocked several down with a stick. At least they wouldn't starve.

They spent the night in a burrowed-out hollow left by deer, staring up at a full, golden moon, the soft grass whispering around them as an evening breeze cooled the bayou. Coleton fell asleep immediately and deeply, exhaustion taking over.

Andy woke at intervals, listening for something other than night sounds. When she did sleep it was somewhere in that place between full sleep and wakefulness. At first light, she ventured out to gather more berries, returning as Coleton was just awakening. He was a little stronger after a full night's rest and insisted they move on, eating berries as they walked.

Midafternoon of the second day, they stopped to rest where the water split into two distinct channels. They drank water and Andy changed Coleton's bandage, washing out the soiled ones. They were both hot, tired, and sticky.

"Would you like a bath?" Coleton asked.

Andy gave him a barely tolerant look. "Of course. Then all I need is soap and a change of clothes." It was meant to be sarcastic, but by that infuriating grin of his, she knew he was ignoring it.

"Would this do?" He tore off a handful of leaves from a bush and handed them to her as she finished rinsing the bandages. She gave him a look that suggested what he might do with those leaves.

"You know, Amanda? Sometimes you are simply too practical. You assume because we're in the middle of the bayou that we don't have some of the comforts of civilization."

He was being smug and she felt like strangling him. "Then perhaps you have a cake of soap hidden somewhere on you. Perhaps it's in the handle of your knife."

"You're holding the soap in your hand."

She looked down at the leaves.

"Rub them together with a little water."

He was baiting her. Determined to prove him wrong, Andy rubbed several of the leaves together between her fingers and added a small amount of water. Her eyes widened in surprise as the sap from the leaves produced a creamy lather.

"How did you know?" She looked up excitedly, all desire for retribution replaced by a desire to be clean again.

The expression on her face was like that of a child, filled with surprise and wonder.

"Cairo taught me everything about the bayou. The

leaves are from the soap bush. The natives use it all the time for lack of the real thing. It works pretty well. Why don't you try it out?"

Andy couldn't resist. Her skin felt as if she were wearing all the slime and dirt of the bayou.

"What about alligators?"

"I'll watch out for them. Go ahead."

Finding firm footing, Andy inched her way into the water up her waist. She immediately began to rub more leaves together, spreading the lather across her shoulders and down her arms.

"It's not bad. It smells like an herb of some kind."

"It's also used for seasoning in stew."

She made a face and turned her back on him. Suggesting she was comparable to a stew!

Andy washed as best she could with her undergarments on. She even lathered her hair when Coleton kept her supplied with more leaves, stealing glances at him outstretched on a fallen tree trunk.

She knew he was tired, she could see the fatigue around his eyes, the drawn look in his face, but he was still the most handsome man she had ever known, now or then. And, she thought with a faint smile, she liked the beard; liked the rich sable color of it, the way it curved around his smile . . . the brush of it against her lips.

Just that simple memory made her warm with desire—his hands in her hair, his lean, taut body easing inside hers, his mouth moving over her with a desperation and passion that took her breath away.

"Amanda." He called to her softly. She followed the direction of his gaze. An alligator slipped lazily from a log into the water, trailing a telltale ripple, its eyes and snout all that broke the surface.

Andy crawled out onto the downed tree trunk and dried her hair in the sun that filtered down through the canopy of trees overhead.

"It's time to go."

She sighed, hating to leave the idyllic place. For this

454

small space of time it had been just the two of them, and it had been wonderful. This is what their life together might have been like—the teasing banter, the easy quiet, the stolen moments when just looking at him brought back all the passion and desire. Was it possible to have it again?

"Do you know where we're going?"

He pointed to the left channel of the bayou. "There's a cabin in that direction. A friend of mine lives there."

They found it just before sundown. It was a small, roughly hewn structure supported on sturdy poles with a deck extending far over the water. Smoke curled from the chimney. Several canoes were tied up at the landing.

Sighing with relief, Andy started down the path toward the cabin. Coleton's hand stopped her.

"What is it?"

"There's something wrong," he warned, his voice low.

Andy looked back at the cabin. "Everything seems all right."

He shook his head. "Old Phillipe has a skiff and a small canoe."

"Perhaps he has guests."

"Maybe." Coleton pointed to the smoke that came from the chimney. "He never uses that stove in the summer. It heats up the cabin too much. He smokes his catch over an outdoor cooker."

Andy's brow wrinkled as she looked back to the cabin. "Maybe it's just easier to cook inside if he has guests."

"You don't know Phillipe. He's Cajun and meaner than a swamp gater. He doesn't *have* people stay for dinner. He doesn't like people."

"How did you come to know him?" she asked, listening to her stomach grumble in response to the aroma from the cookfire.

"He's a friend of Cairo's. We used to come here when we came into the bayou to hunt. He and old Phillipe go back a long time. Come on. We'll go around back."

They came up behind the cabin, shielded by a thicket

of tall, waving swamp grass. Coleton pushed his way closer to the cabin. Andy followed several paces behind. When the heavy growth closed behind him, she stood in momentary confusion, then pushed through in the direction she thought he might have gone. The heavy thicket of tall grass thinned and Andy stepped through.

She would have screamed if Coleton hadn't clamped a hand hard over her mouth and jerked her back into the thicket of grass. She turned and buried her face in the curve of his right shoulder.

"Oh, God!"

Coleton pulled her deeper into the grass. "Take several deep breaths," he instructed as he held her protectively. He'd seen it, too—the body, the head severed from the torso. She had almost walked right into it.

Her hands were twisted into the front of his shirt. Nausea churned into her throat. Andy gulped deep, steadying breaths of air, fighting it back.

"Is . . . it . . . your friend?" she whispered raggedly.

Coleton's voice was hard. "Yes."

Andy shuddered in his arms. "My God, what could have happened?"

"Not what, but *who?*"

They heard voices, and Coleton pulled her farther into the shelter of tall grass. He silently warned her not to say anything as two men passed very close by.

"What about dat shipment?" one man asked the other.

"Forget it. We leave right away."

"But de boss said . . ." The first man was cut off.

"Forget it, Mose. There was trouble. The *Natchez* went down. Duchess sent word to get back to the caves."

"Dat too bad," the man, Mose, responded. "The boss lady sure 'nough goin' to be madder than a wet hen when she hears 'bout this. She was countin' on dat last shipment."

Andy's eyes widened at the man's words. They were talking about the shipment of guns aboard the *Natchez!*

Coleton nodded, indicating he'd heard.

"Hmmm, hmmm, she shore ain't goin' to be happy a-all."

"That's too bad!" the second man grumbled, obviously not too happy, either.

"That shipment is at the bottom of the river, and there ain't nothin' we can do about it. Duchess said we're to cut our losses and get outta here."

"Yeah, boss, but who's goin' to tell the boss lady about it? You know how angry Miz James gets when things don't go they way she wants 'em."

"I'll worry about that later, Mose. For now, let's get outta here." They moved around the corner of the house, their heavy boots making clumping noises up the steps and across the deck before a door slammed.

Andy looked up at Coleton. Miz James? Marilee James? The expression on Coleton's face went to stone.

"I'm sorry," she whispered, knowing how he must feel.

"About what!? The fact that my stepmother is the one who's been impersonating the Gray Fox? It's really very clever when you think about it." He shook his head. "I knew she was greedy. She blamed my father for losing everything when the war broke out—the money, the horses, her fine jewels and gowns. It all went to buy bonds to support the Confederacy. All that was left was Ombre Rose. He even mortgaged her house in Baton Rouge. Then when he died, I was gone, and there was no one else to blame but the Yank Army. And then they came to Ombre Rose. God, how she must have hated them walking all over her fine carpets, drinking her imported wine, stealing all my father's Thoroughbred horses. Possessions! That's all that ever meant anything to her."

"Coleton, I don't understand. How could she possibly have known about the Gray Fox?"

He shook his head. "It was easy enough. My father knew." He laughed a hard, bitter sound. "God, how he loved her, and all she wanted was her fine house in Baton Rouge. She wanted to fill it with the finest of everything from Ombre Rose and then sell off the plantation when she thought I was dead."

Andy shivered in spite of the heat. His voice was cold and filled with such bitterness and hatred.

"What do we do now?"

He said nothing as he moved past her and walked away from the cabin. He followed the channel of water that ran in front of Phillipe's cabin.

"Coleton!" Andy whispered desperately as she tried to keep up.

"Coleton! Please!"

He stopped, but only for a moment as he peered through the trees at the water. He was looking for something and seemed to have found it. They cut through the trees and headed straight for the water's edge.

"Damn you!" Andy whispered with a vengeance. "Will you tell me what is going on?"

Coleton paced the bank, pulling aside heavy undergrowth, pawing his way through waist-high grasses first in one direction, then the opposite.

"What are you looking for?" Andy questioned.

"It's got to be here somewhere." He disappeared into a clump of low-hanging branches and a thicket of wild berries.

"What?" She questioned again.

"This!" he announced as he pulled aside more branches to expose a crudely made canoe. It was long, with a shallow draft, wide enough for only one person to sit.

"Phillipe's canoe," he said by way of explanation. "He kept it here where the channel narrows. Late in the season the water is very shallow. His skiff won't make it back any farther. But this will go anywhere, and it's lightweight. He could carry it overland if he needed to."

Andy slowly shook her head, almost afraid of what might come next. "You're not planning on using that thing?" She gave a look that suggested she considered it completely unreliable, which, of course, was exactly what she thought.

"No, I'm not."

Andy gave a sigh of relief. She'd much rather walk anyway. She already had as many blisters as a person could have.

"You are," he announced firmly.

Andy's gaze snapped back to his. "Oh, no I'm not!"

"Oh, yes you are." Coleton answered in a way that left no doubt that she would do exactly as he intended.

"You can't mean that you expect me to get into that . . . that thing? It will sink."

"I agree it's not much to look at, but it's the finest made on the bayou." Then Coleton gave her a long look. "You did say you could handle a boat."

Andy shifted uncomfortably from one foot to the other. "Well, yes, of course. But . . ."

He cut her off. "Good. Get in."

"Where are we going?"

"*We're* not going anywhere. *You're* getting out of here. Now, get in!"

"Wait just a minute . . .!" Andy started to protest. "I'm not going anywhere without you."

"Get in, Amanda."

It was said low, in a tone that said he wouldn't tolerate any argument.

"Coleton, please. We can both get away."

He reached inside the front of the canoe, wincing with pain as he pulled out a paddle.

"I have no intention of getting away."

"You can't mean that you intend going after those men? My God, you're wounded, and you have only a knife. They have guns, and you don't know how many there are! You can't do this!"

He handed her the paddle. "It's the only chance I have to prove I'm innocent and clear my name. If I can't, Durant will keep after me. I lived that way for over three years. Not any more."

Andy ignored the paddle. "Come with me. We can get help and then go after them. You need a doctor," she

459

pleaded desperately.

Coleton simply shook his head. "They'll move out, fin
another hiding place, and lay low, or leave the area
Then I'll never find them. I can't let them get away."

He'd already made up his mind. Nothing she could sa
would change it. Andy shoved the paddle back at him
"And just how do you plan to stop them!?"

"I'm not certain I can. But I can slow them up—a lot
And I do have one advantage. I know this area bette
than anyone." He pushed the paddle back at her. "I don'
have time to argue with you, Amanda. I need you to ge
to Cairo. Tell him everything that's happened, and tel
him about the caves. He'll get word to Rafe Kelly." Wher
her hand closed over the handle of the paddle he knew
she had at least accepted the logic of his plan. He'
counted on that Yankee practicality of hers and sh
hadn't disappointed him.

He stepped down onto the bank, crouching beside th
canoe. "You've got fresh water. He indicated a fat, bulg
ing skin in the bottom of the canoe behind her.

"Keep to the left of the channel. Eventually the curren
will change. You'll be moving inland, but it will seen
like you're going downstream. That's what gets peopl
disoriented in the bayou. Just let her go with the current
then when you come to a place where a huge water oal
is split and looks like a man could walk through it, go t
the left again. It narrows down from there so that it look
like the channel has dried up completely. When you can'
go any further in the canoe, get out and walk due north.
He pried the compass out of the butt of the knife handl
and handed it to her. "You'll come out right at Hom
Farm. I figure you should make it before dark."

Andy tried one last time. "Coleton, please. I could go
to the authorities. I'll tell them everything I heard abou
Marilee."

There was a pleading softness in her eyes, a sincerity
and openness that tore at him. "The Federal authoritie
want to see me hang. They'll never believe me over

460

Durant. I have to find these men, Amanda." He didn't say that he needed the proof for Phoenix — something tangible to give him or he'd never hold to his part of the bargain.

Andy knew he was right and hated it. It was so dangerous. "There's nothing I can say to change your mind, is there?"

"No. You have to go now, Amanda, before they come out of that cabin."

"You'll be careful?"

He smiled faintly. "I have no choice. There won't be anyone to dig bullets out of me this time."

She knew he meant it as a joke; still, the harsh reality of it tore at her. There were at least six of them and only one of him.

"Be careful."

"I'll try." He started to stand.

"Promise me." Andy leaned forward impulsively, her hand going behind his neck. She pulled him to her, her mouth seeking his in a desperate kiss.

His startled breath mingled with hers, his lips parting in surprise. All pretense was stripped away. As he'd once shown her, she thrust her tongue into the velvet warmth of his mouth with an urgency that was powerful and frightening, conveying both those sensations in a mixture of desire and longing.

She'd begun it, but it was Coleton who deepened the kiss, her words slipping through his senses, igniting a fire and urgency of his own.

Promise me.

The words shattered through him, stripping away every other emotion, every other need except that one.

He ended the kiss, jerking her away from him.

"Get out of here." Without another word, he stood and shoved the canoe away from the shoreline with his booted foot. It drifted, caught the current, and for a moment it seemed she would be pulled downstream past the cabin. But she recovered, dipped the paddle into the water, and

461

began stroking it efficiently through the water, heading the canoe upstream.

Coleton smiled. She hadn't lied; she knew how to handle a boat. Then his smile disappeared as sounds came from the deck of the cabin. The smugglers were preparing to leave.

The current in the channel was slow and meandering; still, it required constant stroking to keep the canoe moving against the flow of water. There was no way for Andy to clearly judge how long she'd been paddling, except for the pinch of growing discomfort between her shoulder blades. Added to that was the oppressive heat as the afternoon wore on.

Sunshine played across the water where it broke through the treetops overhead. Cypress and slash pines lined each bank, drawn up like sentries down a shaded lane.

Grasses and sedges filled the water with decaying vegetation, transforming it into a cushiony bog. In several places the channel seemed to narrow so that she could touch either bank with the paddle. Andy quickly learned it wasn't solid at all, but a spongy black mass, sprouting water plants and small shrubs that quickly gave way to nothing below the surface. The mass blocked the canoe in places. Remembering Coleton's instructions, Andy worked her way slowly through the mass until the canoe drifted freely once more.

The mass seemed to break up, clumps drifting with the current or lodging at the edges. The channel opened up once more, and the canoe moved much easier through the water. She must be very near the place where the channel split.

It was stifling. There wasn't even the breath of a breeze. And it was eerily quiet. She saw an occasional alligator, resting along the banks, seemingly oblivious to her presence. The bayou had quieted as afternoon heat set in. Even the birds had taken refuge. The only sign of life was the constant droning of insects as they buzzed in the still, hot air and an occasional water skeeter that danced across the glasslike surface of the channel.

The thin chemise was plastered to her skin. Andy could feel rivulets of moisture slipping down between her breasts and shoulder blades to pool at her waist. She stopped to rest for just a few minutes, taking the skin of water and drinking deep from it.

The panic at leaving Coleton rose again, and she forced it back. Realistically she knew he was right to send her on. But there was another side that argued she should never have left him. She bound the leather thong about the neck of the skin and took up the paddle once more. Up ahead she saw the tree.

It looked as if it had been struck by lightning. It had no foliage and stood like a giant guardian on a narrow strip of island in the middle of the channel. Just as Coleton had said, the trunk looked as if a man could walk right through it. The small of her back ached and every muscle screamed in protest, but Andy continued on, taking the left fork.

She knew evening was approaching. She felt and heard the subtle changes in the bayou. The heat relented, the air was easier to breathe. The insects were now joined by the croaking song of frogs as their bulging eyes broke the surface of the water along the banks.

The cluster of trees broke and a snow-white ibis soared across a lavender sky, winging its way to shallow water to hunt. To her right, Andy heard a sound she had come to recognize very well—the thrusting glide of an alligator slipping into the water. A gentle breeze lifted streamers of moss. She could see it move across the water ahead, then felt it cooling her heat-dampened flesh.

Andy guided the canoe through the clumped masses of peat and floating bog. It seemed she'd been at this for hours.

Every muscle in her arms and shoulders had gone beyond pain to numbness. She concentrated far ahead, beyond the turns and twists in the channel, willing it to narrow and disappear to land as Coleton had promised it would when she reached the end. But still the water continued until her mind began to play tricks on her and she began to have doubts that she'd followed the right course.

Exhaustion seeped through her, pulling at her, begging her to stop for just a little while. But she knew if she stopped for even a few minutes, she'd never be able to pick up that paddle again. And so she continued, driving herself beyond the point of exhaustion, every thought, each stroke through the water, driven by the knowledge that if she didn't reach Ombre Rose and bring back help, Coleton could well end up dead.

The current was pulling her now, just as he'd said. She dipped the paddle to hurry the pace, struck mud with the tip, and struggled to pull the paddle free. It jerked from her hands.

"No!" Panic-stricken, Andy whirled about in the canoe almost upsetting it, staring in disbelief as the mud and ooze sucked at the paddle, pulling it below the surface as she drifted away from it.

"Please God! What am I going to do?" Her nails bit into the wood at the side of the canoe as she watched the faint rippling of black water where the paddle once had been. In despair, she realized that even if she could somehow manage to turn the canoe, there was little chance of finding the paddle. As she well knew, there were places in the bayou where the water was two feet deep, others where it was twenty.

She buried her face in her hands and wept. Then, tears streaming down her cheeks she threw back her head. "Damn! Damn! Damn! What am I supposed to do now?" she moaned in despair.

The canoe bumped gently into a small island of free-floating peat, momentarily stopping in the water. It was enough to jolt her back to reality.

"No! Dammit, I won't quit! I won't! Do you hear me?" she shouted into the stillness of the afternoon that hung like a heavy blanket over the bayou.

"I won't quit!" she whispered with determination as she knelt on bent legs in the bottom of the canoe. She reached over the sides of the canoe and paddled with her hands.

Alligators be damned! Andy thought with a vengeance, the water dragging at her already aching limbs.

I won't give up! I can't give up! I promised . . . ! Had she dozed? She jerked upright as the prow of the canoe gently bumped into solid ground.

Andy roused slowly, pushing her tangled hair back from her forehead. The canoe must be stuck again. She reached into the water, thinking to dislodge it and continue. Her hand sank into mud. But instead of the shifting, spongy peat, it was solid.

She dragged herself up over the edge of the canoe and stared out before her. There was no water. No water!

Andy edged the canoe closer to the bank; the prow was firmly lodged against a fallen tree. Grabbing a piece of broken limb, Andy probed the bank in all directions. It was wet, oozing mud and water where it fed from a trickle upstream, but the channel definitely ended here.

She grabbed at a longer branch and pulled the canoe alongside the downed tree. Using other limbs for support she pulled herself out of the canoe and up onto the fallen trunk. Then she collapsed, laughing until the laughter went to tears at just the feel of the solid wood beneath her. Wiping away her tears with her arm, Andy took a deep breath and a good look around.

At first she thought it was just that it was darker in this part of the bayou, but as she looked overhead, she saw the fading streaks of pink, lavender, and purple blending into a dusky gray sky. It was almost evening. Andy scrambled to her feet and walked the length of the trunk to the gigantic, exposed roots that gaped out of the ground. Holding up the compass to catch the light, she found due north and began walking.

The fading light and growing desperation drove Andy through the heavy forest. Every few hundred yards she stopped, rechecking her direction to make certain she hadn't strayed in the wrong direction. She swallowed back panic. Surely the forest would thin soon and she would find Home Farm.

She almost ran right up onto the deck. Without any warning, the line of trees broke and opened into the clearing, the roughhewn house at Home Farm seeming to rise right out of the bayou. Andy choked out a sob of disbelief and joy. Nothing had ever looked so good to her. She'd made it. She'd actually done it. This damned Yankee from New York had come through the bayou and made it home. Almost home.

Andy sniffed back tears of relief as she rounded the house and followed the small footpath she'd found all those weeks ago when she first discovered Coleton was living here. The evening star was just rising in the night sky when she broke through the line of trees at the perimeter of the park at Ombre Rose.

She was certain she had no strength left, yet she ran—through the overhanging canopy of fragrant trees and pines, past the gazebo. She hesitated for only a moment, staring at the small marble structure that held so much meaning for both her and Coleton. Then she turned toward the house.

At first it seemed strange to find the main house ablaze with lights. She had thought to find only Cairo and perhaps some of the household staff. But as she crossed the flagstones in the garden and approached the study, she could see that every light on the main floor glowed.

The house murmured with voices as she opened the louvered double doors and stepped inside the study. The room wrapped around her with the familiar scents of lemon oil and rich old leather mixed with fresh tobacco. They were scents that brought back thoughts of Coleton with a sharp pang. She quickly crossed the study, her hand on the handle as the voices drifted to her from the front part of the house.

"I just can't believe it. Surely there must be some mis-

466

take . . ."

Andy was certain it was Lacey's voice. But the words were softly spoken, breaking with emotion when she seemed unable to finish whatever it was she'd begun to say. Andy stepped out into the wide entry hall. She hesitated. Obviously Lacey and several other people were in the drawing room. She looked down at her torn and muddied bloomers and camisole. There would be time for propriety later. Right now, every moment counted if she was to get help for Coleton.

She headed for the lights that glowed brightly from the open doorway to the front parlor. The next voice stopped her.

"Well, of course it is just the most dreadful tragedy." It was a woman's voice with that soft, rich cadence Andy had come to know of the people of Baton Rouge. She listened intently as the woman continued. "First she was abducted. God knows what she had to suffer because of that. Of course, I didn't know her that well, but to get caught up in all this dreadful business. And to die that way." The woman's voice was appropriately tragic.

"Dear Father in heaven. I blame myself."

It was Parker Rawlins.

"If I had just stayed with her that evening until everyone returned . . ." His voice broke and he was unable to continue.

Andy started through the door, but the woman spoke again.

"Well darlin', there was just no way of knowin' what Coleton was up to. All this time he was responsible for all those raids and attacks." There was a faint sniffling sound. "I just couldn't believe it. The latest attack was against General Sheridan himself. God knows I have no sympathy for the man, but murder is just unbelievable. I just thank the Lord that Coleton's father didn't live to see this."

Andy's fingers tightened over the latch of the door to the parlor, fury seething through her. She had no doubt whose voice she was listening to, but she held back, wanting to hear all the lies Marilee James was willing to place at Coleton's feet.

"Of course it's easy to understand his reasons. He just never could accept that the South lost the war, or that *he* lost Ombre Rose. He meant to have it all back, of course, no matter what it cost. And now Miss Spenser is dead, they're all dead."

So that was it, Andy thought. How convenient for it all to be wrapped up so nicely. They'd received word of the explosion. And Marilee wanted very badly for everyone to believe that both she and Coleton were dead . . . That last thought stopped her as Marilee went on.

". . . It's just so dreadful that Miss Spenser had to . . ."

"Had to what?" Andy flung the doors wide open and stepped into the parlor. "Come back? And expose your little plan?"

It was almost perfect, Andy thought. Marilee gave every appearance of the distraught, grieving stepmother. It was a performance to rival anything Andy had ever seen. Except for one very major mistake . . .

"Good God!" August Kittridge exclaimed, his jaw falling open, the cigar he'd been chewing dropping to the carpet.

"Andy!" Lacey gasped as she stood wide-eyed beside her father, her hand at her mouth.

"My God! Amanda!" Parker Rawlins's face was drawn, marked by fatigue and a combination of disbelief and elation.

Andy turned to her other guest. "What, Marilee? No overwhelming joy to see me alive and well?"

"Amanda Spenser! Where have you been?" This from Lacey as she started across the room. "What do you mean, scarin' us all half to death?" Then she stopped midstride and her hand went to the side of her head. "Oh, dear, I do believe I'm goin' to faint."

Andy turned on her. "Lacey Kittridge, you will do nothing of the sort," she ordered firmly, then took her friend gently by the hand. "As you can see, darling, I'm quite real and very much alive. But I need you awake and alert to hear what I have to say. I don't think you'll want to miss any of this." She turned on Marilee James.

Disbelief, shock, utter astonishment—none of those reactions described the expression on the woman's face.

"Damn!" she whispered, then quickly recovered. Her gaze traveled over Andy with something that was hardly relief at seeing her alive.

"Of course we're all so glad to see you. Were there other survivors?"

"I'm certain you'll be glad to hear there are, Mrs. James," Andy informed her firmly. And then Marilee started out of her chair, grief replaced by an expression of panic.

"Sit down. We have a great deal to discuss."

"Amanda . . ." Parker Rawlins came to her, wrapping his coat about her shoulders, "you've obviously been through a great deal. It's just that we're so glad to see you. When I thought . . ." His voice broke as he took her hand and gently stroked it.

The look on his face, the tenderness and genuine caring in his voice was almost her undoing. Dear God, if she believed what she knew to be true, this man was her father! She wondered if he knew, if he sensed anything at all, and somehow believed that he must feel . . . something. The pain she'd seen in his face when she first came in had been too real, too deep. And then the transformation . . .

Andy kissed his cheek gently. "I'm all right. But there are some things that need to be settled."

"Amanda! Where are your clothes? Where have you been? What happened?"

She turned to Lacey. "There isn't time to explain right now." She dismissed the fact that she was clad only in her undergarments as if it were an everyday occurrence.

"Where's Cairo?"

"I am here, Miss Amanda."

469

She turned to find the imperious black man standing in the doorway, his gleaming white robe flowing to the floor about him, making him seem more regal than ever. He didn't seem all that surprised to see her.

"Please come in, Cairo. There isn't much time. Coleton's in trouble. He's headed for a place called the Caves to find the men who work for the person who's posing as the Gray Fox."

There was a strangled gasp behind her. Andy whirled around. Marilee James had sprung out of her chair.

Andy crossed the room and seized her by the wrists, shoving her back into the chair. Cold fury glittered in her eyes. "Come out of that chair one more time and I'll split your lip!"

Marilee shrank back into the damask-covered chair. "It doesn't matter. You'll never get there in time."

Andy whirled back to Cairo. "We'll need men, and Coleton said to get word to Rafe Kelly."

"He left just a short while ago," Lacey informed her friend, the faint sensation vanishing. "He said something about trying to find someone. Coleton had sent him a telegram from New Orleans. He just went crazy when he heard about the explosion, saying Coleton would have found some way of gettin' off that boat."

Andy whirled back to Marilee, planting her dirt-smudged hands on both armrests as she leaned over her threateningly. She knew she must look a sight—barefoot, dressed in what was left of her undergarments, wearing half the dirt out of the bayou. But at that moment she didn't care.

"That raises a very interesting question, Marilee. Imagine my surprise to return home and find everyone mourning my death aboard the *Natchez*. And just how did you manage to find out that little bit of information? Which one of your spies was on board? Was it one of the crew? Or perhaps one of the gamblers who just happened to see Coleton and me on board?"

A look of cool detachment settled across her face. "All

Baton Rouge knows about the explosion. The survivors were comin' into town all day, picked up out of the river. I don't remember who it was told me."

"That's not good enough, Marilee. I know you made arrangements to hide those stolen shipments. I heard two of your men talking about it. It was all part of your plan, wasn't it, including using the disguise of the Gray Fox so that Coleton would take the blame for it."

"That's not true. You're mistaken." She laid her hands on the arms of the chair, her fingers tightening. Then they relaxed as if she had made a decision. "I will not sit here and listen to these wild accusations."

When she looked up, Andy saw hatred gleaming in the tawny depths of her eyes.

"You've been through a great deal, my dear," Marilee said with an eerie smile, "God knows what Coleton did to you. No one would expect you to be coherent after what you've been through."

"He saved my life. I'm alive because of Coleton."

"That's not true. He's a murderer. Everyone knows what he did during the war."

"Of course it's true, Marilee."

"No." Marilee shook her head from side to side. Her gaze came up, searching the room and the faces of the people who stood staring at her.

"No!" She pounded the arms of the chair. "Coleton is the Gray Fox. He's responsible."

Andy kept at her. There was more, something more, and she meant to have it. "Oh, he was the Gray Fox during the war. He never denied that. But he had nothing to do with those raids and stolen shipments."

Marilee laughed, a shrill, desperate sound. "Of course he did."

"He's the one. He's just trying to cover it all up now that Captain Durant is after him."

"It's impossible, Marilee. He didn't commit those crimes because he was with me, here at Ombre Rose."

Marilee's frantic gaze came up to hers. "That's all part

471

of it. He needed proof that he couldn't have committed those crimes, but his men did it." Her hand shook as she pressed her fingers against her temple.

"Amanda . . ." Parker Rawlins came to her. "Perhaps you're wrong."

"No, I'm not wrong. I heard those men. It was Marilee's name they mentioned." She turned on the woman.

"It would have all been so perfect, wouldn't it? God knows Captain Durant wants Coleton because of what happened during the war . . ."

"Yes!" Marilee screamed at her, coming up out of the chair in spite of the earlier warning.

She was trapped, cornered, run to ground like a frightened animal. Andy had heard those men, she knew Marilee was involved, and would make certain the Federal authorities knew it.

Marilee moved in small, agitated circles, wringing her hands as she widened the circles.

"And it would have worked . . ." She whirled on Andy, wide-eyed. Her voice had risen. She was practically screaming now.

"It would have worked if those damned costumes hadn't been switched!"

Andy crossed the room and seized Marilee by the arms. "What did you say!?"

"Nothing . . . I said nothing." Marilee's voice quavered as panic began to set in. She'd made a dreadful error and knew it. She clawed at Andy's hands trying to free herself as everyone else in the room could only stare in stunned disbelief.

Marilee's nails cut into her hands, but Andy's grasp only tightened. She shook Marilee until it seemed her head would separate from her shoulders.

"Say it!"

"No!"

"Say it! What about the costumes!"

Marilee shook her head pathetically. Unable to free herself, she sobbed and dissolved into tears before them.

"It was the costumes . . ." It came out in jerky spasms, they were accidentally switched . . . by the shopkeeper. You should never have received that message."

Instead of loosening her grip now that she had what she wanted, Andy's fingers tightened, leaving marks as her eyes widened at the truth.

Her voice ached in her throat as she shook Marilee. "You couldn't have known about that unless someone told you."

Andy looked first to Lacey and her father, then to Parker Rawlins.

Lacey shook her head. "I was too upset about what happened to you. I forgot all about that."

Andy's gaze came back to Marilee. "You weren't there that night. There's only one other person who knew." As Marilee's gaze fell from hers, Andy knew she had the truth at last.

"You're not the one." She stared in amazement. "You're not the one impersonating the Gray Fox!" She released Marilee, no longer concerned with the woman and her small part in all this as she whirled to Cairo, desperation in her eyes.

"Oh, God, Cairo! He's out there, he's after Coleton. It was him all along."

Lacey came across the room. "What on earth are you talkin' about? If it isn't Coleton, and it's not Marilee, then who is it, for God's sake?"

Andy's gaze met Marilee's, and she knew she was right by the way the woman's eyes darted away from hers. "The one person no one would ever suspect."

Chapter Twenty-three

Coleton watched her leave. There were so many things left unresolved between them. She had become important to him. Somehow he'd learned to care again. It was the last thing he expected, but it was important that she was safe and far away from all this. He had no idea how the rest of it would end. The only thing he could be certain of was her hatred when she finally learned the truth about the bargain he'd struck with Phoenix. He knew she would never forgive him for it.

He heard voices as the men inside Phillipe's cabin prepared to leave. By their unhurried departure he knew they never suspected that anyone was nearby. He hid in the tall swamp grass. There were four canoes, two men in each of the first two, one in each of the last. They called to one another, sharing a crude joke.

Coleton waited until the last canoe glided past him, following in the wake of the others as they followed the inland channel.

He pushed his way through the grass back toward the cabin, where he took the knife from his belt and cut down Phillipe's body. They'd strung him up like an animal and left him to rot in the sun. Coleton had seen too much death to be affected by the grisly sight. But the method did affect him — careless, with no regard for a harmless old man who never did anybody any harm. And they'd done it slowly, skinning the old man before finally putting him out of his misery.

It gave him more information as to the men he was to follow into the bayou. They were smugglers and they'd been after that shipment aboard the *Natchez*. Now . . . they were murderers.

Coleton retrieved a piece of canvas Phillipe had used as a makeshift sail for the skiff. He wrapped the old man's body and laid him on the narrow cot inside the one-room cabin. He twisted several pieces of discarded clothing into a tight knot around the end of a poling stick and thrust it into the smoldering fire in the stove. It smoked, then caught fire. He turned to take one last look at the cabin.

There were a lot of memories here — a boy's memories when Cairo had first brought him into the bayou and taught him to hunt. Phillipe had seemed old then, telling his stories about river pirates sneaking into the bayou at night, their torches glistening on the water.

He remembered one favorite story Phillipe told about a particular pirate who set his ship afire out on the river rather than let those chasing him take his cargo. The old man's eyes had glowed as he laughed with pleasure at the idea of the pirate setting himself afire to keep others from taking his cargo.

"Good-bye, old friend," Coleton murmured as he touched the torch to the oilcloth that hung over the windows, then the transparent netting over the bed. Phillipe had no family anyone knew of. This was the way he would want it — going out in a blaze of glory, taking all his worldly possessions with him.

When Coleton left the cabin, he took just one thing with him — the hand-carved bow Phillipe had taught him to use so many years before. The old man loved to hunt bear, deer, but especially gators. He said it took more skill with a bow.

He smashed the kerosene lantern on the floor, tossed the torch back into the cabin, and watched as it burst into flames. The smoke would be seen for miles around — just as he planned. He wanted those men to know, and wonder.

Coleton slung the bow and the quiver of arrows over his good shoulder and followed the steps down to the lower landing where the canoes had been tied. The fire roared to life overhead. It wouldn't be long before those flames spread down the steps and onto the landing. He ducked his head under the deck and searched the cool shadows where huge posts supported the burning cabin. Coleton's eyes narrowed as he found what he was looking for.

A long rope was tied to one of the wood pillars. The skiff bobbed lazily in the water. No one had bothered to look under the cabin or they would have taken the skiff. He winced with pain as he pulled it to the landing. Phillipe had been wise to the ways of the bayou. The skiff, like the canoe, contained a skin of fresh water, paddles, and a rolled packet of dried food.

"Thanks, old friend." Coleton untied the skiff and tossed the rope into the bow. It wobbled slightly as he stepped inside.

Coleton paddled out into the channel. He looked back only once at the cabin engulfed in flames. Then he turned the skiff and slowly paddled inland. By his guess, there were three, maybe four, hours of daylight left. Evening came early in the bayou, the tall, thick trees blocking the last few hours of daylight.

There was plenty of time to let the men know they were being followed, for them to wonder who it was, and why. After all, he knew where they were headed. He would take his time with them, just like they had with Phillipe.

Hours later, the feeling in Coleton's shoulder had gone from pain to numbness. There was only the warm trickle of the blood he couldn't see but could feel under the shirt, plastering it to his skin.

The last canoe ahead of him disappeared around a snag of trees. He heard the men talking freely among themselves as they beached their canoes.

"What you think dat smoke was? It came from dat old man's cabin."

"Probably just the stove."

"Too much smoke for a woodstove."

"And you talk too much, Mose. Get that canoe up on the bank."

"You want us to make camp and wait for Caleb to bring de mules?"

"We won't be needin' the mules without that shipment. And I ain't waitin' round till mornin'. We got a couple o' hours of daylight left. Pass the word along we'll go ahead on foot. I ain't stayin' here." He hesitated. "I got a real uneasy feelin' about this place."

"Sure 'nuf, boss, but you ain't got no two hours' daylight left. It gets dark real early deep in de bayou," Mose informed him.

"Then we'll use torches. It can't be that far. It only took a couple of hours comin' out the other day. Now, quit jawin' about it and tell the others!"

"Yessir," Mose replied, still muttering to himself as he pulled the canoe up onto dry land.

Coleton beached the skiff, then slipped noiselessly over the side, hiding the small boat in the swamp grass that grew dense along the bank. He crouched low and climbed the bank, peering through the dense foliage. Three canoes were brought ashore and concealed with branches and grass. The two men from the fourth canoe joined them as they walked back from farther up the channel.

Mose had spread the word they were to continue on foot. It was obviously not a popular decision.

"I'm in charge!" the first man reminded them.

Coleton recognized the man as the one who'd given Mose the orders to beach the canoes.

"And I say we go ahead on foot as long as there's light!"

One of the other men spoke up. "Mose says there's no more than maybe an hour's light left. I don't much care to get caught afoot in the bayou."

The first man turned on him. "I give the orders, and I say we go ahead. Or would you rather stay here and sleep with the gators tonight?" He jammed his face into the other man's, his hand going to a pistol snugged at his thick waist.

The man spat out a long stream of tobacco. "I don't reckon that leaves much choice. I never could stand the sight of them critters."

"Good," the leader grunted, stroking the butt of the revolver. "I'm glad to see you agree with me."

"You sure Mose knows the way back?"

The leader tightened his fingers over the handle of the revolver. "He knows the way. Any more questions?"

There was some disgruntled grumbling but no questions asked.

"Get yer gear and let's get movin'. We're wastin' light standing here arguin' about it!" the leader ordered.

The men retrieved guns and packs from the canoes. Then they moved off through the dense trees with Mose in the lead. Coleton made note of their course and smiled slowly. He would give them a substantial lead and then follow at his own pace.

He leaned against the trunk of a cypress tree. Opening the pack he'd found in the skiff, he made a meal of the dried venison and biscuits. His strength slowly returned and with it the pain in his shoulder. He took off his shirt and checked the bandage. It had soaked through with blood.

Coleton tore his shirt into narrow strips and rebound his shoulder. He allowed himself to think of Amanda. If she had followed his instructions she should have reached the end of the channel near Home Farm by now. He smiled. Knowing Amanda, she wouldn't allow herself to fail.

His shoulder throbbed, but he bound it tightly and the bleeding stopped. Then he folded the last strip of fabric lengthwise and bound that around his head to keep the sweat from running into his eyes. The bleeding might have stopped but the fever had returned.

He adjusted the bow and the leather quiver over his shoulder, then checked the blade in the scabbard at his belt. The venison was wrapped and stowed away in the skiff. He would take only the skin of water and the coil of rope used to tie the skiff.

Coleton gazed overhead, his eyes narrowing as he judged the amount of sunlight on the tops of the trees. Those men should have listened to Mose. At best there was only an hour of daylight left. There was no dusk in the bayou. It went from light to dark in a matter of minutes, exactly the way he wanted it. He slipped through the dense foliage of the bayou, expertly picking his way around floating peat onto firm ground as he went deeper and deeper into the forest of the bayou.

Andy had washed and changed her clothes. She buckled the belt of her pants. This time when she went into the bayou, her clothes would be far more practical, she had decided.

She hurried, knowing every second was precious. Even now, Cairo and the men were gathering in the yard below.

Andy sensed her presence before she saw Angeline standing in the open doorway to her room.

Angeline's hands twisted. She made no move to leave, but neither did she come fully into the room. The woman's stricken gaze met hers. Andy could see the pain and uncertainty in her dark, luminous eyes. Angeline clutched at her hands. They were cold as ice. Her lips trembled.

Andy held on to Angeline's hand. "I have to go with them. I can't risk losing him again." She knew Angeline understood as no one else could, for she was the only one who knew the truth—knew that she was Sunny. She'd known from the very first.

"I love him." Andy said it simply, for there was no

479

other way. She crossed the room, grabbing her jacket
Through the opened doors she heard the sounds of horse
and ran out onto the veranda. Cairo and the men were
waiting for her.

"You died because of that love," Angeline whispered
her eyes dark and troubled.

Andy whirled back around, a pleading look in her
eyes.

"I know, even though I don't remember everything yet
Somehow I've been given a second chance and I have to
take it." She laughed a little sadly. "The irony is, he
hates me because he thinks I'm nothing but a damned
Yankee who's stolen Ombre Rose from him." Then she
became very somber. "But I'll make him understand
Angeline. I have to. Don't you see, my life means noth
ing if I've lost his love." The expression in her blue eye
was desperate and determined. "I have to make him un
derstand." And then she was gone, running down the
wide stairs to the men below.

Angeline moved with an agility that belied her years a
she ran down the staircase and out onto the wide lawn
She watched the dance of lights as the riders cut acros
the park at Ombre Rose, torches held high to guide their
way. She whirled on the young stableboy who stood also
watching.

"Where is everybody?"

"Mr. Kittridge and Miss Lacey went into town. I heard
Miss Amanda tell dem to fetch dat man Kelly."

"What about Mr. Rawlins?" Angeline stared after the
riders, their torches now like fireflies in the distance.

"He went with Cairo and Miss Amanda. Said he wasn'
about to let her go back into dat bayou without him."

"Father in heaven, it's happenin' again. Just like be
fore." Angeline clutched at the small cross she wore on a
chain. She whirled on the young boy, making him jump
"Get me a horse, boy! Be quick about it! And I don'
want none of your shilly-shallyin' around."

"A horse?" His huge dark eyes widened. "What you be

480

wantin' a horse for?"

Angeline had turned back to watch those lights, her expression somber but determined. She ignored the question. "Do you know the bayou?"

"My pap and me lived there these past four years." He nodded and smiled.

"Then saddle two horses," she commanded. And when he simply stood there and gaped at her as if he hadn't heard her right, she said sharply, "Move! Or I'll skin you alive!"

Like the gray fox he'd been named for, Coleton had learned to move among the shadows of the night. Now, he hunted.

The men he trailed followed a steady course, moving single file behind Mose. Like their leader, they were all wary, uneasy, one hand kept on their weapons.

They weren't important to him, they were merely the means to move those stolen shipments taken from the Federal arsenals and munitions depots. He now knew Marilee's involvement, and it made sense. But there had to be someone else—someone who had access to times, dates, and deliveries of those shipments. He knew Marilee would never dirty her lily-white hands or risk that beautiful neck.

No, there had to be someone else involved. Someone who knew everything—the man who had impersonated the Gray Fox on all those raids. He wanted that man, and he knew he'd find him at the caves.

Coleton stalked the last man in the column, moving in when he lagged a little behind the others. Caught by surprise, he struggled, his initial reflex to grab at the hand that clamped down over his mouth. It was a fatal mistake. As his hand came away from the revolver, Coleton sunk the knife between his ribs. The smuggler slumped noiselessly into the knee-high grass, his companions unaware as they walked ahead.

481

Coleton thought of old Phillippe and he felt no remorse. He resheathed his blade and slipped back into the forest.

The night closed around them. They stopped to light their torches and drink water. The small clearing glowed with the firelight.

"Pass them skins forward, Dooley," the leader commanded.

"Sarge? . . ."

He whirled around. "I told you never to call me that," he grumbled as the man called Dooley came running up to him. "What the hell's the matter with you?"

"It's Tanner."

Slightly agitated, Sarge flicked a brief glance over his men. "What about him?"

"He's gone." Dooley danced nervously from one foot to another.

"What do you mean *gone?*"

"He's just plain gone. I can't find him nowhere. He just ain't back there."

"He has to be."

"I swear, Sarge . . . er, uh, sir." He continued stammering. "He was right behind me, and then when I looked around . . . he was gone."

"He probably just stepped off the trail to relieve himself." Sarge muttered an oath, then walked back past the rest of his men to the end of the column. He cupped his hands. "Hey, Tanner! Dooley's been missin' ya. Come on out, boy."

The crude remarks met only with silence. The men shifted uneasily, their faces shadowed with doubt in the flickering light from the torches.

"Maybe he forgot somethin' and doubled back," one of the other men suggested hopefully.

"Or maybe the bayou got him." Mose stepped from the front of the column to stare past the men into the darkness that surrounded them.

Sarge whirled on him. "What the hell are you talkin'

482

about?"

Mose shrugged his shoulders, his dark eyes widening. "The swamp ain't no place to be at night. Dey's some folks believe dey's spirits in the forest. Dat's why I didn't want no part in killin' dat old man."

Sarge glanced around the circle of worried men. "Shut up, Mose. We know the trail well enough. Tanner knows it, too. He'll be along. But for now we got to get to the caves. Get yer gear!" he shouted to the men. "And the next one I hear mention anythin' about spirits I'll cut his tongue out myself." He stomped back to the head of the line. "Mose, get yer black ass up here and let's get movin'."

A murmur of discontent passed among the men but none dared challenge their leader. One by one they fell into line behind the sarge and Mose. Now instead of watching the trail in front of them, they watched the dark shadows surrounding them.

Before the second smuggler even realized it, Coleton slipped up behind him and snapped his neck. Now there were four.

"Christ! Sarge! Jessup's gone now!" The three men in front of Dooley stopped and whirled around.

"Damn! What the hell's goin' on?"

"Quiet! All of you be quiet!" the sarge bellowed, the sound scattering night creatures from their perches in the trees. Bats squealed as they winged frantically away from the light of the torches.

"I don't like this! I don't like it at all!" another man muttered nervously, his fingers working over the butt of his revolver.

"I tried to warn you," Mose piped up. Sarge charged at him, grabbing the front of his shirt in ham-shaped fists.

"I told you to shut up. We go on. In two's! Now move!"

"But what about Tanner and Jessup? They ain't both out relievin' themselves."

"You wanna stay around and look for them?" Sarge

growled as he shoved Mose away and sneered at the other man.

"No, sir."

"All right, then move out!"

They moved up the trail in pairs; the sarge and Mose in the lead, Dooley and the fourth man only a few paces behind.

Coleton knew exactly where they were. They'd been climbing a slight incline for almost half a mile. He listened. The sound came from off to his left. Water from the creek that fed the bayou tumbled lazily this time of year over rocks. He stopped to rest, mentally blocking out the searing pain in his shoulder. Fever burned through him, but he wouldn't stop.

He looked up at the clear night sky that blanketed the bayou overhead. The familiar stars winked back at him through the canopy of pines. A crescent moon was just coming up behind the peak of a distant hill. He visually marked a line between that peak and the tip of the cup of the Big Dipper. He moved to his left and worked his way ahead of the men.

Coleton made a loop in the rope snare and knelt in the darkness beside the trail to wait.

He let Sarge and Mose pass. He wanted the other two men. Fear made them walk close together — a critical error. Too late they realized it as Coleton yanked the loop of the snare. The rope snapped around both men's ankles and jerked them high in the air. One man's revolver thudded to the ground.

Coleton retrieved the revolver and jammed it into his belt. Then he drew one arrow through the string of the bow and took aim. He only needed one.

"Lawd Almighty!" Mose screamed as he came running back down the trail with Sarge. He jolted to a halt, his eyes almost popping out of their sockets at the sight of the two dead men dangling by their heels, one arrow impaling both.

"I'm gettin' outta here!" He whirled around.

"Damn you, Mose! Get back here!"

"No, sir! I warned you! I tried to tell you. Somethin' out there wants us dead. If you hadn't killed dat ole man—"

"If they wanted us dead we would already be dead. Mose? Mose!" he shouted after the black man as he disappeared down the trail.

"Damn you! You worthless son of a bitch! Get back here!" Sarge bellowed into the night. Then he whirled around, wide-eyed, his gaze scanning the forest about him.

Coleton let Mose go. From what he'd heard, the man had nothing to do with Phillipe's death. He would let him live. He watched as the sarge pulled the revolver at his belt and whirled around, brandishing it in several different directions.

"Come on out! Come and get me! I'll fight!" he shouted. "Show your face, you filthy cowards! What is it you want? The shipment?" He laughed. "It's at the bottom of the river! Do you hear that?" He spun around in the opposite direction.

"Did you hear? There ain't no shipment! It's gone! Blown up!" There was nothing but silence.

"I'll make you a deal! I'll cut you in! We got a lotta stuff hidden!" Sweat poured off him. A bat squeaked through the night air as it winged past him. He jerked around and fired at it, the loud report sending hundreds of bats from dark perches.

"Do you hear me?" Sarge whirled around and around, leaping in first one direction then another, frantically waving his torch in one hand, the revolver in the other.

Coleton shoved the tip of his knife up under Sarge's chin, drawing a trickle of blood as it pricked the skin when he came up behind him.

"I hear you," he growled low in his throat, pressing the tip of that blade up a little higher, forcing Sarge up on his toes. "Now, hear me. Drop the gun."

The revolver thudded to the ground.

485

"The knife," Coleton commanded, glancing down briefly at the man's belt, knowing without even looking there was one there. Sarge grabbed for it.

Coleton jerked the tip up another fraction of an inch. "Slowly!" The knife fell beside the revolver.

"These are the rules. Walk, and don't try to get away or you'll end up like your men." He motioned to the two who dangled by their ankles.

"Don't call out." He turned the blade a notch for emphasis of what Sarge could expect. "Or you'll end up like your men."

"In short, don't do anything, except walk ahead slowly. Is that understood?" He twisted the tip again, and Sarge nodded as emphatically as he could with the blade poking him.

"Put your hands behind your back," Coleton ordered and quickly tied them, leaving a lead of rope to hold on to. "Make one wrong move, say anything at all," he jerked the rope, pulling Sarge backward, the blade moving through the air in an arc only an inch from the man's throat, "and you're a dead man."

Sarge nodded frantically that he understood.

"Good. You're smarter than you look."

It wasn't much farther to the caves.

As a boy they had been a source of intrigue and fascination. Few people knew of them, mostly believed them to be part of pirate legend. Supposedly a band of pirates out of the gulf discovered the caves over a hundred years ago and hid their gold and silver in them.

Cairo had first showed him the caves. He'd explored them as a child, determined to find that pirate's gold, but he never found any. Now they hid a different bounty — the stolen arms shipments.

Coleton jerked on the rope as they approached the small clearing at the mouth of the caves. A glow came from inside. His arm went around the front of his captive's chest, pinning his arms. The knife was clenched in his other hand. Pain tore through his shoulder as he brought the knife up under the man's throat.

"What's the signal?"

Sarge cleared his throat uneasily. "An owl's hoot; twice."

Coleton pressed the knife at his throat. "Go ahead. But," he pressed the knife until beads of blood appeared at Sarge's throat, "if you try anything, you're the first to die.

Sarge gave the signal, his eyes closing in what had to be silent prayer as they stood and waited. A shadow emerged from the entrance of the caves.

"That you, Sarge?"

Coleton prodded him.

"That's right."

"Come on ahead."

Coleton pushed his captive ahead of him. He'd already taken a quick inventory. There were two guards at the cave entrance.

"Somethin' wrong?" the man called out, coming forward a few paces with one of the guards.

Sarge fumbled. "I, uh . . ."

"Hold it right there!" Coleton called out. He pushed Sarge to the ground and shoved his booted foot across his neck. He brought the revolver up and aimed it at the man who came toward them.

"What the . . . ?"

The guard pulled back the hammer on his revolver.

"I'll get both of you before you get me," Coleton promised, digging the heel of his boot into Sarge's throat. A smile began slowly as he recognized the man who stood only a few feet away. He'd first seen him at the auction in Baton Rouge. He'd bid against him for Ombre Rose. The second time he'd seen him was aboard the *Natchez*.

"Sergeant Meachum, I believe. Of the Union Army?" Coleton leveled the pistol at him. "You had access to information about all those shipments, and Marilee had the social connections for interested buyers. The French? the Mexicans, the Indians, maybe even the Union Army, the same government you stole them from in the first place.

At a very handsome profit."

Coleton fought back the weakness from the fever and the pain that pulsed through his shoulder. He had what he wanted. Now he had to get Meachum to Phoenix. "It was all so perfect. Wasn't it, Meachum?"

"It still *is*, Major James."

Coleton heard the distinct sound of a revolver being cocked behind him. Then he heard a voice he'd memorized that night three years ago when he'd hidden in a fallen tree with stolen documents and earned the name Gray Fox.

Bootsteps crunched over dry pine needles. Cold sweat mingled with that of the fever. Coleton knew he'd made a grave error.

"Sergeant, may I introduce the *real* Gray Fox." There was cold laughter. "I've waited a long time for this."

At the edge of the park, instead of heading back into the bayou the way Andy had originally come from Home Farm, they followed a wagon road. It bordered the freshly harvested cane fields on the east, the dense pine forest on the west—the same pine forest Andy had once argued about with Coleton.

It was dark when they left Ombre Rose. Lacey and August Kittridge had gone into Baton Rouge to find Rafe Kelly. There were nine of them, riding in groups of two or three where the road allowed, falling back into a column of single riders when they left the road and followed Cairo into the forest.

The men Cairo brought were armed. Andy didn't ask where they acquired guns when the entire South had supposedly surrendered all its weapons at the end of the war.

Angeline caught up with them on the wagon road, accompanied by one of the young stable boys who was a son of one of the men who rode with them. Andy was especially fond of him. He was quiet and kept to himself. His name was Sobe. He was the fifth son in his family.

His mother had desperately wanted a daughter. When she was told she'd had another son, she'd been at a loss for a name and simply said "So be it". From then on he was called Sobe.

Angeline rode behind Andy, with Sobe behind her. It was a ride Andy knew she would never forget. If she thought her journey out of the bayou was dangerous, she soon realized it was nothing compared to the trail Cairo followed.

The trail was difficult at best, exhausting to both horse and rider. They cut through dense stands of trees, branches whipping at them, threatening to unseat any rider who didn't pay strictest attention. They carried torches, but at best they gave light to the man who carried it and little to the one trailing behind. Andy gave up trying to guide her horse and simply held on, hoping he had the sense to follow the horse in front of him.

There were moments when the trail seemed to disappear altogether as they came face-to-face with a solid wall of trees. There were others when the incline was so steep Andy was forced to cling to the neck of her horse to keep from slipping off. It became a task of holding on with arms, legs, and ankles until every muscle, bone, and joint ached with the effort.

Branches tore at her hair and clothes and cut her cheeks. She alternated cursing the horse, the trail, and herself for not being a better rider. But underneath it all was the driving desperation that Coleton might die if they didn't get to the caves in time.

They rode for hours. Andy was certain they must be riding in circles. No one could possibly know their way through here, much less at night with only the torches to guide the horses.

She heard the sound of rushing water almost the same instant they crossed the wide stream. It seemed they followed it for miles. Then it was on the left and she had no idea how it might have happened except that she must have dozed upright in the saddle.

Andy had become so used to the motion of the horse beneath her that she was practically unseated as they all came to a halt.

"We go without the torches from here," Cairo announced, dousing his torch in the stream. The other riders did the same, their torches hissing in the night air. Then they were plunged into darkness with only the waning light of a sliver of moon to guide them.

Guns were checked and made ready, rifles laid across saddles before the riders. And silently they moved forward as Cairo led them.

Dawn stole silent fingers of gray light into the forest, turning green pine needles to silver. A breeze stirred through the trees. An owl fluttered through the crowning treetops, returning from the hunt to perch and sleep. Cairo turned his horse and rode back to Andy.

"The caves are just ahead, there may be guards. We go on foot from here. I will take two of the men and go on ahead. You will stay here with the others." He turned to leave.

Andy grabbed at his arm. "No! I'm going with you," she insisted.

He met her defiant gaze stoically, then he looked past her to Parker Rawlins. "Keep her here," he ordered the man. "There may be trouble."

"Cairo!" she whispered desperately after him, but he paid no attention as he silently signaled to two of the men from Ombre Rose to follow him. They dismounted and tethered their horses. Cairo gave instructions to one of the men who was to remain behind, then turned with his companions. They disappeared noiselessly into the forest. Andy brought one leg over the front of her saddle and slipped to the ground.

"Amanda!" Parker Rawlins whispered angrily. "Where do you think you're going?"

"I'm going with Cairo," she announced, pushing past the hot, sweating horses that blocked the trail. One of the men from Ombre Rose tried to stop her, and she pushed past him as well. She ran down the trail after Cairo.

"Amanda! Amanda, please!" Parker caught up with her, catching her arm and spinning her around.

She whirled to face him, and some vague memory resurfaced. This wasn't the first time there had been anger between them.

"I have to go with them!"

For the first time in almost twenty years father and daughter confronted each other.

Chapter Twenty-four

Time hung suspended between them. For those few moments they both saw the past as it had been — when Parker Rawlins was a younger man, and Andy had lived another life. Her hand closed over his as he grasped her arm.

"I have to go to him," she said softly.

Parker Rawlins was not a well man. The ride had taken its toll. Yet he had insisted on coming. Had he known the truth when he made that decision, or had he only guessed? It didn't matter. All that mattered was this moment.

She knew the battled feelings that had lain dead for almost twenty years. She could see the anger, pain, and helplessness. And she saw something else behind his tired eyes. She saw understanding — something he hadn't been able to give her all those years ago.

"I'm coming with you," he announced, his mouth trembling with unspoken words.

Andy ran down the trail Cairo and the others had followed. The hill rose to their left, the thinning trees ringed with soft halos of morning mist as it rose off the bayou down below.

Cairo and the two men stood at the edge of the clearing. Coleton was standing in the middle with Durant's men surrounding him. His shirt was gone. The bandage at his shoulder was muddied and bloodstained. His hands were bound behind his back, pulled back in an awkward position that she knew must be agonizingly painful to his wounded shoulder.

He stood, feet planted in a military stance. His head was up, his face was etched with pain, the twitching muscles in his jaw completing the hard mask. Dirt smudged his chest, sweat ran in rivulets down his chest. Andy knew the fever had returned, heat pouring through his battered body. But his eyes were like shards of ice. She tried to go to him.

Cairo grabbed her back. "Not yet!" he warned. "There are too many of them. If we go in there now, they will kill him."

"They'll kill him anyway! We have to do something!"

"There aren't enough of us."

"Amanda, please. He's right."

She watched helplessly from their hidden position at the end of the clearing, watching as Durant slowly circled Coleton like an animal stalking its prey. Coleton had walked right into a trap.

"It's been a long time, Major James." Durant slowly drew off his buff military gloves. "But I swore this day would come." His voice was cold, deadly.

"And now I will have my revenge." He slowly walked across the glade, then turned and faced Coleton. "Revenge for Gettysburg. Every time we launched an assault, we were met by a superior Confederate force. We moved a dozen cannons to a battlefield and were met by twenty. We shifted our troops to another sector to surround a Reb battalion and found ourselves facing an entire regiment." He turned to pace back to Coleton.

"Someone knew all our movements before we made them — someone the Confederates called the Gray Fox."

"My career was at stake. I was offered a promotion in exchange for the Gray Fox." Slowly, he paced the clearing, his gloves dangling from his hand.

"For months I planned your capture. But time after time," each word was emphasized by a slap of those gloves against his blue-clad leg, "you eluded me. Except . . . for once."

He turned back around, his eyes glittering with hatred from under the brim of his military hat. "I sprang my trap and caught the Gray Fox." He whirled on Coleton, his hand shaking with rage as he pointed at him accusingly. "You should have hanged! Yes, by God, you should have hanged. Instead you escaped, but not before I left my mark on you."

It was then she knew—Durant was the one who'd ordered him beaten. And he obviously took delight in the scars that remained. It wasn't enough.

"You destroyed my military career," Durant screamed, his words hard and bitter. "West Point, a brilliant record, commendations, all of it gone. I was overlooked the next time promotions were handed out by General Grant. It was 'suggested' that I volunteer for the position of adjutant to General Sheridan during the military occupation after the war and thereby redeem myself for something that should never have happened. So you see, Major James, it was a matter of pride and honor." He'd circled the clearing once more as he continued his tirade. Now he stopped before Coleton.

"Pride and honor." He circled round and faced Coleton. "Isn't it true that honor is everything to a southerner?" Durant was deliberately goading him.

Andy's stricken gaze fastened on Coleton. Durant was toying with him, like a cat played with a mouse before killing it. Her fists clenched at her sides with helplessness. Where were the others? Had Lacey and her father been unable to find Rafe Kelly? It was taking too long. They should have been here by now.

"Sergeant!" Durant yelled across the clearing to a plain-clothed man Andy immediately recognized as the man who had bid against her and Coleton for Ombre Rose!

"Bring the pistols."

Sergeant Meachum disappeared inside the entrance to the caves and quickly returned with a large, flat box carried under his arm. He placed it atop the stacked crates and stepped back. Durant slowly strode across the clearing. He caressed the fine rosewood box, then turned, his brutal eyes fastening on Coleton.

"I've always admired a fine weapon, Major. I think you'll agree these are among the finest, and you should recognize them. I took them from Ombre Rose."

Coleton's gaze snapped to the case as Durant raised the lid

494

of the box and revealed the twin dueling pistols nestled in midnight-blue velvet. His only response was the hardening muscle at his jaw.

Durant removed one of the pistols and held it aloft as he examined it. Andy stared at the deadly weapon. Dear God, what was he doing? Then she had her answer.

Durant circled Coleton. "I'm going to give you the chance to avenge that stupid honor you Confederates prize so highly." Taking a knife from one of his men, he cut the rope around Coleton's wrists. Then he walked away from him.

Her gaze followed Durant. What was he talking about?

Slowly Durant turned, raised the pistol, aimed it straight at Coleton, and pulled back the hammer.

Andy would have run to Coleton, but Parker Rawlins stopped her.

"Amanda!" he whispered desperately, pulling her back against him. "If you make one move toward him, Durant will kill him."

"He'll kill him anyway," she whispered desperately, trying to break his hold.

"There may be a chance!" he warned her. "We need time for the others to get here!"

Time. That one little word burned into her thoughts. He was right, and she knew it. But she was afraid there was no more time. Durant wanted Coleton dead and he was mad enough to do it—but not without making a horrible game of it. She stared, disbelieving as Durant delivered his challenge.

"A duel, Major, to the death. Your last opportunity to regain some small measure of your . . . honor."

Andy's gaze fastened on Coleton. *No!* her frantic thoughts cried out. *Don't take it! Don't do it! It's what he wants you to do. Don't give in to him! Please, don't do it!* But she knew he would.

Coleton's eyes were cold as death, and they never left Durant. She watched, horrified as Coleton reached out and slowly took the pistol in his left hand.

"Oh, God, no!" Andy sobbed softly. Coleton was left-handed. With his injured shoulder he could never hope to raise that pistol, much less fire it. And Durant knew it. The duel was a mockery, a horrible game that he had no intention of losing.

Perhaps it was breath of rising wind that slowly filled the trees and made a soft, stirring sound. Or perhaps it was the first gray light of dawn that spread across the floor of the glade, swirling streamers of mist from off the bayou.

Weakness poured through Andy, engulfing her senses. It began like the buzzing of bees on a warm summer morning. Then it grew louder and louder, until the sound was a deafening roar that made her head ache. She clasped her hands over her ears trying to close it out.

"No! Please, not now! This can't be happening again." But it *was* happening again. And no matter how she fought it, Andy felt herself being drawn into that dark, cool place she'd been before. If she left now, if she slipped into the memories of her other life she might lose him forever in this life. And God only knew if they would ever be together again.

Even as the deafening sound persisted, she stared across the glade at Coleton and concentrated on staying there with him no matter what happened. But she was powerless to control it, just as she had been before.

One moment she was staring at Coleton, reaching out as if she could physically hold on to him and the images of the people in that glade. In the next moment, it was as if she were viewing everything from very far away, with darkness closing all around her, as if she was looking through that long, dark tunnel. Coldness swept through her, numbing her senses, suspending her in a dark void where there was no sight, no sound, no feelings.

Then the darkness burst into vivid color. It was as if she were traveling backward through her memories. Images slipped past in a kaleidoscopic blur of brilliant reds, blues, greens, and blinding whites. The pictures of her memory spun faster and faster, taking her into the past.

It was blinding and painful. She was leaving her present life behind. Amanda Spenser had become a blur until it seemed she ceased to exist at all. Then the images focused, not as Amanda Spenser, but as the person she had once been — Sunny Rawlins.

"Now darlin', you know my reasons," her father was softly explaining to her as he sat at his large desk. *"I have asked you not to see Coleton James again. It simply is not proper. You simply don't understand your feelings."*

"But I do understand, Papa. I love him." She clenched her fists in the fold of her morning dress. She'd worn it especially for Coleton.

"Sunny, we have spoken of this before," he reminded her. *"I asked you to refuse him when he calls on you. If he persists, I shall have him put out."*

"You wouldn't, you can't."

"Sunny, you know I would. I simply won't allow this to continue."

I won't allow it!

Her father's words echoed over and over, burning through her with all the old pain and anguish.

There were other images. She felt as if she were spinning past countless windows. When she looked in each, she saw scenes, bits and pieces from her other life.

She was Sunny; she was Amanda; she was both, experiencing both lives at once. It was as if all her memories and emotions as both Sunny and Amanda were playing out side by side. They overlapped, separated, then ran together, weaving together the past and the present.

It was like waking from a dream, but like the times before, she knew she hadn't slept. She took a deep breath, feeling the cool air fill her lungs. Her legs were folded under her and she was curled over her knees. It was painful at first, and the thought occurred to her that it must be a little like being born and dying all at once.

She slowly brought her head up and stared out across the glade. She felt the restraint at her arms, and saw everything as it had been just those few moments before, but she saw something else as well — she saw the past.

It was as if transparent images of her other life were laid out over the images of the present. She saw the pine trees that surrounded them, and she also saw the image of the gnarled oak, streamers of Spanish moss dripping from the branches.

The cold gray dawn spilled into the glade, now as it had before. Shadows lengthened and separated as the two men stood shoulder-to-shoulder. The mist swirled around their legs, making them seem almost like ghosts as each clutched a gleaming pistol.

She saw the brilliant blue of Durant's uniform, the corded muscles across Coleton's scarred back. They were of an even height, both soldiers, trained to lead . . . and to kill. But there was a lean intensity in Coleton, an animal wariness that hinted, even though he was wounded, blood soaking through the stained bandages, unable to fire a gun with his left hand, that he was dangerous and deadly.

Then the images faded and changed. Once again she saw two men standing in the middle of the glade. But one was older, the weariness of age in his bent stance. The other man was much younger, hardly more than a boy, and his pale gray eyes smoldered with the fire of passion . . .

They were the images from her drawings, memories from Sunny's life that had emerged through her art.

Durant's voice jolted her back to the present.

"At the signal we will each take ten paces, mark and turn. Each man will fire a single shot."

"No," Andy whispered. "This can't be happening."

"There's nothing you can do, child," Parker Rawlins whispered to her desperately.

The sergeant gave the signal to begin. She stared horrified as they slowly paced away from each other. Almost simultaneously they stopped. She watched disbelieving as they turned.

She could almost feel the tension in taut muscles as arms were raised, the hard, smooth steel of the pistols, the cold breath of fear that hung suspended in time as their fingers slowly squeezed back . . .

"No!" Andy sobbed as she broke free from Parker Rawlins. Fear choked into her throat as she ran between them. Tears flooded her eyes. Every thought fragmented into only one: She couldn't let Coleton die.

"Amanda!"

She heard Parker Rawlins's warning a fraction of a moment before the deafening blast of gunfire roared across the glade. And in that one moment, it seemed time had stopped.

She reached Coleton. Her hands clasped at his arms as she stared up into the startled gray of his eyes, no longer the boy.

Coleton saw her break free of Rawlins's grasp, but there was nothing he could do to stop her or prevent what he suddenly realized would happen. It was his worst nightmare, and it was truly happening . . . all over again. The agony and pain he'd carried for almost twenty years crystallized into that one memory — Sunny.

Everything was just as it had been that morning nineteen years ago. He felt it, sensed that moment of silence when it seemed everything about them hung suspended in some void in time.

She was running to him. He saw the light catching the soft gold of her hair and the desperation in her eyes, just as he'd seen it that day. She called his name, as he'd heard it a thousand times since in his dreams. The shot rang out across the glade.

"Coleton," she gasped as pain slammed through her shoulder, driving the breath from her lungs. She stared up at him wide-eyed, knowing in that instant what it was she had never been able to remember . . . the gunshot.

His right arm went around her, taking her slender weight against his body, the pistol still clutched in his left hand, unfired.

"Coleton James!" Durant roared across the glade. Even now, he fought to reload the single shot pistol.

"I'll kill you, James! I swear I'll kill you . . . !"

Coleton raised his pistol, and took aim. His hand shook, then steadied as he slowly squeezed back the trigger. The single shot cracked sharply.

The pistol dropped from his fingers. Coleton stared down into her upturned face, saw the trembling of her lips, the fear that was softened by unwavering love in her eyes, felt the soft brush of her breath. And in that moment he knew that he held both the past and the present in his arms.

He went down on one knee, cradling her, unaware that several mounted soldiers led by Rafe Kelly had charged into the clearing.

"Sunny." His voice broke as Coleton held her, and she felt the desperation, heard it in his voice, and she clung to him.

He simply held her, disbelieving, and at the same time desperate to believe.

She closed her eyes, the heat of his body stealing through her, tasting the salt-sweatiness of his shoulder as she kissed him. He was real, he was here, and he was holding her.

Coleton's fingers plunged through her hair as he cradled her head, holding on to her as if she were life itself. Then, still unable to comprehend, he held her away and stared searchingly into her eyes.

"You are real."

She nodded, tears spilling from her lashes as she reached to caress his cheek, the faint lines at his eyes, the soft brush of his mustache above his lips.

"How?"

"I don't know. I only know it's happened, and in spite of everything, I found you." Her arms went around his neck and she buried her face at his throat. "Please, just hold me and never let me go."

Coleton closed his eyes and he felt himself come alive, truly alive for the first time in nineteen years.

"Dear God!" He shuddered, pressing his cheek against her hair. "When I saw you just now, it was as if it was happening all over again."

"I know." She breathed a tremulous sigh, reaching up to hold his handsome face between her hands, laughing faintly at the soft growth of his beard. He'd been so young. She'd been so young.

She stroked the soft sable of his mustache, and his lips burned against her fingertips.

"All I could think was that somehow I had to keep it from happening," she murmured. "Oh, Cole. I couldn't bear the thought of having a second chance and living it without you. But I didn't remember what had happened until the gunshot . . ."

Andy's eyes darkened. She realized now that *she* was the one who'd been shot that day so long ago. *She* had taken the bullet meant for Coleton and the other man had been . . . her father!

She twisted in Coleton's arms and stared back across the clearing.

"Oh, God, no!" Andy ran to the crumpled body that lay between Coleton and Durant.

She fell to her knees beside her father. Angeline sat cradling his head in her lap, blood trickling from his pale lips.

She met Angeline's soft, dark eyes.

"Now you understand what happened that day, child."

Andy nodded as she took Parker Rawlins's hand in hers. With her other hand, she stroked back the silver hair from his forehead.

His eyes fluttered weakly as they opened and slowly focused.

"Sunny?"

"Yes, Daddy. I'm here."

"Then it is true—you are my Sunny."

She nodded, fighting back the tears. "Yes, Daddy," she whispered. He'd run after her and pushed her out of the way when Durant fired his pistol. He'd saved her life.

"Oh, Daddy, why did you do it?"

He smiled weakly, then coughed, bringing up crimson spittle. Angeline wiped at it with the hem of her skirt.

He held on to Andy, his fingers tightening. "I think I always knew, from the first moment I saw you. There was something . . ." He stopped, the coughing coming again, harder. There was more blood. Andy's stricken gaze searched Angeline's. The older woman simply shook her head.

"I had to do it, child." He reached up, pressing a hand against her cheek. "Somehow I had to make up for what I

501

did . . ." His voice broke. "I never meant to hurt you, Sunny. Dear God, you have to know that. I loved you more than anything in this life. I know now that I was wrong. I should never have tried to keep you apart." He slowly looked past her to Coleton. "Can you both forgive me?"

Andy felt the pressure of Coleton's hand on her shoulder. She looked up at him, love and pleading in her eyes. She knew her father was dying. They'd lost each other once before and reclaimed some small piece of time these last weeks. But she and Coleton had a lifetime to share. *Please, dear God, let it end here.*

"There's been enough hatred," Coleton whispered, his voice thick with emotion.

Andy covered his hand with hers, knowing how difficult it was for him to give that much.

Her father sighed. "Then I can die a happy man, finally at peace."

"Daddy . . ." Andy sobbed, unable to hold back the tears.

"No, no, sweetheart," he comforted her. "You mustn't cry for me. I was given a gift of time these last months. I have no regrets, Sunny." His fingers tightened over hers. Andy bent over his hand, rubbing it against her cheek. "I love you . . ." he murmured, then his fingers slowly released hers.

Andy looked up. He was gone. Tears slowly slipped down her cheeks.

"Major James?"

Coleton looked up at the young corporal and the two other soldiers who stood with him. "We'll take him, sir, if that's all right with the lady."

Andy's questioning gaze met Coleton's.

"It's all right, sweetheart. These are the men Rafe brought back with him."

Andy looked to the three soldiers in bright blue uniforms. They made no move toward Coleton. She slowly nodded, watching protectively as they carefully lifted her father for the return trip. She finally released his hand.

"Major James?" The young corporal hesitated. "Phoenix is waiting for you, sir. At the train. I can take you there."

At Andy's questioning look, Coleton slowly brought her to her feet.

He nodded, he'd been expecting this. He just didn't think it would be this soon.

Coleton reached inside his pocket for the medallion Phoenix had once given him. He started to hand it to the corporal.

"Give this to Phoenix."

Andy stared at the medallion that spun at the end of the chain that dangled from Coleton's fingers. She grabbed it, staring up at him.

"Where did you get this?"

Coleton gave her a puzzled look. "Phoenix gave it to me."

"Phoenix?" she whispered, disbelieving as her thoughts raced back to when she was fourteen and she had given an identical medallion to her brother. There was no other like it; she'd had it especially made for him because of his love of the myth of the Phoenix.

"My God, Stephen?" Was it possible after all these months of emptiness and loss. She whirled on the corporal.

"Take me to the man who calls himself the Phoenix."

The startled corporal looked from her to Coleton. "That's not possible, ma'am."

She lunged at the poor young soldier, clutching the medallion in one hand, her other twisting the front of his uniform.

"Take me to him!"

The train sat in the shadows of overhanging oaks at the same remote siding Coleton remembered. They had both been blindfolded as they were led to Phoenix's location. His thoughts churned. That brief moment back in the glade, he was certain Amanda was either overwrought with grief over Parker Rawlins's death or exhausted beyond reason.

Now he stood at the far end of the railroad car and watched Amanda in the arms of another man.

"Why didn't you tell me?" Andy buried her tear-streaked face once more in Phoenix's shoulder—the man she knew as

503

Major Stephen Spenser, now Colonel Stephen Spenser.

Stephen shifted his weight to his good leg as he held his weeping sister. He stroked her back, feeling all the guilt of the last months wash back over him.

"I couldn't," he said simply. "I was under orders. There was this damn conspiracy . . ."

"Orders?" Andy stared up at him incredulously. "Orders? And you couldn't just write a note—something to let us know you were alive?" She knew she was screaming at him and didn't care. "Do you know what you put us through? Aunt Lenore had a huge memorial service for you, there was a full color guard . . ." She stopped when she realized what she'd said. The Army had been in on it all along. "Damn, the Army!"

"Amanda . . ." He gestured helplessly. "I'm sorry. You'll never know how sorry I am. But I couldn't, not even when I knew you were in Baton Rouge—at Ombre Rose, right in the middle of all this. It would have given everything away."

He looked over her shoulder to Coleton, who slumped wearily against the end wall of the car.

"I had to rely on Major James. He was the only one I could trust."

"You mean the only one you could blackmail into breaking the conspiracy," Coleton corrected him.

"The choice of words is yours. I thought you might be motivated to breaking it." Stephen met the steady gaze of the man who had once been known as the Gray Fox—a man he respected, in spite of the different color of their uniforms.

"Blackmail?" Andy looked from Coleton to Stephen, then back again. Coleton wouldn't meet her gaze.

"What are you talking about?"

Stephen released a heavy sigh. He knew his sister's temper and just exactly what her reaction would be.

When he'd finished explaining the deal he had made with Coleton, he realized he didn't know her quite as well as he thought he did.

Andy turned to Coleton. Now she understood everything. He'd originally come to Ombre Rose intending to have it back no matter what it took. But what it took was a deal with the United States government to break the weapons conspiracy. And his reward for exposing the man posing as the Gray Fox was Ombre Rose.

The official documents were drawn up. Once again the government had stepped in, just as it had when officials in Washington had convinced Stephen to go underground and keep his identity a secret when he was officially listed as dead after that battle in Virginia.

Now the United States government would give Coleton James his reward for a job well done. He would have both his full pardon as a war criminal and Ombre Rose. But there was so much more that wasn't resolved. Had he forgotten everything that had happened in that glade?

Andy's voice was thick with emotion. "I guess you have won after all. It's all yours—Ombre Rose . . . everything." Her bottom lip trembled as she searched his gray eyes, trying to understand what she saw there. She bit at her lower lip.

Coleton saw that endearing gesture and it wrapped around his heart. It was such a small thing, but it was so typical of who she was—who she'd been all along, and what she was to him.

His voice broke as he looked at her, remembering everything and scared as hell she would walk away from him now. He knew what Ombre Rose meant to her, had watched her fight to keep it, and knew how stubborn and proud she could be.

Would that hardheaded Yankee stubbornness she'd been raised with in this lifetime destroy what they'd begun in another?

"I don't have anything unless I have you," he whispered softly. "It's meaningless without you. Everything I am, everything I've ever done or wanted is because of you."

Andy's eyes pooled with tears. It wasn't what she was prepared for, and it reminded her that Coleton had changed from the young man she once knew. She wanted very much to know all about the man he was now.

"You're certain?" She took a tentative step toward him.

"I was certain then; I've never changed my mind." Coleton held out his hand to her as he had almost twenty years ago and countless times in his dreams since.

"Now wait just a minute," Stephen protested. "Amanda? You can't just go with this man. You know nothing about him. After all, he made a bargain to take that plantation away from you."

Andy slipped into Coleton's arms, burying her face against his chest. She closed her eyes, feeling safe, protected, and loved. Then she breathed in slowly and raised her eyes to his as she spoke to her brother.

"It's all right, Stephen," she said as she looked up at Coleton, "we're married."

"Married? I don't understand. When in the hell did all this happen?" Stephen started around his desk, brotherly indignation written in the hard lines of his face.

"A long time ago," Coleton answered, remembering that brief ceremony in a dimly lit chapel when they had stood together and promised their lives to each other. She had kept her promise.

"A lifetime ago," he whispered against her soft golden hair as he held her tight and silently vowed he'd never let her go again—not in this life or any other.

"Coleton?"

"Yes, little one?"

"Is it really over?" she asked.

"It's over, little Yank." He closed his eyes against the weakness and pain from the wound at his shoulder, wanting only to hold her. He kissed her hair, his eyes growing damp as he realized he'd never thought to feel that silken softness again.

There were moments, like now, and over the past months when he had looked at her and actually saw Sunny. It was something in her eyes. They were Sunny's eyes; wide and unafraid one moment, laughing at him with mischief another, then darkening with stubbornness and more pure mule-headedness than he could ever have imagined.

More than anything, it was the stubbornness that seemed

so different about her. But then when he'd known her at fifteen, she was hardly more than a young girl. He'd had no inkling of the woman she would become. Amanda Spenser was that woman. And though he'd loved her for over twenty years, he was only just beginning to know her. It was a second chance.

"Cole?" She looked up at him, those blue eyes dark with love. "Please take me home."

His fingers trembled against her skin as he cradled her face in his hands, remembering so many moments out of the past and more recently. He searched her face. Who was she now? Sunny or Amanda? Would he ever be certain?

He saw only love and emotion choked into his throat as he lowered his mouth to hers and tenderly kissed her, tasting tears and unbelievable sweetness.

"Yes," he whispered, breathing her in as his mouth traced hers. "I'll take you home."

His arm went around her shoulders and he leaned heavily against her as they turned to go. Then he stopped and looked back at Colonel Stephen Spenser, alias Phoenix.

"We will have a proper wedding, of course," he assured his future or present brother-in-law—he wasn't certain which. Then he looked down at Amanda and knew he held his entire world in his arms.

"A proper wedding, with a white gown for the bride, in the gardens at Ombre Rose, and," he whispered to her alone, "the gold wedding ring I've always kept for you."

Andy's fingers trembled as she traced his lips, the beard at his cheek. "Yes, love. I've waited so long to wear it again."

Epilogue

"Daddy, I want to hear it again," the child's voice called sweetly in the dusky evening night that enveloped the grand, sprawling house.

"You've already heard it before, my stubborn little Yank."

"Why do you call me that?" Four-year-old Shauna Spenser James asked inquisitively, not at all ready for bed. Her wide blue eyes searched her father's gray ones with a mixture of impish delight and wide-eyed innocence. Coleton James had a feeling he was being had.

"Because you're just like your mother when you make your mind up about something."

"Tell me about Gray Fox, and Uncle Stephen who was really the Phoenix and the captain who stole all the guns and about the time the alligators almost ate Mommy and how Uncle Rafe stole away Aunt Lacey to Mexico."

"That's a very long story."

"All right." She propped her small chin on a finger. "Then tell me about Sunny," she said by way of compromise, nestling with childish delight into a pillow made of her soft gold hair. She patted the coverlet across her wide four-poster bed insistently.

"Sunny was a very special young lady. And she was loved very much by a young man. But there was a tragic accident. . . ." Coleton began tentatively.

His daughter picked up the story as she always did, embellishing it with her vivid imagination. "And she was hurt and died," she stated, understanding with the blissful innocence

508

of a child's simplistic outlook.

"That's right. But before she died, she asked the young man to promise that he would love her forever." Coleton continued the story, reaching to stroke his daughter's face as she yawned sleepily.

"And did he?" she asked drowsily, already knowing the answer. The dark fringe of lashes drooped over eyes that were exactly like her mother's.

Coleton smiled tenderly, thinking how very special and wondrous his daughter was. She was like her mother must have been at this age, full of curiosity and impudence one moment, melting and fragile the next. She always asked that particular question even though she knew the story by heart and could have recited it herself.

"Yes," he answered softly, "he loved her with all his heart, always." He would love this one no less.

"And then what happened?" She yawned again, curling into a tight little kitten-ball on her side.

Coleton smothered back another smile. "He loved her forever, and he never forgot her. And his life was very empty. And then one day many years later, he saw a young woman. And there was something very special about her that reminded him very much of the girl he had once known." He paused, thinking she might have dozed off.

"I'm not asleep," she murmured thickly.

"And he knew in his heart that it was she."

"And he called her Sunny," Shauna finished sleepily.

"Yes, he called her Sunny."

"Just like you sometimes call mama Sunny, because you love her that much."

"Yes, Shauna, because I'll love her forever." He bent and kissed his daughter, thinking as he often did that she was a precious gift, and he was going to have his hands full. She was so much like her mother. She giggled softly and turned to wrap her small arms about his neck.

"Your mustache tickles."

"Does it?" He pretended to frown. "Maybe I shouldn't kiss you then."

509

Her eyes opened, shadowed soft blue with sleep. "That's all right. I like it. So does Mama."

"Is that right?"

"Uh huh, she told me so. And besides, she always lets you kiss her."

"Well, you better get to sleep, or Mama will be unhappy that you're still up so late and won't let me kiss her at all." Coleton tucked her in and rose to leave, dimming the gas lantern at the wall.

"Daddy?"

"Yes, little one?"

"Was she really Sunny?" Her question stopped him. In all her childish innocence and whimsy she had struck unerringly at the truth. Ah, the wisdom of children.

"Yes, she was, Shauna."

"But how, Daddy? How could she die and come back to life again?"

"Perhaps it was because their love was so strong that she came back to be with him. Good night, little Yank."

Obviously satisfied with that, she sighed. "Good night, Daddy." But Coleton knew she would ask to hear the story again. He stopped in the doorway to look back at her. She was already fast asleep.

"That was a very long, bedtime story."

He turned at the sound of Amanda's voice, feeling as he always did that sweet rush of desire and longing at just the nearness of her. He slipped his arm around her waist, newly slender after the birth of Reeve Parker James, who now slept in the small nursery that adjoined their bedchamber. He kissed her hair, loose and tumbling to her waist.

She smelled of sweetness from his son's bath and the soft jasmine fragrance she wore. The satin dressing gown barely closed over the swell of her breasts, full and supple beneath his hands. Every moment with her was a gift, something rare and precious that had once seemed impossible and now made him wonder at every one they shared. He had spent so many years without her. The last five years with her had not made up for even one day of that time apart. He needed an eter-

510

nity, and then maybe, just maybe . . .

She tilted her lovely head back, those blue eyes reaching his in the soft glow of lamp light from the hallway. "What story were you telling her tonight?"

"She wanted to hear about Sunny."

"And what did you tell her?" She wrapped her arms around him and laid her cheek against his chest where his shirt fell open. She could feel the beating of his heart, and her own joined the rythym. He was her lifeblood.

He chuckled softly, caressing the fall of hair that cascaded down her back. "She told me the truth."

She lifted her head. "She has a vivid imagination."

"She has her mother's hardheaded practicality."

"And what are you going to do about it?"

"I'm going to explain it to her one of these days, when I think she's ready."

"And what will you tell her that won't make you sound like a raving madman?" She gazed up at him with a soft smile.

His hands came up to steal tenderly through the hair at her temples, his fingers caressing her. "I will tell her that our love isn't enough for a dozen lifetimes." His mouth came down on hers with stirring heat.

She came up on her toes, arching her body into his, feeling the tendrils of desire that curled through every part of her. Her mouth opened, taking him fully inside, only to trap him there with the tender stroking of her tongue.

Coleton drew back, desire darkening the soft gray of his eyes. "I'll never have enough of you." His voice was ragged, the need sharp and hungering.

"Then promise me."

"Anything."

She nibbled at his lower lip, then reached to trace his mustache with her tongue. "Promise you will love me forever."

"I promise. Forever." The need was too great, the desire burning through him like liquid fire. Coleton bent and swept her into his arms.

"Where are we going?" she whispered thickly as her arms closed around his neck and her mouth caressed his throat.

"We're going where I can have you all to myself."

"The children . . . ?" She started to protest, but it was smothered by the heat of his mouth. And she gave in to it, knowing Angeline would take care of the children should they awaken.

He swept her down the stairs, never hesitating as he carried her through the study and out the double doors that opened out onto the garden. In long, purposeful strides, Coleton carried her into the park, beneath the spreading canopy of pines and magnolias. The moon guided him, casting silvery light on the rolling lawn that spread to the edge of the bayou.

White marble gleamed in the soft light like an opalescent jewel. Coleton pushed open the gate of the gazebo and carried her inside to this sheltered world, abloom with small white Cherokee roses and star jasmine. It was their world, a place apart where it all began, where promises were once made by a young boy and girl and fulfilled by the strength of that love.

Coleton gently laid her down on the cool marble, her dressing gown falling back from her slender legs. He lay beside her, pulling her to him with the desperation of a man who has known what it is to lose his soul and find it again. He drew away the gown as she pushed back his clothes, until they lay naked, entwined on the cool marble floor, desire banked by slow caresses.

His fingers wove through her hair as if he could trap the soft gold and hold it forever.

"Promise me," he whispered against her throat.

"Anything." Her eyes closed, feeling the rush of desire and need she'd known with only him.

"Promise you will love me forever." He wanted desperately to hear it, just as she had asked him all those long years ago.

"I promise I will love you forever."

His hands cradled her face as he caressed her with long, soul-robbing kisses. "You are my Sunny, my very own Sunny."

"Yes, my love." And it was Sunny who answered.